Caste, Tribe and Gender

Caste, Tribe and Gender

Politics of Self and the Other

Edited by
Vulli Dhanaraju

RAWAT PUBLICATIONS
Jaipur • New Delhi • Bangalore • Guwahati • Kolkata

ISBN 978-81-316-0829-6

Published by
Prem Rawat for **Rawat Publications**
Satyam Apts, Sector 3, Jawahar Nagar, Jaipur 302 004 (India)
Phone: 0141 265 1748 / 7006 Fax: 0141 265 1748
E-mail: info@rawatbooks.com
Website: www.rawatbooks.com

New Delhi Office
4858/24, Ansari Road, Daryaganj, New Delhi 110 002
Phone: 011 2326 3290

Also at *Bangalore, Guwahati* and *Kolkata*

Typeset by Rawat Computers, Jaipur
Printed at Chaman Enterprises, New Delhi

For

My Beloved Teachers

Prof. Y.A. Sudhakar Reddy and Prof. Kanaka Durga,

Centre for Folk Culture Studies,

University of Hyderabad, Hyderabad

Contents

Part IV
Other Marginal Identities and Politics

Foreword

Gail Omvedt

Question of self and the other is a basic question of the root of existence of human beings. Even when there were no caste, class or gender divisions, human beings couldn't have gotten away from dealing with this question. In precaste and pregender societies, there existed two binaries: one, men and women as independent parts of human beings having natural sexual division of labour. Women were the other for men, and men were the other for women. In the same way, human beings as a whole faced with the rest of nature as the big other as a part of total nature. These binaries have become part of the complex fabric of identities today in the form of various selves and various others. Today identities are based on nation, country, linguistic states, ethnic groups, genders, race, religion, sects, classes, castes, geographic areas, geopolitical situations, ecological situations and so on.

While dealing with this issue today, we have to have two approaches. One is historical development of selfness and otherness as concepts. Second is how these concepts, while developing themselves, went through the practical process of various cultures, mode of productions and so on, and acquired the character of today. But this is also not sufficient because in the contemporary situation all social, economic and cultural relations are in the process of change. It is a tendency today not to take serious note of these changes taking place in the life and relations of exploitation and domination related to identity formation. Many approaches deal with these issues on the basis of old realities that are no more existent. For example, if we take the question of caste identity, the concept of self in relation to caste identity, the concept of other and so on, most writings deal with these on the basis of caste relations that existed at the time of Phule and Ambedkar. When various caste groups are leading their lives as classes in modern capitalism, they also experience the caste hierarchy, caste oppression and caste-based political identities in a modern way. There are only exceptional attempts to deal with this contemporary situation. So people go on talking about all these issues on the basis of the terminology used for analysing *varna* system and old form of the caste system. The same is true about tribal/adivasi women, 'bahujans', racial minorities, religious minorities and other minorities.

So it is obvious that we should take note of radical changes brought about by the ravages of modern capitalism and imperialism affecting the social-economic and cultural relations on which the identities of self and others emerge. First we have to take note of the nature of imperialist globalization today, which shapes and gets shaped in relation to the existence of not only classes but all these sections having different identities as well. So we have to identify a dialectical relationship between these different processes for taking note and analysing the contemporary nature of various 'selves' and 'others'. Capitalism as a system cannot sustain itself without continuously renewing itself. It will do it on its own basis. Critiques of capitalism can and should analyse this and identify which are the aspects in the change in capitalism which will have an adverse effect on the liberator aspects of marginalized people's identities helping them to go towards liberation. At the same time they should be able to analyse the aspects of the same changes that might be used by these groups for positively going towards creating a new society which would be a society of socialized humanity.

An understanding of interrelationship between the identities of marginalized themselves is a very important aspect to be dealt with. Here again we should take the example of the caste system and refer it to the related character of class and gender relationships. As Dr Babasaheb Ambedkar correctly said, the caste system is a system of a graded hierarchy and it is a division of labourers. This creates two problems that need to be solved by all these oppressed castes. One problem is to dissolve the walls created by the caste system between oppressed caste sections for becoming a new self for caste annihilation. The second problem is related to this dissolution of identities itself. If they want to dissolve these identities, the obstacle in front of them is not only that of dissolving the walls between them but also solving the problem of the hierarchical relations among them. Further, these relations are not only culturally hierarchical, but they are economically exploitative also, and in that sense it becomes a question of ending of exploitative relations between the toiling castes that are the main exploited mass of the caste system as a whole.

Mahatma Phule talks about what he termed as the necessity of formation of *ekmey lok* out of 'stri-shudra-atishudras' to create a new identity as a nation. He was dealing with the same question mentioned above, dissolution of contradictions and identities into a single unified humanity for the task of getting liberated from all kinds of oppression and exploitation. So he brought forward an alliance of what he called 'stri-shudra-atishudras' but this formation of alliance would have to give independence and autonomy to all three sections mentioned and at the same time create a new unified identity as a combination of the three. So for Phule it was not only a question of analysing the separate identities and their nature but also dealing with solving the question of how these people along with their different identities can go towards getting liberated from the clutches of slavery.

Dr Babasaheb Ambedkar has identified this problem in his own way. In *Annihilation of Caste* he talks about intermarriages as one of the means of going towards dissolving the separate and hierarchical identities of the oppressed castes. But he questions the prognosis of this process and comes to the conclusion that the root cause of keeping these hierarchical identities is in the religion and thought processes and strictures brought in by religion. He proposes the idea of castes being a notional existence; if it is a notion, then the question arises 'from where this notion comes into existence?'. To abolish this notion, one has to abolish the faith in religion that creates this notion? And that is why he proposes to go towards a religion like Buddhism that would create a new identity out of all these divided and hierarchical identities. If we go to the history of acceptance of Buddhism and its progress up to now, we would see that identities of caste and sub-caste are not dissolved even today among the people who went to the refuge of Buddhism. Intermarriages between the people who had different castes are still impossible among Buddhists and in many places even inter-sub-caste marriages cannot become a reality. With the development of capitalism in India and South Asia, the *jajmani* or *balutedari* jobs, which were supposed to be done by various castes, have not remained as a thing on the basis of which people live. People are doing various jobs of the modern capitalist society, which cannot be defined as caste jobs. Even in this new scenario, caste and sub-caste identities are not dissolved. On the contrary, they are politically and socially consolidated. This shows the complexities and difficulties in grappling with the question of selfness and otherness in the practical transformative process.

One can relate this problem to the question of gender as well. In South Asia, the question of gender is also related to the question of caste division among women or, one can say, within the gendered identities. Mahatma Phule has compared the practical life experiences of a Brahman woman with a peasant woman and expresses his opinion about the sea-differences between the character of oppression as women experienced by Brahman and non-Brahman women. Within non-Brahman women, the degree of sexual oppression at a family and social level differs in greatly. Here also it becomes a question of dissolving the differences in gender oppression for creating a new identity as women for getting together in a women's liberation movement. Without disrespecting the specificities of the situation from which the specific experience of women's oppression is shaped, one has to create this new identity.

Adivasis or tribal identities bring forward altogether different issues. In this respect, it is not only the question of trying to dissolve the identities of self and other but also a question of offering many aspects that form these identities for making a new humane identity of all marginalized groups. It is because of the fact that at least in the remote 'undisturbed' areas of adivasi communities, the values and practices revealing equality, community feeling, cultural creativity, relatively more autonomy and rights for women and so on are seen or experienced and could be offered to the other marginalized groups who lack this positive character. But even in adivasis for the last few years, there is a great stratification on the lines of class and gender, which in them has endangered the equalitarian or liberatory values that are carried forward for generations together. Adivasis are not really part of the scheme of caste hierarchy but with the intermingling of adivasis with caste society it has gone on becoming as a 'caste' and treated like that by the non-adivasi society. Like the great adivasi radical poet Waharu Sonawane mentions in one of his poems that 'our settlement is considered as inferior and cast-away settlement'. The experience of the movement in his area of northern Maharashtra shows that adivasis considered untouchable castes as lower than them, and untouchable castes considered adivasis as 'cast-away' and backward community. These are the complexities without solving which one cannot go forward on the issue of self and other problematic.

The question of nationality so far as India goes relates with the nationalities in the Northeast, which never got the feeling of oneness with the emergence of India as a nation, is a unique question related to self and other problematic. Their cultural values, their relation with nature and their own understanding about their identity are not only related with languages like other states but also related to overall geopolitical ecological and social-cultural milieu in which they live. They have always felt that India is something other, which has encroached upon their self. If one goes into the history of the emergence of India as a nation and the behaviour of the Indian state with these nationalities, one can definitely understand why this kind of feeling is there in the minds of these nationalities. The question of nationalities and their autonomy and freedom on the basis of their identity itself is a marginalized question along with the marginalization of these nationalities themselves. That is why it is necessary to bring this issue into the mainstream of theoretical thinking in radical academia. Today it is an almost forgotten question for any rigorous theoretical treatment.

The relation between human social formations and remaining nature has gone on becoming complex with the complexities created by modern production processes in the uses of material from natural resources, whether they are renewable or non-renewable. Like Marx said, in *Capital Volume I*, that capitalism not only saps labour by exploiting it but also saps nature of its resources by creating imbalance in the exchange between humans and nature, and thus erodes the base of the existence and continuation of the basic production process in general that goes on shaping humanness of the human society. This relation between human society and nature also has the aspect of self and otherness. Since human society has become exploitative within itself, it went on ruthlessly behaving towards nature, considering it not as part of the overall nature including human but as some outside thing, the other that could be defeated, dominated, sapped, polluted and so forth. This contradiction between humans and nature if continued in the same way might lead towards the destruction and degeneration of both. That is why the autonomy of both and dialectically complementary relation between both should be emerging to avoid this disastrous future.

This could be done in two ways. First, is the way which is presented by the so-called 'eco-capitalism' where capitalism – which has an exploiting practice and attitude towards humans – takes the approach that there should be a new form of capitalism that only takes ecological balance of nature including humans. But if one goes by this way, you cannot avoid the relation of domination between eco-capitalism and nature on the one hand, and eco-capitalism and exploited people on the other hand. This cannot achieve the aim of harmonious and dialectically enriching relations between humans and nature. The second way could be adopted only when humans take the route of ending exploitation among themselves by giving autonomy and freedom to the varieties of identities on the one hand and creating a new identity of all humans on the other hand. This is a much more difficult and complex kind of process because it involves the emergence of multicultural, multivalued but still harmonious social identities of liberated humanity on one hand and on the other hand inventing the processes through which exchange of matter between nature and humans becomes not only balanced and harmonious but also healthy.

The relation of domination between humans and nature is also a complex reality. Even if humans go on thinking in a capitalist exploitative society that they are dominating and submitting nature to their wishes, nature retaliates and shows it could not be dominated in this manner and on the contrary it would be disastrous for both nature and humans. This signal given by nature should teach enough lessons for changing the behaviour of human society towards nature. This whole situation brings forward the dissolution of identities of two aspects of nature, that is, human society and the rest of nature. This is an impossibility. But it is definitely possible to evolve a broad new identity of nature by keeping independent identities of humans and rest of nature intact in a non-contradictory form.

This complex issue is not related really to technology as such, but modern technology is involved in dealing with this issue because technology should flow from the general theoretical point of view, which is implicit in this approach. This theoretical point of view cannot but deal with the question of decentralized control of the creative productions by clusters of human groups. This is related to the creation of free opportunity for creativity of humans and establishing democratic relations between the creative production on one hand and humans and nature on the other hand. So the concepts of 'sustainable development', appropriate technology and renewable-based production processes are not sufficient for evolving such a theoretical viewpoint because this viewpoint should base itself on the cohabitation of humans and nature and creating and enriching relations between them that would protect both the identities. The nature of technology will follow on this basis.

Only then hierarchical relations in a so-called sustainable renewable production processes could be avoided.

The problematic of self and otherness is philosophical issues on the one hand and ideological questions and practical problems faced by humanity on the other hand. The concept of self cannot come without humans becoming self-conscious of them, that is, humans identifying themselves as distinct from the rest of nature. This can only happen when humans go beyond subconscious understanding of them and start recognizing themselves as something different from the rest of nature. In other words, they have to stop considering themselves as nature and call themselves as human beings and call the rest of nature as 'nature'. This self-consciousness is the first step towards the concept and practice of self on the one hand and defining otherness on the other hand. Within humans, up to the point they don't identify implicit sexual division of functions they cannot possibly have two selves within themselves: one, men and the other, women. When this happens not only are sexual functions identified as defining factors for self and otherness, but also they go further in defining sexual division of labour and distinct feminine and masculine values, thereby defining themselves as two kinds of human beings. This lays the basis for further separation of identities and developing this separation into the relations of reverence and domination between these two halves. Once the fixed location of their livelihood enters in their lives with the advent of stable agriculture or defined area of gathering resources, there enters the factor of identifying themselves as a group of men and women related to a particular space, necessitating the protection of the area. This need of protection goes on taking away the 'magic' of creation that is attached to the feminine functions, which are related to creating new things, and defines feminine gender now as a weaker gender for constantly being ready for the function of protection of the space-defined community. This transforms the relation of self and other between men and women into a relation of domination and exploitation, masculinity and femininity, laying the basis for patriarchy. At this point the whole relation of human society with nature also transforms itself into a domineering relation of human society over nature. The end of the identities of self and other, playing the role of obstacles in the road to liberated humanity, could be removed only by creating a healthy democratic space for non-domineering identities of various selves and others in the process of human development.

Preface

The issues of self and the other have been the subject of much academic debate in the study of subaltern/marginal identity politics all over the world. This debate addresses several questions. What is a social identity? How marginal identities are different from others? How the self is contested with the other politics? In keeping view these questions, social identity can be defined as the sense that people make of themselves through their subjective feelings based on their everyday experiences and wider social relations. The politics of self and the other identities have been undermined due to the globalization and social network revolution that enabled the subaltern communities to look into their own identities and resist the power and hegemony of the agencies in the name of social identity movements. As a result, caste, tribe and gender identities that have all arisen are some way from a redrawing of the otherness and everyday experiences in the society.

Indeed, the constructions of subaltern/marginal identities have become an important issue in academic debates. It is not a matter of surprise, therefore, that social/historical inquiries into their conditions have attracted the attention of several scholars. The social scientists identify that the peculiarity of Indian society is laid in caste. The adivasis or tribes do not have that sort of importance in the society, except in the tribal belts. The gender question on the other hand has also attracted a lot of attention, particularly, because of the rise of the feminist movement in post-independence period. Like other social categories, women also have been involved in collective actions equipped with their agenda, leadership, ideologies and organizations in order to have their proper and dignified place in all aspects of life.

The forces of new technologies, social network revolution and globalization have played an important role in the representation of local/personal identities as social construction. It enabled the growth of identity politics after 1980s. The identity politics have resisted to not only universal hegemonies but also contesting within the same identity in many aspects that extensively played an important role in the weakening of their own identities, although the self-respect movements emerged as an alternative force in representing subaltern politics.

In this context, this book proposes to explore the nature of social subordination and its diverse forms of subordinations in the study of personal experiences/struggle and structural domination within the same social identities. The interface between contemporary state and social identities on the one hand and relationships among personal identities on the other hand provided the context within which social discrimination or subordination is practiced. Social marginalization, contestation and discrimination has existed in Indian society since time immemorial. But the self-respect movements after 1980s heralded the process of major changes in the social identity movements, which remoulded many of the pre-existing social discriminations.

The book is divided into four thematic sections covering 16 chapters. The four themes are (1) Politics of Self and Other; (2) Caste and Tribe; (3) Gender; and (4) Other Marginal Identities and Politics. Each section has covered core theme of the book. Thus, this book will help us to construct the self and the other in study of caste, tribe and gender identity politics and contextualize the debates related to these identity politics from different perspectives. The idea of self and the other is used by postmodern social scientists and cultural theorists to emphasize how social identities are contested. This book also used these concepts in order to understand the contested nature of subaltern/marginal politics and its relation with the state and other hegemonic institutions.

Vulli Dhanaraju

Acknowledgements

Like any other work, this edited book is a collective endeavour. This book is an outcome of International Conference on 'Contesting Self and Other: Identities of Caste, Tribe and Gender' organized by the Department of History and Anthropology, Assam University (Central University), Diphu Campus, Assam, during 27–28 March 2015 in collaboration with Maulana Abul Kalam Azad Institute of Asian Studies (MAKAIAS), Kolkata and Indian Council of Social Science Research (ICSSR), New Delhi. At the very onset, I would like to express my thankfulness to all the contributors. Without their cooperation and support, this book would not have been a reality.

I wish to express my gratitude to the Maulana Abul Kalam Azad Institute of Asian Studies (MAKAIAS), Kolkata and Indian Council of Social Science Research (ICSSR), New Delhi, for their collaboration and financial assistance in organizing the International Conference at the Department of History and Department of Anthropology, Assam University (Central University), Diphu Campus, Assam. I extend my gratitude to the Assam University (Central University), Diphu Campus, Assam, for giving me an opportunity for organizing the International Conference at the Diphu Campus.

I am very grateful to Prof. Gail Omvedt, eminent social scientist, for accepting my request to give keynote speech at the conference. Interacting and engaging with her at various occasions has been a great learning experience and source of intellectual enrichment.

I am deeply indebted for all the help from my loving family and the support they gave me throughout my academic career. I wish to express my deep sense of gratitude to my favourite teachers and ideal couple, Prof. Y.A. Sudhakar Reddy and Prof. Kanaka Durga, Centre for Folk Culture Studies, University of Hyderabad, who have even helped me to overcome hurdles in personal life and supported me to sustain in the difficult times of life. Their erudition and characteristic unassuming style provided me inspiration and encouragement. Without their exceptional generosity and scholarly support, this book would not have been possible. My indebtedness to them could not be expressed in words. I am dedicating this book to this ideal couple.

I owe an intellectual debt to Mr Dharam Singh Teron, Eminent Writer and Director, Centre for Karbi Studies, Karbi Anglong, Assam; Prof. Yagati Chinna Rao, JNU, New Delhi; Prof. P. Kesava Kumar, University of Delhi, Dr B. Eswara Rao, University of Hyderabad; Prof. B.C. Dash, Assam University, Diphu Campus and my friend, Chittibabu Padvala, IIT Mumbai. I also extend my gratitude to Dr Kh Narendra Singh, Associate Professor, Department of Anthropology, Assam University, Diphu Campus, and also the co-coordinator of the conference for his cooperation and support.

I thank the entire faculty and staff of the Department of History, Assam University, Diphu Campus, Assam, for all the academic and administrative support. Words fail to express my gratitude to Dr R.K. Bijeta, Department of History, Assam University, Silchar. She is known for her unfailing support without reservations or conditions throughout and without a shred of tiredness and she has always gone out of her way to help me. I also extend my thanks to the Research Scholars in the Department of History, Assam University, Diphu Campus, particularly, Ms Rupali Rongpipi, Ms Junmoini Hansepi, Ms Nukshirenla and Ms Rashmi Engipipi for their assistance in proofreading this book. My friends and students have always encouraged me and inspired me to expand upon new ideas that constantly helped me in the preparation of this book in the present form.

This endeavour would not have come to fruition but for the support that I have received from my family members especially my mother and sisters.

No words are left to express my gratitude to Rawat Publications, for their keen interest in the publication of this book.

Vulli Dhanaraju

Contributors

Sunitaa Saikia, Research Scholar, Centre for Historical Studies, Jawaharlal Nehru University, New Delhi.

Suniti Ahuja, Associate Professor, Department of English, D.A.V. Centenary College, Faridabad, Haryana.

Binod C. Agrawal, Professor of Eminence and Director General, TALEEM Research Foundation, Ahmedabad, Gujarat.

Maggie Katharpi, Assistant Professor, Department of English, Diphu Government College, Diphu, Assam.

Vulli Dhanaraju, Assistant Professor, Department of History, Assam University, Diphu Campus, Assam.

Riju Devi, Research Scholar, Department of Sociology, Tezpur University, Assam.

Abheeshta Nath J.R., FDP Substitute Lecturer, Department of English, Government College for Women, Trivandrum, Kerala.

R.K. Bijeta, Guest Faculty, Department of History, Assam University, Silchar, Assam.

Thiyam Rabikanta Singh, Assistant Professor, P.G. Department of Anthropology, D.M. College of Science, Imphal, Manipur.

Tahir Hussain Ansari, Assistant Professor, Department of History, Assam University, Diphu Campus, Assam.

Tripti Soni, Research Scholar, Department of English Literature, M.G.S. University, Bikaner, Rajasthan.

Rini Banerjee, Assistant Professor, Department of English, Women's College, Tinsukia, Itanagar, Arunachal Pradesh.

Bijayani Mishra, Research Scholar, Centre for the Study of Social Systems, Jawaharlal Nehru University, New Delhi.

Biman Kumar Nath, Research Scholar, Department of Economics, Rajiv Gandhi University, Arunachal Pradesh.

Jhumpa Dey, Senior Specialist (Institutional Management and Commerce and BCC), World Bank Project, PHED, Government of Assam, Assam.

Sekhar Kanti Sarkar, Research Scholar, Department of Law, Assam University Silchar, Assam.

Prasad R., Research Scholar, Loyola College of Social Sciences, Trivandrum, Kerala.

Introduction

Vulli Dhanaraju

The issues of self and the other have been the subject of much academic debate in the study of subaltern/marginal identity politics all over the world. This debate addresses several questions. What is a social identity, how are marginal identities different from others? How the self is contested with the other identity politics? Keeping view these questions, social identity can be defined as the sense that people make of themselves through their subjective feelings based on their everyday experiences and wider social relations. The politics of self and the other identities have been undermined due to the globalization and social network revolution that enabled the subaltern communities to look into their own identities and resisting the power and hegemony of the agencies in the name of social identity movements. As a result, caste, tribe and gender identities have all arisen in some way from a redrawing of the otherness and everyday experiences in the society.

Self identity is the idea that one possesses about himself/herself as a unique individual. Collective identity on the other hand is one that somebody shares with a group of people as a member of a large social group such as a linguistic, faith, cultural or ethic group. The term *otherness* is often used in the understanding of struggles of caste, tribe and gender identity in contemporary society. For example, being Indian may be most easily articulated in terms of not being colonial white and to be a dalit (oppressed) may be conveyed in terms of not being upper caste in Indian context. The same dalit identity is contested with elite dalit identity. It is the same case with tribe and gender. Dalit or elite dalit and tribe or other tribal identities can be seen as relational. This relational position reflects wider ideas surrounding the identity being viewed in relation to an 'other' or others who are seen as possessing a different identity. It can be said that self-identity is defined in terms of difference from the objectified other.

The construction of otherness identity politics has become an important issue in academic debates. It is not a matter of surprise, therefore, that social/historical inquiries into their conditions have attracted the attention of several scholars. The adivasis or aboriginal tribes do not have that sort of importance in the society, except in the tribal belts. The gender question on the other hand has also attracted a lot of attention, particularly, because of the rise of the feminist movement in post-independence period. Like other social groups, women also have been involved in collective actions equipped with their agenda, leadership, ideologies and organizations in order to have their proper and dignified place in all aspects of life.

I

How do we understand the concept of identity? There are several broad categories that are used normally in social science discipline. The people use different identities in contemporary India such as national identity, cultural identity, political identity, linguistic identity, gender identity, ethnic identity, regional identity, religious identity and so on.

The formation of identity is essentially a question of perception by the other. Our identity lies in a manner in which we are perceived by others. This implies that when applied to marginalized communities, the formation of identity is dependent upon their perception by the non-marginalized groups. The issue of the formation of identity, therefore, involves mainly the following questions:

- What is the process through which identities are formed?
- What are the constitutive elements which shape the identity formation of the marginal sections?
- What is the relationship between the marginal communities and the hegemonic communities?
- What are the significant markers that distinguish the marginal identity from the mainstream people?

These group markings, within which an individual normally defines himself, can and does change over different historical periods or as societies evolve in relation to each other. For instance, the industrial revolution in England had changed the way people identified themselves. From being farmers, yeoman or serfs and nobility, modern

England created the worker, the industrialist and other professional identities. Similarly, 200 years of English colonialism created a modern Indian identity quite separate from its traditional variant. When cultures come in contact with each other, they also come in contact with a different value system and a different way of viewing the world. This implies that above all identity is not unchangeable. Identity formation must be viewed as a dynamic process that changes with historical changes.

One significant way in which identity formation underwent a change historically was in the relationship between the individual and the society. In premodern and modern societies, it was the community whether based on caste, religion or any other identity, which formed the basic unit of identity in the society. A person was known primarily by his membership in the community that he belonged to. Individual identities did not acquire a position of centrality. But the postmodern world has led to the creation of an atomized society where the individuals constitute the basic units of identity along with other forms of identities.

Another important point to be noted is that understanding identity is relational. One is aware of one's identity only in relationship to the other. This operates at all levels of identity whether it is national or individual. For example, Indian identity exists only in relation to British or French or some other national identity. Similarly, identity of religion exists mainly in relation to each other. Identity is, therefore, not just a simple sense of the self. A study of identity formation means examining different processes through which this sense of the self is arrived at and how it manifests itself. Thus, identity could be defined as a general consensus based on commonly accepted social customs, taboos, which connects life together and marks groups of people and individuals therein.

Richard Jenkins (2008) argued that ideas of similarity and difference are central to the way in which we achieve a sense of identity and social belonging. Identities have some element of exclusivity. Just as when we formally join a club or an organization, social membership depends upon fulfilling a set of criteria. It just so happens that such criteria are socially constructed (that is, created by societies and social groups). As such 'we' cannot belong to any group unless 'they' (other people) do *not* belong to 'our' group. Sociologists set out to study how societies manage collective ideas about who gets to belong to 'our group' and which types of people are seen as different – the outsiders of society.

However, the identity formation among the marginal communities is not an accidental affair. It has evolved through several forces in the past. However, reconstruction of their history is a very difficult task, precisely because they have had no written records by themselves. Whatever records are available, they are written by others, with different interests and compulsions. These are mostly divorced from the objective and subjective conditions of the marginal people.

II

The present section will conceptualize the concept of self and the other in the understanding of social identities. The concepts of self and the other are a central in the understanding of marginalized identity struggles in India. This is because the representation of different marginalized groups is controlled by groups that have cultural/political hegemony. In order to understand the notion of the other, we need to put a critical analysis in which social identities are constructed. Rather than talking about the individual characteristics or personalities of different individuals, which is generally the focus for psychology, sociologists focus on social identities (Jenkins, 2008). Social identities reflect the way individuals and groups internalize established social categories within their societies, such as their cultural (or ethnic) identities, gender identities, class identities and so on. These social categories shape our ideas about who we think we are, how we want to be seen by others and the groups to which we belong.

George Herbert Mead's (1934) classic text, *Mind Self and Society* (1934) established that social identities are created through social interaction with other people such as observing and interacting with others, responding to others' opinions about oneself and internalizing external opinions and internal feelings about oneself. The social aspect of self is an important distinction because other sociologists and psychologists of Mead's time felt that the self was based on biological factors and inherited traits. According to Mead, the self is not there from birth, but it is developed over time from social experiences and activities.

The concept of the self has long been salient in feminist philosophy, for it is pivotal to questions about personhood, identity, the body and agency that feminism must address. That is why Simone de Beauvoir's, *The Second Sex* (1977), work quoted in highlighting the distinction between men and women that 'He is the subject, he is the absolute – she is the other'. To be the other is to be the non-subject, the non-person, the non-agent-in short, the mere body. In law, in customary practice and in cultural stereotypes, women's selfhood has been systematically subordinated, diminished and belittled, when it has not been outright denied.

Since De Beauvoir's idea of the other as a construction opposing and thereby constructing the self, the concepts of the other, othering and otherness has taken root in areas of thought and inquiry ranging from nursing science to cultural geography (Brons, 2016). De Beauvoir's 'other' was not an entirely a new idea, however, as she acknowledged herself, and was heavily influenced by Hegel's (1807) dialectic of identification in the encounter of the self with some other in his 'Master–Slave Dialectics'. He has explained the master–slave dialectic relations in his *Phenomenology of Spirit*. It is a basic principle of Hegelian philosophy. He stated that the development of self-consciousness as such in an encounter between what are thereby (i.e. emerging only from this encounter) two distinct, self-consciousness beings; the essence of the dialectic is the movement or motion of recognizing, in which the two self-consciousnesses are constituted each in being recognized as self-conscious by the other. This movement, inexorably taken to its extreme, takes the form of a 'struggle to the death' in which one masters the other, only to find that such lordship makes the very recognition he had sought impossible, since the bondsman, in this state, is not free to offer it.

Muhammad Kamal (2004) has reviewed the master slave relations as it follows. First, the master needs the slave for recognition. That is what objective certainty means. But this recognition is not reciprocal, as the master is recognized by someone whom he does not recognize, and recognition from one side is not sufficient (Hegel, 1807). The master wants to act as a self-conscious being by directing his desire towards another self-conscious being. This issue as we see is problematic because at the end of the fight the slave will not be recognized by the master as another self-conscious being and is reduced to a thing. The desire of the master is directed towards an objectified desire or an object, and therefore, the master is not recognized by another self-conscious being. His objective certainty is not confirmed by another self-conscious being and will never get satisfaction by being recognized by a slave or a thing.

Second, there is no master without a slave. A self-conscious being becomes a master by possessing slaves. Accordingly, the master depends on the slave to become a master. That may be called formal dependence to distinguish it from material dependence.

Third, the master depends upon the slave materially. His superiority over nature is realized in the slave's labour. Labour is placed between the master and nature and transforms nature into the desired objects of the master. The paradise in which the master lives is bound by the products of the labour of the slave. Whatever the master has is produced by the slave. The master is, therefore, not an independent being, but rather dependent on the slave and slave's labour.

One interpretation of this dialectic is that neither a slave nor a master can be considered as fully self-conscious. A person who has already achieved self-consciousness could be enslaved, so self-consciousness must be considered not as an individual achievement or an achievement of natural and genetic evolution, but as a social phenomenon (Moran, 1988). As philosopher Robert Brandom argues (2008) that

> Hegel's discussion of the dialectic of the Master and Slave is an attempt to show that symmetric recognitive relations are metaphysically defective, that the norms they institute aren't the right kind to help us think and act with – to make it possible for us to think and act. A symmetric recognition in this way is authority without responsibility, on the side of the Master, and responsibility without authority, on the side of the Slave.

And Hegel's argument is that unless authority and responsibility are commensurate and reciprocal, no actual normative statuses are instituted. This is one of his most important and certainly one of his deepest ideas, though it's not so easy to see just how the argument works (Borossa, 2003).

However, the master and slave relationship influenced numerous discussions and ideas in the twentieth century, especially because of its supposed connection to Karl Marx's idea of class struggle as the important force of social development. Moreover, Hegel's master–slave relations, and particularly the emphasis on recognition, has been of crucial influence on Martin Buber's (1925) idea of relational schema in *I and Thou*, Simone de Beauvoir's account of the history and dynamics of gender relations in *The Second Sex* and Frantz Fanon's (1952) analysis of the colonial relation in *Black Skin, White Masks.*

Zygmunt Bauman (1988) writes that the notion of otherness is central to the way in which societies establish identity categories. He argues that 'identities are set up as dichotomies'. Such as woman is the other of man, animal is the other of human, stranger is the other of native, abnormality the other of norm, deviation the other of law-abiding, illness the other of health, insanity the other of reason, lay public the other of the expert, foreigner the other of state subject and enemy the other of friend.

Postcolonial theory is built in large part around the concept of otherness. The term *otherness* includes doubleness, both identity and difference, so that every other, every different than and excluded by, is dialectically created and includes the values and meaning of the colonizing culture even as it rejects its power to define. Bhabha's (1990) concept of otherness is derived from Jacques Lacan's (1977) other and Fanon's idea of the other as binary opposition between the white and the black. The significance of his theory lies in his suggestion that colonial authority is rendered 'hybrid' and 'ambivalent' in the postcolonial era. Here Bhabha opens the spaces for the colonized to subvert the master discourse. In his essay, 'The Other Question: The Stereotype and Colonial Discourse', he emphasizes on how the colonial subject is taken as 'other leading to the construction of a stereotype in colonial discourse'.

Though the term *other* refers to the colonized subject, it is not a plain term as it is more ambiguous. This is related with a number of approaches to epistemology and cultural identity. The term *Other* is used by many theorists such as Sartre, Derrida and Lacan in their writings. The term used by Sartre explains the relation between self and the Other. This use of the term is helpful in creating an awareness of self and identity. Freud applies this term as the formation of subjectivity. As the psychoanalyst and cultural theorist, Lacan makes a distinction between 'Other' with capital 'O' and the 'Other' with small 'o'. Here the small 'o' designates the other who resembles the self, which the child discovers when it looks in the mirror and becomes aware of itself as a separate being. The capital 'O' refers to the great other in whose gaze the subject gains identity. According to Homi Bhabha, the other with capital 'O' can be compared to the empire (the empirical centre) that makes the colonized subject conscious of one's identity as somehow other and dependent. This thinking reminds Gayatri Spivak's (1988) coinage of the term *othering*, which means that the empirical centre creates its others. In other words, the colonizing other gets established when the colonized others are treated as subjects.

Homi Bhabha states that 'colonial discourse' depends on the ideological construction of otherness. He further states that it gives rise to 'the stereotype'. Here he says that an important feature of colonial discourse is its dependence on the concept of 'fixity' in the ideological construction of otherness. It is this process of ambivalence central to the stereotype that my chapter explores as it constructs a theory of colonial discourse. Bhabha evaluates the complete question of colonization: that is, how the colonizers came to build their colony and colonized the native people, who are now termed the other. By studying this situation, he states that the stereotype image of the colonized is a negative one. In other words, they are considered inferior to the colonizers in colour, race, knowledge and culture. Here he states that colonial discourse is an apparatus of power. He further states that: 'The objective of colonial discourse is to construe the colonized as a population of degenerate types on the basis of racial origin, in order to justify conquest and to establish systems of administration and instruction. Despite the play of power within colonial discourse and the shifting positionalities of its subjects (for example, effects of class, gender, ideology, different social formations, varied systems of colonization and so on), I am referring to a form of govern mentality that in making out a 'subject nation', appropriates, directs and dominates its various spheres of activity. Therefore, despite the "play" in the colonial system which is crucial to its exercise of power, colonial discourse produces the colonized as a social reality which is at once an "other" and yet entirely knowable and visible'.

Here he points out that colonial discourse highlights the inferior status of colonized before the colonizers. It also states the power politics of the colonizers that always try to dominate the colonized in all sense. Many critics have studied the work of Homi Bhabha and expressed their views to locate his position in Indian literary critical history. Robert J.C. Young (2001) argues that 'If Bhabha changed his interpretative methods in response to the objections of his critics, he would no longer be Bhabha, the brilliant insights would be lost, and he would become a conventional cultural or historical critic'. Young refers Bhabha as one of the 'Holi Trinity' of postcolonial theory, alongside Edward Said (1995) and Gayatri Spivak (1988). He further compares Bhabha with Ashis Nandy (political psychologist) and states: There are parallels, influences and convergences of which we should be aware when we consider postcolonialism. Both critics in their writing characteristically violate the historical integrity of the theoretical tradition from which they draw and thereby deinstitutionalize its scope.

Thus, the above discussion on the self and other highlights how many societies create a sense of belonging, identity and social status by constructing social categories as binary opposites. This is visible in the social construction of marginal identities in India. It is argued that no group ever sets itself up as the one without at once setting up the other over against itself.

III

Recent writings appreciate the close relationship between caste, tribe and gender that got manifested in many ways. Various social scientists argue that the peculiarity of Indian society is laid in caste. They also saw that there was a section in society, namely the aboriginal tribes, which had not been brought into caste society. The structure of caste society differed from tribal society in many respects. Gender was one important aspect in which the organization of a tribe differed from that of a caste. The following section conceptualizes the identities of caste, tribe and gender while presenting the various arguments from different perspectives.

Caste is the most debatable issue that has enthralled and divided scholars who wished to study this system of stratified social hierarchy in India. There is an enormous body of academic writing and political polemic on the issue. These are basically the part of debate on the transformation of Indian society under the impact of colonialism and its administrative mechanisms. Some argue for the continuities of precolonial social structures including caste. Others stress on the basic qualitative changes introduced by the colonial rulers. Let us assess the different views on the ideology of caste in Indian society.

Structural functionalist theories highlighted the integrative role of caste. In structural-functionalist writings, caste is viewed as a system of interdependence and reciprocity, and not as inequality or exploitation. The same emphasis is also found in the structuralist approach of Louis Dumont (1980). His famous book, *Homo Hierarchicus*, constructed an image of caste based on Hindu texts. In this image, two opposing conceptual categories of purity and pollution are the core elements of caste structure. These unique core principles of caste hierarchy, according to Dumont, are observed in scriptural formulation as well as the everyday life of all Hindus. In other words, these values separate Indians culturally from the Western civilization, making India a land of static, unchangeable, 'oriental' Brahmanical values. According to him, Brahmanism represents a core civilizational value, and caste is the central symbol of this value. It is the basic expression of the precolonial traditions of India.

Following Dumont, Michael Moffatt (1979) maintains that the lower castes share with the higher castes the basic assumptions and values of the caste structure. They recreate among themselves the entire set of institutions and rank relations from which they have been excluded by the higher castes. He thus sees cultural consensus at work from the top to the bottom, which includes the principles of inclusion and exclusion, complementarities and replication.

In order to counter Louis Dumont's view of caste, a number of studies were also conducted from the perspective of lower caste that demonstrates the difference between the socio-religious ideologies of the lower castes and the upper castes (Berreman, 1979). They point out that lower castes do not accept the unclean and demeaning status assigned to them in the caste hierarchy. The lower castes have diverse notions of their own as to how and why the caste system developed, most of which refer to the superior wealth and power of the higher castes rather than their purity. Due to socio-economic compulsions, therefore, lower castes seem to subscribe to the dominant ideology rather than being in consensus with it.

It is also very important to note that Ronald Inden (1990), Nicholas M. Dirks (1987, 2001) and other subaltern scholars such as Partha Chatterjee (1989) have challenged Dumont's notion of caste. They argue that it was the colonial ruling class that established the caste system in its ossified form. In order to break Indian people's resistance, the colonial state used knowledge and culture apart from economic and political means. According to this view, power relations and command over men and resources were more important. Nicolas Dirks, in his *Castes of Mind* (2001), argues that caste is a product of 'colonial modernity'. By this he does not mean that caste did not exist before the advent of British. He is simply suggesting that caste became a single, unique category under the British rule that expressed and provided the sole index of understanding India. Earlier there were diverse forms of social identity and community in India. The British reduced everything to a single explanatory category of caste. It was the colonial state and its administrators who made caste into a uniform, all-encompassing and ideologically consistent organism. They made caste as a measure of all things and the most important emblem of traditions.

Susan Bayly (1999) has criticized this line of thought of Nicholas Dirks from her point of view (which we can definitely criticize) and has argued that Brahminism and its hegemony were not a product of colonialism, though they were certainly strengthened by it. The Brahmins played a significant role in the construction of this colonial knowledge, and the collaboration of the colonial state and native elites could be discerned throughout this entire process. The collaboration between the colonial state and the native elites and feudal classes was neither an imagination nor a construct, but was a stark reality.

Abhinav Sinha (2013), in his recent article, vehemently criticized the line of thinking of Nicolas Dirks and other subaltern studies' arguments, which are mentioned in the earlier. He argues that orientalist/colonial construct of caste is a kind of subjectivism. No state can ever make a construct of any such divide from the above, unless that division has a history of its own. It must certainly be accepted that the fetish of the British ethnographic state to count, enumerate, classify and systematize the castes did indeed shake the division and hierarchy in the castes once and made it rigid in a new way.

The celebration of the precolonial past by historians of subaltern studies and the academics motivated by orientalism of Edward Said (1995) and postmodernism in the name of opposing modernity and enlightenment is a flight of imagination and a mental construct of these historians (Sinha, 2013). Sumit Sarkar (2005) argues that this cultural critique of colonialism ultimately aligns itself with the revivalism of the extreme Right, though it also superficially terms communalism as a colonial construct (which is more accurate in this context as compared to caste). This whole logic is circular and a self-defeating one.

Thus, caste has not been identified or institutionalized by colonialism; the foreign travellers have also described the nature of Indian society in their works. The works of the Greek ambassador to the court of Chandra Gupta Maurya, Megasthenes, in the third century BC, and Al-Beruni, the historian–companion of Mahmud of Ghazni in the eleventh century, have reflected the social structure of India. This shows that caste systematized in India since time immemorial. Megasthenes, the Greek traveller in the third century BC to India, mentions two of the features characterizing the institution of caste. He says 'It is not permitted to contract marriage with a person of another caste or to undertake an occupation other than ancestral nor for the same person to undertake more than one, except if he is of the Caste of Philosophers, when permission is given on account of dignity' (Ghurye, 1969).

Nonetheless, colonialism reconstructed cultural forms and social institutions like caste to create a line of difference and demarcation between themselves as European modern and the colonized Asian traditional subjects. In other words, British colonialism played a critical role in both the identification and production of Indian 'tradition'. The colonial modernity devalued the so-called Indian traditions. Simultaneously, it also transformed them. Caste was recast as the spiritual essence of India that regulated and mediated the private domain. Caste-ridden Indian society was different from the European civil society because caste was opposed to the basic premises of individualism as well as the collective identity of a nation. The salience of this precolonial identity and sense of loyalty could easily be used to justify the rule by the colonial modern administrators.

IV

Second, tribal history in India is largely a product of colonial ethnography. Though the early sources of information about the tribals were the accounts of travellers, administrators and Christian missionaries, a systematic study of these people in India begins with the establishment of the Asiatic Society of Bengal. Anthropological studies in India until independence were confined to the study of tribes and were geared largely to the need of colonial administration, with its years of experience in governing the 'nature' and some administrators realized fairly well the importance of anthropology in all works relating to the people under their charge. The following section briefly discusses the idea of self and other in the construction of tribal identity by the study of various arguments that have been a source of knowledge in the Indian society.

Tribal identity mainly focuses on ethnic identity. This means that ethnic homogeneity, along with other factors, characterizes a tribe. Tribe represents a historical continuity and exclusiveness. Groups that had been living together without losing or diluting their specific characteristics were formed into a tribe. The formation of the tribal identity, as indeed that of tribes, was a product of territorial, economic, ecological and technological isolation. In other words, human groups of a similar ethnicity that remained isolated from the rest of the world through geography, or the use of a specific primitive technology or through economic specificity were formed into a tribe and came to acquire a tribal identity.

Identity formation among the tribals must be perceived as a dynamic process that can be dealt with historical changes. There have been extensive research on the tribal identities in colonial period but very few studies have been done on the precolonial period. Neeladri Bhattacharya (1999) has criticized them for the little interest they have shown on the precolonial tribal situation. He stated that

> the social lives and practices of forest dwellers and peasants, shifting cultivators and pastoralists, were crucially affected by the way they were seen by state and society, as well as the self-conceptions of their own practice. Research on the theme, limited as it is, has tended to focus on the colonial period, and arguments about dramatic changes in state

> attitudes have often been made on the basis of implicit unexplored assumptions about precolonial societies.

This makes it imperative to at least take a quick look at the precolonial dominant constructions of the tribes.

However, social scientists have focused on various tribal movements to indicate the nature of social structures that determined popular protests led by tribals. In this regard K.S. Singh (1985) has produced seminal works on the protest movement led by Birsa Munda. Ranajit Guha (1983) who had studied the popular aspects of tribal/peasant insurgency between 1783 and 1900 has provided an analytical framework. He has shown that official documentation was indicative of 'power discourse' that helps us to identify the self and other identities among the tribal people of India. He has argued that as the rebel was conscious of starting revolt against dominant groups so he was an insurgent. However he found his identity at the level of dominant groups. That's why he possessed negative consciousness. Ranajit Guha's work definitely helps in understanding social ties, intellectual and spiritual beliefs that went into the making of tribal insurgencies. Though scholars have questioned his concept of negation and the categories of dominant and subaltern groups, the remains that he has produced a new argument on the nature of popular protests. K.S. Singh in his analysis has pointed out the changing nature of various protest movements. The presence of millenarian trends in popular uprisings has been studied by Stephen Fuchs in his 'Rebellious Prophet'. The emergence of messianic leaders who emerged during the times of ruptures between traditional and alien cultural norms has been highlighted by him.

The subaltern perspective not only analysed the tribal insurgencies but also put forth a framework for studying such tribal revolts as an academic discourse. An important approach to the study of tribal movements has been enunciated by Ranajit Guha. His approach seeks to restore a balance by highlighting the role of the politics of the people against elite politics played in Indian history. The whole thrust of subaltern historiography is on reconstructing 'the other history', that is, history of people's politics and movements and their attempts to make their own history. As a brilliant demonstration of how the 'other history' could be constructed, Guha has offered us a study of the tribal insurgency in colonial India. The study provides with a useful framework for studying social movements in general and tribal/peasant insurgencies in particular.

V

The concepts of self and other are crucial in the understanding of gender relations. The concept of the other highlights how many societies create a sense of belonging, identity and social status by constructing social categories as binary opposites. This is clear in the social construction of gender in Western societies and how socialization shapes our ideas about what it means to be a 'man' or a 'woman'. There is an inherently unequal relationship between these two categories. Note that these two identities are set up as opposites, without acknowledging alternative gender expressions. In the early 1950s, Simone de Beauvoir (1977) argued that 'otherness is a fundamental category of human thought'. Thus no group ever sets itself up as the one without at once setting up the other over against itself. Gender identity is in the sense of self-associated with cultural definitions of masculinity and femininity. Gender identity in this sense arises out of a complex process of interaction between self and others.

In recent times, the feminists processed their ideology and perceptions through postmodernist and poststructuralist discourses and shifted their concern from women centred or women stand point to postmodern feminism wherein the emphasis is on difference and critique of sameness. They deconstruct the gender and power relations transforming or reconstructing social values and institutions. Several feminist scholars have been influenced by the ideas conceptualized by the postmodern scholars, Foucault (1978, 1980) and Derrida (1982). Postmodernism focuses on diversity and difference, and critiques grand narratives. The meta-narratives of modernist period that privileged the universal knowledge are abandoned and a search for previously silenced voices, specificity of power of language and their relation of knowledge, context and locality began in the intellectual world. Judith Butler (1990) holds that no subject can be its own point of departure. Individual subjects experience and understand life within a discursive and material context. By this, Butler means that the language or discourse that 'explains' the concrete experiences of daily life influences and shapes the way individuals interpret 'reality'. The self is not merely reflections of reality or experience but also formed under complex socio-historical circumstances that must be analysed and understood as such.

Colonialism and the nationalist movement played a crucial role in the construction of gender in India. The education reforms of the late nineteenth and early twentieth century widened the horizons of women and produced a 'new woman' with interests beyond the private realm (Forbes, 1996; Vijayalakshmi, 2005). Nationalism was a neutralizing force in resolving the conflicts of social reform during the nineteenth century by portraying the modern woman as an embodiment of spiritual superiority of the nation, with qualities of self sacrifice, devotion and religiosity. Feminist activism in the early twentieth century saw the first of the organizing of women, and addressed issues such as gendered construction of the social and political domains, their changing boundaries and the challenges they posed. Feminist activism could bring into public discourse some of the crucial issues and politicize them at a time when India was under colonial rule, and the political climate was less favourable than under postcolonial India.

In Indian patriarchal system, cultural ideas have been used as a tool of the powerful in making of gender relations. Men in general have constructed ideologies that define women as inferior to justify their inferior treatment. Culture is so powerful that it operates gender identity. Feminist scholars have recognized that Indian women are disadvantaged by widely shared gender ideologies of Hindu culture that restrict women's movements outside the home and limit women's interactions with their husbands within the homes. Accounts such as women' subordinate economic position, the rigid boundaries of a caste system or joint-family living, all these Hindu social structures help to form gender ideology. Hindu men and women confront every day the structure of gender inequality. It is evident that men realize the advantages that are gained by controlling women and that they consciously act and talk to maintain those advantages.

Scholars such as Janaki Nair (1994), Mrinalini Sinha (1997), Uma Chakravarti (1998) and Patricia Oberoi (1996) reviewed sexuality within a complex of interrelated social and political phenomena, and they avoid restricting it to only individual psychological referents. Chakravarti conceptualizes sexuality as a relation between the caste systems and the sexual conduct of women. Sinha points out the colonial masculinity's dependence on notions of female chastity. Nair and Oberoi blame it to the changes in laws and social reforms. These scholars have connected sexuality within the domains of economy, national identity, communal cohesion and forms of the state.

Gender ideology accompanies gender division of labour. In India, gender ideology recognizes appropriate female behaviour that emphasizes modesty, obedience, self-sacrifice and attachment to the home. Precisely speaking Hindu gender ideology consists of the elements such as restrictions on women's movement outside the home, limitations on their interactions with powerful men within the home, everyday interactions that constitute women as vulnerable intruders outside the home, men's perception that restricting women advances their own interests, restrictions on interactions between husband and wife, and men's interest in limiting women's power within the household. These are factors that contribute to women's position in India.

Culture is a process of domination, and Indian women's practices also shape the gender order. Scholars such as Kandiyoti (1988) argue that in societies like India, China and the Muslim Middle East, women's strategy is never independent of men's ideas. Scheff (1990) argues that structures of domination are often joint accomplishments of both super ordinates and subordinates. Liddle and Joshi (1986), Calman (1992), Gail Omvedt (1980) and so on perceived women to be strong and dominant. The working-class women and the powerful images of female goddesses in Indian religion imply women's actions that most clearly contest the dominant gender ideology.

In recent times, the subaltern theories have analysed and explained the way in which the powerful (coercion) and the weak (consent) interact during 200 years of British rule. In their attempts to explain hegemonic processes, subaltern scholars have uncovered the articulated stories of suppressed people. Gayatri Spivak in her article, 'Can the Subaltern Speak?', states that 'it is problematic to write the history of colonial women because, women as object of colonial historiography and as subject of insurgency, the ideological construction of gender keeps the male dominant. If, in the context of colonial production, the subaltern has no history and cannot speak, the subaltern as female is even more deeply in shadow'. Subaltern studies conceptualize the colonial state as incapable of affecting the domain of intimate relations. To subalterns, it was the village councils and the larger community who ruled over sexuality.

The decade of 1980s was marked by ignition of caste identity and consciousness and theoretical and political issues involved in the debate on caste and its role in social transformation came to be debated (Kothari, 1994). Relationship between dalit and feminist politics is an important issue around which many of the debate of contemporary dalit politics are based. The emergence of autonomous dalit women's organizations in the 1990s gave rise to a politico-ideological platform called dalit feminism, thereby giving rise to an intense debate around the issue of caste and gender and their interrelatedness.

In this context one may also point out that during the 1980s and the 1990s, politics of difference was gaining vast prominence in the world feminist movement, with increasing affirmation of black feminist and Third World feminist identities. Gopal Guru (1995) argues that 'in a situation, where the organization of politics around difference has become a major feature of feminist politics, the organization of Dalit women around the notion of difference is bound to be a logical outcome'. This independent assertion, as Guru argues, should not be perceived as divisive by dalit men, 'instead, it ought to be seen as carrying positive emancipatory potential' that can 'lead to a meaningful engagement of their creative energies'.

Sharmila Rege is the scholar whose work on the interplay of patriarchy and caste oppression is important for understanding Indian feminism. Rege rewrote the book on feminist studies by showing that patriarchy here is about caste and about keeping its hierarchies intact. Delving into the history and politics of social movements, particularly of lower caste struggles, she showed that gender and caste are intertwined deeply. Her books, *Writing Caste, Writing Gender: Reading Dalit Women's Testimonios* (2011), and her recent work, *Against the Madness of Manu: B.R. Ambedkar's Writings on Brahmanical Patriarchy* (2013), as well as several essays and activist interventions, nudged the feminist debate in India towards critical engagement with questions of caste.

The dalit feminist argues that Dr B.R. Ambedkar not only championed the cause of social justice for the downtrodden and underprivileged sections of Indian society but also worked diligently throughout his life to challenge the legitimacy of orthodox Hindu social order that defends iniquitous gender relations in an institutionalized manner. His mission in life was to reconstruct Hindu society along the modern democratic ideas of liberty, equality and fraternity. Ambedkar played an important role in the emancipation of social status of women in the Hindu society. His ideas are very relevant in the contemporary feminist discourse on gender equality. His main argument is that gender relations are artificially constructed under Hindu social order, which not only moulds attitude of Hindus towards their women but also conditions women to confirm to a stereotype feminine behaviour.

Remarkable changes have taken place regarding the status of women since independence. The Constitution promised complete equality to women. Women like men also got right to vote. B.R. Ambedkar, the law minister after independence, submitted a bill that raised the age of consent and marriage, upheld monogamy, gave women right to divorce, maintenance and inheritance and treated dowry as *stridhan* or woman's property. This bill faced stiff opposition from the conservative section of society. The bill had to be postponed because of this. Finally important sections of the bill got passed in four separate acts: The Hindu Marriage Act, The Hindu Succession Act, The Hindu Minority and Guardianship Act and The Hindu Adoption and Maintenance Act. The extension of legal rights to Hindu women was not sufficient but it was definitely a bold step. This can be gauged from the stiff opposition faced by the government while extending the same legal rights to women from other religious communities.

In 1985, the Supreme Court granted a pittance to Shah Bano, a divorced Muslim woman; the conservatives among Muslim community created so much of furore in the name of interference in the Muslim personal law that Rajeev Gandhi's government wilted and introduced a bill in the parliament to negate the Supreme Court judgment. Some legal rights have been exercised even as some have remained on paper. The right to vote has been taken seriously by women even in rural areas. Many times they take decisions independent of their husbands about whom to vote. The 73rd and 74th Constitutional Amendment Acts have provided for reservation of 33 per cent seats in local self-government institution both urban and local for women. It has played an important role in correcting gender bias in our political and social life. But the promise to reserve seats in parliament has not been met yet.

A recent debate in gender identity is the identity of third gender. On the 15 April 2014, India's Supreme Court legally recognized a third gender, declaring that those who identify themselves as neither male nor female should be entitled to the same educational, welfare and employment rights as other men and women. Third is usually understood to mean other, a word which is often seen on application forms and official pieces of documentation as a catch-all category when the standard options provided are inappropriate.

In India, the declaration of a third gender is primarily connected with the *hijra* community, the collective description used for transsexuals, transvestites, cross-dressers, eunuchs and transgender people. This community has often lived on the fringes of society, ostracized because of their gender identity and denied basic rights – a situation which the new ruling attempts to address. However, India is not the first country to legally recognize a third gender, Nepal taking the same step in 2007, and Bangladesh in 2013. In November 2013, Germany became the first European country to allow a third gender designation on birth certificates. The expression third gender has various interpretations, the strictest being as a category that is completely independent of male or female. Others include the state of being both man and woman, being neither man nor woman, being in an intermediate state between man and woman, or the ability to cross or swap genders.

VI

The forces of new technologies, social network and globalization have been playing an important role in the representation of local/personal identities as social construction. It enabled the growing of identity politics after 1980s, otherness identities expose their resistance to not only universal hegemonies but also contesting within the same identity in many aspects that extensively have been playing an important role in the weakening of these identities. The otherness identity question has been emerged as an alternative force in presenting their experiences in the mainstream society. The otherness and their experiences and their struggles are different from region to region and country to country as well. In this way, we need to assess the nature of identity struggles of otherness in the study of personal experiences from grass-root levels. This will help us to construct otherness identities and contextualize the debates related to identities from multidisciplinary perspective.

Globalization can be seen as an ideology committed to production for profit, which leads to relative or absolute deprivation of women, colonies and marginal groups and communities (Sociology Essays, 2015). Globalization has brought profound transformation in the lives of people everywhere, and it has immense potential to affect social, political and economic conditions globally. Globalization is also transforming people's definitions of selfhood and identity. Globalization is generally agreed to result in an increasing overall homogeneity, and an increase in standardization, in broad terms, across the world, due to the swapping of local business and media by multinationals. The globalization, in this sense, is a force that inspires enabling of the multiple narrative development of a sense of self, through searching, creatively, for a sense of one's own identity. The globalization of ideas, of information, has thus been a great enabler of the postmodern development of self-identity, in terms of opening up the number of possible narratives and providing evidence that alternative narratives are not only possible, but also desirable. The globalized world enables such self-directed participation, as active creators of one's own identity, where an individual will 'fit in' somewhere, due to the re-defining of social space as a variety of niches, all of which are open for new members who have defined their reflexive self on the basis of that particular narrative.

According to David Lyon (1999), the postmodern social condition is dominated by two realities: the rise of new media technologies and the dominance of consumerism in society. The combination of these two dynamics causes identity to come to the foreground as a question that has no final answer. This is both a source of exhilaration (we are free to construct ourselves) and anxiety (we really don't know who we are at the deepest level).

According to Foucault (1975, 2009), identity is a creation of power knowledge (the way the circulations of power created discursive fields which construct identity). He stated: 'Power produces knowledge ... power and knowledge directly imply one another ... there is no power relation without the correlative constitution of a field of knowledge, nor any knowledge that does not presuppose and constitute at the same time power relations'. He also stated: Truth is not outside of power, or lacking power: contrary to a myth whose history and functions would repay further study, truth isn't the reward of free spirits, the child of protracted solitude, nor the privilege of those who have succeeded in liberating themselves. Truth is a thing of this world: it is produced only by virtue of multiple forms of constraint. And it induces regular effects of power. Each society has its regime of truth, its 'general politics' of truth: that is, the types of discourse which it accepts and makes function as true; the mechanisms and instances which enable one to distinguish true and false statements, the means by which each is sanctioned; the techniques and procedures accorded value in the acquisition of truth; the status of those who are charged with saying what counts as true.

According to Lacan, the self – born vulnerable – forms identity through identifying with 'images' on a doomed quest for a unified, stable sense of self. According to Paul Ricoeur (1995), the self is essentially a fiction through which we understand our lives as coherent stories (narrative identity). We are the stories we inhabit and tell about ourselves.

Dichotomies of otherness are set up as being natural, and often times in everyday life they are taken for granted and presumed to be natural. But social identities are not natural – they represent an established social order – a hierarchy where certain groups are established as being superior to other groups. Individuals have the choice (or agency) to create their identities according to their own beliefs about the world. Yet the negotiation of identity equally depends upon the negotiation of power relations. Andrew Okolie (2003) argues that 'social identities are relational; groups typically define themselves in relation to others'. This is because identity has little meaning without the other. So, by defining itself a group defines others. Identity is rarely claimed or assigned for its own sake. These definitions of self and others have purposes and consequences. They are tied to rewards and punishment, which may be material or symbolic. There is usually an expectation of gain or loss as a consequence of identity claims. This is why identities are contested. He also stated that: Power is implicated here, and because groups do not have equal powers to define both self and the other, the consequences reflect these power differentials. Often notions of superiority and inferiority are embedded in particular identities.

Social institutions such as the law, the media, education, religion and so on hold the balance of power through their representation of what is accepted as 'normal' and what is considered other. British sociologist Stuart Hall argues that visual representations of otherness holds special cultural authority. The notion of otherness is used by sociologists to highlight how social identities are contested. We also use this concept to break down the ideologies and resources that groups use to maintain their social identities. Sociologists are therefore interested in the ways in which notions of otherness are managed in society. For example, we study how some groups become stigmatized as outsiders, and how such ideas change over time. As Dutch-American sociologist Philomena Essed argues (1991, 1996), the power of othering includes opting out of 'seeing' or responding to racial discriminations. He stated that

> Power exists as long as the group stays together against the 'others' ... Exercising power over other people affects them, through action or inaction ... whether or not those who exercise power are aware of the success or consequences of their practices and whether or not the other party is aware of the power being exercised over him or her.

Thus, the concepts of self and the other are used by postmodern social scientists and cultural theorists to emphasize how social identities are contested. This book also used these concepts to understand the contested nature of marginal identities and its relation with the state and other hegemonic institutions.

VII

The book is divided into four thematic sections covering 16 chapters by scholars, social science researchers and other experts on identities of caste, tribe and gender. In each section, four chapters are included, each touching upon the main theme of the book. Thus, the readers will find this book dealing with self and the other in the study of caste, tribe and gender identity politics.

Section I

Politics of Self and Other

Sunitaa Saikia's chapter, 'Contestation of Identities in a Globalizing World', tends to explore the interface between contemporary state and social identities and also shows how the development of technology, globalization and social network revolution proves to be a harbinger of the process of major changes in the social movements and identity contestations. She argues that our place in the society is determined by our identity, which is a relative term because – though it is a marker of who we are – it actually tells us how we relate to others in the world we live in. And since we interact within a plethora of systems, our identities are essentially multifaceted, stemming from a number of cultural classifications, such as ethnicity, nationality, social, class, gender, sexuality, and so on. Suniti Ahuja in her chapter, 'Conceptualizing "Self" and "Otherness" Identity', argues that in the present scenario, people from all walks of life are facing extremely intense and stressful lives. Newer and bigger challenges are experienced every day. Peace of mind is torn into pieces. Physical science has enabled us to guide the missiles but has done nothing to guide our own mind. It will only be possible with the true knowledge of our own identity (SELF) and the identity of others. She argues that

> in order to conceptualize the self and otherness identity in real, we will have to understand our true real identity which is: S-Spiritual, E-Energy, L-Light, F-Form, i.e. we all are spiritual energy in light form. If we think minutely on this, then we will find that each human individual has to be a unique expression of that universal element; each human being is both unique and universal. He has in him an element of the divine as also an element nature. When the two things get integrated, then it is that you call a human being a fulfilled and perfect human being. So without imbibing the divine values in ourselves, we will not be in a position to realize our own true identity as well as the identity of others. This brings out the issue of divinity through the self construction.

Binod C. Agrawal in his chapter, '"Self" and "Other" of Hindu Identity in National and Global Perspective', argues that self in each context is specifically defined in a given situation and contextually presented for the purpose of other. The boundary of other keeps shifting, and each time it is redefined for social action. The symbolic interaction has been compounded by the colonial hangover of caste and tribe classification, and related laws such as the '1850 Caste-Disabilities Removal Act' which was enacted by the colonial rulers remain unchanged in independent India is used as a strategy for electoral victory in parliamentary democracy, though in both situations social action of self and other remained on shifting sand. He also argues that the issue of contesting self and other identities of caste, tribe, gender and beyond from the perspective of 'symbolic interaction' helps fathom individual social action to suggest amicable solution of socio-political conflict and alternate method to solve the issue. Maggie Katharpi's chapter, 'Reflections in Understanding the "Self": Transforming Hegemony and the (un)Seen "Other"', attempts to focus on identifying hegemonic elements that have eventually resulted in recreating the Other in the image of the 'self'. Much as in similar categories identified as affected with hegemony, the natives of Karbi Anglong are found to be undergoing through several phases of intergenerational transmission of the Other, at times under vicious and the so-called 'unseen' avoidable circumstances. The natives despite being called the 'Columbus of Assam' reflect an inchoate peoples' group. Accepted that the concept of domination is a vital and essential mechanism in the entire process of hegemony, what about elements that stabilize the noun/adjective. Where does a common man sense a political strength, a growing economy, an efficient civil/military force and the capability to lead and enforce.

Section II

Caste and Tribe

Vulli Dhanaraju's chapter, 'Debating the Caste in Indian History', proposes that caste is the most debatable issue that has enthralled and divided scholars who wished to study the system of stratified social hierarchy in India. There is an enormous body of academic writing and political polemic on the issue. These are basically the part of debate on the transformation of Indian society under the impact of colonialism and its administrative mechanisms. Some argue for the continuities of precolonial social structures including caste. Others stress the basic qualitative changes introduced by the colonial rulers. In this context, this chapter assesses the different views on the ideology of caste in Indian academics. Riju Devi's chapter, 'Caste-based Exclusion of the 'Damais' among the Nepali community in Assam', looked at the issue of caste system among the Nepali communities. The social order of the Nepali community is exclusionary due to its classification into groups as distinct castes within the broad framework of the Hindu system of the four *varnas* based on concepts of ritual purity and pollution. She argues in her chapter that apart from these divisions in Hinduism, there are other subcastes within these when it comes to the Nepali community, depending on the setting. Rigid rules of avoidance between castes, and denial of contacts that are regarded as contaminating, happen to prevail in villages. Generally, within the Nepali caste system, the process of patronization of the high castes by the lower castes is very prevalent. The distance in terms of contacts is strictly maintained and the concept of purity and pollution is imbibed, not just in the hierarchical structure but also in the day to day rituals. Abheeshta Nath J.R.'s chapter, 'In Search of the Myth and the Real "Ishi": The Last Man of Yahi Tribe', is an attempt to seek 'Ishi' – the individual and the representative of his tribe through the various works that came out in his name, and also the contentions in these works as they are the outputs of the Occidentals writing about the 'Oriental Other'! She has brought out the very interesting discussion about the last of man of *Yahi* Tribe. On 29 August 1911, a 'wild man' entered into the occidental world of Oroville, California, from the wilderness of the neighbouring foothills. Shadowed with hunger, isolation, exposure and fright, he appeared wretchedly near death, at a slaughterhouse in the outskirts of the city. The curiosity of local whites compelled the county sheriff to lock him in jail. Newspaper stories concerning 'The Primitive/Stone Age Man' brought him to the attention of the anthropologists, Alfred Kroeber and Thomas Waterman. They identified him as the last man of the *Yahi* Indian tribe, whose population dropped drastically in the infamous California Gold Rush (1848–1855). He could speak no language except for a Yana dialect. He had no name and hence they gave him the name 'Ishi', which meant 'man' or 'person' in Yana language. They managed to have him released to the care of the Museum of Art and Anthropology of the University of California. Thus, Ishi, the last *Yahi*, came to live his final years in a museum room and finally succumbed to TB in 1916. This chapter argued that ever since his appearance to his death and, thereafter, Ishi has gained the attention of men from various disciplines. Their unnatural interest in him almost evolved him into a cult with a number of biographies, scholarly studies, documentaries, movies and so on coming out in his name. He even became the hero of some children's literatures. R.K. Bijeta's chapter entitled 'Raids, Resistance and Sovereignty: A Study of Naga–Ahom Relations' narrates the Ahom–Naga relations in pre-colonial Northeast India. The sporadic conflicts of the Ahoms with the Nagas were one of the main characteristics of the history of Assam throughout the entire period of Ahom rule. Raids were the means through which Nagas articulated their resistance, restiveness, objection, power and sovereignty. It was hence a political deal rather than a guerrilla tactics of terrorizing as is often supposed. Raids were also countered by raids called expedition or punitive expedition. In this sense, raids and counter raids were the feature of pre-colonial Ahom–Naga relationship. It was followed by reasons of sovereignty, clash over scarce resources, and requirement of rites and resistance to an advancing power. In all cases, the weapon that was used by the Nagas to express their hostility was raids.

Section III

Gender

Thiyam Rabikanta Singh's chapter, 'Masculine Gender Identity and Man's Modern Right among the Meiteis of Manipur', argues that generally, masculine gender role identity is established from the early age of a boy. A Meitei boy's 'maleness' not only being a biological male, but also as male gender is structured culturally to achieve the male's self-image as a gendered being. Masculine identity that is sharply maintained in rural agrarian economy, however, is to certain degree coexists with mixed identity in urban surroundings. The socially prescribed gender role is challenged by certain individuals as they cannot bear the stigma of gender stereotypes in fighting the practical way of life in the present situation. Nevertheless, in the Meitei tradition, there are certain feministic social roles such as *maibi*, the spiritually possessed priestess that can be adopted as a transsexual role by her anatomically opposite sex. Some males step outside the bound of male occupations and take up feministic occupations even though the society marginalizes them. In addition, there are also man's modern rights telling the grievances of male gender that can be pledged to every ear in human society. The qualitative study among the Meiteis tries to discourse the development, shift of masculine ego ideal as well as man's rights of the concerned people. Tahir Hussain Ansari's chapter, 'Situating Women in Muslim Society: Study from Personal Experiences', highlights the issue of women's question in Muslim society from his personal experiences. Muslims in India have often felt to be structurally and systemically alienated from the mainstream. The Sachar Committee Report brings forth the hard hitting fact about the situation of Muslims in India. The report says that Muslims are doing worse than Scheduled Castes (SCs) and Scheduled Tribes (STs). And the absence of any affirmative action to redress this has worsened the scenario. Concerns like how one understands the situation of women in a more patriarchal religion like Islam have taken centre in many debates. But sadly the experience of Muslim women is often seen as the same with Muslim men or other women. Either gender overdetermines or community overdetermines the Muslim women's question. Whatever work is done on Muslim women, religion is seen as dominating in every aspect. He argues that the need to talk about

Muslim women when one talks of marginalized communities rises from the fact that Muslim women is a doubly marginalized community – being women and being Muslims. Tripti Soni in her chapter, 'Does Sexuality Define Identity? An Expository Study on Bar Dancers, Prostitutes and Eunuchs in the Works of Literature', raises the issues of identities in the lives of bar dancers, prostitutes and eunuchs. They are ostracized from the society and their identical issues are beyond from caste, tribe and gender identities. Their identity is rather related to sexuality. At one side, society looks down to the bar dancers and prostitutes for their explosive sexuality, and on other side eunuchs who do not belong to any gender are deprived of passionate love and physical contact. Their struggle is not for money, land and power rather they seek to establish their personal identity. This chapter focuses on two issues. First, the fact that how a sense of your identity is essential to being able to truly loved. Second, it also elucidates the terms such as bigender and third gender in the works of eminent writers such as Jeet Thayil, Suketu Mehta, Anchee Min, Jia Yinghua, Germaine Greer, Jason Goodwin and many more. Rini Banerjee's chapter, 'Role of Societal Norms in the Creation of Identity of a Female: A Study of Aruni Kashyap's The House with a Thousand Stories', focuses on Oholya, the matriarch who establishes her own identity or rather tries to establish her identity by herself within the family by her activities. This chapter highlights the different aspects of her personality that went on in the creation of her identity without a male relation apart from her father as well as the reasons behind her becoming the unmarried matriarch of the large extended family. She happens to be the powerful matriarch of the well-known Assamese family of Mayong. In creating such a character, Kashyap has rejected those stereotyped female characters that find a place in almost every Indian literature.

Section IV

Other Marginal Identities and Politics

Bijayani Mishra's chapter, 'Conceptualizing Nature of Identity Movement: An Analysis of Telangana State', analyses people's aspiration of Telangana for identity and self-rule, the process by which an identity has been constructed and throws light on different factors that contributed to the ever popular identity movement in India. Telangana Movement has been a strongly mobilized movement in India. This movement is not a struggle for identity based on either language or religion. Telangana people's movement could be analysed in historical and developmental context. In Andhra Pradesh, rather than just language they cherish their history and cultural synthesis as their identity. Both language and culture are crucial to identity, and Telangana people are not an exception to it. The sub-regional identity grew when the factors of 'internal colonialism' generated and promoted inter-regional disparities and different phases of discrimination. During colonial period, settlers not only occupied Telangana but also acquired permanent settlement on land and continued their rule on Telangana population. The formation of linguistic state and the process of urbanization both ended in widening the social, cultural, economic disparities and imbalanced and unplanned growth. Many of the sub-regions despite being rich in resources have remained economically underdeveloped due to sheer neglect of their development by the state. One region has been survived at the cost of other through resource and earning transfers. This is the main reasons for demand of identity and a clarion call for separate Telangana state. Biman Kumar Nath in his chapter, 'Occupation of the Marginalized: A Study of Urban Informal Sector in Tezpur Town of Assam', focuses on the issues of the marginal section in informal sector. The informal sector is characterized by low level of organization, long working hours, absence of employer–employee contract and predominance of unskilled workers that leads to low productivity. The rapid urbanization process in different corners of India fuelled the growth of informal sector, which is better labelled as urban informal sector in the development literature. Such trend of urbanization is also reflected in Tezpur town of Assam, which is situated in the north bank of Brahmaputra valley of Assam. A survey is made with 200 workers in urban informal sector works as self-employed and working in other enterprises. Canvassing pretested questionnaire to the workers yields various interesting results. The employment situation of the respondents is highly disturbing. Moreover, their earnings and working conditions are vulnerable. Jhumpa Dey and Sekhar Kanti Sarkar's chapter, 'Social Networking Sites: A Born or Curse for Society', argues that social networking is a network of expanding the number of one's social contacts or for business by making connection through individuals. Social networking can be done for business purposes or for social reasons or for both. Since the introduction of social networking sites like Orkut, Myspace, Facebook, LinkedIn, WhatsApp and other social networking sites offer its user to connect and communicate with other users of these sites or its members. These sites are also called social media sites. In the present age, social media is defined in terms of mobile and web-based technologies to create a social network in a virtual world through a collection of online communication channels. Social media are those virtual worlds where people interact freely, sharing and discussing ideas and information, know about each other and their lives, sending messages and so on by using a multimedia mix of personal words, pictures, videos and audios. In this context, this chapter finds out what constitute social networking or social media sites, whether social networking sites are a boon or a curse for society in the present context and to what extent it is protecting the rights of the marginalized gender, that is, women section of the society. Prasad R.'s chapter, 'Conceptualizing "Self" as a Social Product: An Analysis among the Migrant Labourers in Kerala', is divided into two parts: the first section of the chapter deals with the theoretical understanding of the self in the sociological discourse through reviewing the existing literature. On the basis of this theoretical framework, the second part investigates the identity of the migrant people in the destination region. India, although, considered as an emerging world power, however, is also known for its large-scale socio-economic disparities. It is characterized by widespread inland and foreign migration. For a better living, people are in search for green pastures. While the skilled are moving outward, the unskilled people are trying their luck through migration within the county. For the latter category, Kerala is now considered as a prominent destination region for many. It is estimated that more than 25 lakh migrant labourers from the states of West Bengal, Bihar, Assam, UP, Orissa and other states are employed in the labour market as manual labourers. But, within Kerala these people are indeed being very vulnerable and marginalized. These people, although, are a major part of the overall socio-cultural setting, at the same time being exposed to large-scale maltreatment and social discrimination. In this scenario, this chapter is an attempt to capture the extent of this problem linking it with the problem of 'identity' and 'self'.

Thus, the edited book proposes to explore the nature of social subordination and its diverse forms of subordinations in the study of field experiences/struggle and structural domination among various social identities. The interface between contemporary state and social identities on the one hand and relationships among personal identities on the other hand provided the context within which social discrimination or subordination is practiced. Social marginalization, contestation and discrimination have been playing an important role in the construction of social identities in India. Although the formation and development of technology, globalization, and social network revolution heralded the process of major changes in the social identity movements, which remoulded many of the pre-existing social identities, thus, this book will explore the identity struggles in understanding contestations within self and other identities of caste, tribe and gender.

References

Bauman, Zygmunt, *Post-modernity and Its Discontents* (London: Polity Press, 1998). http://othersociologist.com/otherness-resources/(19 May 2015).

Bayly, Susan, *Caste, Society and Politics in India from the Eighteenth Century to the Modern Age* (New York: Cambridge University Press, 1999).

Berreman, Gerald D., 'The Brahmanical View of Caste', *Social Stratification,* (ed.), D Gupta (New Delhi: Oxford University Press, 1991).

Berreman, Gerald D., *Caste and Other Inequities* (New Delhi: Ved Prakash Vatuk, 1979).

Bhattacharya, Neeladri, 'Introduction', *Studies in History* Vol. 14, No. 2 (1999): 165–171.

Borossa, Julia, and Caroline Rooney, 'Suffering, Transience and Immortal Longings: Salome Between Nietzsche and Freud', *Journal of European Studies* Vol. 33, Nos. 3/4 (2003): 287–304.

Brandom, R.B., 'Untimely Review of Hegel's Phenomenology of Spirit', *An International review of Philosophy* Vol. 27 (2008): 161–164, http://www.pitt.edu/~brandom/(20 June 2015).

Brons, Lajos, 'Othering: An Analysis'. http://www2.hu-berlin.de/transcience/Vol6_No1_2015_69_90.pdf (February, 2016).

Buber, Martin (1923), Martin Buber wrote his famous essay on existence, *Ichu and Du* (later translated into English as *I and Thou*), and in 1925, he began translating the Hebrew Bible into the German language.

Butler, Judith, *Gender Trouble: Feminism and the Subversion of Identity* (London: Routledge, 1990).

Calman, Leslie, *Toward Empowerment: Women and Movement Politics in India* (Boulder: Westview Press, 1992).

Charsley, Simon, 'Untouchable: What Is in a Name?', *Journal of the Royal Anthropological Institute* Vol. 2, No. 1 (1996): 1–23.

Chakravarti, Uma, *Rewriting History: The Life and Times of Pandita Ramabai* (New Delhi: Kali for Women, 1998).

Chatterjee, Partha, 'Colonialism, Nationalism, and Colonialized Women: The Contest in India', *American Ethnologist* Vol. 16 (1989): 622–633.

de Beauvoir, Simone, *The Second Sex* (Harmondsworth: Penguin Books, 1977).

Deliege, Robert, 'Replication and Consensus: Untouchability, Caste and Ideology in India', *Man* Vol. 27, No. 1 (1992): 155–173.

Derrida, Jacques, *'Difference': Margins of Philosophy* (Chicago: University of Chicago, 1982).

Dirks, Nicholas B., *Castes of Mind: Colonialism and the Making of Modern India,* (Princeton: Princeton University Press, 2001).

Dirks, Nicholas B., *The Hollow Crown: Ethnohistory of an Indian Kingdom* (Cambridge: Cambridge University Press, 1987).

Dumont, Louis, *Homo Hierarchicus: The Caste System and Its Implications* (Chicago: University of Chicago Press, 1980).

Essed, Philomena, *Diversity: Gender, Color and Culture* (Amherst: Mass Press, 1996) Cited in 'What is Otherness'? http://othersociologist.com/otherness-resources/(12 April 2015).

Fanon, Frantz, *Black Skin, White Masks* (*Peau noire: masques blancs*, 1952). It is a sociological study of the psychology of the racism and dehumanization inherent in situations of colonial domination.

Fanon, Frantz, *Grolier Encyclopedia of Knowledge* Vol. 7 (1952).

Forbes, Geraldine, *Women in Modern India* (Cambridge: Cambridge University Press, 1996).

Foucault, Michel, 'Body/Power and Truth and Power', *Michel Foucault: Power/Knowledge*, (ed.), C. Gordon (UK: Harvest, 1980).

Foucault, Michel, *Discipline and Punish: the Birth of the Prison* (New York: Random House, 1975).

Foucault, Michel, *Power/Knowledge: Selected Interviews and Other Writings, 1972–1977* (New York: Vintage, 1980a).

Foucault, Michel, *The History of Sexuality* (London: Penguin Books, 1978).

Ghurye, G.S., *Caste and Race in India* (Bombay: Popular Prakashan, 1969).

Gough, Kathelin, 'Brahmin Kinship in a Tamil Village', *American Anthropologist* Vol. 58, (1973): 826–853.

Guha, Ranajit, *Elementary Aspects of Peasant Insurgency in Colonial India* (New Delhi: Oxford University Press, 1983).

Guru, Gopal, 'Dalit Women Talk Different', *Economic and Political Weekly* Vol. 30, Nos. 41/42 (1995): 2548–2550.

Hegel, G.W.F., *Encyclopaedia of Philosophical Sciences* (translated by William Wallace) (London: Oxford University Press, 1985).

Hegel, G.W.F., *Phenomenology of Mind* (translation of Hegel, 1807 by J.B. Baillie) (London: Harper & Row, 1967).

Homi Bhabha, K., 'The Other Question: Difference, Discrimination and the Discourse of Colonialism', in *Out There: Marginalization and Contemporary Cultures*, (ed.), Russell Ferguson (New York: New Museum of Contemporary Art, 1990).

Inden, Ronald B., *Imagining India* (Oxford: Basil Blackwell, 1990).

Irvine, Judith, and Ronald B. Inden, *Marriage and Rank in Bengali Culture: A History of Caste and Clan in the Middle Period Bengal* (Berkeley: University of California Press, 1975).

Jenkins, Richard, *Social Identity (Key Ideas)* (London: Routledge, 2008).

Juergensmeyer, Mark, *Religion as Social Vision: The Movement against Untouchability in 20th Century Punjab* (Berkeley: University of California Press, 1982).

Kamal, Muhammad, 'Master-Slave Relationship in Hegel's Dialectics', *Hegel Summer School* (2004). http://ethicalpolitics.org/seminars/master-slave.htm (22 June 2015).

Kandiyoti, Deniz, 'Bargaining with Patriarchy', *Gender and Society* Vol. 2, No. 3 (September 1988): 274–289.

Kothari, R., 'Rise of Dalits and the Renewed Debate on Caste', *Economic and Political Weekly* (25 June 1994): 1589–1594.

Lacan, Jacques, *The Four Fundamental Concepts of Psychoanalysis* (New York: W.W. Norton and Company, 1977).

Liddle, J., and R. Joshi, *Daughters of Independence Gender, Caste and Class in India* (New Delhi: Kali for Women 1986).

Lyon, David, *The Post Modernity: Concepts in Social Sciences* (Open University Press, 1999).

Mead, George Herbert, *Mind Self and Society from the Standpoint of a Social Behaviorist* (Chicago: University of Chicago, 1934) (Cited in Feminist Perspectives on the *'Self'*, (First published 28 June 1999) (Substantive Revision 27 January 2010).

Mencher, Joan, 'The Caste System Upside Down, or The Not-So-Mysterious East', *Current Anthropology* Vol. 15, No. 4 (1974): 469–493.

Moffatt, Michael, *An Untouchable Community in South India: Structure and Consensus* (Princeton: Princeton University Press, 1979).

Moran, Philip, *Hegel and the Fundamental Problems of Philosophy* (Holland: Gruner, 1988).

Mosse, David, 'Idioms of Subordination and Styles of Protest among Christian and Hindu Harijan Castes in Tamil Nadu', *Contributions to Indian Sociology* Vol. 28, No. 1 (1994): 67–106.

Okolie, Andrew, 'Identity', *An International Journal of Theory and Research* Vol. 3, No. 1 (2003).

Omvedt, Gail, *We Will Smash this Prison: Indian Women Struggle* (London: Zed, 1980).

Philomena Essed, *Everyday Racism: Reports from Women in Two Cultures* (Claremont: Hunter House, 1990).

Philomena Essed, *Understanding Everyday Racism: An Interdisciplinary Theory* (Newbury Park: Sage Publications, 1991).

Ricoeur, Paul, *Oneself of Another* (Chicago: University of Chicago, 1995).

Said, Edward W., *Orientalism: Western Conceptions of the Orient* (London: Penguin, 1995).

Sargiacomo, M., 'Michel Foucault, Discipline and Punish: The Birth of the Prison', *Journal of Management and Governance* Vol. 13, No. 3 (2009): 269–280.

Sarkar, Sumit, *Beyond Nationalist Frames: Postmodernism, Hindu Fundamentalism, History* (New Delhi: Orient Blackswan, 2005).

Scheff, Thomas J., *Micro Sociology: Discourse, Emotion and Social Structure* (Chicago: Chicago University Press, 1990).

Silverman, Max, *Frantz Fanon's 'Black Skin, White Masks': New Interdisciplinary Essays* (Manchester: Manchester University Press, 2006).

Singh, K.S., *Birsa Munda and His Movement* (Delhi: Manohar, 1985).

Sinha, Abhinav, 'Historiography of Caste: Some Critical Observations and Some Methodological Interventions' (Paper presented at the Fourth Arvind Memorial Seminar on Caste Question and Marxism, Chandigarh, India, 12–16 March 2013).

Sinha, Mrinalini, *The Manly Englishman and the Effeminate Bengali in the late Nineteenth Century* (New Delhi: Kali for Women, 1997).

Sociology Essays: Postmodernism Identity Formation (23 March 2015). http://www.ukessays.com/essays/sociology/postmodernism-identity-formation.php (26 May 2015).

Spivak, Gayatri, 'Can the Subaltern Speak', *Marxism and the Interpretation of Culture*, (ed.), Cary Nelson and Larry Grossberg (Chicago: University of Illinois Press, 1988).

Uberoi, Patricia, *Social Reform, Sexuality and the State* (New Delhi: Sage Publications, 1996).

Vijayalakshmi, V., 'Feminist Politics in India: Women and Civil Society Activism', Working Paper No. 161 (Institute for Social and Economic Change, 2005).

Young, Robert J.C., *Postcolonialism: An Historical Introduction* (Wiley-Blackwell, 2001).

Part I

Politics of Self and Other

1

Contestation of Identities in a Globalizing World

Sunitaa Saikia

The word 'identity' can claim to be one of the most litigious words today, particularly when identities and their connotations have become contested at levels ranging from individual to perhaps universal, in an era of globalization and the concomitant mixing of peoples and cultures. Identities are not just essentialist notions existing as scientific or biological facts but also social constructions emerging from discursive practices, and they form in association to something else. Derrida (1974) proposed that identities are constructed through what they aren't, through difference and exclusion (Derrida, 1974). Identity 'is not the opposite of, but 'depends on', difference' (Woodward, 1997) or in Hall's terms, 'identities are constructed through, not outside, difference' (Hall and Gay, 1996). Relational power includes the authority to classify things into inclusion and exclusion. Binary oppositions present the most extreme picture of dissimilarity, often leading to stereotyping, as the many degrees of relationship that exist between the poles are almost ignored in toto. Often group identities are constructed through contrasting a notion of self with an 'other', as in dichotomous categories of the West and the Orient, the 'colonizers' and the 'colonized', the higher caste and the 'untouchables', generically, the 'us' and 'them' mindset.

Our identity determines our position in the society; it makes us aware 'of who we are and of how we relate to others in the world in which we live' (Woodward, 1997). We assume different roles and our identities are necessarily multifaceted, as we interact within a number of social systems. Identities stem from a number of classifications, such as gender, sexuality, social class, ethnicity, nationality and so on. Consequently, the whole is hardly ever cohesive but remains fragmented and even conflicted. A focus on the process of social construction means a recognition that identities are constantly in flux and are continually being defined and redefined through strategic interactions at all levels of states and societies. A person is located in the social space by virtue of the relationships that these identities imply. These identities are symbols whose meanings vary spatially and temporally. One's perception of oneself is in direct relation to how others perceive one, and further, it is in relation to the other that identity is constructed and reinforced.

Our preference of certain identities through which we wish to represent ourselves always function within the socially constructed world of identities that we are push into. Questions of identity arise today even in virtual spaces. With new technology, it has become much easier to present new identities in cyberspace that rupture some of these limits and to assume group identities unbounded by geographic restrictions. Many people play with their identities taking an advantage of invisibility, and take up online identities that are different from their offline identities. In the absence of any monitoring, those with culturally stigmatized or marginalized identities or ideological orientations take the opportunity to interact anonymously with others. These participants also most often experience greater self-acceptance, though these identities are often short of discursive power outside e-space.

The identity of each one of us is a potpourri determined by gender, age, class, caste, religion, region, ethnicity, race, nation, history, sexual orientation and myriad aspects that cannot be fitted into an unambiguous category. Anthropologists and historians underscore the fluidity and intricacies of social identity and problems of imposed categories. Also, our subcontinent has seen a horde of conquests and conflicts. Political theorist Rajeev Bhargava (2002) applies the metaphor of the palimpsest here; the idea that something is altered yet bears traces of its original form. Thus, the contours of caste, regional or ethnic identity has been shifting in our subcontinent. For instance, we can trace the changing view of Indian society with regard to the system of caste.

The Orientalist view of the caste system emphasized the broadest ideological category of the system of the *varnas*, referring to an idealized hierarchy of *brahmins, kshatriyas, vaishyas, shudras,* and, below all of these, the *avarna* (castes outside the *varna* order), sometimes referred to as 'untouchables' or dalits. These divisions, codified in ancient writings of the subcontinent such as the *Vedas* (1500–1000 BC) and the *Manava Dharmasastra* (first century of the Common Era), are associated with different occupations and come with a set of laws. The last century has seen the meaning of the *varna* order transforming for its actors, with a heightened opportunity for social mobility. Additionally, there is the cultural category of *jaat,* which has no structural reality in terms of corporate activities nor does it directly affect the behaviour of those who are classified under it. But there have been efforts to mobilize people around this category for political and educational purposes, in the last few decades. A *jaat* would still mean 'caste'. In reality, caste divisions are more ambiguous and regionally varied than the codifications suggest; nevertheless, caste continues to play a major role in the lives of many Indians, often having a profound effect on opportunities in terms of residence, education, occupation, social interaction and marriage. One cannot conclude that inconsistencies do not occur – occasionally, a wealthy caste has a low ritual position, just as a caste having a high ritual position is poor. Historically, it has been very hard to change the structure of caste politics in India.

Previously known as the 'depressed classes', the SC category was created by the colonial government in 1936 in order to implement the 1935 Government of India Act, which gave special electoral representation to certain minority groups, including untouchables. The STs, also known in parts of India as *adivasis,* are 'those groups distinguished by 'tribal characteristics' and by their spatial and cultural isolation from the bulk of the population' (Galanter, 1984). Although the term *tribe* evokes a 'problematic legacy of evolutionary anthropology', tribes in some cases have 'transformed it from a stigmatized label into a political asset and collective identity' (Karlsson, 2001). In spite of such instances of social interaction and mobility, they are among the most socially and economically disadvantaged groups in India (Karlsson, 11). The ST category was also listed and included as a protected minority in the 1935 Government of India Act and later recognized in the Indian Constitution for policy purposes including reservations. No method is specified in the constitution to define a third category in India, the Other Backward Classes (OBCs), except that the President should appoint a Backward Classes Commission (Article 340). The Mandal Commission Report (1980) served as a basis for extending reservations in central government jobs to the OBCs in 1990. The term *Backward Classes* has had a variety of local usages, but notably, in spite of the use of the word 'class', the category has generally not been defined by applying solely economic criteria to individuals. By and large, the OBCs are economically and socially depressed castes or communities, such as lower castes that are not considered untouchables or other similarly disadvantaged non-Hindu communities.

In India, identities are often asymmetrical, ranked or graded, and hierarchical, and the social environment is characterized by limiting identities, biases, exploitation, domination and marginalization. The striking feature of hierarchy is *varna* and much of the scholars have talked about *Manusmriti*, the scripture that sanctifies this hierarchy and gives an elaborate picture of the principle of *varnas*, their origin, assigned duties and responsibilities, their status and order of things. Hierarchy is not only ranking but a principle in which the elements of whole are ranked within the whole. The idea of hierarchy is based on the binaries of 'purity' and 'pollution', which correspond to Brahmin and dalit, the two social poles. The hierarchy of *varna* is not limited to caste only, but extends its tentacles to the other identities as well in a hierarchal manner such as ethnic communities and gender. In a patriarchal society, there is social difference between men and women: men are privileged and women are subdued. Likewise, many ethnic identities are kept under perpetual surveillance. Inferior and low ranking identities are today contesting these ideologies that legitimize such hierarchy and conflict.

In the various ancient treatises on caste, dalits have been referred to as *achhuts* (untouchables), *avarnas, panchamas, atishudras* and *antyajas*, and during freedom movement Gandhiji called them *Harijans* (children of God). And since Britishers enlisted such castes, later these were recognized in the Indian Constitution and are named as SCs (Karlsson, 133). This isolated culture and socially, economically and politically deprived status marked the identity of dalits. Post-independence, the SCs have undergone various changes and acquired different significance through reform movements or *sanskritization,* whereby lower-caste people adopt lifestyle of upper-caste people in social hierarchy, and also by the process of westernization. The identity of SCs has not only remained a social and cultural identity but also a political identity in Indian society (Karlsson, 154).

The hierarchy of caste and its role in politics and access to power and resources has created a society of patron–client relationships along the caste lines. This has resulted in the practice of vote banking, where voters back only candidates who are from their caste, or officials from whom they expect to receive some kind of benefits. Several castes have demanded a lower rank to avail privileges that are conferred on the lower castes by our constitution. India is facing competing demands to combine caste, class, tribe and gender considerations in legislative reservations. But can a state empower its citizens by simply classifying them? As Frantz Fannon (1967) aptly puts it, 'Where am I to be classified? Or, if you prefer, tucked away?' (p. 113)

Thus, identity politics in India is seen as hitherto a growing challenge to the dominant ideologies of hierarchy, hegemony and patriarchy in dialectic manner. Identity politics is witnessing a struggle in India for recognition and cultural autonomy in the various domains over a period of time – caste politics, ethnic and linguistic community, Backward Classes, SCs/STs, dalits, gender identity and so on. Identity politics makes people aware of pluralism and differences, and this presents challenges to the hegemonic ideology. However, though exclusive in nature, identity politics is more often than not, self-defeating and does not bear any constructive results. In the words of Bhabha (1994), '(I)dentity is never a priori, nor a finished product; it is only ever the problematic process of access to an image of totality' (p. 51).

Vivek Kumar (2007) has attempted to understand exclusion of dalits from the institutions of governance and politics of development in contemporary Indian society in the socio-political context of globalization, when job opportunities in private sector are spreading and in public sector it is shrinking. He takes one of the most important elements of social structure of Indian society for deliberating dominant role of caste in the shaping of Indian administrative structure. It is true that traditional social structure of Indian society influences modern social structure and it directly influences the bureaucracy and judiciary. The untouchables, tribals and even *shudras* have always been left out of the institutions of governance in the Indian society. In defining governance, sociological principles of policies, programmes, formulation and implementation, and distribution of social and economic resources among the masses on the universalistic principles and institutions of governance such as bureaucracy, legislature and judiciary should have fair representations of all social groups without monopoly of one group or the other. Kumar has shown relationship of governance and dalits in the past and present in High Court judges, Class I government jobs, Indian High Commission offices and the educational profiles of dalits in different Indian states as well as central universities in different periods of time.

Social identities are embedded in socio-political contexts. Social identity theory focuses on the extent to which individuals identify themselves in terms of group memberships (Tajfel and Turner, 1986). The central tenet of the social identity theory is that individuals define their identities along two dimensions: social, defined by membership in various social groups, and personal, the characteristics that distinguish an individual from others. Deaux (1993) argues for an inseparable interplay between the two. Since people are motivated to evaluate themselves positively, they tend to evaluate positively those groups to which they belong and to discriminate against groups they perceive to pose a threat to their social identity. But strong identification with a group need not, in principle, be correlated with out-group hostility, unless there are conditions of competition and intergroup threat (which could as well be assumed). Social identity theory maintains that it is in-group identification that causes out-group bias. Realistic conflict theory, on the other hand, maintains that out-group threat and hostility lead to in-group identification (Le Vine and Campbell, 1997). There are regional variations in the identity of groups, which are produced in different ways. There is a greater sense of association between separate groups today due to their formation into larger bodies and their uniqueness marks the level of everyday living. Different groups, while drawing on regional traditions and patterns, construct their identity in exclusive and intricate ways.

Identity movements may also generate explicit social movements. One influential theory of social movements hypothesizes a collective identity that motivates group action (Taylor and Whittier, 1992). This identity requires a perception of membership in a bounded group, consciousness about that group's ideologies, and direct resistance to the prevailing order. Langman (1998) evaluates how identity constructions serve hegemonic ends and legitimating ideologies create identities that obscure an understanding of injustice. Collective identities generally do offer social and emotional compensations for inferior categories upholding systems of inequality. The location of a caste also plays a pivotal role. If a lower caste were concentrated enough in one area, it could then translate that pocket of concentration of its caste members into political power and then challenge the hegemony of locally dominant upper caste. Those identities have a fundamental content defined by a common origin or a common structure of experience, and often both are a general supposition. When identity struggles arise, they generally take the form of redefining negative images as positive, or of bringing forth the 'authentic' identity. An alternative approach emphasizes the impossibility of authentic identities based on a universally shared experience or origin (Grossberg, 1994); identities are relational, defined by their difference from something. But Hall (1996) argues that identity is something that cannot be thought about in the 'old way' but without which certain key questions cannot be thought about at all: 'identities are points of temporary attachments to the subject positions which discursive practices construct for us' (Hall, 1996). Traditional literature reflects a modernist approach to identities, casting them as specifiable, measurable, structured and, in some sense, rational. This approach sees identities as generally stable, although responsive to social milieu, as pertinent both for individuals and for social groups and as motivators for social action. The deconstructionist literature reflects a postmodernist approach to identities, casting them as manifold, processual, relational, unstable and possibly political. Although this identity is elusive, Hall's comment that certain questions cannot be thought about without the concept of identity is well taken. What those questions address is the possibility of agency and social action.

Frable Des (1997) calls for 'seeing people as whole', referring to the need to address gender, racial, ethnic, sexual and class identities as multiple identities of whole people. In the same vein, seeing people as a whole means recognizing that both our everyday lives and the larger cultures in which we operate shape our senses of who we are and what we could become. The details of our everyday lives are relatively predictable and orderly, but the details of our larger cultural environments may be markedly more unsettled and shifting. But what is important is that both the milieu shape our experiences of identities.

K.S. Singh (2002) talks about the construction, existence and relevance of segmented identities in India with its truly collective and shared cultural heritage. These identities or new experiences emerge in such variations of the global society and result in an alternative experience of unity through the use of perpetual process of dialogue, assimilation and accommodation. Pathak (2006) says that identities often appear to be natural but the fact is that identities are constructed through socialization and cultural practices in a complex domain. The identity of a Brahmin is socialized and trained to be separate from a 'non-Brahmin'. Likewise ethnic identity depends on the intensity of cultural practices. An individual from an ethnic group grows with the self-perception of celebrating cultural practices allowed by his or her cultural/ethnic group and this ascribes his or her identity.

Now, talking about the global diaspora, the economic and social aspirations have been noticed as driving force for migration of various sorts of professionals to the Western countries – Europe, America and also to the African and Middle East nations. The migrants seek to transplant/transform cultural boundaries and recreate new representations of their selves and their past in their new environment (Rayprol, 1997: 2). In the contemporary movement of people between nations, the identities and culture get delocalized but the memories of past places and times rarely unfasten, and finally the desire for newly constructed identities arise out of such migration. Scholars have described that the immigrant communities face cases of epistemological nature, changing legal and political system, ruptures in families, tensions between older and newer social and cultural values and struggles for economic mobility. But Indian immigrants maintain extensive ties with India in contemporary times because of their comparative affluence and worldwide improvement in communication. Marriage arrangements, kinship networks, property and religious affiliations keep many migrants well linked to their places of origin in India. It is interesting to see that region, religion, caste, language, family and others still play important role in their identity formation in all parts of the world. These lead to the growth of larger social network, and associations on these lines of caste, religion, region, language and so on provide a setting for meeting and helping people coming from the same region who speak the same language, belong to the same region and religion and practice the same socio-cultural lifestyle for maintaining a separate Indian identity.

Rayprol (1997) talks of religious identities and gender relations in the context of the Indian diaspora settled in the United States, with special focus on gender relations after migration. To compete with the process of acculturation, immigrants carry imagined cultural roles with them in the alien environment. And they prefer to retain their ethnic distinctiveness and they cope up with the alien environment by remaining allied with it on the one hand and on the other hand they also try to integrate with host and parent culture as it provides opportunities for development of self-esteem and identity. Whatever strategy they adopt, they are primarily concerned with 'cultural reproduction' or the process by which they seek to transmit their knowledge, value system, belief system and behavioural norms to the next generation. To resolve this crisis, immigrants establish indigenous social and cultural activities in the new society. By the middle of the twentieth century, religion was firmly institutionalized. However, several studies have shown that Indian immigrants have retained religious values and other forms of cultural expression regardless of the community they have emerged in. The religious institutions of immigrants have not been only centres of worship but they serve various cultural and social activities, which bind them in a close-knit community. It makes them 'authentic' and feels as they were in India. And women with their traditional role as transmitters of culture take more active apart in giving concrete shape to their memories in the forms of festivals, ethnic food, traditional dress, religious practices and language classes. Women more often than men tend to serve as unpaid keepers and embodiment of memory. Women are expected to stay in the past culture and men more on the fast track of individualism.

In the late twentieth century, nostalgia served as a 'consumerist' frame as for Indian immigrants' desire for latest ethnic fashion, jewellery, spices and specificity of food, which they can acquire through global capitalism, which are embedded in a consumerist culture. All expressions of nostalgia among Indian immigrants in the group or subgroup form, share a common ancestry, a common history, a common pursuit and a common immigrant situation. Indian immigrant community is merely a moral community in the sense of religious group but is also known as a 'community of memory'. In Durkheimian view, the idea of religion performs social functions as a mode of social reality, as both the system of communication of ideas and sentiments and a mode of specifying and regulating social relationship. Immigrants in the United States stay in nuclear family but when they meet on cultural or religious occasions, they are like one big extended family and also behave in that manner. This clearly shows the desire for identity formation.

Forces of globalization, telecommunication revolution and the emergence of market economy have led to the awakening of consciousness of identity among minorities, ethnic groups and weaker sections of the society. Consequently, there is a new process of culture change through emergence of an 'information society'. If we take the example of India, we can see the impact of globalization in the nature of the cultural identities of the local, regional and national levels and also the extent of their inner resilience to withstand the forces of globalization (Singh, 2000). The rise in popular culture in the process of globalization has a direct bearing on the cultural identity and its felt crises by way of changes in lifestyle. Cultural changes are taking place at both institutional and ideological level. There have been changes in the structure of the community in both rural and urban India, and the relationship between modernity and ethnicity is also perceived in a fresh light today.

The feeling of cultural domination, process of cultural conflict, movements for seeking legitimacy for one's cultural practices and the gradual adoption of newer cultural traits with a tension in values are very common within a society at local, regional or national level. Globalization only expands the pace and scope of cultural interactions across boundaries, and there is intense cultural, social and economic interaction due to the emergence of the cultural diaspora. Such cultural contacts result in cultural assimilation, adaptation, interaction or conflict. Cultural globalization possesses a threat to the cultural identity by the way of homogenization of styles and practices. This can be seen in the upcoming fusions in styles, contents and forms in the various fields of language, music, painting, dance, architecture and other areas. One cannot say that traditional or original forms and styles of cultural continuity and creativity have ceased to evolve and that there is no replacement of original forms with experimental ones. There is assumption of new meaning and significance, since globalization not only brings several cultures and their institutions together but also enkindles sharper consciousness of cultural identity. Globalization results in the formation of a trans-global identity and the creation of infinite hybrid identities. As consumer's appropriate global culture in local ways and local culture in global ways, identity is arising not within particular national boundaries but in the relationships between cultures and identities, forming an infinite variety of hybrid identities. Geographic space is no longer the defining element, which raises the question of difference and how we are to define identities without falling back on national boundaries or a constructed organizing dichotomy, such as East versus West.

Intensification of globalization has given rise to the promotion of politics of identity instead of citizen-based politics of nation building. In Indian society, opposition to globalization as a new hegemonic development is seen in micro movement with a view to check onslaught on the interest of farmers, women, artisans and poor, and it has raised a new discourse on democracy, that is, participatory which is beyond conventional institution of election and political parties. However, India is confronted with the dilemma of joining global race on the one hand and retaining its distinct national character on the other hand, as transnational activities of globalization process touch almost all aspects of Indian social fabric including religion, media, migration, economy, polity, gender, labour, family, culture and community. The local or micro movement in India or localization does not mean necessarily obstructing modernization of the economy; migration and mobility of people and its benefit to the poor depend on how the strength of local and indigenous economy provides security and employment to its members.

National identities develop through the concept of internationalism, through relationships of one of 'us' among many of 'them'. In Anderson's (1991) terms, a nation is, in fact, an imagined community, constructed and maintained by those who claim its membership. The first challenge of a new nation is to gain international recognition, to demonstrate how it is both similar to and different from other nations. The national flag becomes symbolic of this difference (Billig, 1995). Conversely, national identities become fractured when the historical narrative is ruptured. National identities are more than their geographic outlines, economies, technologies and industries, with culture as an additional characteristic. National culture is the site of contested meanings, with the groups who wield more relative power and are able to define national identities and affect national regulatory bodies, which means national identity becomes closely linked to the notion of cultural identity. In a globalized world, geographic place no longer provides a strong sense of cultural identity, and conflating national and cultural identities becomes particularly problematic. Combined with geographic displacement is the flow of ideas through new communication technologies, forming 'a new communications geography' (Morley and Robins, 1995), which brings the issues of the relationship between culture and identity to the fore. When cultural communication is no longer based on shared history or space, it becomes difficult to define who constitutes the other in networked societies (Castells, 1996).

Nationalism in all its forms (ethnic, racial, linguistic or religious) seeks to transform the creative and accommodative flow of cultures into static or rigid ideas of cultural purity and exclusion. In our subcontinent, these forms of nationalism are frequently violent and seek to expunge from the social record the evidence of simple neighbourliness. There is tension between the lived experience of cultural (or religious) tolerance (as not only respect for, but also interest in difference), and the deployment of culture or religion for nationalist purposes. With the emergence of different kinds of nationalism in South Asia, there is reification or hardening of identities and socio-religious practices throughout the region, transcending narrow community, regional or political identities.

Though some may say that the importance of ascribed identities such as caste and religion is gradually eroding, actually these biases have remained resilient in India even in the face of substantial economic development and increasingly heterogeneous cities. Yet, such simple dichotomy understates the complexity in characterizing social biases in India. New forms of bias may emerge while other forms fade away. While social biases often result from prejudice or chauvinism, they may also result from legitimate apprehensions about, or (imagined) threats from another social group. The very process of development and change in India may be generating new forms of social and economic competition that manifest themselves in terms of social bias. A modernizing India may trigger the erosion of certain traditional hierarchies, while opening the way for new cleavages based on the social and economic contestation.

References

Anderson, Benedict, *Imagined Communities: Reflections on the Origin and Spread of Nationalism* (London: Verso Books, 1991).

Bhabha, Homi, *The Location of Culture* (London: Routledge, 1994).

Bhargava, Rajeev, Presentation at International Conference on 'Living Together Separately: Cultural India in History and Politics', organized by the Academy of Third World Studies (Jamia Milia Islamia, New Delhi, 19–21 December 2002).

Billig, Michael, *Banal Nationalism* (Sage Publications, 1995).

Castells, Manuel, *The Rise of Network Society: The Information Age: Economy, Society and Culture*, Vol. 1 (Oxford/Maiden: Blackwell Publishers, 1996).

Deaux, K., 'Reconstructing Social Identity', *Personality and Social Psychology Bulletin* Vol. 19 (1993): 4–12.

Derrida, Jacques, *Glas*, translated by John P. Leavey, Jr., and Richard Rand (Lincoln/London: University of Nebraska Press, 1986) (Original French, Paris: Galilée, 1974).

Des, Frable, 'Gender, Racial, Ethnic, Sexual, and Class Identities', *Annual Review of Psychology* Vol. 18 (1997): 176–206.

Fannon, Frantz, *Black Skin, White Masks* (New York: Grove Press, 1967).

Galanter, Marc, *Competing Equalities: Law and the Backward Classes in India* (Berkeley: University of California Press, 1984).

Grossberg, L., 'Identity and Cultural Studies: Is that All There Is?', Hall and Du Gay, *Questions of Cultural Identity* (1994): 87–107.

H., Tajfel and J., Turner, 'The Social Identity Theory of Intergroup Behaviour', S. Worchel and W.G. Austin, (eds), *Psychology of Intergroup Relations* (Chicago: Nelson, 1986): 7–24.

Hall, S. , 'Introduction: Who Needs 'Identity'?', *Questions of Cultural Identity*, (eds), Stuart Hall and Paul Du Gay. (London: Sage Publications, 1996).

Hall, Stuart and Du Gay, Paul, (eds), *Questions of Cultural Identity* (London: Sage Publications, 1996).

Karlsson, Bengt G., 'Indigenous Politics: Community Formation and Indigenous Peoples' Struggle for Self-Determination in North-East India', *Identities: Global Studies in Culture and Power* Vol. 8, No. 1 (2001): 7–45.

Kumar, Vivek, 'Governance and Development in the Era of Globalisation', *Globalisation, Governance. Reforms and Development in India*, (ed.), Kameshwar Chaudhary (New Delhi: Sage Publications, 2007): 241–258.

Langman, Lauren, 'Identity, Hegemony and Social Reproduction', *Current Perspectives in Social Theory* Vol. 18 (1998): 185–226.

Le Vine, R. and Campbell, D., *Ethnocentrism, Theories of Conflict, Ethnic Attitudes, and Group Behaviour* (New York: Wiley, 1997).

Morley, David and Robins, Kevin, *Spaces of Identity: Global Media, Electronic Landscapes and Cultural Boundaries* (London: Routledge, 1995).

Pathak, Avijit, *Modernity, Globalisation and Identity: Towards a Reflexive Quest* (Delhi: Aakar Books, 2006).

Rayprol, Aparna, *Negotiating Identities: Women in the Indian Diaspora* (Delhi: Oxford University Press, 1997).

Singh, K.S., *People of India: Introduction* (New Delhi: Oxford University Press, 2002).

Singh, Yogendra, *Culture Change in India: Identity and Globalisation* (New Delhi/Jaipur: Rawat Publications, 2000).

Taylor, Verta and Whittier, Nancy, 'Collective Identity in Social Movement Communities: Lesbian Feminist Mobilisation', *Frontiers in Social Movement Theory*, (eds), Aldon D. Morris and Carol McClurg Mueller (New Haven: Yale University Press, 1992): 104–129.

Woodward, Kathryn, *Identity and Difference: Culture, Media and Identities*, Open University Series, Vol. 3, (Sage Publications, 1997).

2

Conceptualizing 'Self' and 'Otherness' Identity

Suniti Ahuja

When I say 'I am Ram or Rahman', I mean the name of my body by which I am identified and called. If I say my father, my brother, wife or friend, it indicates their relationship with me. When I say my house, my car and my table, all these indicate my belongings. When I say I am a doctor, an engineer or a teacher, it indicates the acquired scientific and systematic knowledge for becoming a professional to earn livelihood. When I say my head, my ears and my eyes, I mean these are the organs of my body. My relations, my body and my possessions are different from me, though they belong to me. I make different uses of my body and its organs. Even the brain cannot think, decide, perceive and perform on its own. It is an inanimate component of the 'being', which performs these functions with the help of the brain and gross body.

As all goods are meant for other's use, similarly the physical body is not created for its own use. It is for the use of the conscious entity known as 'being or soul'. The soul is a sparkling point of conscious energy that empowers the entire body to monitor and perform all physical activities. The soul harmonizes the growth of body. When the soul (the master) leaves the body, the latter loses its awareness, ability to think, decide, act, react and experience. All including bodily functions ceases with the departure of 'being' from human. So soul is the life force in the living human body.

If you minutely think about the deep meaning of above two paragraphs, then it clearly shows that there are two separate entities. 'I' is separate and my belongings and possessions are separate. Then, who am I in original?

In today's scenario, we have forgotten our real selves completely. We have started considering ourselves as body, not that the power that runs the body. We have forgotten that as all goods are meant for other's use, similarly the physical body is not created for its own use. It is for the use of the conscious entity known as 'being or soul'. Soul or being is the real SELF, which is the master of the body. It is that energy or power that controls and runs this body. Even, the full form of SELF itself gives the true identity:

S: Spiritual
E: Energy in
L: Light
F: Form

Now we will try to understand the true attributes of SELF. No need to mention that requirement of 'body' is quantitative, which are food, cloth and shelter. But, the requirement of 'being' (soul) is qualitative. The qualities of soul can be classified into the following two categories:

Primary Qualities of the Soul

We are originally a point of sentient light fully charged with spiritual (metaphysical) energy that naturally manifests as truth (knowledge), peace, love, joy, purity, power and bliss (balance) when we first come into this world. These innate qualities or attributes of the soul are so basic that they themselves are the basis of all virtues and powers. Now we will think about the detailed description of these virtues.

Secondary Qualities of the Soul

Virtues are secondary qualities springing from myriad combinations of the seven basic attributes mentioned above. Another aspect of the secondary qualities, which come into play more frequently in our day-to-day life, is that these are linked to human relationships. These are as follows:

- Honesty
- Generosity
- Orderliness
- Reality
- Good Wish

- Truthfulness
- Politeness
- Equality
- Self-confidence
- Humility
- Sweetness
- Serenity
- Coolness
- Contentment
- Simplicity
- Tolerance
- Appreciation
- Determination
- Fearlessness
- Egolessness
- Sobriety
- Worrylessness
- Benevolence
- Cooperation
- Obedience
- Farsightedness
- Aloofness
- Purity
- Mercifulness
- Asceticism
- Observer state
- Royalty

It is ironical that we are completely in a state of ignorance about true identity of self and also degrading the primary and secondary qualities of a soul. In fact, human ignorance about his primary and secondary qualities are profound. Immense regions of our inner world are still unknown.

Conceptualizing 'Otherness' Identity by Conceptualizing Ourselves First

Whenever we reduce ourselves to mere things and objects, we do not try to realize that we are also subjects with the quality of being, of intelligence and of freedom. The major reason behind not conceptualizing the otherness identity is that we are not conceptualizing our own identity. We constantly dehumanized ourselves and then become mere cogs in the wheel. The need of the hour is that we all have to realize that we are human beings – a subject – who are able to transform the world, to mould history and to determine the goal to which we all should move.

We all will have to take some concrete steps. We have also to do something else; remove the cause of disparity among the human beings of our society. Similar kind of common purpose will have to be instilled into the hearts of people of the world. The causes of disparity will have to be removed and we have to develop understanding among societies, so that they feel allegiance to one common humanity as they now feel towards societies.

At first, we all will have to create a new man who will feel humanity as a whole. Now just think who will be the new man whom we want to create, no doubt if you want a change world you will have to start from yourself. Because improvement always begins with 'I'. This change in man requires inward change.

We are constantly quarrelling with other peoples, not having enough love for one another, but having enough hate. If we really want to enlarge our minds, to enrich human hearts as a whole, the process of transforming the nature of man has to be effected. It is that change which will be symbolic of the change in the world. We must believe ourselves to be true citizens of the society. We can only bring about inward change by discipline and meditation. That is what we have to undertake, if we are to be the true inheritors of the new world, where the arts of ages, books and classics from every part of the country are available to us. We must, therefore, try to understand each other and recognize them as good or as bad as ourselves. That is what all academics and universities stand for: intellectual solidarity, mutual understanding, peace on earth and goodwill among societies.

In this critical period of human history, we will have to understand that as a human being we are born to love and create – not to hate and destroy. We will have to upgrade our state above the strife, above the battle, where we all can think ourselves as the servants of God and humanity. By raising our own spirits, each individual becomes the symbol of divine. We will able to see the dwelling light in ourselves. We cannot be regarded as deserted by the Supreme. If the Supreme is there, that Supreme protects every individual in this world and nobody is deserted by Him.

By understanding this in detail, we will be able to overcome the real conflict of the minds of men. If we really become faithful to the inner voice of conscience – the divine law – then we will understand the moral law that binds the members of the human family together and give us a new sense of responsibility for the safety and happiness of the whole human family. By being ourselves, we best serve the interest of others.

It is unfortunate that we are constantly losing faith in ourselves. We all are suffering from a feeling of utter helplessness. We seem to have lost our initiative and judgment. We live in an age that seems to be purposeless, greatly concerned but unconvinced. Our mind is at conflict with ourselves.

So in this crucial moment, we will have to overcome from the contradiction of human nature in order to settle down the happy home for humanity. In this regard Rabindranath Tagore stated: 'Obstinate are the trammels that bind me, but my heart aches when I try to break them. The shroud which I put on I know is a shroud of dust and death, yet I hug it in love'. We can treat this as a real contradiction. We know the right; we know that our fundamental loyalty is to the world community; we know that we should not work for groups, not for sections, not for races, but for the whole of humanity. Humanity is no doubt above all nations.

So what the world requires today is spiritual orientation. We developed so many things in this world, and yet we are afraid of what is likely to happen. Spiritual freedom should be the root of this universe and from that freedom intelligence, mind, life, matter, all arise. By understanding the deeper meaning of spiritual orientation and freedom, we will able to discipline ourselves and others. In this way we will able to get rid of anger, hatred, pusillanimity and pettiness, while dealing with others and will be able to see God face to face.

In this fast dissolving world, it is very necessary to understand that without abiding spiritual values in ourselves, the goal realizing our own true identity will remain unfulfilled. To make our thoughts conform to spiritual wisdom, to make our will in accordance with the realization of the universal purpose of fellowship, to mould our emotions into harmony with world unity, that is the great purpose that is the will of the ages. It is the will of providence, it is the meaning of history, and that we should move forward to fellowship and friendship, to raise ourselves to higher spiritual status.

Conclusion

In this age of scepticism and materialism, few people bother to know about our true self. Without thoroughly understanding our own identity, we will not be able to understand the identity of others. It is the sole reason behind the conflicts of human mind that they neither try to realize their own identity nor give proper attention to the identity of others. The capacity of knowing ourselves provides us a chance for justifying our virtues and vices too. So at first try to enrich human life, which is a blessing of God Almighty, with the primary and secondary qualities of a soul. After enriching our own lives and broadening our own mind, try to enlighten our fellow beings in the best possibility. It should be the purpose of our human life, and we can achieve it by blending spiritual orientation and spiritual freedom.

References

Andrew, Harvey, *Hidden Journey*, Rider (London: Random House, 1991).

Bruce, Rita, *Love of Conscience* (Puttaparthi: Sri Sathya Sai Books and Publications, Prashanti Nilayam, 2003).

Chandra Shekhar, B.K., *Science of Mind Simplified* (New Delhi: Diamond Books, 2008)

Chandra Shekhar, B.K. and Mishra, Renu, *Personality Development* (New Delhi: Mahaveer Publications, n.d.).

Cohen, S.S., *The Maharishi as I Saw Him* (Tiruvannamalai: Ramanasramam, 1991).

David, Godman, *Padamalai* (Tiruvannamalai Ramanasramam, 2004).

de Caussade, Jean Pierre, *Self-Abandonment to Divine Providence* (England: Sydney, 1931).

From Amma's Heart, Conversations with Sri Mata Amritanandamayi Devi (Kollam: Kerala, September 2003).

Ganesan, V., *Direct Teaching of Bhagawan Ramana* (Tiruvannamalai: Sri Ramanasramam, 2011).

Haraldsson, Erlendur, *Miracles Are My Visiting Cards* (Bangalore Sai Towers Publishing, 1997).

Hemadpant, Dabholkar, *Sri Sai Satcharita* (Shirdii: Shri Sai Baba Sansthan Trust, 2012).

Murphet, Howard, *Sai Baba Avatar* (New Delhi: Macmillan India, 1994).

Narayanswamy, Ramnath, 'Explaining Guru Tatvam', *The Deccan Herald* (Bangalore, 28 March 2013).

Narayanswamy, Ramnath, 'Realize the Mahatma Within', *The Deccan Herald* (Bangalore, 4 April 2013).

Narayanswamy, Ramnath, 'Sri Ramana on Self-realization', *The Deccan Herald* (Bangalore, 17 January 2013).

Narayanswamy, Ramnath, *The Global Mission of Sadguru Sri Sharavana Baba,* (Bangalore: Om Sharavana Baba Seva Foundation, 2010).

Pradip, *Path of Unity* (Puttaparthi: Sri Sathya Sai Books and Publications, Prashanti Nilayam, n.d.).

Sarvepalli, Radhakrishnan, *The Creative Life* (New Delhi: Orient Paperbacks, 1976).

Sri Ranmanasramam, *Sat-Darshana Bhasya and Talks with Maharishi,* (Tiruvannamalai: Sri Ranmanasramam, 2010).

Swami Sri Yukteshwar, Sri Sri, *The Holy Science* (Kolkata: Yogoda Satsanga Society of India, Kolkata, 2011).

Web Sources

http://www.iimb.ernet.inresearchsitesdefaultfilesWP%20No.%20434_0.pdf

http://www.iimb.ernet.in/research/sites/default/files/wp%20434_0.pdf

http://mcnellie.com/525/readings/heydtsherman.pdf

http://www.ignou.ac.inuploadBswe–003%20Block–4-UNIT–16-small%20size.pdf

3

'Self' and 'Other' of Hindu Identity in National and Global Perspective

Binod C. Agrawal

The question of 'self-identity' has been raised both in Anthropology and Sociology to a large extent in the context of colonial history of India for conflict resolution and creation of inter-religious animosity and clash. At the same time, issue of self-identity has been contested at various levels within global, national regional, provincial and local perspectives having cultural, socio-political and economic ramifications. In recent past, a large number of debates have centred around 'marginal identity', it being advocated by civil rights workers and champions of democratic governance for equitable and just sharing of resources and political power among all within the democracy of India.

The notion of other in opposition to self is basically emanated from an alien philosophical tradition strongly promoted by Judo-Christian tradition and thought process introduced in the nineteenth century colonial India. The architects of British colonial empire, it seems had a limited and bizarre understanding of the Indian civilization, its historical and philosophical specificities. In order to unfold the notion of Hindu identity within the Indian civilization, I like to turn the leaf of few forgotten socio-psychological well-established theoretical formulations in the contemporary democratic India. The term *Hindu civilization* knots a composite multi-lingual, multi-religious culture that evolved over 5 millennia with multiple written languages, urban formations and highly specialized occupational guild and philosophical tradition. Today, it is spread across South Asia and beyond. First, I will discuss the 'symbolic interaction' proposed by Herbert Blumer (1969) for understanding of self and other.

Symbolic Interaction of Self and Other

Herbert Blumer (1969) brought a collection of articles written on different occasions on 'Symbolic Interactionism'. The book remains a classic and controversial at the same time in sociological theory and practice for all times to come. 'Symbolic interaction' according to Blumer (1969: 78–79) has

> peculiar and distinctive character of interaction as it takes place between human beings. The peculiarity consists in the fact that human beings interpret or 'define' each other's action instead of merely reacting to each other's actions. Their 'response' is not made directly to the actions of one another but instead is based on the meaning which they attach to such actions. Thus, human interaction is mediated by the use of symbols, by interpretation, or by ascertaining the meaning of one another actions. This mediation is equivalent to inserting a process of interpretation between stimulus and response in the case of human behaviour.

Earlier, George Herbert Mead thought 'the act of interpretation implies for an understanding of human being, human action and human association' (referred by Blumer 1969: 79).

In declaring that human being has a self, Mead had in mind chiefly that the human being can be the object of his own actions. He can act towards himself as he might act towards others. '(Further) ... human action is built up step by step through a process of such self-indication ... The human individual pieces together and guides his action by taking account of different things and interpreting their significance for his prospective action' (as quoted by Blumer, 1969: 81). These two essential features emerged out of Mead's analysis of the basis of symbolic interaction that is being applied in the understanding of self and other while presenting Hindu identity in the context of the Indian civilization.

Within this formulation, Blumer (1969) thought that the analysis of social interaction was very important as it allows the presentation of self and other in responses of the meaning. Further, Blumer (1969: 10) believes

> that the 'worlds' that exist for human beings and for the group are composed of 'objects' and that these objects are product of symbolic interaction ... (symbolic interaction) is seen ... as a process in which people, as they meet in their different situations, indicate lines of actions to each other and interpret the indications made by others.

British Colonialism and Issues of Self and Other

Impressed by the wealth of India and craftsmanship, the British began to make in-roads in several parts of declining Mughal India and in small kingdoms of India. Michael Edwards (1967: 32) reported that 'Towards the end of (17th) the century the British were becoming conscious of a sense of racial superiority. The easy social relations they had had with Indian began to decline, though first only in Kolkata. In other parts of India, where English society was numerically small and fashionable attitudes slow to arrive, the old relations with Indian continued'. The symbolic interaction between the individual Indians and the individual British officials and their families generated a new social action that lead to change in social relationships and atmosphere. In 1810, it was visible to a visitor in Calcutta that Britons appeared to pride himself on being outrageously a John Bull while working with East India Company (Edwards, 1967). This process got intensified by 1820, and the British community in India began to develop distaste for Indians and their way of life. The evangelical Christians working in the company started feeling that things that were done by Indians were evil (Edwards, 1967). The personal diaries and historical records of 1857 War of Independence known as 'Mutiny' narrated by British soldiers and officers in India documented that the Indians were like Negro and hence inferior human beings as opposed to white Britons.

Social action of British self as opposed to the Indians other was seen as racially, intellectually and socially inferior beings required to be educated, civilized and self propagation of monotheistic Christianity was considered essential to other Indian having polytheistic *Dharma* (religion) living in multi-religious India. It also reflected their strongly held sense of social superiority in white man social action. At this point of time, the other had to be defined in a social category that would make sense in self British White World and elsewhere in Europe. The other largely included Indian multi-religious, multi-lingual and hierarchical India. The other was a social reality that lived in large part of India controlled by British and in more than 500 small autonomous kingdoms after Queen Victoria's proclamation on 18 November 1858 in declaring India as British colony directly under the Crown.

In 1871, the British colonial rulers at the time of the first Census of India carried out applied 'civilized' society inductive method to identify distinct social categories as a unit of identification for recording them in the census. This led to the classification of India for the first time into caste and tribe and within each category further division and identification of caste and tribe depending upon the understanding of the census enumerator. Earlier, Todd while describing Kingdoms of *Rajputana* (now Rajasthan) treated all Rajputs of Rajasthan as 'tribes'. The amount of confusion and misunderstanding that was created at that time of Census of India 1871 is yet to be resolved even after 140 odd years. The fact is that the confusion, misunderstanding and misinterpretation continue to compound within socio-political fabric of the Indian civilization.

In British India, social action of self was largely characterized by conscious effort to abstain from interference in socio-cultural and religious life of the India, though in reality British officials continued to temper the Indian life by their social action especially in political domain and in socio-economic and religious arena. The outcome of these social actions was emergence of other layer of 'middle-class' Indian who demonstrated their loyalty to British colonial power that continued until India achieved its independence in 1947.

Recorded history of over last 200 years as discussed earlier has been responsible for several conflicts between self and other individual, family, caste, religion and territory. Even after the partition of British India, on the basis of religion, in 1947, and further partition of Bangladesh and Pakistan in 1971, the symbolic interaction and the process of conflict between self and other continued to be unabated.

Hindu Identity

History of India provides an ample evidence to show that the term *Hindu* is of very recent origin and not even 300–400 years old. International literature in English, French, Portuguese and German languages started using the term *Hindu* only after their firsthand contact with India. Of course, other Asian travellers and invaders had used the term *Hindoo* to designate or 'label' the inhabitants of the subcontinent of India. The term *Hinduism* as the derivative of Hindu is to signify the religious belief system different from Christianity and Islam. It has been used widely for designating other religions such as Buddhism and Jainism.

Renou thinks:

> Hinduism is indeed a complex and rich religion. No founder's initiative, no dogma, no reform have imposed restrictions on its domain; on the contrary, the contributions of the centuries have superimposed without ever wearing out the previous layers of development ... Life is looked upon as a rite; there is no absolute dividing line between scared and the

> profane. In fact, there is no Hindu term corresponding to what we call 'religion'. There are 'approaches' to the spiritual life and there is *dharma* or 'maintenance' (in the right path) ... (1962: 17–18)

Earlier Agrawal (2011) argued that 'the closest term to religion not necessarily equivalent is *dharma*' in Hinduism. In the *Upanishad,* one finds statements such as 'There is nothing higher than *dharma*'. According to Radhakrishnan (1988: 341), *Dharma* is the immanent order. It denotes the laws of nature, the chain of causation, the rule for the castes .... It is absolute infallible righteousness of which our earthly justice is but a shadow'. *Upanishad* or 'Approaches' 'are collection of texts developing the ritual or cosmogonic data of the Veda in a strongly speculative direction and installing on new foundations the ancient equivalence felt between the human and the divine world' (Renou, 1962: 86).

Hence, in the context of the Indian civilization, the closest term to religion, not necessarily equivalent is *Dharma*. Anthropologists believe that religion is a cultural universal, and it exists in every human society in one form or the other (Kottak, 2011). Wallace (1966: 5) defined religion as 'belief and ritual concerned with supernatural beings, powers and forces' (as quoted by Kottak, 2011: 286). Largely, the scholars and laypersons view religion as 'faith'. Religion is transmitted and kept alive from generation to generation, through enculturation. In the process, of enculturation, religion changes over a period of time. Religion incorporates new elements and few new aspects are also modified. In this way, religion discourses continue to take place for promoting few traditions.

The issue of Hindu self and other is much recent in origin and also in the context of *Dharma* within the multi-religious frame of discourse of all levels of symbolic interaction and social action. At global or regional level of symbolic interaction with the citizens of other countries and governments, it is confined to national identity and is dealt within political boundary of the country in which religious identity is largely either hidden or not asked until questions of culinary or food taboos are enquired by the other. Within the national context self, the Hindu identity vis-à-vis other comes in sharp focus in multiple layers of linguistic groups, religious groups and caste groups. In a way, the 'Hindu identity' which is differed within each of the social actions and categories is subjugated and submerged within any of the groups without any explicit reference to Hindu self identity. At village level or community level beyond defined groups, the Hindu identity is uttered. Hence, the self refers to caste and other social groups in which 'daughter and sister' can be exchanged and other is referred to rest of the village or community in which reference has been made.

Irawati Karve (1968) has brought out the distinction of self and other while defining *Jati.* Karve sees the importance of *Jati* only for the purposes of finding a bride or a groom. The patterns of symbolic interaction and social action of Hindu self and other shows near universal acceptance, though a great deal of variation can be found within the broad patterns of Hindu self and other. Deviation from the pattern of social and symbolic interaction may lead to marginalization of several members of a caste group or few families, thereby upsetting their social position. Economic factors and economic power further contributes in the caste social marginalization regardless of the religious status of the individual. Emergence of new social categories such as 'Scheduled Tribes' and 'Scheduled Castes' and other social categories more or less follows the same symbolic interaction and social action while asserting their identity of self and other (Agrawal ed., 1982).

The brief analysis presented so far brings out that British constructed Hindu identity began to vitiate and multiple new factors got incorporated after India's independence. The new distinct Indian identity emerged by adding multiple layers of Hindu self and Hindu other. In addition, the Hindu self and non-Hindu other within multi-religious and multi-lingual India began to emerge giving rise to multiple new identities at national, regional and global levels.

Current socio-political crisis of self and other and marginalization of several social and caste groups are the result of these historical misconception, misinterpretation and imposition of Judo-Christian logic on an ancient civilization having distinct 'Indic' logic of self and other for over several millennia.

Symbolic Interaction after Independence

The Constitution of India declared India as a 'Sovereign Secular Democratic Republic with a parliamentary system of a government'. The Republic is governed in terms of the constitution, which was adopted by Constituent Assembly on 26 November 1949 and came into force on 26 January 1950. The constitution provides fundamental rights to all citizens with special provisions for STs, SCs and OBCs. The addition of names of STs and SCs has been continuously revised in the last 67 years, which has marginally helped them at the same time and created a whole lot of economic, political and psychological problems. The political leaders of STs and SCs want to capitalize on the original British Sin with no end to the problems.

The advantage of self was seen first in religious categories. The religious self by and large, in the process of symbolic interaction tried to identify itself with the other members of the same religious group beyond the boundaries of village, district, state and nation and in international gatherings. A Christian belonging to a particular part of India remains with his or her religious group living within a linguistic social boundary. For him or her anyone beyond the social boundary is the other and seldom it is crossed. At another level, regardless of religious commonality, a Christian belonging to a linguistic region considered his or her self within the linguistic boundary. The Christian outside this boundary is treated as the other.

At a national level, for no political gain all Christians treat their self as opposed to the other Hindu or Muslim. Moreover in global prospective, though religion still plays an important role, self-identification with the country of origin remains most important as self. In this respect, the religious boundaries get blurred and national identity becomes most dominant in any symbolic interaction of self with the other. It holds true in spite of a great deal of commonality among the religious groups belonging to different countries both in their symbolic interaction and socio-economic negotiation and in political discourses. The Prime Ministers of Fiji and Mauritius may belong to Hindu religion, but they remain the other for a citizen of India who happens to be a Hindu. Similar situation between self and the other can be found between a citizen of United Kingdom and United States.

The political forces and economic competitions superimposed on various SCs and various STs have emerged and evolved leading to changes in the definition of self and the other. The changes are generally to maximize profit or gain in a variety of ways within economic, political and religious realms, which Blumer (1969) calls it as peculiar and distinctive character of symbolic interaction. Scheduled Castes and Scheduled Tribes in India define their social action of self as oppose to the other. There has been a regular and excessive use of symbol to ascertain the meaning of social action of self and the other. The same holds true for the other religious groups.

Use of cross as oppose to *Swastika* gives specific understanding of deeply held religious values and other related philosophical views of self and the other to interpret distinct meaning and content. The same holds true for white robe of a Christian priest as oppose to saffron robe for Hindu *Sadhu*. In contemporary India, the symbolic interaction between self and the other in the political arena is being fought tooth and nail for gain of political maximization and self-interest. Under the protection of the Constitution of India, STs and SCs and minorities project themselves to maximize their benefit and interest at a state and national levels. So is the case with other castes and social groups for the protection of their self interest. In multi-lingual India, linguistic groups also rally around their language groups to create self against the other for protecting and preserving their interest.

Historically a large part of India lives in the diverse mosaic of the Indian civilization for over five millennia having continuous crises and conflicts accentuated by uninterrupted immigration of other cultures from Central Asia, West Asia and North and South-East Asia who have brought with them methods of symbolic interaction. External invasions from time to time have generated conditions for induced and forced new features of self and the other, diversity and tolerance within the subcontinent of India.

A close analysis of symbolic interaction between STs of Northeast region or between Hindu and Muslim and lately between Hindu and Christian in Indo-Gangetic plain manifests a variety of symbolic interaction between self and the other leading to conflict be it religion, caste, tribe, territory or natural resources. The whole of India has been experiencing the conflict of self and the other. It can be observed at village, district, state and region apart from religion in the last 67 years after India's independence. In order to reduce conflict and to fulfil the aspirations of diverse linguistic and social groups, efforts to minimize the distinction between self and the other may help bring about peace and prosperity. Otherwise, symbolic interaction between self and the other may turn into perpetual conflict without any end in sight.

In a recent book, Ashok Kaul (2011) discussed Kashmir contested identity who termed contemporary political situation of Kashmir as a state of 'perpetuated sickness'. Kaul concludes that 'Kashmir 'ailments' can be cured through 'demystification of regenerative politics, awakening of masses on the prerequisite of the new social order, launching a social movement for internal reform and bringing political transparency' (Mahajan, 2012). Similar observations were reported in the case of Bihar by Bholey (2011) while discussing caste conflict arising out of symbolic interaction among various SCs. Current situation in Northeast region witnessed in the recent past can be seen in the same prospective.

Today in India, self in each context is specifically defined in a given situation and contextually presented for the purpose of the other. The boundary of the other keeps shifting and each time is redefined for social action. The symbolic interaction has been compounded by the colonial hangover of caste and tribe classification, and related laws such as the Caste Disabilities Removal Act 1850 enacted by the colonial rulers that remain unchanged in independent India is used as a strategy for electoral victory in parliamentary democracy, though in both situations social action of self and the other remained on shifting sand.

Finally this chapter argues that the issue of contesting self and the other identities of caste, tribe, gender and beyond from the perspective of 'symbolic interaction' helps fathom individual social action to suggest amicable solution of socio-political conflict and alternate method to solve the issue.

References

Agrawal, Binod C. and Khan, Irfan Md., 'Hindu Dharma Satellite Telecast in a Multi-religious South Asia: An Analysis' (Paper presented in the International Conference on Media Religion Culture 2012, Eskisehir, Turkey, 8–12 July 2012).

Agrawal, Binod C., 'Culture, Communication and Health in North East Region: An Anthropological Perspective' (Keynote address delivered at the National Seminar on Culture, Health and Development – The Situation among the Tribes of North East India, Diphu, Assam University, Diphu Campus, 20–21 October 2012).

Agrawal, Binod C., 'Learning Hindu Dharma from Television Cartoons: An Analysis of school Children in the Indian Civilization' (FABC-OSC Roundtable on Religion and Social Communication: Relations and Challenges, Thailand, 2011).

Agrawal, Binod C., (ed.), *Anthropological Approaches to the Study of Complex Societies* (Lucknow: Ethnographic & Folk Culture Society, 1982).

Bholey, Mihir, *Caste Conflict and Social Justice the Discourse and Design* (Manheim, Germany: Lambert Academic Publishing, 2011).

Blumer, Herbert, *Symbolic Interactionism Perspective and Method,* (Englewood, Cliffs, New Jersey: Prentice-Hall, Inc., 1969).

Edwards, Michael, *British India 1772–1947* (New Delhi: Rupa Publications, 2011): 1967.

Karve, Irawati, *Hindu Society – An Interpretation* (Bombay/New York: Asia Publishing House, 1968).

Kaul, Ashok, *Kashmir: Contested Identity – Closed Systems, Open Choices* (Jaipur: Rawat Publications, 2011), Reviewed by Chakravarti Mahajan In

Sociological Bulleting, Journal of the Indian Sociological Society Vol. 62, No.3 (September–December 2013).

Kottak, Conrad Phillip, *Cultural Anthropology, Appreciating Cultural Diversity*, 14th (ed.), (New York: McGraw-Hill, 2011).

Mahajan, Chakravarti, Book Review of *Kashmir: Contested Identity – Close Systems, Open Choices* by Ashok Kaul (Jaipur: Rawat Publications, 2011) in *Sociological Bulletin* Vol. 63, No. 3 (2012): 286–288.

Mead, George Herbert, Quoted by Blumer, Herbert *In Symbolic Interactionism Perspective and Method* (Englewood, Cliffs, NJ: Prentice-Hall, 1969).

Radhakrishnan, S., *Buddhism, Reader, An Anthology*, (eds), Rao Nagaraja P. and Gopalaswami K. Ramakrishnan (Bombay: Bharatiya Vidya Bhavan, 1988).

Renou, Louis, *Hinduism* (New York: George Braziller, 1962).

Wallace, A.F.C, *Religion: An Anthropological View* (New York: McGraw-Hill 1966).

4

Reflections in Understanding the 'Self'

Transforming Hegemony and the (un)seen 'Other'

Maggie Katharpi

This chapter focuses on the many hegemonic elements affecting the culture, language, local customs and laws in accordance with our constitution. Through many decades since Independence, the ethnic identity, ethnic rights and protection/security provided under the constitution is found to require urgent attention.

The natives of Karbi Anglong remain an ethnic tribe of great antiquity. Since antiquity, they have established communities in many regions, far as well as near. In addition to Karbi Anglong, the natives have scattered themselves in many places such as Sonitpur district, Dima Hasao, Kamrup, Morigaon district, Golaghat, Karimganj, Lakhimpur, Arunachal Pradesh, Jaintia Hills, East Khasi Hills and Dimapur (Nagaland). Also, very interestingly, it has been affirmed that there are Karbis inhabiting places such as Lhasa (Tibet), Thailand, Nepal and Bhutan. The newest hypothetical theory tells us their inception might have taken place in some parts of Armenia. According to many, this is a remote possibility.

> The migration pattern of the Karbis is that they came to Assam, wave by wave, consisting of small groups. Therefore, one of the groups might have taken the Tibet, Nepal, Bhutan route and reached Assam.[1]

Their diasporas from its original homeland remains unknown whether it's due to imperialism, trade or labour migrations, relationships with other ethnic communities, natural calamities, dearth of food or for the worse, if at all it was due to lack of integrity. But one thing remains certain that this erstwhile ethnic group of people is antiquated, they had travelled long and hard and on many occasions have been geographically marginalized and dislocated. Their quest for a greener pasture, peace and identity had brought them this far. The Chinthong version, thus, narrates the exodus of this indigenous group in these verses:

> *Lasi pirthe la achethe adim, mindar la achethe adim*
> (Then earth's this navel, navel of universe this)
>
> *Ahem la kimpi dam lonang lepu, arit kimpi dam lonang lepu*
> *(Home thus begins to be built, hearth thus begins to be built)*
> *Ansi Karbi aso atum, ansi Karbak aso atum*
> (Then Karbi followers)
>
> *Ahem kimpi dampo kepu, arit kimpi dampo kepu*
> (Home they commit to build, hearth they commit to build)
>
> *Lasi loti jokje lepu, tovar jokje lepu*
> (Then passage not being free, access not being free)
>
> *Lasi sadu jokje lepu, lasi same jokje lepu*
> (Then road not being free, route not being free)
>
> *Bang inglong komchen tangte lepu, bang arlok komchen lepu*
> (They mountain surrounded, they canyon surrounded)
>
> *Ji atum dothip lepu, Hova atum dothip lepu ...*
> (Ji in their strength resided, Hova in their strength resided ...)[2]

Their journey was never easy; they had to overcome various giants and battle through the storms. Being the pristine sojourners to have entered Assam, Bishnu Prasad Rabha – the great artist-scholar – referred to the Karbis as the 'Discoverer of Assam'.[3] Unfortunately, the natives despite being called the Discoverer/Columbus of Assam reflect an inchoate peoples' group.

In 1996, a native by the name Borsing Tisso on his trip to Kathmandu met Karbi natives therein (in Rani Pauwa). Their names and surnames are the same as the ones in Karbi Anglong; *Lunse Timung, Sarmen Timung, Kania Terang, Kangnep Terang* and *Mohori Teron*. Unfortunately, they do not speak the language except few words. According to Rev. Kamalsing Timung, there are several village names akin to Karbi words – for instance, *Ko Longki, Chetung,*

Mungling, *Langthang*, and *Lohan*. Another Karbi gynaecologist from West Karbi Anglong on his trip to Lhasa met Karbis. They believed they were the only remnants of the tribe. If one were to go into detail about the origin, exodus and diasporas of the natives, a book wouldn't suffice. These few instances are to project the marginalized status of the natives in the hands of the many giants that they had had to battle. The battle continues and the fight for the self still remains unreached.

The Karbis are the major tribal community in Karbi Anglong and is enumerated as the third largest tribal community in Assam. Being the principal ethnic group, it may be assumed that they enjoy power, authority and wealth. Partially it may be so but in actual, there's nothing of the sort. The self are mere puppets in the hands of the Other. Elements of hegemony and marginalization are replete in their culture and society. Much as in similar categories identified as affected with hegemony, the natives of Karbi Anglong are found to be undergoing through several phases of intergenerational transmission of the Other, at times under vicious and the so-called 'unseen' avoidable circumstances.

> The power of cultural hegemony lies in its invisibility. Unlike a soldier with a gun or a political system backed up by a written constitution, culture resides within us. It doesn't seem 'political,' it's just what we like, or what we think is beautiful, or what feels comfortable. Wrapped in stories and images and figures of speech, culture is a politics that doesn't look like politics and is therefore a lot harder to notice, much less resist. When a culture becomes hegemonic, it becomes 'common sense' for the majority of the population. (Gramsci, 1971).

What Gramsci had said is aptly applicable to the natives of Karbi Anglong. Culture as he had said dwells within and depends much on how one feels and would react to certain things in life. Complacency has been embraced in lieu of assertion. People's consciousness does not prick, and one remains numb and void amidst all the prevailing turbulences. The following will help in understanding as to where cultural hegemony have been found to be extant.

Karbi cuisine comes in the form of *kangmoi, kalangdang, hanthor, 'kemung, ke-u, kephi* and so on. Nowadays, we have less of these cuisines on the Karbi dining table. Fried chicken, chow mein, dumplings and different dishes of the Other are considered better than one's own. 'From the KUT to the KFC, the Karbi kitchen has undergone a metamorphosis beyond recognition'.[4] Not many can prepare these cuisines with precision and taste now. Many might consider this as part of multi-cuisine and multiculturalism but this is one step moving towards (unknowingly) loss of one's culture. Such practices reflect the dominance of a superior power, seen or unseen. The subtle intricate elements and tastes lead to that stage where aggression and expansion of command and control gradually reflect the Other rather than the self. The art of keeping and practicing *phelo bisir* is hardly found. One would rather buy soda from the market, as easy as that. The people hardly use *long* and *lengpum* (mortar and pestle respectively) to pound rice; all thanks to modern amenities. Many people have remained unemployed because pounding of rice was or is one of the sources to acquire money or employment to sustain livelihood.

On the surface or perhaps for the lucky few, the moment is less stressful and convenient. It is, to be precise, a dream woven to open the delicate threads of questions of survival of the dominated. Much have been forgotten and lost. If only one would still practice them to keep this tradition alive.

> Politics is not only fought out in state houses, workplaces or on battlefields, but also in the language we use, the stories we tell, and the images we conjure – in short, in the ways we make sense of the world. (Duncombe, 2007)

The natives, according to linguists, linguistically belong to the Tibeto-Burman group. The language is rich and is highly esteemed by those who understand it. Though the language reflects few in its vocabulary, yet it remains rich and beautiful in nature. In the past, both English and Assamese were considered *Recho alam* (meaning king's language). Very unfortunately, it is still (unconsciously) considered the same. Universality of language is an important facet in life while losing one's language at the cost of the Other is entirely a different agenda. But the people have, very wistfully, conjoined these two concepts into one, making it 'common sense'. As of now, one may not refer to it as *Recho alam* but it remains reflected in their everyday conversation. It has been observed and almost everybody will agree to this that the natives are more comfortable in using Assamese and at times, English, in expressing themselves. They are able to express themselves better by using the Other words. Common everyday words of the natives are replaced with words of the Other. Most of the commonly used words are as follows:

Po/pei	–	Papa/mama
Choro lo	–	Thank you
Alir	–	Rong/colour
Isi/hini/kethom	–	Ek/dui/tini
Aduli	–	Athona (fifty paisa)
Sika isi ra aduli	–	Arhoi toka (a rupee and fifty paisa)
Sika hini ra aduli	–	Der toka (two rupees and fifty paisa)
Urmi/Durmi	–	Monday/Tuesday/Humbar/Mongolbar (all of the days of the week)
Arkoi/Thangthang	–	January/February (all the months are used in English)
Phang ok ong	–	Gorom ong (it's very hot)
Ko-an lo	–	Keita (how many?)
Ni	–	Baido
Asai	–	Kam
Hong	–	Bahera
Akele	–	Besi besi
Chepaklang	–	Dekhai/show off
Apor/porphai	–	Baji/time
Hithi	–	Bojar
Kulat	–	Dukan
Saihem	–	Office
Inghap	–	Dorja
Keng-op	–	Juta
Him	–	Biscuit
Bong	–	Bottle
Birta	–	News/khobor

An example in which a native shopkeeper asked for a five rupee change from the writer:

Paas	toka	change	do	ma?
(Five	rupees	change	have	do)
Assamese	Assamese	English	Karbi	Karbi

This is just the way how the natives often use other words to express themselves. David Foster Wallace said,

> but the fact is that in the day to day trenches of adult existence, banal platitudes can have a life or death importance. (2005)

The simple things we say, the words we use to express and the deliberate or unintentional words/sentences we utter to convey 'meanings and messages' to people around have its repercussions.

We often consider the words we use everyday will warrant little or no attention because of its commonality or banality, which isn't true rather it produces 'life' or gives way to 'death'. The more one uses the Other language, the more it gives life to it and vice versa. It is this serious.

Padmashree Rongbong Terang writes,

> Many Assamese words have entered the Karbi language and have been endeared by the Karbis.[5]

Sounds common sense and one might consider usage of their words wouldn't distort or deconstruct one's language. But it begins with a word, moving onto two and gradually increasing in its number, finally devouring the entire self. In this process, the Other spaces become more defined and constructed.

The Assam Official Language Act of 1960 prescribes,

> Official language for official purposes of the State of Assam without prejudice to the provisions of Article 346 and 347 of the Constitution of India and subject as hereinafter provided, Assamese shall be used for all or any of the official purpose, of the State of Assam: Provided that the English language, so long as the use thereof is permissible under Article 343 of the Constitution of India, and thereafter Hindi in place of English, shall also be used for such official purposes of the Secretariat and the offices of the Heads of the Departments of the State Government and in such manner as may be prescribed.[6]

This language act created furore among the many tribal linguistic groups residing in Assam and it was vehemently opposed but no steps were taken to rectify the matter. Nowhere is it written that a particular linguistic group should abandon his or her mother tongue but it clearly prescribes that one has to follow as written therein. In the last few years, many of the native veterans had attempted to standardize the Karbi language; unfortunately, all their attempts went in vain. The Other seems to be more concerned with the natives 'ch' and 'th', dictating the natives whether they should be considered as individual letters or as blends. They seem to know more on the language rather than the self. Their concern is not for the well-being, upliftment and comfort of the natives or for the standardization of the language. They are solely bent on hindering the growth and upliftment of the self. If one were to adapt the Devanagari script, generations would be affected. The decision, as in this case and according to the writer's understanding, should not be taken by the Other but should be decided by the self. They should be given the liberty to weigh its pros and cons and take necessary measures on behalf of the society. Also due to this language problem, the natives have not been successful in the UPSC examination so far. Being in Assam, one has to opt for either Assamese or Hindi for the language paper. So even if they were to clear all other papers, language paper obstructs them from moving further. This aspect has hindered the possibility of quantifying and qualifying results in the examination, in the standardization process as well as in the everyday conversation of the people. The Mizos and the Khasis are not intimidated with this problem so they've been successful over the last few years. Also Manipur is the only state that enjoys to opt for Alternative English (MIL) through a special UPSC ordinance. It has been found that certain benefitting steps have not been taken up for all indigenous groups settled in Assam regarding the language paper. The natives have been, therefore, not only linguistically marginalized but also hegemonized.

Hegemonic encroachment is not only seen in the linguistic pattern but also in the traditional attires of the natives. Attires woven elsewhere are more preferred than the ones locally woven. This has not only undermined the natives' growth in traditional attire but also been a setback in the local economy. There used to be many local weavers and entrepreneurs but many have closed down because of this encroachment. *Pini, pekok, blouse, sator, choi hongthor, pe-um, pelu, peba* and other traditional clothing are less woven locally. There is no question of innovation and beauty but the ones woven elsewhere are preferred because it's cheaper and can be obtained faster. Also the intricate designs on the *pini* (lower wraparound garment), *pekok* (upper garment pinned on the right shoulder) and *choi hongthor* (jacket for men) are hegemonized with the intricate designs as used by the Other. It is believed that it's good to blend in. All these are being done in the name of multiculturalism. It is, therefore, important that one reconsiders their steps because it is during such times the unseen Other is recreated in the self.

> Leavis believed that mass culture, along with industrialization, had destroyed an authentic, unified culture, replacing it with a synthetic, divided one.[7]

The designs and patterns woven on the traditional attires all carry and symbolize a life, an idea or a series of pattern of their indigenous lifestyle. About 80 per cent of its originality is lost and is no longer woven. The people are stranded somewhere in the middle:

> Following Antonio Gramsci's approach, it is therefore wrong to think that people as much in the west as the non-west want either tradition or modernity, either continuity or change, either traditional dress or fashion, either the local or the global, but rather want both/and. (Kaiser, 2012)

And in this process, much have been lost and forgotten – not realizing that we forge our very identities and sense of the self by blending in with the Other, all in the name of 'newness' and 'nowness'. Many wouldn't know what *barlin pho* or *barlin kethom pini* are. Contemporary weavers aren't bothered much as to which design or series should follow a particular pattern. Originally, certain series of designs need to be followed while weaving a *pini*, *pekok* or any of the traditional clothing. That's traditional. Also a female's marital status was previously identified only through her attire. The natives are religiously animistic in their belief so married women do not put on vermilion on their forehead. They put on *pesarpi*, *pe seleng* or *pe jangphong* while young girls put on *duphirso* (*pekoks* that are woven in red and orange chequered designs). Traditional attires, therefore, play an important role in the making of culture. It should be sustained not only by the wearers but also by the weavers. Modern attires should be encouraged; conglomeration of designs is also welcome. Tradition and modernity should move parallel but it should not corrupt tradition itself.

Identity crisis is yet another calamity faced by the natives. There are natives living in Nogaon district, who've been rechristened as Koch, Bora, Das and other names, either by coercion or through other forms of persuasion. The writer's grandfather was also at one point of time christened as 'Bongsidhar Medhi' while in Jorhat (Majuli). He remained a Medhi from 1920 till 1929. During the conversion/christening ceremony, cow dung was put on his head and was made to drink the water which was used to wash the priest's legs. In 1929, he became a Christian and was rechristened as Basa Ingti Kathar. Mental subjugation has been the sole reason behind identity crisis. There are many who wouldn't dare identify themselves as natives if they were in places such as Guwahati, Nogaon and others. Perhaps considering it to be a shame to be a native. Herein, it is pertinent to mention that the (un)seen Other have used words such as 'Mikir okora' (previously the Karbis were referred to as Mikirs) in books. This came out in one of the Assamese textbooks. The students were made to recite the lines in the form of a poem repeatedly. For the Others, it might have sounded amusing while for the self, this purely inflicted pain and completely demoralized them. Because fear and shame gripped them so they naturally desired to emulate the speech and nature of the Other because it was/is made to think they're superior. Accepted that the concept of domination is a vital and essential mechanism in the entire process of hegemony, what about elements that stabilize the noun/adjective. Where does a common man sense a political strength, a growing economy, an efficient civil/military force, the capability to lead and enforce. Obviously, it all lies in the eyes, ears and senses of the beholder.

It becomes more important to be accepted by the other. So the stress was more on speaking their language and tuning one's song according to theirs. It is natural to desire to be a part of a greater community – the natives, in this manner, are mentally coerced to recreate oneself in the image of the other. They were at several times referred to as 'monkeys' in schools because of the piece of cloth worn by men to cover their lower part. Do people even realize that all of our forefathers were at one point of time primitive in nature? This sort of mental subjugation served in demoralizing them. It has, therefore, become a matter of discomfort to even identify oneself as a native. Many would rather merge with the other, losing the self. Unity in diversity is one thing but losing one's identity is another. There was a time when all school teachers and students were directed to wear *mekhela chaddar*. That was an uproarious time. Many opposed it while many abided by it. There's nothing wrong in wearing a *mekhela*. But how would one feel if one is told to dress regularly in a Karbi traditional attire to school and college without respecting the rights and sentiments of other ethnic groups? One would surely say 'no' – That's not me – it's not the 'self'.

It is still a big question as to why *Cannabis indica* has been extensively planted in some parts of Karbi Anglong. The areas ranging the Langpi, Kopili and Barapani rivers are overgrown with it. Due to this, many of the natives have taken to marijuana, have become lethargic and lazy and this tradition has been intergenerationally transmitted. The habit of intake of marijuana and drinking of wine have affected generations. Partaking wine in the name of religious and customary rituals have disabled them from discerning what's right or wrong. We do see the presence of wine on several important occasions and perhaps they should be restricted only for those purposes. But that's not the way wine is being used; gallons of wine are used not for completion of the rituals but to be consumed. After every occasion, many can be seen in a deplorable state. Whether its marijuana, bhang or wine, they do not make, they destroy.

As an ethnic tribal group, the constitution also provides certain rights and provisions for the people. Moving governance of tribal areas in Assam, Tripura, Meghalaya and Mizoram, according to the Sixth Schedule, is to help address, redress and salvage the demand for autonomy. Each clause in it was minutely scrutinized. The drafting committee wrote down each clause judiciously and with far-sightedness, keeping in mind the views of the needs and requirements of the ethnic tribals living in India. Unfortunately, the clauses and laws remain unimplemented, obscure, re-amended as and when the Other wants and has remained dysfunctional like a maimed body or like a paraplegic human. Why would the natives cry for statehood if all's well? Evidences show the people have been time and again marginalized. Cultural hegemony has seeped into the lives of the natives without their knowledge in the name of 'common sense'. Nothing's right or adequate. The cry for autonomy continues because they feel unsafe and not cared for by the so-called parent government. Erstwhile leaders had given their say in these few words,

> Karbi Anglong and Dima Hasao districts are the most backward district of the country, and are facing serious threat of marginalization in every sphere.

What is the use of a law that does not discern between right and wrong, good and evil or even between a simple black and white? What is the point in having a law that sees or feels only the colour and smell of money respectively? Many have passed away without getting justice. Extremism is just an excuse. Because they wear uniforms and terrorize people, we think they are the main issue or problem. But in actual (it is a reiteration), extremism is just an excuse. There's so much more than just what meets the eye. We have been taught to embrace a culture, a law or a belief considered to be postmodern wherein vice become virtue and vice versa. Like what Gramsci said that everything becomes 'common sense' – this is what the natives have been taught to embrace. And that's what the Other has planned it strategically. Gramsci also spoke of 'a long march which started with 'consented' coercion, moved to a situation where a crisis called for the masks of consent to slip away, revealing the first of force'. The natives are bound to that vicious cycle of its first force. It looks beautiful; but it's absolutely beautiful trouble (Boyd, 2012). This looks and feels beautiful from the outside but it's trouble within.

Conclusion

> There are these two young fish swimming along, and they happen to meet an older fish swimming the other way, who nods at them and says, 'Morning, boys, how's the water?' And the two young fish swim on for a bit, and then eventually one of them looks over at the other and goes, 'What the hell is water?' (Wallace, 2005)

This is an excerpt taken from one of David Foster Wallace's keynote addresses given to a group of college students. According to him, the most obvious, ubiquitous, important realities are often the ones that are the hardest to see and talk about. Everything's right at the front and it's there. Likewise the natives do not seem to see or realize it.

At the close of this chapter, it is a clarion call to the people to analyse and re-analyse oneself. The self has been dislocated and marginalized – like the two young fish, do the natives still ask 'What is water?'.

Cultural hegemony can be seen in the traditional attires, everyday conversation and in the recent 1st Assam Ethnic Festival 2015. Are the natives still singing 'What is water?'

Common sense is not always common sense after all. It's important to understand, interpret and critically evaluate the sense of self. Anything that should hinder upliftment or the promotion of the self should be opposed. Multiculturalism is common sense but not at the cost of losing one's own culture and identity. It's pivotal to understand the self. Unless one understands this, it's impossible to transform hegemony.

So what should be sustained? The self or the (un)seen Other?

Notes

1. Teron, Dharamsing, (ed.), *Karbi Studies Karbi Studies, Reclaiming the Ancestors' Voices* Vol. 2 (Guwahati: Assam Book Hive, 2011).
2. Teron, Dharamsing, (ed.), *Karbi Studies, Memories, Myths, Metaphors*, Vol. I (Guwahati: Assam Book Hive, 2012).
3. www.metastatic.org (2005).
4. www.neportal.org (2002).
5. Waugh, Patricia, *Literary Theory and Criticism* (Oxford: Oxford University Press, 2006).
6. Terang, Rongbong, *A Glimpse of Karbi Literature and Culture* (Diphu: Sahitya Sabha, 2010).

7. The Sentinel, *Separate State Is Our Motto: Hill State Democratic Party* (5 December 2012).

References

Boyd, Andre, *Beautiful Trouble: A Toolbox for Revolution* (New York: OR Books, 2012).

Duncombe, Stephen, *Re-Imagining Progressive Politics in an Age of Fantasy* (New York: The New Press, 2007).

Gramsci, Antonio, *Selections from the Prison Notebooks* (translated and edited by Quitin Hoare and Geoffrey Nowell Smith)(New York: International Publishers, 1971).

Kaiser, Susan B., *Fashion and Cultural Studies* (New Delhi: Bloomsbury Publishing, 2012).

Wallance, David Foster, *Consider Lobster and Other Essays* (New York: Little Brown, 2005).

Part II

Caste and Tribe

5

Debating Caste in Indian History

Vulli Dhanaraju

The term *caste* in India is often regarded an unchallengeable and closed system of social stratification. This term refers, paradigmatically, to a social institution in India in which endogamous descent groups, known as *castes* or *sub-castes/Jatis*, are hierarchically ranked. It has also been used to describe hereditary forms of social stratification. Caste and hegemony are central part of Hindu ideology. No scholar could challenge to ignore this reality in Indian society. The caste and ideology have undergone significant changes in different historical periods. Modern and postmodern scholars have also revealed the hegemonic ideology of Hinduism for exclusion of marginal sections in history.

I

Caste is the most debatable issue that has enthralled and divided scholars who have wished to study this system of stratified social hierarchy in India. There is an enormous body of academic writing and political polemic on the issue. These are basically the part of debate on the transformation of Indian society under the impact of colonialism and its administrative mechanisms. Some argue for the continuities of precolonial social structures including caste. Others stress the basic qualitative changes introduced by the colonial rulers. Let us assess the different views on the ideology of caste in Indian society.

Structural functionalist theories highlighted the integrative role of caste. In structural functionalist writings, caste is viewed as a system of interdependence and reciprocity, and not as inequality or exploitation. The same emphasis is also found in the structuralist approach of Louis Dumont (1980). His famous book, *Homo Hierarchicus*, constructed an image of caste based on Hindu texts. In this image, two opposing conceptual categories of purity and pollution are the core elements of caste structure. These unique core principles of caste hierarchy, according to Dumont, are observed in scriptural formulation as well as the everyday life of all Hindus. In other words, these values separate Indians culturally from the Western civilization, making India a land of static, unchangeable, 'oriental' Brahmanical values. According to him, Brahmanism represents a core civilizational value, and caste is the central symbol of this value. It is the basic expression of the precolonial traditions of India. Following Dumont, Michael Moffatt (1979) maintains that the lower castes share with the higher castes the basic assumptions and values of the caste structure. They recreate among themselves the entire set of institutions and ranked relations from which they have been excluded by the higher castes. He thus sees cultural consensus at work from the top to the bottom, which includes the principles of inclusion and exclusion, complementarities and replication.

In order to counter Louis Dumont's view of caste, a number of studies was also conducted from the perspective of lower caste that demonstrate the difference between the socio-religious ideologies of the lower castes and the upper castes (Berreman, 1979). They point out that lower castes do not accept the unclean and demeaning status assigned to them in the caste hierarchy. The lower castes have diverse notions of their own as to how and why the caste system developed, most of which refer to the superior wealth and power of the higher castes rather than their purity. Due to socio-economic compulsions, therefore, lower castes seem to subscribe to the dominant ideology rather than being in consensus with it.

It is also very important to note that Ronald Inden (1990), Nicholas M. Dirks (1987, 2001) and other subaltern scholars such as Partha Chatterjee (1989) have challenged Dumont's notion of caste. They argue that it was the colonial ruling class that established the caste system in its ossified form. In order to break Indian people's resistance, the colonial state used knowledge and culture apart from economic and political means. According to this view, power relations and command over men and resources were more important. Nicolas Dirks, in his *Castes of Mind* (2001), argues that caste is a product of 'colonial modernity'. By this he does not mean that caste did not exist before the advent of British. He is simply suggesting that caste became a single, unique category under the British rule that expressed and provided the sole index of understanding India. Earlier there were diverse forms of social identity and community in India. The British reduced everything to a single explanatory category of caste. It was the colonial state and its administrators who made caste into a uniform, all-encompassing and ideologically consistent organism. They made caste as a measure of all things and the most important emblem of traditions.

Susan Bayly (1999) has criticized this line of thought of Nicholas Dirks from her point of view (which we can definitely criticize), and has argued that Brahminism and its hegemony were not a product of colonialism, though they were certainly strengthened by it. The Brahmins played a significant role in the construction of this colonial knowledge, and the collaboration of the colonial state and native elites could be discerned throughout this entire process. The collaboration between the colonial state and the native elites and feudal classes was neither an imagination nor a construct, but was a stark reality.

Abhinav Sinha (2013), in his recent article, vehemently criticized the line of thinking of Nicolas Dirks and other subaltern studies arguments which they mentioned earlier. He argues that orientalist/colonial construct of caste is a kind of subjectivism. No state can ever make a construct of any such divide from the above, unless that division has a history of its own. It must certainly be accepted that the fetish of the British ethnographic state to count, enumerate, classify and systematize the castes did indeed shake the division and hierarchy in the castes once and made it rigid in a new way.

The celebration of the precolonial past by historians of subaltern studies and the academics motivated by Orientalism of Edward Said (1995) and postmodernism in the name of opposing modernity and enlightenment is a flight of imagination and a mental construct of these historians (cited in Sinha, 2013). Sumit Sarkar (2005) argues that this cultural critique of colonialism ultimately aligns itself with the revivalism of the extreme Right, though it also superficially terms communalism as a colonial construct (which is more accurate in this context than caste). This whole logic is a circular and a self-defeating one.

Thus, caste has not only been identified or institutionalized by the colonialism but foreign travellers also have described the nature of Indian society in their works. Even in the works of the Greek ambassador to the court of Chandra Gupta Maurya, Megasthenes, in the third century BC, and Al-Beruni, the historian–companion of Mahmud

Ghazni in eleventh century, have reflected in their tour writings about the social structure of India. This shows that caste has been existed in India since time immemorial. Megasthenes, the Greek traveller in the third century BC to India, mentions two of the features characterizing the institution of caste. He says 'It is not permitted to contract marriage with a person of another caste or to undertake an occupation other than ancestral nor for the same person to undertake more than one, except if he is of the Caste of Philosophers, when permission is given on account of dignity' (Ghurye, 1969). The term *caste* has been defined differently by different people.

II

Colonialism reconstructed cultural forms and social institutions like caste to create a line of difference and demarcation between themselves as European modern and the colonized Asian traditional subjects. In other words, British colonialism played a critical role in both the identification and production of Indian 'tradition'. The colonial modernity devalued the so-called Indian traditions. Simultaneously, it also transformed them. Caste was recast as the spiritual essence of India that regulated and mediated the private domain. Caste-ridden Indian society was different from the European civil society because caste was opposed to the basic premises of individualism as well as the collective identity of a nation. The salience of this precolonial identity and sense of loyalty could easily be used to justify the rule by the colonial modern administrators. So, according to Dirks, it was the colonial rule of India that organized the 'social difference and deference' solely in terms of caste.

The Portuguese travelogue, Duarte Barbosa's work, *An Account of the Countries Bordering on the Indian Ocean and Their Inhabitants* (1518) and translated it by M.L. Dames (1916) was among the first works to peruse the social institutions of India. But the first to envisage 'the caste system' was the French Missionary, Abbe J.A. Dubois in his work entitled, *Description of the Character, Manners and Customs of the People of India, and of Their Institutions, Religious and Civil* (1816). It was translated subsequently by Henry K. Beauchamp as *Hindu Manners, Customs and Ceremonies* (1906). Abbe Dubois had referred to the caste system of India. He said, 'I am persuaded that it is simply and solely due to the distribution of the people into castes that India did not lapse into a state of barbarism and that she preserved the arts and sciences of civilization whilst most other nations of the earth remained in the state of barbarism'. Other Christian missionaries did not share his favourable view of the civilizational value of caste and the Madras Missionary Conference of 1850 held 'caste to be one of the greatest obstacles to the progress of the gospel in India'. Indian social reformers, while unwilling as yet to condemn the caste system as a whole, also dwelt on some of the harmful social consequences of the institution.

The colonial construction of India began by the early Orientalists with their own cognitive maps and with texts explained by *pandits*. Their social model was *varna*-based Brahmanism of Manu. The early admiration of a golden age gave way to a condemnation of Brahmanical tyranny. William Jones translated and published *Manu Dharmasastras* or *The Laws of Manu* (1794). Manu was concerned with such topics as the social obligations and duties of various castes (*varnas*), the proper form of kingship as upholder of *varna*, the nature of sexual relations between males and females of different castes and ritual practices related to domestic affairs. It became the main authority in imagining of Indian tradition as based on *varnasrama dharma* (social and religious code of conduct according to caste and stage of life). Scholars have questioned the attempt to codify Indian social relations according to this single, orthodox Brahmanical text. The text, compiled by Brahman scholars, depicted a caste society under the exclusive domination of Brahmins who reserved for themselves pride of place in the caste hierarchy. The prescriptive text also became the basis of actual description of Indian social order. James Mill, in his *History of India*, viewed caste as a prime example of an Indian social institution based on priesthood and adapted to oriental despotism. Mill borrowed from Jones' work despite his attack on the Orientalists. Max Muller also based his interpretation of caste on textual sources. He suggested that the caste in Vedic period was different from caste in the later degraded periods. For Muller, the soul of Indian civilization was that of the Vedic age, while the later distortions began in the time of Manu.

Orientalists saw the Hindus as victims of an unchangeable, hierarchical and Brahmanical value system. The basic objective of the colonial state was to procure data about Indian social life so as to frame the laws and policies for India. The British colonialism played a critical role in both the identification and production of Indian 'tradition'. It did serve the colonial interests as by condemning the 'Brahmanical tyranny', colonial administration could easily justify their codes to 'civilize' and 'improve' the 'fallen people'. The Orientalists treated *shastra* texts as the authoritative sources on 'native' law and custom. Such informants had an incentive to argue that India was a land of age-old Brahmanical values. Many nineteenth-century Orientalists saw priestly Brahmans not only as an important but also as pernicious force in the society. They doubted the veracity of claims of these indigenous literate specialists.

Ram B. Bhagat (2001, 2006) argues that there were several reasons why the British Government started census in India. From an administrative point of view, clear knowledge of the composition of Indian society was necessary to exert control and extract revenue. During this time, a new classificatory trend in the European intellectual tradition was also emerging which motivated the British government to develop taxonomy based on their perception of Indian societies primarily belonging to primordial categories. Census consolidated the imperial ideology of caste by meticulously gathering data about castes. Caste as subject of social analysis not only organized many administrative concerns from famine relief to criminality, but also constituted the Brahmanical ritual system. There was a general consensus among most of the enumerators that caste should be the basic category to classify diverse population of India. Risley adopted a procedure to organize castes on the basis of 'social precedence' in 1901 census. As a result of this, a number of caste associations emerged to contest their assigned position in the official hierarchy, each demanding a higher position and organizing their fellow caste members in the colonial public space. After 1931, the colonial state found it difficult to ignore the political implications of the caste-oriented census. It abandoned the use of caste for census counting altogether. The idea of an all-India census was first seriously contemplated in the mid–1850s. It had a number of precedents. There were regional household counts, an attempt in 1846 to test population estimates that had been derived from land settlement records, and presidency-wide census of Madras before 1851.

Dirk's (2001) critically argues that 'the way British officials understood caste reflected in the census categorization and enumeration, and it affected the way caste was practiced. This led to some quite innovative relations between *Jatis* (castes) all over India'. Contrary to this proposition, some researchers also believe that it is not correct to say that colonialism created the religious and caste categories in India; they were already present before the arrival of the British, but it did make a difference in the formation of communal and caste identities in the country (Gupta, 2004). In recent years, it has been a subject of great interest with the proposition that census has not only counted people and communities, but in the process of counting, it has also been involved in creating communities or fundamentally altering the traits of existing communities (Cohn, 1987).

III

Other than these sociological interpretations, the study on caste system done by G.S. Ghurye also made a significant contribution. On the whole, Ghurye put stress on the racial origin of the caste system. Besides him, there were some other sociologists also, such as N.K. Dutt, D.N. Majumdar and R.P. Chandra, who supported this idea of racial origin. These people are of the opinion that the Aryans invaded the Indian subcontinent at its north-western area and subjugated the people of Dravidian origin. To keep these subjugated people under a structural subordination, the Brahmins constructed the theory of purity/pollution. With this theory at the base, the caste hierarchy was designed according to relative purity/pollution in comparison to the Brahmins, and thus came the caste system into being. But as Suvira Jaiswal (1998) has argued, there is no evidence to substantiate this theory.

Ghurye's understanding of caste is functional and Indological as well. Unlike his contemporaries, he doesn't glorify or condemn caste, rather he considers caste as a product of Indian culture, changing with the passage of time. Hence, it is a subject of sociological interest. In his book *Caste and Race in India*, he agrees with Sir Herbert Risley that caste is a product of race that comes to India along with Aryans. Ghurye considers it as unfortunate that caste system is mostly understood in terms of Brahminic domination. Caste has gone through the process of fusion and fission in different ways in Indian history. During Vedic period caste was a product of race. Aryans distinguished themselves from non-Aryans just in terms of colour but subsequently different ethnic groups developed alliance/relationship with each other and Hindu culture and values moved from Aryan community to non-Aryan communities. Aryans never introduced themselves as Brahmins or as a superior race as against non-Brahmins. Aryan society itself practiced different kinds of occupations which were allocated to different individuals and families. On the basis of their occupation caste names were allocated to different groups. Therefore, Aryans society had architects, peasants, warriors and artisans, and their society was highly disciplined, organized and progressive. Ghurye argues that it may be a matter of fact that caste evolved in India with the advent of Aryans, as their racial character was different from Indians. But at the same time there were different racial categories present in India prior to coming of the Aryans. India was not the home land of one racial group. Aryans advent added one more race to the already existing ones.

Racial theory cannot be accepted as the exclusive theory of the origin of caste system in India. Caste system should not be confined to India. It should be found in all such societies which have experienced the conquest by other racial groups. Second, it is quite natural that whenever two or more distinct races come into contact, some sort of segregation results. But this may not always lead to untouchability. Third, the practice of hypergamy may be a reasonable factor contributing to the formation of caste system. But this is not the sole reason. If we relate the origin of caste exclusively to the race, it will neglect many other possible factors.

M.N. Srinivas (1956, 1959) studied mostly about the caste and religion to highlight the structural functional aspects and the dynamics of caste system. According to him, there are basically two ways of understanding society. These are book view and field view. Book view is to understand the society from the books and literature available and is otherwise known as Indological approach. But he has emphasized more on field view, where understanding society from field work is considered as important. He coined the term *Sanskritization* to reflect the social mobility present in Indian Society. According to M.N. Srinivas,

> Sanskritization is a process by which a 'low' Hindu caste, or tribal or other group, changes its customs, ritual, ideology, and way of life in the direction of a high, and frequently, a 'twice' born caste. It is followed by a claim to a higher position in the caste hierarchy than traditionally concealed to the claimant caste by the local community. Such claims are made over a period of time, sometimes a generation or two before they are conceded.

On the other hand, Suvira Jaisawal (1998) argues that postcolonial sociological studies ignore the aspect of history in the study of caste/*varna*. The whole stress goes into the study of the intricacies of the contemporary nature of caste, but they do not venture to delve into its origin or at least do not do so sincerely. To a great extent, this analysis seems to be correct. Since while studying the caste system, these sociologists ignore its evolution and origin, and see it in its contemporaneity only, they arrive at extremely divergent and incomplete conclusions. Undoubtedly, these studies provide several insights regarding the contemporary caste system. But, while they are unable to use these insights, historians use them.

IV

Ambedkar's idea of caste can be seen in his works such as *Caste in India*, *Annihilation of Caste* and *Who Were the Sudara?* In these works, he has critically analysed the caste system from the historical and sociological perspective. While framing his own understand of caste, he has referred Ketkar, Senart, Nesfield and others definitions of caste. Finally, he said that 'everyone failed to encompass its various facets in one single definition'.

While analysing ethnographers/colonial administrator's definitions of caste, Ambedkar has developed his own understanding of caste. He defines caste as 'an artificial chopping off the population into fixed and defines units, each one prevented from fusing into another through the customs of endogamy'. The essence of the caste, according to Ambedkar, is endogamy; caste is not merely a division of labour. It is a hierarchy in which division of labourer is graded one above the other. Caste system involves an attempt to appoint tasks to individuals in advance, selected not on the basis of trained original capabilities, but on that of the social status of the parents, i.e. absence of intermarriage. In a system where intermarriage is prohibited, it tends to alienate itself from others and convert itself into an enclosed social unit having an independent identity of its own. According to Ambedkar,

> the problem of caste, then ultimately resolves itself into one of repairing the disparity between the marriageable units of the two sexes within it. The husband may die before the wife and create a surplus woman, who must be disposed of; else through intermarriage she will violate the endogamy of the group. In like manner, the husband may survive his wife and be surplus man, whom the group, while it may sympathized with him for the sad bereavement, has to dispose of, else he will marry outside the caste and will break the endogamy. Thus both the surplus man and surplus woman constitute a menace to the caste if not taken care of for not finding suitable partners inside their prescribed circle very likely they will transgress the boundary marry outside and import offspring that is foreign to the caste.

The study of the caste problem by Ambedkar emphasizes that it is to be noted in four points: (1) that in spite of the composite make-up of the Hindu population, there is a deep cultural unity; (2) that caste is a parcelling into bits of a large cultural units; (3) that there was one caste to start with; and (4) that classes had become castes through initiation and excommunication. He further said that caste did not result in economic efficiency. It had not improved the race. It had completely disorganized and demoralized the Hindus. He found that there was no Hindu consciousness as such. In every Hindu, the consciousness that exists was the consciousness of the caste. Hindus did not even form a federation. Their habits and customs, beliefs and thought were not enough to constitute them into a society. Men constitute a society because they had things, they possessed in common. The caste system prevents common society and by preventing it, it has prevented the Hindus from becoming a society with a unified life and a consciousness of its own being. There is only individual share or part in the associated activity. According to him, castes are autonomous and there was no authority anywhere to compel caste to admit a new corner to its social life. The Hindu society being a conglomeration of castes and each caste being a close corporation, there was no place for a convert. The Hindu religion ceased to be a missionary religion when the caste system grew up among the Hindus. Caste was inconsistent with conversion. So Ambedkar said, 'So long as castes remain, Hindu religion cannot be made a missionary religion and *shuddhi* will be both a folly and futility'.

Ambedkar vehemently refused the racial theory for the origin of *varna*/caste. It is commonly accepted that the Aryans came from outside India and they are racially different from the natives. But Ambedkar argues that the term *arya*, which occur in the Vedas, had not been used in the racial sense at all. So far as the *Rigveda* was concerned, there was not a particle of evidence suggesting the invasion of India by the Aryans. The theory of the Aryan race is just an assumption by Westerners. The theory of invasion in an invention is necessary because of a gratuitous assumption, which underlies the Western theory. The assumption is that the Indo-Germanic people who are the purest of the modern representative of the original Aryan race. The distinction between the aryas, on the one hand, and the Dasa and Dasyus, on the other hand, was not a racial distinction of colour. It was the European scholars who held that the white race is the best race and insisted that the word *varna* meant colour. He concludes that there is no evidence in the Vedas of any invasion of India by the Aryan race, and there is no racial distinction between the upper-caste Hindus and the lower-caste people.

Ambedkar also presented his views on *varna* system and the origin of shudras. He argues that there were only three classes in the past and at that time a member of one clan had the freedom of changing one's clan. The origin of the *varnas* may be traced back to the well-known struggle for supremacy that took place in ancient past between the Brahmins and Kshatriyas, the conflict is conflicted in the allegorical story of the many long wars between them which was rooted in the question of and is superior in matters relating to the institution of priesthood. In this conflict, Raja Shudras – the supporter of Viswamitra – held the key position. However, Visista was the ultimate winner, and the celebration of his triumph was followed by the degradation of the progeny of shudras to menial ranks that led them to occupy the lowest place in the social ladder. The technique employed by the Brahmins for the degradation of the shudras, according to Ambedkar, was that the Brahmins refused to perform *upanayana* ceremony for them.

Ambedkar also gave his arguments for the causes of the origin of untouchability. According to him, there are mainly two reasons for the origin of untouchability. They are concept of Buddhism and beef eating. The emergence of Buddhism and beef eating are said to be the cause of the origin of untouchability. Since Hinduism had the practice of caste system, broken people left Hinduism and embrace Buddhism. Their acceptance was only to get rid of the caste system and practice of untouchability. When there was a large number of a conversion into Buddhism, Brahmins could not digest it. Then Brahmins began to hate both, the untouchables as well as the Buddhists. They considered untouchables very low caste because of beef eating. Since then the concept of the untouchability came into existence.

The untouchables hated the Brahmins because the Brahmins were enemies of Buddhism. Since lower caste was called untouchables they converted to Buddhism. Hence it is possible to conclude that the root cause of untouchability is Brahmins themselves and their jealousy. According to this, beef eating is the reason for the spread of untouchability. Ambedkar quoting various instances from early Hindu scriptures asserts that the slaughter of the cow was not prohibited in the early Vedic period. *Yajna* of the Brahmins was nothing but killing of animals. Manu too did not regard cow as a sacred animal; on the other hand, he regarded it as an impure animal whose touch caused ceremonial pollution. He had whatsoever no objection at all against the killing of the cow. The reason why lower-caste people were untouchables was only because they were eating beef, which Brahmins did not like. Brahmins worshipped the cows.

In order to put down Buddhism and to regain their lost position, the Brahmins gave up the habit of beef eating and made the cow a sacred animal. Thus, the goal of the Brahmins in giving up beef eating was to snatch away their social prestige from the Buddhist. Having adopted this means, the Brahmins declared all those who eat beef as untouchables. The untouchables having no choice left behind continued their beef eating.

The caste hierarchy and the practice of untouchability find justification in religious scriptures. The Hindus widely believed that persons belonging to the untouchable community were originally from non-Aryan races, they were of lowly origin and they have no capabilities. Ambedkar wanted to refute these misunderstandings. He argued that originally only three *varnas* existed: Brahmins, Kshatriyas and Vaishyas. The shudras were a powerful tribe belonging to the Kshatriya *varna*. Conflict between the shudras and the Brahmins resulted in the shudras' degradation from Kshatriya status because the Brahmins denied them the rights of *Upanayana*, sacrifice and kingdom. Thus, the shudras became the fourth *varna* below the other three. He shows how the religious and ritual power of Brahmins caused the downfall of the shudras. This indicates the overall supremacy of the Brahmin *varna* in the ancient society. Untouchability resulted from the conflict between Brahminism and Buddhism.

Ambedkar denies that untouchables were originally non-Aryans. In fact, he argues that in the Indian society, we find a mixture of various races. Therefore, the idea that the untouchables were belonged to some inferior or defeated race was untenable. He provides a socio-logical answer. Originally there existed a number of unsettled tribes. They came into conflict with other wandering tribes. These wandering tribes were defeated and their members scattered. These scattered people finally became attached to various settled tribes. However, their status in the tribal societies remained subordinate to the settled tribes. Thus, the wanderers stabilized as outsiders. The next round of conflict between these outsiders and the settled tribes took place on the issue of religion and subsequently beef eating. Ambedkar argues that to meet the challenge of Buddhism, Brahminism adopted complete non-violence, total renunciation of meat-eating and deification of the cow. The outsiders who were followers of Buddhism traditionally ate meat of dead animals including cow. Since they did not suspend the practice of beef-eating, they were ex-communicated by the settled tribes under the influence of Brahmins. This ex-communication was later justified by incorporating it in religious scriptures. Thus, untouchability became a permanent and sacred part of religion.

Although some of Ambedkar's interpretations have been debatable, nobody denies that untouchability first came into existence and then became a part of religion. Moreover, the most important task that Ambedkar's research has fulfilled is to create self-respect among the lower castes and untouchables. He convinced them that there is nothing shameful in their past, nothing inferior or inglorious in their heritage. He convinced them that their low status was not due to any disability on their part, but it was a result of social mechanism under the influence of Brahminism. His interpretations, above all, convinced everyone that a scrutiny of the religious foundations of Hinduism was necessary.

However, Ambedkar knew that all this involved a total change in Hinduism, which would take a very long time. Therefore, along with this suggestion for basic change, he also insisted on many other ways for the uplift of the untouchables. Under the influence of tradition, the untouchables had completely surrendered to the domination of the upper castes. They had lost all spirit to fight and assert themselves. The myth of inherent pollution also considerably influenced the minds of untouchables. Therefore, it was necessary to arouse their self-respect. Untouchables should realize that they are the equals of caste Hindus. They must throw away their bondage. Therefore, he repeatedly announced that an ideal society will be based on liberty, equality and fraternity. What are the forces operating against these three principles? Caste is an obstacle in achieving these three principles. Finally, Ambedkar's idea of caste is very useful to all the social scientist in the understanding of peculiarity of caste.

References

Ambedkar, Dr Babasaheb, Writing and Speeches, '*Annihilation of Caste*', Vol. 1 (Bombay: The Education Department, Government of Maharashtra, 1989–1991).

Ambedkar, Dr Babasaheb, Writing and Speeches, '*Castes in India*', Vol. 1 (Bombay: The Education Department, Government of Maharashtra, 1989–1991).

Ambedkar, Dr Babasaheb, Writing and Speeches, '*The Untouchables. Who Were They and Why They Became Untouchables?*', Vol. 7 (Bombay: The Education Department, Government of Maharashtra, 1989–1991).

Bayly, Susan, *Caste, Society and Politics in India from the Eighteenth Century to the Modern Age* (New York: Cambridge University Press, 1999).

Berreman, Gerald D., 'The Brahmanical View of Caste', *Social Stratification*, (ed.), D Gupta (New Delhi: Oxford University Press, 1991).

Berreman, Gerald D., *Caste and Other Inequities* (New Delhi: Ved Prakash Vatuk, 1979).

Bhagat, Ram B., 'Census and Caste Enumeration: British Legacy and Contemporary Practice in India', *Genus* Vol. 62, No. 2 (April–June 2006): 119–134.

Bhagat, Ram B., 'Census and the Construction of Communalism in India', *Economic and Political Weekly* (November 2001): 4352–4355.

Charsley, Simon, 'Untouchable: What is in a Name?', *Journal of the Royal Anthropological Institute* Vol. 2, No. 1 (1996): 1–23.

Chatterjee, Partha, 'Colonialism, Nationalism, and Colonialized Women: The Contest in India', *American Ethnologist* Vol. 16 (1989): 622–633.

Cohn, Bernard, 'The Census, Social Structure and Objectification in South Asia', in Bernard Cohn (ed.), *An Anthropologist Among the Historians and Other Essays* (Delhi: Oxford University Press, 1987): 224–254.

Deliege, Robert, 'Replication and Consensus: Untouchability, Caste and Ideology in India', *Man* Vol. 27, No. 1 (1992): 155–173.

Dirks, Nicholas B., 'Colonial Histories and Native Informants: Biography of an Archive', *Orientalism and the Postcolonial Predicament: Perspectives on South Asia*, (eds), Carol A. Breckenridge and Peter van der Veer (Philadelphia: University of Pennsylvania Press, 1993).

Dirks, Nicholas B., *Castes of Mind: Colonialism and the Making of Modern India* (Princeton: Princeton University Press, 2001).

Dirks, Nicholas B., *The Hollow Crown: Ethnohistory of an Indian Kingdom* (Cambridge: Cambridge University Press, 1987).

Dubois, Abbe J.A., *Description of the Character, Manners and Customs of the People of India, and of their Institutions, Religious and Civil* (London: Longman, 1816).

Dumont, Louis, *Homo Hierarchicus: The Caste System and Its Implications* (Chicago: University of Chicago Press, 1980).

Gellner, David, 'Low Castes in Lalitpur', (eds), David Gellner and Declan Quigley, *Contested Hierarchies* (Oxford: Clarendon Press, 1995).

Ghurye, G.S., *Caste and Race in India* (Bombay: Popular Prakashan, 1969).

Gough, Kathelin, 'Brahmin Kinship in a Tamil Village', *American Anthropologist* Vol. 58 (1973): 826–853.

Gupta, D., 'Introduction – The Certitude of Caste: When Identity Trumps Hierarchy', *Contributions to Indian Sociology* Vol. 38, Nos. 1/2 (2004): v–xv.

Inden, Ronald B., *Imagining India* (Oxford: Basil Blackwell, 1990).

Irvine, Judith, and Inden, Ronald B., *Marriage and Rank in Bengali Culture: A History of Caste and Clan in the Middle Period Bengal* (Berkeley: University of California Press, 1975).

Jaiswal, Suvira, *Caste: Origin, Function and Dimension of Change* (Delhi: Manohar, 1998).

Juergensmeyer, Mark, *Religion as Social Vision: The Movement against Untouchability in 20th Century Punjab* (Berkeley: University of California Press, 1982).

Mencher, Joan, 'The Caste System Upside Down, Or The Not-So-Mysterious East', *Current Anthropology* Vol. 15, No. 4 (1974): 469–493.

Moffat, Michael, An Untouchable Community in South India: Structure and Consensus (Princeton: Princeton University Press, 1979).

Mosse, David, 'Idioms of Subordination and Styles of Protest among Christian and Hindu Harijan Castes in Tamil Nadu', *Contributions to Indian Sociology* Vol. 28, No. 1 (1994): 67–106.

Said, Edward W., *Orientalism: Western Conceptions of the Orient* (London: Penguin, 1995).

Sarkar, Sumit, *Beyond Nationalist Frames: Postmodernism, Hindu Fundamentalism, History* (New Delhi: Orient Blackswan, 2005).

Sinha, Abhinav, 'Historiography of Caste: Some Critical Observations and Some Methodological Interventions' (Paper presented in the Fourth Arvind Memorial Seminar on 'Caste Question and Marxism') (Chandigarh: March 12–16, 2013).

Srinivas, M.N., 'A Note on Sanskritization and Westernization', *The Far Eastern Quarterly* Vol. 15, No. 4 (1956): 481–496.

Srinivas, M.N., 'Sociology in India and its Future', *Sociological Bulletin* Vol. 43, No. 1 (1994).

Srinivas, M.N., 'The Dominant Caste in Rampura', *American Anthropologist* n.s. 61, No. 1 (1959): 1–16.

Srinivas, M.N., *Caste in Modern India and Other Essays* (Bombay: Asia Publishing House, 1962).

Srinivas, M.N., *Caste: Its Twentieth Century Avatar* (New York: Penguin, 1997).

6

Caste-Based Exclusion of the '*Damai*' Caste Group among the Nepali Community in Assam

Riju Devi

Every society is characterized by stratification, be it in a subtle or an extreme form. The study of inequalities in society has always been one of the important areas of sociology. The *Oxford Dictionary of Sociology* defines stratification as being 'usually applied to studies of structured social inequality; that is, studies of any systematic inequalities between groups of people, which arise as the unintended consequence of social processes and relationships' (Scott and Marshall 2009: 735). The term *stratification* is used by sociologists to describe inequalities that exist within the human societies between the individuals and groups where they enjoy unequal rewards and status depending on which position they occupy within the system or society (Giddens, 2009). Caste, class, race, ethnicity and gender are some of the important categories of social hierarchy and differentiation.

This study is an attempt to understand the caste system of the Nepali community living in Assam with special reference to Sonitpur district. The term *caste* has been used to mean different things by different people in a variety of situations. Sometimes it implies a small and more or less localized group; at other times the same word is used to refer to a collection of such groups. Andre Beteille defines caste as

> a small and named group of persons characterized by endogamy, hereditary membership and a specific style of life which sometimes includes the pursuits by traditions of a particular occupation and is usually associated with a more or less distinct ritual status in a hierarchical system, based on concepts of purity and pollution. (1996: 46)

The social scientists working in or on Indian societies have often assumed that the process of modernization initiated by the colonial administration would eventually break up the caste system and the ideologies revolving around it and give way to the class system. However, modernization has not been able to break the basic foundation of the caste system. The fact that some considerable changes have been witnessed in the caste system also cannot be denied, as it no longer is practiced as rigidly as ancient times (Jayaram, 1996). 'The caste system has been the most flexible of the primordial institutional arrangements in the world, and it has shown an extra ordinary capacity to adapt itself to a variety of changing, and often apparently contradictory, socio-economic conditions' (Jayaram, 1996: 70). The acknowledgement of the changes in the caste system however doesn't deny the fact that such process is not uniform throughout the country. While in certain regions we see flexibility in day-to-day practices, in some other regions caste system is characterized by conservation and orthodoxy.

Since the present chapter intends to shed light on the caste system of the Nepali community in Assam, which is a migrant community, it is important to understand the history of their migration and settlement. The connection of Assam with Nepal is historically very old. Assamese historian Kanaklal Barua wrote that Assam had matrimonial alliances with Nepal since the early ages. But it was only during the colonial times that migration of the Nepalis to Assam took place with serious socio-political implications (Nath, 2003). An organized migration from Nepal hills to the frontiers of Assam was triggered by the British. A.C. Sinha provides two reasons for such major human movement. First, for some, life became difficult in Nepal due to certain factors such as the repressive regime during the mid-eighteenth century that meted unequal treatment to the subjects based on caste hierarchy. Also, the lack of arable land made life in the hills difficult that led them to move out of the country. Further, there were several factors that attracted the Nepalese people to the British ruled India where they realized their demand (Sinha, 2003).

Lopita Nath in her article Migration, Insecurity and Identity: The Nepali Dairymen in India's Northeast states that

> The Nepali dairy farmers are the later group of migrants who began to migrate in the last part of the 19th century. They followed the 'beaten paths' followed by the Gurkha soldiers recruited by the British to defend the Eastern Frontier and the skilled and unskilled labourers who came to work in plantations, coal mines and oil fields from the middle of the 19th century onwards. (2006: 130)

The number of such migrants kept on increasing contributing to the population of the Nepali community in the Northeast India. Chandan Kumar Sharma in his article 'The Immigration Issue in Assam and Conflicts Around It' states how the growing presence of the Nepali community in the Northeast and specially in Assam created the need among the leaders of the anti-foreigners movement to campaign against the Nepali 'foreigners'. This demand, however, did not gain such momentum. Even in the subsequent years no such movement against the Nepali community has been seen; rather both the Assamese and the Nepali communities have maintained an amiable relation (Sharma, 2012).

For the study, I would like to draw from multiple approaches. My work will be largely informed by Dumont's understanding of the concept of hierarchy where he focuses on the rigidity of caste position at each end of the hierarchical spectrum. For Dumont, the dominant principle of the Hindu caste system is hierarchy, which is informed by great religious significance, so are the principle keys of purity and impurity (Subedi, 2010). This understanding would be relevant in the area of study to understand the concept of purity and pollution in their day-to-day practice.

The Weberian perspective too is relevant for the study because he emphasizes on caste as a predominant phenomenon in the Indian society. He mentions that caste is more than of mere occupational specialization. Weber interprets caste as a special and extreme case of status groups, which is constituted by honour and prestige. Caste according to him is an ideal variety of closed status group. He further states that the decisive forces that lie in the core of caste system is to be found in ideology, that is, religion, and not in economy, or material conditions.

The Nepali Caste System

The Nepali ideological and cultural institutions are much influenced by the caste system. Similar to any other Hindu society, the social order of the Nepali community is exclusionary due to its classification into groups as distinct castes within the broad framework of the Hindu system of the four *varnas* based on concepts of ritual purity and pollution (Subedi, 2010). According to M.N. Srinivas,

> The layman is unaware of the complexities of Varna. To him it simply means the division of the Hindu Society into four orders, viz., Brahmana (Brahmin, traditionally priest and scholar), Kshatriya (ruler and soldier), Vaishya (merchant) and Shudra (peasant, labourer and servant). The first three castes are 'twice born' as the men from them are entitled to don the sacred thread at the Vedic rite of *upanayana,* while the Shudras are not. The Untouchables are outside the *varna* scheme. (Gupta, 1992: 28)

Each of the above *varnas* is constituted by many castes and sub-castes within them, which is true of the Nepali community too. Besides the general features as given by G.S. Ghurye in his book *Caste and Race in India* (1969), there are several small rules in the customs and religious practices specific to the Nepali community.

The knowledge of the caste system leads to the understanding of the contemporary Hindu society and provides us an insight to the society that practices it. In a general sense, the Nepali caste system pertains to all the above-mentioned features. However, the significant regional differences cannot be ignored. There are several sub-castes specific to different linguistic areas of the country. The Nepali being a migrant community in Assam has its own specificity in terms of the transformations in the institution of caste, owing to its interaction as well as adaption to the local setting of Assam. This chapter examines how the *Damai*, an occupational shudra caste, are marginalized within a multicaste settlement and excluded from the everyday affairs of village life.

Caste has undergone significant changes in different societies over a period of time. It is significant therefore to cite the works of scholars such as Srinivas who have discussed about these changes in the caste system. Srinivas, in order to explain such social changes has formulated the concepts of sanskritization and westernization. Srinivas defines sanskritization as 'The process by which a 'low' Hindu caste, or other group, changes its customs, ritual, ideology and way of life in direction of a high and frequently 'twice-born caste' (Srinivas, 1966: 6). Generally, within the Nepali caste system the process of patronization of the high castes by the lower castes is quite prevalent. The distance in terms of contacts is strictly maintained and the concept of purity and pollution is imbibed, not just in the hierarchical structure but also in the day-to-day rituals. The acceptance of their exclusion by the lower-caste groups as fate and their submissive nature makes the caste hierarchy still strong. Hence, even if the members of the lower-caste groups progress in other fields, their social status continues to be marked by their caste identity.

The *Damai/Darjee* Caste and Their Exclusion

Damai/Darjee meaning 'tailor' is a sub-caste that falls under the shudra category of the Nepali caste system. This chapter will try to explore the discrimination of the *Damais*, specially from the religious and socio-cultural points of view, and is based on the qualitative analysis of a small village. Hukai Gaon is situated in Sonitpur district in the north-central Assam near a town called Jamugurihat. This village is under the Pub-Borbhogia Panchayat in Na-Duar block which is populated mostly by the Nepali community.

Situated 4 km from Jamugurihat centre with a total population of 447 out of which 221 are male and 226 are female (Census, 2011). This village has 103 households and is populated by families which belong to the *Brahmin (Sharma), Chetry, Newar, Kami* and *Damai/Darjee* caste groups. There is also a small population of Assamese community. Even though their caste name suggests that they are a tailoring caste, only two families in the village make a living by sewing clothes. Two families have members working in the defence services and Indian Railways. Few also work as part-time instrument players in a local band that plays in marriages. Most of them make their living as agricultural labourers.

Although the process of modernization India is going through, the people of higher caste and older generation do not easily want to give up power that they traditionally exercise over those below them. In Hukai Gaon, persistent traits of caste discrimination can be still witnessed in village life. Such discrimination is evident with respect to denial of entry to the lower caste groups by higher castes into their houses, temples, workplaces and other places. None of the households in the village which belong to the higher castes bearing surnames such as *Sharma* or *Chetry* provide access to the *Damai* people inside their homes. Any kind of business or conversation is to be done from the verandah or the yard. The high-caste people do not enter into kinship including inter-caste marriages. In the village, so far there is no instance of inter-caste marriage between the *Sharma/Chetry* and the *Damai* caste group.

Concept of pollution or contamination (*jutho*) among Hindus is vested with taboos when associated with food and drinks. Distance is also communicated through preferences and restrictions on commensality held by members of particular caste and religious communities. A higher-caste person may have friends and workmates from lower-caste communities, whom he meets in the village and at the local market. But he neither visits their house nor takes meal with them nor invites them into his own house. The avoidance of close relationship with members of other communities is based on differences in food habits and restrictions following an ideology of what they can consume and what they have to avoid according to their caste and religious affiliations. The habits and taboos which are culturally determined are important in the sense that they keep members of different ethnic groups in different social strata. Generally, the higher the status of a caste, the more rigid it is in the matter of accepting food from others. Thus, Brahmans do not accept cooked food from non-Brahmins, although the latter accept it (Subedi, 2010). Also there are minute rules as to what sort of food or drink can be accepted by a person and from which caste. But there is great diversity in this matter (Ghurye, 1969). All food is divided into two types: *kachcha* and *pakka*, the former refers to any food in the cooking of which water has been used, and the latter to any food cooked in ghee. As a rule, 'a man will never eat *kachcha* food unless it is prepared by a fellow caste man, which in actual practice means a member of his own endogamous group'. To take *kachcha* meal with someone is to imply intimacy and approval (Dumont, 1980: 83–85).

The *Damais* commonly face caste-based discrimination by high-caste people on various religious and socio-cultural occasions, especially during festivals, feasts, marriage processions and funerals. During any kind of feast (personal/public) in the village, they have to eat separately or at the end as the higher castes consider it polluting to eat together with the *Damai.* When asked about the same, many expressed that they face humiliation during wedding parties as they have to eat separately and at a distance from high-caste people. While many other cite *sanojaat, hami ta bhindai khanu paro ni* (being lower caste, we surely have to eat separately). Generally, in the Hindu caste system, untouchability is widely practiced around the concept of water pollution of water and use of public drinking water source. The *Damai* caste group does not fall under the untouchable category, however they belong to the *pani nachalne jaat* (water polluting caste). Upper-caste members do not drink water touched by them. Now however they have access to public drinking water (public well, hand pumps and water supply tap). Few families also allow them to collect water from their personal wells/hand pumps, while few still hesitate.

One reason of this is the fact that now almost every household belonging to the *Sharma* and *Chetry* households has their own source of drinking water and, hence, they do not have to share the public sources of drinking water with the *Damais*. They are also regarded as 'polluted' by the higher castes due to their food habits and lifestyle. The *Damai caste group* eats pork and makes their own rice beer which is not accepted by the higher castes.

Settlement structure of the village also manifests the caste-based discrimination practiced in the village on everyday basis. The *Damais* of the village state that the lower castes are generally not welcome in and around the settlements of the higher castes. Even if a *Damai* family settles within an area dominated by the higher castes, they feel isolated as they are excluded from almost every public and private function.

The discouragement in terms of formal education among the *Damais* also has its roots in their families. In spite of formal schooling and the basic amenities of education being free, the children of the *Damai* families are hardly motivated towards studies. Most of the parents are themselves uneducated and hence fail to understand the importance of education. When asked why their kids do not go to school, few replied by saying 'he/she doesn't listen and hence we have stopped saying anything'. In most of the families, girls are seen helping their mothers in the household works. Boys on being asked said, *Bangalore jaanchu, kamauna* (will go to Bangalore to earn money). There has been a trend of young boys from the village migrating to South Indian cities in search of jobs. A visit to the school revealed that the students were not asked to sit separately or even eat separately during the mid-day meal. However, discrimination by peers could be seen as the children were playing in different groups segregated by caste. Such discrimination even at the primary level shows how such exclusive and discriminatory ideas are imbibed into a child's mind by seeing their parents practice the same.

It is no surprise that the *Damais* face discrimination in community leadership as well. Representation in the community organizations is one of the best indicators of participation in the development process. In Hukai Gaon, the *Damais* claim that they are not given any role in the decision-making of the community organizations. Not only is their leadership not accepted, but not even a single member of the *Damai* caste group has ever been a part of any village committee or the school management committee as well. The higher castes find it insulting to take instructions from the lower castes and hence avoid involving them in any group. When an elderly Brahmin man was asked for the reason of this, he responded by saying that it is the lower castes that are supposed to seek their advice and follow their instructions, not the other way round. Also, the representation of the *Damais* in the political sphere of the village is negligible. Although they have been active voters, none of their members have ever been nominated or elected in the local self-government elections. One reason is their small population as compared to the other higher castes in the village.

The Nepali community with its cultural, ethnic and religious diversity is majorly a Hindu and a patriarchal, patrilineal and patrilocal society, where a women's life is strongly shaped by the male members of the family. However, the relative status of women varies from one ethnic group to another. Although the contribution of women in the family is significant, it goes relatively less noticed, probably due to the traditional 'expressive' role attributed to her, which again is taken for granted. Moreover, most of the work done by women is not regarded as economic activity, eventually establishing their work as less important in a wider sphere. Like their counterparts in other societies, Nepalese women are not a homogenous group. They are heterogeneous in nature. Thus, democratic practices in private sphere and forms and intensity of discrimination and inequality at private and public spheres vary enormously from one group of women to another. Women usually are victims at different levels. The upper-caste Brahmin and *Chetry* women are victim of gender discrimination alone, while the lower-caste women are double victim of gender discrimination as well as caste-based discrimination. Nepali women's status or positions and roles or functions are mostly based on prescription by patriarchy rooted in religion and culture. In most of the groups and community-based organizations such as credit groups and self-help groups, 'high-caste' women have more access to and control over resources. Lower-caste women are either excluded or even if they are included they are dominated by the 'high-caste' women in such groups (Bhattachan, et al., 2009). In Hukkai, the self-help groups formed by the women belonging to *Sharma* and *Chetry* categories do not include women from the *Damai* category. Nor are they included in any of the religious activities conducted by the women of the higher caste. *Damai* women are confined to performing domestic works and child bearing and caring. They have limited or no access to and control over resources such as land, house and cash. They experience violence including physical and psychological. In most of the *Damai* families in the village, wives are beaten by their husbands after they get drunk. To make their ends meet, many women work as agriculture labourers as well as household maids. For them the labour is double as they also have to do all the household works. When a woman was asked what she did when her husband hit her, she replied, *galigarchu, tara hath uthaudina. Budo ho jastai bhaini* (I scold, but never raise a hand. After all he is the husband).

The *Damai* caste group in Nepal falls under the dalit category. Derogatory terms, such as *pani nachalne* (water polluting), *acchoot* (untouchables), *dom, pariganit* and *tallojat* (low caste), are used to refer to the lower-caste groups (Bhattachan, et al., 2009). However, in India as well as in Assam, the *Damais* do not fall under the official dalit (SC) category. But they are referred to as *pani nachalne/tallojat jaat* (water polluting/low caste). In spite of the discriminations faced by them, they do not enjoy the benefits that are enjoyed by other dalit groups. The *Damais* fall under the (OBCs) category. There also has not been any kind of protest or any form of organized consciousness so far in order to claim the Schedule Caste status in Assam. However, a process of changing their surname to 'Das' is quite prevalent among the *Damais* of the village as a form of passive resistance. They do this as an attempt to evade humiliation as well as in the hope to avail the facilities as enjoyed by the SCs. The common surname among the *Damais* is *Damai/Darjee*. However, it is found that many students in the local schools have *Das* as their surname. Das – an inclusive surname – is used by them to evade humiliation. When asked why does he write the surname *Das*, a person named Bittu said that it sounds better and less humiliating than *Darjee*. Another young boy named Bikash who studies in a junior college added that most people who have *Das* as surname fall under the SC category and can avail facilities of reservation. He too hopes to access the same in the course of his higher studies.

Due to growing market economy in urban centres and intensified efforts by the dalit movement, caste-based untouchability is declining but has not yet been eliminated (Bhattachan et al., 2009). Even though the *Damais* are not regarded as untouchables, they continue to suffer from other exclusionary practices. The higher castes of the village do not provide them with any kind of services. The *Damais* even have their own 'priests' in order to conduct all kinds of religious functions as the Brahmins, the priestly caste, abstain from any kind of connection with them. With such discrimination and exclusion it is still humiliating for the members of the *Damai* caste group to exist in the society along with the other (upper) caste groups. Although rationality and universal perspectives have begun to replace and question age-old beliefs and customs, those occupying the higher positions in the caste hierarchy continue to protect it. And with no intervention or initiative from the state to compensate the loss undergone by the lower castes, there is a chance that their status remains stagnant for a long time.

References

Beteille, Andre, *Caste, Class and Power* (New Delhi: Oxford University Press, 1996).

Bhattachan, Tej B. Sunar, Yasso K. Bhattachan. 'Caste-based Discrimination in Nepal.' *Working Paper Series, Indian Institute of Dalit Studies* Vol. 3, No. 8 (2009): 1–49.

Census of the Pub-Borbhogia Panchayat under the Na-Duar Block, 2011, Sonitpur District, Assam.

Dumont, Louis, *Homo Hierarchicus: The Caste System and its Implication* (Chicago: Chicago University Press, 1980).

Ghurye, G.S, *Caste and Race in India* (New Delhi: Popular Prakashan Pvt. Ltd., 1969).

Giddens, Anthony, *Sociology* (New Delhi: Wiley India Pvt. Ltd., 2009).

Gupta, Dipankar, (ed.), *Social Stratification* (New Delhi: Oxford University Press, 1992).

Jayaram, N., 'Caste and Hinduism: Changing Protean Relationship', *Caste: It's Twentieth Century Avatar*, (ed.), M.N. Srinivas (New Delhi: Penguin Books India (P) Ltd., 1996).

Nath, Lopita, *The Nepalis in Assam* (Kolkata: Minerva Associates (Publications) Pvt. Ltd., 2003).

Nath, Lopita, 'Migration, Insecurity and Identity: The Nepali Dairymen in India's Northeast', *Asian Ethnicity*, Vol. 7, No. 2 (August 2006): 129–148.

Quigley, Decan, 'Is a Theory of Caste Still Possible?' *Contextualizing Caste: Post Dumontian Approaches*, (eds), Mary Searle-Chatterjee and Ursula Sharma (Jaipur: Rawat Publications, 2003).

Scott, John and Gordon Marshall, *Oxford Dictionary of Sociology* (New York: Oxford University Press Inc., 2009).

Sharma, Chandan Kumar, 'The Immigration Issue in Assam and Conflicts around It', *Asian Ethnicity*, Vol. 13, No. 3 (April 2012): 287–309.

Singh, Yogendra, *Social Stratification and Change in India* (New Delhi: Manohar Publishers and Distributors, 1997).

Singh, Yogendra, *Modernization of Indian Tradition* (Jaipur: Rawat Publications, 1986).

Sinha, A.C. 'The Indian Northeast Frontier and the Nepali Immigrants', *The Nepalis in Northeast India: A Community in Search of Indian Identity*, (eds), A.C. Sinha and T.B. Subba (New Delhi: Indus Publishing Company, 2003): 31–66.

Srinivas, M.N., *Social Change in Modern India* (New Delhi: Orient Blackswan, 1966).

Srinivas, M.N., *Village, Caste, Gender and Method* (New Delhi: Oxford University press, 1998).

Subedi, Madhusudan, 'Caste System: Theories and Practices in Nepal', *Himalayan Journal of Sociology & Anthropology*, Vol. 4 (2010): 134–159, http://www.nepjol.info/index.php/HJSA/article/viewFile/4672/3886 (5 January 2015).

Subba, Tanka Bahadur, 'Living the Nepali Diaspora in India: An Autobiographical Essay' *Zeitschrift für Ethnologie*, Vol. 133, No. 2 (2008): 213–232, http://www.jstor.org/stable/25843148 (2 December 2014).

7

In Search of the Myth and the Real 'Ishi'

The Last Man of Yahi Tribe

Abheeshta Nath

In the August of 1911, a man named 'Ishi' shot to fame in the American history neither due to his excellence in any discipline nor because of his notoriety. But he was identified by the Occidental world as the last man of the Red Indian *Yahi* tribe which was thought to be extinct sometime ago.

The *Yahi* tribe was a sub-group of the Yana tribe, which was a group of Native Americans, indigenous to Northern California in the central Sierra Nevada Mountains, on the western side of the range. The Yana comprises mainly four groups namely the Northern Yana, the Central Yana, the Southern Yana and the *Yahi*. They were hunter gatherers who lived in small egalitarian bands without centralized political authority. Their territory was approximately 40 miles by 60 miles and was rich in natural resources. Each group had relatively distinct boundaries, dialects and customs. The Yanas were around 3,000 in number, out of which 400 were *Yahis*. They were leading a rather peaceful, reclusive life until James. W. Marshall, the Anglo-American discovered gold in the American River in California on 24 January 1848, where the Yanas had their settlement. It set the stage for the notorious Californian Gold Rush – where tens of thousands of gold miners and ranchers flocked into the Yana territory. They plundered their resources, fought with the tribals for territory, killed them in multiple raids, enslaved and raped their women (rape unknown to the *Yahis* till then). Many of them even succumbed to the invasive diseases (also venereal) which these invaders brought with them. Thus the Yana population began to reduce drastically and the *Yahis* were the most affected. In a span of three decades, the *Yahi* tribe almost became extinct except for the relatives of Ishi and himself. But soon in another raid Ishi lost them and then for almost three years he lived all alone in hiding among the foothills of his homeland.

Now this is what the poor tribals – the *Yahis* – encountered when the whites moved into their territory and monopolized their land and resources. It was nothing but genocide – to call a spade a spade – though the Occidental historiographers may go for many euphemisms to describe the massacre, which exterminated a whole tribe into obscurity. Now let us see, what happens when the last man of the *Yahi* tribe steps into the world of the whites.

So, after surviving for three years all alone, starving and with nowhere to go, at the age of 48 or 49, on 29 August 1911 Ishi walked out into the Occidental world. In a wicked irony, he took shelter in a local slaughter house in the outskirts of Oroville city, California. He was captured stealing meat there. The wild man immediately caught the imagination and attention of thousands of onlookers and curiosity seekers. After the native was noticed by town people, the local sheriff took the man into custody for his protection. He was in fact put into a jail for the insane. It was soon learnt that he spoke neither English, Spanish nor any locally recognized Indian language. Newspaper stories concerning this 'wild man' brought him to the attention of Alfred Kroeber and Thomas Waterman, anthropologists with the Parnassus Heights Museum, University of California. Kroeber confirmed and referred to him as the 'Last Stone Age Indian in North America'. They identified his language as the Yana dialect and gave him the name 'Ishi' which meant, man or person in Yana language. For, they knew that according to the *Yahi* traditions, a *Yahi* would reveal his name only to a friend, and never to a stranger.

They took charge of him and managed to release him to the care of Californian University Museum. Thus Ishi, the last *Yahi* came to live out his final years in a museum. In the next five years, thousands of visitors watched him chip arrow heads, shape bows and make fire by the age-old techniques in the halls of the modern museum where he oddly made his home. Thus he was literally exhibited there as a living specimen of his tribe – the rarest of the rare species – the aesthetic other.

There he was studied closely over the years and interviewed at length to help reconstruct *Yahi* culture. He described family units, naming patterns and the ceremonies that he knew. He identified material items and showed the techniques by which they were made. He provided valuable information on his native Yana language, which was recorded and studied.

We have innumerable accounts of him being treated very kindly by the authorities, many of them becoming close friends with Ishi. Ishi adopting himself into the modern world appears in suits and coat, wears a tie and works as their research assistant and stuff.

But the truth that he was just a specimen, a research object or a guinea pig for them is clear, as they don't even spare his dead body!

Ishi having come to live in the modern world and having no immunity to the 'diseases of the civilization' was often ill, and finally, after five years he died of TB, on 25 March 1916. Against the *Yahi* traditions which demanded the body to be kept intact, the doctors of California University did an autopsy on his body and not just that, they managed to take away and preserve his brain. Then they gave him 'a decent cremation' according to the *Yahi* traditions, including the remains of one of his bows, five arrows, three rings and his other belongings.

Thus after his death in 1916, Ishi passed out of public view and was largely forgotten by the mass media (probably because the whole world was preoccupied with the trauma and splendour of the two world wars) until the appearance in 1961 of Theodora Kroeber's (wife of Alfred Kroeber) book, *Ishi in Two Worlds: A Biography of the Last Wild Indian in North America*. It soon triggered an unnatural interest in Ishi again. It influenced several works on Ishi by other writers. Theodora Kroeber herself revisited them in a 1964 novel for adolescents entitled *Ishi: The Last of His Tribe*. A number of plays, documentaries and movies also came out in his name. He even became a hero in children's literatures. Ishi almost evolved into a cult with the distinction between the 'real' Ishi and the 'myth' Ishi blurring in his case.

The sorry phase of all these is that most of these outputs were from the side of the Occidental whites writing about the 'barbaric other' and hence mostly ethnocentric, even when they made a conscious effort not to prove so in their writings.

Kroeber's works are its best examples. Kroeber claims that it is he who named 'the wild man' Ishi. We know that to name a person means to exercise power on him. It means to monopolize the individual and be its authority. Ishi's future life also doesn't prove otherwise! But

Kessler's *How We Found Ishi* has a variant explanation of the way in which Ishi acquired his name – he claims that it is an abbreviated version of 'who is he?' – the frequently asked question put forth by the visitors in the museum.

Also in her second work, *Ishi: Last of His Tribe*, which takes the form of a novel, Ms Kroeber conveniently omits any indication that Ishi was not the protagonist's original *Yahi* name. *Ishi in Two Worlds* does good justice in showcasing the life of *Yahi* tribe, their customs and traditions. It brings our attention to many interesting things such as the existence of separate dialects for men and women in Yana language; how boys as babies learn their mother's dialect and then as boys learn their second language, that is, the father's dialect; how boys and girls do not sleep under one roof after puberty and so on.

But all throughout the book right from the preface, the superiority of the Occident justifies themselves in their actions and even subtly laughs at the simpleton lives and ways of the *Yahi*.

It is true that the ensuing text does not gloss over the horrors inflicted upon the *Yahi* by the invading whites. In fact, the book dwells on its horrors in detail. But the preface of this work stands contrary to this.

The history of Ishi and his people is inexorably part of our own history. We have absorbed their lands into our holdings. Just so we must be the responsible custodians of their tragedy, absorbing it into our tradition and morality.

The sanitizing diction of the epigraph itself initiates that process here: what might more appropriately be the term *invasion* is referred to as 'absorption' and what was to speak more accurately as 'the extermination' of Ishi's people is labelled as 'their tragedy'.

Today even the anthropologists' argument about Ishi as the last *Yahi* man is contended. Some research has brought evidence that as a *Yahi*-Yana Indian his closest living descendants are the Yana people of North California. So, even Ishi's last-ness – Ishi's status as literally the last of his tribe is therefore speculative. It can be accepted at face value unconditionally only if it is understood to mean that he was the last to have been closely observed by the dominant white culture. Even Ishi's identity as a *Yahi* is being questioned in some circles since then. He was identified by Kroeber and Waterman as a *Yahi*, and Ishi never denied it either. But some of his cultural traits, especially his production of projectile points, more resembled those of the historic Wintu/Nomlaki groups. Meanwhile his physical appearance seemed closer to the Mandu Indians with whom the *Yahis* were not on good terms historically.

Kroeber's *Ishi in Two Worlds* closes with what may have been the dying Ishi's last words, 'You stay, I go!', followed by a reproduction of the signature of his Western name that he had been taught to inscribe. For the society that appropriated unto itself the right to 'stay' while attempting to exile forcibly the native population, it is a very comforting envoi!

The alive Ishi served their research purposes well as a specimen and a window to the dead *Yahi* culture. But we further see the cannibalism of the imperialist self as it doesn't spare Ishi's body either. Every human being deserves a dignified death and burial according to his customs. Ishi was denied a dignified *Yahi* burial when his body was autopsied and his brain taken away. Ishi who trusted and befriended his white companions, though out of helplessness, got nothing but a bestial treatment in return. Kroeber tries to wash his hands off this unethical behaviour by saying that he couldn't stop it, though he really wanted to, for he was in New York when Ishi died and his letter opposing even an autopsy arrived late. Nonetheless it is this very person who had earlier referred to as his obligation as a friend to respect Ishi's wish to be buried whole, when on returning to California, instead of adding the brain to the ashes of the cemetery decided on sending the brain off to the National Museum on 5 January 1917 and it was recorded as a gift from Department of Anthropology, University of California. It was again Theodora Krober's book that revealed the secret about the autopsy on Ishi's body and the removal of his brain. But it did not provide any whereabouts about the location of its preservation. The saga of Ishi has taken a new turn. In 1997, the Butte County Native American Cultural Committee launched a campaign for the return of Ishi's remains for reburial in the *Yahi* homelands in northern California. Although his body's ashes were known to be in a niche in Olivet Cemetery just south of San Francisco, the Native Americans learned that the details about his brain has never been recorded anywhere in the many publications about him, including the detailed medical charts and autopsy report which is now archived in the Health Sciences Library at the University of California, San Francisco. Finally, after much delay and denials, the world came to know that the brain is preserved in Washington's National Museum. The event generated so much controversy over the years that in 2000, the Smithsonian Institution had to part with his brain in spirit of the National Museum of the American Indian Act of 1989 (NMAI), which required all of Ishi's remains to be handed over to the Redding Rancheria and the Pit River Tribe, Ishi's closest relations. Thus in 2000, he was given a reburial by the designated Native American people according to their customs.

The act might have healed the wound, but the scar still remains as the memories of what was done to Ishi and his people!

Although the violence and injustice suffered by the *Yahi* and many other groups in Native California cannot be undone, there now appears to be consensus among non-Indians and Indians alike that removing Ishi's brain was wrong and that it should be rejoined with the ashes of his body. To quote Nancy Rockefeller, a medical historian at the University of California, 'He has been admired for his resilience and heroism and now he is a symbol of the repatriation struggle. There are many Ishis'. Yes, the issue of Ishi encouraged repatriation struggle so much that, since 1991 the Smithsonian's Repatriation Office had to return more than 4,000 sets of remains to more than 40 Native American groups.

Now to sum up the entire Ishi–white affair, let me quote a conversation from the film drama *The Last of His Tribe* directed by Harry Hook. It is between Kroeber and Henreitte (a sensible voice in the play).

H: 'So tell me more about your Mr Ishi. What will you do with him?'

K: 'Legally I suppose, he will be our ward'.

H: 'Surely there are other Indians who can look after him'.

K: 'No other *Yahi*, darling, not a single one. And that's why he is such a big prize'.

H: 'You make him sound like just another artifact for your museum'.

K: 'He is much more valuable than that, I can assure you. I'm the only person who can understand him; without me everything these people were, their language, their stories, art, religion would be forgotten. I'm going to write a book'.

H: 'Alfred, I was just wondering may be there is something that ought to be forgotten. Things we aren't worthy to know'.

K: 'Well, you have just dispensed with the entire field of Anthropology'.

Yes, as Henrietta put it 'There are some things that ought to be forgotten. Things we aren't worthy to know'; for us to accept and preserve the mutual dignity and divinity of man universally; to live in universal harmony and understanding with the realization that it is the same blood which flows through all of us and the same air that we all breathe in and finally that we all will turn to a bag of ashes today or tomorrow.

But coming to terms with reality, the life of Ishi and the history of *Yahi* tribe will repeat itself in any part of the world as long as these aboriginal subalterns are heard through these Occidental historiographies and as long as they do not find a voice of their own!

References

Heizerand, Robert F., and Kroeber, Theodora, (eds), *Ishi the Last Yahi: A Documentary History* (Berkeley: University of California Press, 1979).

Kroeber, Theodora, *Ishi: Last of His Tribe* (Berkeley: Bantam Starfire, 1973).

Kroeber, Theodora, *Ishi in Two Worlds: A Biography of the Last Wild Indian in North America* (Berkeley: University of California Press, 1961).

Merton, Thomas, *Ishi Means Man* (Greensboro, North Carolina: The Unicorn Press, 1976).

Vizenor, Gerald, 'Ishi and the Wood Ducks: Postìndian Trickster Comedies', in *Native American Literature: A Brief introduction and Anthology*, G. Vizenor (New York: Harper Collins, 1995).

8

Raids, Resistance and Sovereignty

A Study of Naga–Ahom Relation

R.K. Bijeta

Raids were not new in Northeast India. Prior to the advent of the British, the area was subjected to various raids. The precolonial Northeast India had a number of polity formations. There were large states like that of the Ahoms, Meitei, Tripura and Dimasa (Cachar), whereas there were also smaller states like that of the Jaintias, Khasis, Tiwas and Bodos. Adjoining them were the chieftainship of the Lushais, Nagas, Arunchalese and countless other hill tribes. The tribal frequently committed raids on the territory of the larger states for diverse reasons. Most relentless raids were committed by the Nagas and various tribes of Arunachal on the Ahom territory, whereas the Lushais and Kukis committed raids on the Cachar, Tripura and Bengal territories. This chapter tries to examine the raids committed by the Nagas on the Ahom territory.

The Nagas were one of the most powerful tribes of Northeast India living on the Valley of Kopili River in the west to the Burhi-Dihing in the east. Their habitat consisted of the hilly areas bordering the district of present Nowgong, Karbi Anglong, Sibsagar and Dibrugarh of Assam. A number of Naga tribes occupied the Patkai hills range. It was here that the Ahoms came across the Nagas for the first time while passing through the Patkai hills. In fact the Nagas were one of the first tribe who defied the Ahom incursion of Brahmaputra valley. On the other hand, it was not trouble-free to identify the Nagas by their present identity. Nagas were recognized to the plainsmen by the names given to them by the plainsmen, which were a depiction relatively than a genuine ethnic name. This made the classification of the tribe in contact of the precolonial times with their present ethnic character.

In the precolonial period, most of the tribes were not conscious of their tribal identities (Downs, 1994: 222–236) and their world was confined to their family, clan, *khel* and village. Terms such as Noga, Abor, Chulikata, Banferia, Kapur-shor and so on were given to them by non-tribal plains people (Devi, 1968). Even the major tribal groups in Naga Hills such as Ao, Angami, Lotha and Konyak got their names from other tribes (Dubey, 1982: 4). An assessment of the north-eastern situation will amply demonstrate it. For instance, the Nagas – one of the major tribes of north-eastern India – were not aware of themselves being Nagas. They had their personal distinctiveness for themselves. They identified themselves by their identities, which afterward became sub-tribal names, for example, Ao, Angamis, Chakesangs, Konyaks, Sangthams, Yimchungers and so on. Each of the village was a state (*ang*) or *Khunbao* (chieftaindom) or *Tatar* (Ao council of elected headmen), which was autonomous and often matched up to Greek city-states of the Ancient World. Fascinatingly the majorities of these were at war and frequently dedicated fierce raids on each other captivating an intense toll on its demographic potency. They were called Nagas (pronounced as Noga) by the bordering plainsmen of Assam. It is not known why they were called Noga but according to the existing theories the word *Noga* came from the Sanskrit word Naga meaning naked, or because the nature of hostility they perpetrated (Naga Gha or Naga Jalakiya) have been fallacious. Amusingly, most of Nagas cannot utter the alphabet 'G' so for them Naga is Naka. In fact even the Assamese people who coined the description *Naga* very rarely called the Nagas as Nagas. They were referred to as *Khamjangias, Aitonias, Tablungias, Namchangias* and so on. Sometimes they were not mentioned by the name of the Naga tribe or clan but by the names of a number of villages against which expedition was launched. Originating from the west between Dayang and Dikhow rivers, the Naga tribes were branded by the Assamese as *Panihatias* (those who come by water), the *Torhatias* (those who come by land) or *Dayangias*, the *Hatigorias, Assyringias, Dupdorias* and *Namchangias.* The first two were part of the Lotha Nagas and the rest of the Aos. Between the Dikhow and Burhi-Dihing river, the Naga tribes were famous as *Tablungias Jaktoongias, Mooloongs, Changnois* (also known as *Bhitor Namchangias*), *Jabokas* or *Abhaypurias, Banferas* and *Mutonias* (or Kooloongs). *Paniduarias, Barduarias* and *Namchangias* (or *Jaipoorias*) were not connected with the *Namchangias* (division of Ao) who inhabited the low boundary hills on the left side of Dikhow. A number of these tribes were more expansively positioned thinning out over a number of villages (*Tablungias* over 13 villages but some tribes over few villages, *Jobokas*, *Banferas* and *Mutonias* each with four or five villages only). These Naga tribes were the Konyak and Nocte tribes who resided between Dikhow and Burhi-Dihing bordering plains. The names of these Naga tribes stemmed either from the *duars* or passes through which they stirred down into the plains or from the important Naga villages or seats of the plains located at or close to the aperture of the passes. In face the Ahom state appointed some officers to manage and deal with each of these tribes.

Pre-Ahom Situation

The Nagas seemed to have animated a very controlled and private life prior to the Ahom occupation and subjugation of the Brahmaputra Valley, autonomous and independent without much contact with the neighbouring states. But on every incident when there was any intimidation to their sovereignty or their economic requisite, they did strike back. The major states that emerged in Brahmaputra Valley earlier than the Ahoms was that of the *Kacharis* (*Dimasa*) and *Chutiyas*. The Kachari Kingdom seems to have extended up to Mohong (Devi, 1968), which lay in the land of the Borduaria and Paniduaria Nocte Naga tribes. The Kachari Kingdom 'in the 13th century appears to have extended towards the east up to the Dikhow only' (Gait, 2011). It appeared thus that the Kacharis who had for a short while occupied Mohong, which possessed nearly all the important salt wells, could not put into effect the suzerainty for long time over the Naga tribes living between the Dikhow and the Burhi-Dihing. Salt springs had enormous implications in the Naga and Brahmaputra Valley liaison. The hills of the Nagas where they lived did not have any source of salt, which was one of the most important consumer items. As against this, the Brahmaputra Valley had a number of salt springs under the control of the different powers that ruled the area. The Nagas often attacked and raided the plains only to take control of these salt springs. Kachari state had a number of salt springs in its frontier with the Nagas. To take control of these springs, the Nagas had driven them out of Mohong long before the advent of the Ahoms and took possession of the salt springs. The Chutiya kings whose dominion extended up to the Disang only did not seem to have exercised any suzerainty over the Nagas living between the Dikhow and the Burhi-Dihing. The Chutiya kings too had a number of salt springs around Sadiya but did not seem to have felt the necessity of taking possession of the salt wells lying in the land of the Nocte Nagas adjacent to the south-western fringe of their kingdom. This was perhaps due to the abundance of supply. These facts implied that the Naga tribes living between the Dikhow and the Burhi-Dihing were outside the political control of both the Kacharis and the Chutiyas. Because of these circumstances, they resented very much the newly established political suzerainty of the Ahom kings over them when it emerged from the thirteenth century. The new state not only compelled them to share the produce of some of the salt wells with the Ahom government, but also compelled them to acknowledge the overlord ship of the Ahom kings by paying annual tributes to them. The compensation that they received in lieu of it from the Ahom government in the shape of lands and fishing waters along with retainers on the plains was considered by them to be too insignificant in comparison to their loss of independence. So long the Ahom government was sufficiently powerful to keep their prestige intact by displaying their spirit in repelling foreign invasions and quelling disturbances within the kingdom, these Nagas remained peacefully submissive to their Ahom power. Hence the neighbours were now poised for the series of confrontation.

The Ahom Rule and Naga Raids

The Ahoms were one of the major Shan tribes of Burma who migrated under the leadership of a chief named Chukapha. They ruled Assam up to the eighteenth century. The Ahoms were a branch of this *Shan/Tai* race of Burma. The *Shans* were occupying the northern and eastern hill tracts of upper Burma and western Yunnan (Gait, 2011: 66), where they formed a group of states called *Mung-mau* or *Pong*. As a result of inter tribal rivalry among various Shan states in Burma, there were constant migratory movements of these tribes towards northern and eastern directions. One of the reasons for such migration was that unlike many other tribes of the region, Shans were a wet rice cultivating community. As states burgeoned, population exploded and internecine rivalry increased, the Shans began to look for new lands for settlement and wet rice cultivation.

The migration of the Ahoms were one such migratory movement of one of the Shan tribes of Burma who due to interstate rivalry and search for land were moving towards the Brahmaputra basin under the leadership of a chief named Chukapha. The country from which Chukapha came was called 'Maolung.' In 1228 AD, the Ahom pressed by the Burmese in the Maulung district of upper Irawadi crossed the Patkai range and entered into the eastern part of the Brahmaputra Valley, and Chukapha was the chief of this martial group of the Ahoms (Gait, 2011: 71–73). Chukapha was said to have left Maolung in 1215 AD. The iterant community had a contingent of 15 nobles, 9,000 fighting men, 1 tusked elephant, a female elephant, an elephant keeper and 300 horses with covered eyes (Devi, 1968: 5–6). The number of nobles and soldiers who had accompanied Chukapha varied from one *Buranji* to another.

According to some *Buranjis*, 8 nobles and 3,000 soldiers accompanied him, while according to others only 1,080 soldiers and a few nobles (number is not stated) accompanied him. In view of the hazardous journey that he had to undertake through the hilly country of the Patkai and many battles he fought with the tribes such as the Naga, the number of soldiers seemed to have been much greater than these *Buranjis* state (Devi, 1968). On the way Chukapa halted for a few days in the kingdom of the Nara Raja of Mogaung or Mungkong and after stealing the image of 'Somdeo', the tutelary God of the Shans, from him, he moved towards Assam. It was during this movement from Burma towards the Brahmaputra Valley that they trespassed through Naga habitat and encountered fierce resistance from the Nagas.

The first tribes whom Chukapha encountered on entering Northeast India were the Nagas of Patkai range such as the Wanchos, the Tangsas and the Noctes. But it was not the Naga resistance that brought hostility between the two but the intermittent raids that the Ahoms committed into Naga territories that caused the friction. The Ahoms wandered in the Patkai Hills range for about 13 years since their departure from their homeland in search of new lands for settlement or roads leading to such lands. In course of these 13 years, they often raided the Naga villages of the Patkai Hills and plundered their habitat. The Nagas were helpless victims of these raids. They were a small conglomeration of villages weak in demography or military skill against a highly sophisticated military community. But soon raids turned into invasion as Ahoms trespassed into Naga territory. These Nagas resisted the advance of the Ahoms through their land in several places. The resistance was a natural reaction of the Nagas to the trespassing of their habitat but the Ahom response was equally violent.

> For thirteen years he (Chukapa) wandered about the hilly country of the Patkai, making occasional raids on the Naga villages and in 1228 AD he

> came to the Nongnyang Lake. He then came to Namtillikkangtai. He crossed the river Khamjan and halted near a lake (the Nongyang Lake). It was on the arrival at Nongnyang Lake that Chukapha gave orders to his soldiers to fight with the Nagas. (Devi, 1968: 6–7)

It is not known why Chukapa had to order an expedition against the Nagas. It was probable that some of the Nagas had attempted to resist his advance. Gunabhiram Barua stated that they resisted the advance of the Ahoms. The Ahoms therefore had to force their way through the land of the Nagas.

The *Buranji* (the Ahom Royal Chronicle that actually provided minute details of the Ahom rule) provided the details of the expedition,

> The Nagas of the villages Kharukhu, Pungkang, Tithang, Binglao, Latema, Lampang and Taru acknowledged submission. The two villages Lunkam and Luka were destroyed. Then Chukapha conquered the Nagas of Taputapa. He placed Kangkhrumung (belonging to the family of the Bargohain who accompanied him) in charge of the country khamjang. Thus was created the post of the Khamjangia Gohain. Chukapha then ordered Kangkhrumung, the Khamjangia Gohain, to pay regular tributes to him with the articles produced in the surrounding Naga villages conquered by him and then left the place. (Devi, 1968: 11–12)

He arrived at Daikorang (the ancient name of the Patkai) where he stopped and ordered his chiefs to conquer the Nagas of both the plains and hills. As a consequence, the Nagas of the village Papuk, Tengkham, Khunkhat, Khuntung, Tangching and Jakhang were attacked. A great number of the Nagas were killed and many more were made captives. Though the Nagas offered valiant resistance, *Buranjis* report that many Nagas 'were cut to pieces and their flesh cooked. Then the king made a younger brother eat the flesh of his elder brother and a father of his sons'.

The colonial historians looked at this cruelty as ghastly and barbaric (Gait, 2011: 77). According to Edward Gait,

> 'Some Nagas resisted his advance, but he defeated them and arrived in Khamjang. He crossed a river called the Khamnamjang in rafts and came to the Nongnyang Lake. Some Nagas attempted to resist his advance but he defeated them and perpetrated frightful atrocities on them. He caused many of them to be killed and roasted and compelled their relatives to eat their flesh. Such ghastly barbarity created such widespread terror that the other Nagas of the neighborhood all hastened to make their submission. Leaving one of his nobles to rule the conquered country Chukapa proceeded to Dangkaorang, Khamhangpung and Namrup. (1968: 77–78)

Through these measures, therefore Chukapha not only destroyed the Naga villages but also morally through sheer cruelty forced its inhabitants to acknowledge his suzerainty. The conquered Naga chiefs were ordered by Chukapha to pay regular tributes to him with the produce of their hills.

The Ahoms never wanted to settle in the hilly terrain, and the above-mentioned details are sufficient evidence to that. Despite wandering for 13 long years in the hills and then conquering the tribal habitat too they did not settle in those lands. They had devastated the Nagas so much that they were left traumatized. They left the Nagas under one of their officers and marched ahead for the desired place. The reasons were obvious. The Ahoms were wet rice cultivators, they needed plain lands and river basin. Therefore, they did not settle in the Patkai and came down the hills in search of plain lands. But Nagas were not people who could be easily conquered. The moment the Ahoms left the Pataki, it was Nagas's turn to declare their sovereignty which they did by committing raids. Till the time the Ahoms were settled, the Nagas remained quiet perhaps due to the terrible inhumanity meted out to them. But by the turn of the fifteenth century when Nagas realized that they needed to announce their sovereignty, they began the perpetration of raids on the Ahom territory.

The Early Confrontation

In the eighties of the fifteenth century, by which time the Ahoms had firmly settled in Brahmaputra Valley and formed their own polity, the Nagas of Tangsu (or Tangasu) village revolted the reign of Chuchenpha (1439–1488 AD) in 1487 AD, the records called it a revolt but does not provide the nature of revolt or the nature of its manifestation. It appears that there was a raid on the Ahom territory. An expedition was sent against them, which defeated the Nagas (Barua, 1985: 52), but the Ahoms lost 140 men along with the two *dangarias* (i.e. ministers) in the battle. According to some *Buranjis*, however, some Khampa Nagas requested the help of the Ahom king against the Tangsu Nagas who were troubling them by raiding their territory (Devi, 1968: 8). They too confirmed the loss of two *dangarias* and 140 men. There is still another version that says that the Tangsu Naga made a present of swords as a token of their apparent submission but killed a great number of Ahoms using the opportunity through a sudden raid. A punitive expedition was sent that defeated the guilty Tangsu Nagas but as the expedition progressed, the Nagas in their characteristic way raided a detachment of the Ahoms and cut off the head of the Bargohain named

Chaokanbanruk who was in command. In the following expedition however, the Nagas were in retreat and some Naga children, spears and other things along with three Tangsu Naga families, were taken as booty by the Ahoms. These Tangsu Naga were most probably the 'Tangsa' Naga tribe living in the Tirap Division of Arunachal Pradesh on the Assam–Burma border.

This was the first recorded Naga hostile activity against the Ahoms since their first encounter. The Tangsus were the same Nagas whom Chukapha devastated on his way to Brahmaputra Valley. This was the Naga's way of revenge and a declaration that they no longer acknowledged the Ahom suzerainty over them. It took almost two centuries for the Nagas to rise up from the wreckage caused by the Ahoms and then emerge to declare their sovereignty. The casualties that they caused to the Ahoms through their raids also demonstrated that they had upgraded their war technology and strength to fight up a mighty military power. Up to the end of the fifteenth century, therefore, the Nagas had maintained their grievance and hostile attitude towards the Ahoms who tried to keep them forcibly down. The Tangsu Nagas however, in spite of their defeat, did not conclude a peace with the Ahoms.

But the troubles were brewing from the other side as well. The Nagas living on the northern slopes of the Patkai mountain gave much more forceful and continuous quandary to the Ahoms than others. These Nagas were known as Khamjangia Nagas as they lived around the Khamjang forest area. They were conquered by Chukapha on his way to Assam from Burma by the most important low pass over the Patkai mountain via the Nongnyang Lake (Shakespear, 1914) and instituted the post of the Khamjangia Gohain to rule the country of Khamjang that stood just on the way on this pass on the other side of the Patkai mountain and also its neighbourhoods. The Ahom government claimed suzerainty over the Nagas living in the low hills south of Sibsagar and Dibrugarh districts from Dikhow to the Burhi-Dihing by compelling these tribes to pay taxes of slaves, elephants' teeth, spear-shafts, clothes and cotton.

In the year 1530, the Namchangia and the Tablungia Nagas raided and plundered an Ahom force and took into custody several guns. They also killed some 23 Assamese subjects in another raid in the year 1692. The Ahom king Gadadhar Singha effectively took stern actions against the Nagas and obliged them to admit defeat and proffer two Naga princesses to the king. Such subjugation of the Nagas was a very exceptional occurrence. But Gadadhar Singha was a very powerful Ahom who not only stretched out his territory but also cowed a number of tribes in the valley. There were always sporadic clashes between the Nagas and the Ahoms throughout the entire period of the Ahom rule till the time of Purandar Singh. Such clashes were in the form of raids and counter raids that took always place in the border areas and not in the interior of the Naga Hills, which remained always impenetrable to the Ahom (Bhuyan, 1974). Thus the mass of the Naga tribes could not be fully subjugated by the Ahoms. The Ahoms followed a policy of conciliation using duress and force whenever necessary. The Ahom rulers considered it adequate to receive the submission of the Nagas and to allow them to enjoy their tribal autonomy so long as the Nagas – living near the plains, who were granted revenue-free lands and fishing waters along with retainers in the plains – did not raid Ahom territories and the Nagas on the Indo-Burma frontier did not collaborate themselves with the enemies of the Ahoms beyond the Patkai range to put at risk the Ahom kingdom.

The Ahom–Naga relation during the seventeenth century however demonstrated some kind of progression. During the reign of Chuchingpha (1644–1648 AD), some Khamjangia Nagas came to the Ahom Garhgaon and sought the help of the Ahom king against some rival Naga villages such as Khamteng, Sikidu, Titu, Khama and Luma who were harassing them (Barua, 1985: 134–139). The Ahom king took the opportunity of settling gain with rival Nagas that troubled the Ahom kingdom for some time. An expedition was sent against the Nagas who tried to resist the expedition but retreated as soon as they perceived the size of Ahom army. Instead of resisting the Nagas of the villages, Thaokhen, Rukhru, Latema, Khampin and Chaokha along with Khamteng strategically surrendered. They sent several men with two goats, two cages of fowls and two pots of liquor as tributes. The Ahom army marched forward and attacked the Khamtengia Nagas who fled away. The Ahoms obtained possession of 20 *mithuns*, 160 Naga caps, 6 blankets, 16 women and 2 young men of the enemy as war booty. Twenty Naga captives were presented and punished publicly by the king. The Khamtengia Nagas then offered the king two gongs, a packet of poison and some other gifts. This time the brother of the Khamtengia Raja (the Naga chief) also came to the Ahom king at Garhgaon. Thus, for the first time, one of the restless Naga tribe of the Patkai mountain, who gave trouble to the Ahom rulers, visited the Ahom king at his capital and established friendly relations with him. The Ahom king also on his part received these Nagas cordially in spite of their repeated rebellious raids against Ahom authority.

But such armistice lasted only till Chuchingpha lived. Soon after his accession to the throne, King Jayadhvaja Singha (1648–1663 AD) had to send three envoys to negotiate with the Nagas who it was reported had refused to obey the order of the king (Devi, 1968: 4–5). The envoys went to Khamjang, and according to the instructions given to them, they collected the Khamjangia Nagas and held them responsible for disobeying the Ahom monarch. The Nagas as usual regretted the conduct and begged pardon of the king and requested him not to punish them considering them to be the slaves of his ancestors. In response for this act of kindness pleaded for, the Nagas assured to look after the well-being of the Khamjangia Gohain, the Ahom officer who was in charge of these Naga locales. Actually the Ahoms humiliated the Nagas by making them eat the scraps thrown off from the dishes of the Ahom princes. This was followed by the submission of the Khamjangia Nagas along with the Khamjangia Gohain Tyaorai Thaokhen who came to the king to pay their homage. They brought with them many presents consisting of gold vessels, silver vessels and varieties of cloth, Japis (cane hats), black Japis and feathers of a species of wild bird known as Kairangcha. Jayadhvaja Singha also reciprocated, and they went back with appropriate commands and expensive gifts from the king. By the middle of the seventeenth century, it was therefore evident that the Nagas of this region were converted into systematically acquiescent and from this time they did not gave the impression to have given any more trouble to the Ahom head of the state in later times. The Nagas by paying their annual tributes on a regular basis continued to be at peace with the Ahoms that also helped them to uphold their friendly associations. It therefore took almost one and a half centuries of skirmishing from the commencement of the sixteenth century that these Khamjangia Nagas were brought down and enforced to surrender.

The Ahoms were also enormously troubled by the Nagas from the other side of the boundary. The Nagas who existed close to the plains also often raided the Ahom area. During the reign of Chuhungmung, the Dihingia Raja (1497–1539 AD), Tablungia, Jaktoongia and Namchangia Nagas, divisions of Konyak Naga tribes living on the eastern side of the Dikhow River, raided the Ahom territory and hence an expedition was sent in 1536 AD against them (Devi, 1968). Namchangias were of two categories: the Namchangias and *Bhitar Namchangias* (Nagas from the interior). The *Bhitar Namchangias* or the Changnois inhabited the low border hills on the right bank of the Dikhow River on the Sibsagar border, and the Namchangias lived beyond the Sibsagar frontier, that is to say, in the Lakhimpur district, who are also known as Jaipurias. The *Buranjis* have the reference of the Naga villages of Jaktoong, Changnan (i.e. Changnoi or Bhitar Namchang), Janphan (Jenphan) and Chantai (or Shanchai of Ahom Buranji) waging a unified attack on the Ahom army. These cohesive attacks by the Nagas compelled the Ahom troops to recoil, leaving behind four guns in the Naga territory.

The Nagas triumph was however short-lived since they complied and made peace with the Ahoms by returning the guns. Despite the fact that the Nocte and the Konyak Nagas existing close to the plains brawled with the Ahoms on various occasions akin to the Nagas of the Patkai mountain, nevertheless some of them ascertained close associations with the Ahoms; and some of them established affable relations once they were beaten. It is quite apparent that these Naga tribes accepted the over lordship of the Ahom ruler and were in the habit of giving presents to the Ahom king which might be regarded as annual tributes. By the middle of the sixteenth century, these Banfera Nagas apparently on the potency of the secure friendship with the Ahom kings set out to the extent of asking for the help of the Ahom king Chuklengmung (1539–1552 AD) the successor of Chuhungmung in their inter-tribal squabbles.

Struggle over Salt Springs

Livelihood apprehensions were mostly to be held responsible for the antagonism with the Nocte Nagas of the Tirap Frontier Division of Arunachal Pradesh who lived on the low hills close to the plains of Sibsagar and Lakhimpur districts. This region had its livelihood significance to both the Nagas and the Ahoms as it possessed a number of salt wells. The Ahoms got hold of extraordinary custody of some of these salt wells and also the right to certain other wells by grappling it from the Nagas. But the Nagas were very much offended by this and appeared to have half heartedly approved the idea to share with the Ahom government the produce of the salt wells. The Nagas intermittently committed raids upon the people of the salt mines that were under the control of the Ahoms. On the other hand, the Ahom government in order to preserve their privileges as far as these salt mines were concerned had to send punitive expeditions against these Nagas. This financial interest of the Ahoms in the salt mines thus was one of the most important reasons of the conflicts between the Ahoms and the Naga tribes of this area as it implicated upon their livelihood matters.

As can well be perceived from the above that the Nagas raided not only to pronounce or affirm their autonomy or for the purpose of vengeance but also to obtain consumable products that were not available in the hills. One such product was salt. The Ahoms had abundant of salt springs and rock salt hills in their territory. And usually the Nagas acquired and relied on these free sources of salt to meet their requirements. However with the rise of the Ahom state and along with it the practice of positioning boundaries restricted the natural passage of the Nagas to acquire these valuable items. It's worth mentioning here that the Nagas also had quite a few numbers of salt springs in their own territories which the Ahoms with their coming forcibly staked claim on. Hence these had now to be acquired through raids in the form of pillages. This was for the reason that the salt springs and salt wells and all other sources of salt that the Ahoms had within their territory was not even adequate to mete out their requirements. The Assamese by and large accumulated salt from the salt springs, which were not sufficient for the whole Ahom inhabitants. Consequently the Ahom subjects in general developed a skill by means of which they produced a substance called *Khar* which they used as an alternative for salt. The salt springs were therefore the bone of contention between the Ahoms and the Nagas throughout the precolonial period.

According to some *Buranjis*, in the year 1458 saka (1536 AD) the Ahoms obtained possession of one salt well in Mohong by defeating the Nagas, which the Nagas had wrested from the Kacharis earlier (Devi, 1968). The Borduarias and Paniduarias were Nagas living at the eastern extremity of the Sibsagar district who were also called Mohongias (Grierson, 2005). For the Nocte Nagas, the Mohongs was one of the most imperative salt generating places of their land. Hence, economic concern of the Ahoms also obligated them to exchange blows against the Mohong Nagas living between Borhat and Jaipur. In the due course of time, the Ahoms got hold of an exclusive ownership of a number of salt wells and they also had to launch numerous voyages in opposition to the Nagas to hold on to their rights in the salt wells unharmed.

In 1692 AD, during Gadadhar Singha's reign the Namchangia Nagas cut 23 persons at the salt mine (Devi, 1968). Tamcheng Chinghai Phukan, the commander of the former expedition, was selected by the Ahom king to be sent to proceed to the Borduar (i.e. main pass) of the Namchangia Nagas. Moreover one more person Laling Phukan was ordered to leave for the Borduar of Borhat. Together the Phukans undertook united deed against the Nagas. The Nagas were overwhelmed, and incalculable Nagas together with their Raja were incarcerated. Every single one of the Nagas was decapitated in the neighbourhood of the Jamuna in the village Langkek. According to the Ahom *Buranji*, the brother of the Khunbao (Naga Raja) named Latha was made the Raja. The Nagas connecting the Dikhow and the Burhi-Dihing, nevertheless, sustained to offer hitches to the Ahoms, the raid being unswerving in the salt mine. Dr S.K. Bhuyan identifies these Namchangia Nagas with the Namchangias living by the side of the Dikhow who are a branch of the Ao Nagas. About the year 1563 AD, the Ahom king Chukhampha, Khora Raja (1552–1603), rewarded the Tablungia Nagas, one of the Konyak Naga tribes living by the side of the Dikhow, with *beels* (large natural ponds) on the plains in recognition of some valuable services rendered by them to the Ahom king. Besides they were also consigned fishermen *paiks* (Dom-bahatias) as well as to supply them with the dried fish from the *beels*.

In the reign of the next Ahom king Rudra Singha (1697–1714 AD), in the beginning of the eighteenth century in December 1701 AD, a *Jugi* (Hindu mendicant) merchant of Bandarkhel killed approximately 60 Nagas at Borhat who had entered the Ahom fort guarding the salt mine there. During the confusion which followed the Nagas also killed a large number of people of Ahom tribe at the Lonsal or salt mine. King Rudra Singha at that moment was absent from the capital and was halting at Biswanath on his return voyage from Koliabar. He was explained of the happening at hand. He recommenced his voyage upstream the Brahmaputra towards the beginning of March 1702 AD. As Laxmi Devi mentions in her book that:

> In consultation with the Dangarias and the Phukan the king propelled an army under the leadership of Basang Phukan to fight with the Nagas. The Phukans advanced and stopped in the plains to the north of the Dilih opposite Borhat; from there he sent a few men to the Naga villages to convince the Nagas to come to terms. They accomplished their operation and brought with them a number of Nagas who bowed down in front of the Ahom king. The king pardoned them and sent them back with present. Undoubtedly these were the Nocte Nagas; nevertheless it was not probable to ascertain whether they were Borduarias, Paniduarias or Namchangias unquestionably. The strategy of urging employed by Basang Phukan confirmed to be exceptionally thriving, as no Naga raids were heard of until the commencement of the 19th century when the Ahom kingdom was on its way to decline.

The intermittent Naga raids however still continued. As a result, the next King Pratap Singha (1603–1641 AD), with a view to stop the raids of the Naga tribes on the borders of Sibsagar and Lakhimpur, constructed a fort called 'Naga-garh' and forbade the Nagas to enter inside the fort unaccompanied by the *chaotangs* or interpreters (Devi, 1968). As most of the Naga tribes were deficient in the supply of foodstuffs, King Pratap Singha granted the chiefs of these tribes or lands along with retainers called *Khats* in order to put a stop to their raiding operations upon the Assamese villages bordering on the hills. These estates were called Naga-Khats and were administered by Assamese agents called Naga-Katakis and the produce of those lands were used to provide the tribes with foodstuffs. The Nagas of each pass (or *duar*) in lieu for the lands granted to them had to forfeit an annual mark of respect to the Ahom king in the shape of *mithun* (wild cows), painted goats, red hair, red cane, salt and a variety of other articles produced in the different passes.

Head Hunting Raids

The purpose of the Naga raids projected in the writings of the colonial historians was to look for human heads. Even though the British were discussing concerning their own colonial times where they showed that the Nagas perpetually raided their territory and killed British subjects because the Nagas by tradition were a head hunting tribe and such raids were made to kill plainsmen and to accumulate human heads as their reward which were essential for various rationales such as proof of masculinity, tribal ritual of fertility, morturial rites of dead chiefs and so on. Naga raids were therefore perceived by the colonial historians as an extension of Naga history of raids from the precolonial periods.

Headhunting has been perceived as a common institutionalized performance of anthology of human heads by a number of tribes of Northeast India on the foundation of which they have been brandished as 'wild', 'savage', 'barbaric', primitive' and so on. It is this headhunting and related raids of the tribes that have been presented as the reason for an incessant bloody war in opposition to the tribes which lasted approximately a hundred years. Head hunting as a practice was revealed only in the colonial era. In fact, previously than that hunting for survival was not seen as an attribute of savagery. 'No notion of hunting-gathering existed before 1740's. Rather the discourse centred on "natural man versus civilization ..."' writes Allan Barnard (1999) of Edinburgh University. He depicted various stages of hunting-gathering:

Foraging: Living by victuals produced by nature such as trees.

Food Production: Through commerce and violence. In the seventeenth century, reports of ferocious giants were common place among the intellectuals. Montesquieu and Herder classified hunters as savage people or people who do not cultivate land. Lewis Henry Morgan (1877) divided culture into three stages: savagery, barbarians and civilization. Alan Barnard (2000) asserts that it was Frederick Engel (1884) who followed Morgan rather than Karl Marx in this scheme of evolution.

It was in both phases that some tribes practiced head hunting according to the author.

Since the Ahoms were the predecessors to the British in Assam, let us look at the nature of raids perpetrated by the Nagas on Assam for such head hunting. The raids that were discussed so far had been for various reasons as has been conferred above. There was no verification of Naga raids in the pre-Ahom period but most possibly this was owing to the fact that Nagas did not raid on the plains as there was no recognized state there. Most of them were tribal states in the Assam plains, which did not have much to offer to the Nagas in terms of treasures to be captured. Some Naga tribes had not set up till they migrated in the region.

The raids carried out by the Nagas were by and large on each other, one tribe to another and the raids on plains were not considerable enough in conditions of loss to receive mention. The preliminary encounter between the Nagas and Ahoms was essentially an altercation between two adversaries. The ensuing raids were to stop the progress of the Ahom expansion into the Naga areas and also to display their independence. Several Naga raids were to guard their salt springs or protect the land, water bodies or forest resources. None of them however were for collection of human heads. The first record of a Naga raid on the Ahom territory for human heads was in the seventeenth century.

After the Burmese invasion, however, they rekindled their raiding operations. Thus, throughout the reign of the last Ahom king Purandar Singha (1832–1838 AD) who was installed as the king of the whole of upper Assam, the Malauthupia (or Malanthupia) Nagas, who were now taken notice of for the first time, killed a number of villagers in the Ahom kingdom and pillage their properties in 1836 AD (Golap Chandra Barua). The Neog Phukan summoned a Naga-Kataki and asked him to go to the Malauthupia Nagas and win over them to come to him. The Kataki arrived with a number of Nagas. The Neog Phukan made an enquiry and found that the Nagas implicated in uprising and confined the Nagas. But the Malauthupia Nagas took vengeance by unexpectedly attacking the Ahom army, which took life of a number of men. The sepoys in addition opened fire on the Nagas and killed a number of Nagas and the remaining fled away.

Conclusion

As the above narrations of Ahom–Naga relations confirm, sporadic clashes of the Ahoms with the Nagas was one of the main characteristics of the history of Assam throughout the entire period of Ahom rule. Most of these were with the Naga tribes living on the Patkai mountain around the country of Khamjang and the Nagas living between the rivers Dikhow and the Burhi-Dihing. Several reasons seem to have contributed towards this development. Initially it was the clash between a native settled community and an invading power. It was followed by reasons of sovereignty, clash over scarce resources and requirement of rites and resistance to an advancing power. In all cases, the weapon that was used by the Nagas to express their hostility was raids. Raids were the means through which Naga articulated their resistance, restiveness, objection, power and sovereignty. It was hence a political deal rather than a guerrilla tactics of terrorizing as is often supposed. Raids were also countered by raids called expedition or punitive expedition. In this sense, raids and counter raids were the feature of precolonial Ahom–Naga relationship.

An important reason of raids was the issue of sovereignty. The Nagas had tremendous sense of independence. They resented very much their subordinate status. The route from Burma to Brahmaputra Valley was through the Naga country. Hence it was very much important both for strategic and other reasons. That's why they did never allow the disturbances of this region to gain gigantic proportions so as to jeopardize their kingdom. They took prompt action in every case, though it was very difficult to fight in the hills and there was very little to gain, such as some mithuns and buffaloes, in the shape of war booty. Friendly relations however developed between the Ahom rulers and some of these Naga tribes whose chiefs were in the habit of visiting the Ahom kings at their capital and also of inviting the armed intervention of the Ahom government against one another in their own inter-tribal conflicts.

References

Assam Buranjs (S.K. Bhuyan's, *Deodhai Assam Buranji & Tungkhungia Buranji,* Harakanta Barua's, *Assam Buranji,* S.K. Dutta's, *Assam Buranji*, Kasinath Tamuli Phukan's, *Assam Buranji*).

Barnard, Alan, 'Images of Hunters and Gatherers in European Social Thought', *The Cambridge Encyclopedia of Hunters and Gatherers*, (eds), Richard B. Lee and Richard Daly (Cambridge: Cambridge University Press, 1999).

Barnard, Alan, *History and Theory in Anthropology* (Cambridge: Cambridge University Press, 2000).

Barua, Golap Chandra, (ed.), *Ahom Buranji: From the Earliest Time to the End of Ahom Rule* (Guwahati: Spectrum Publications, (Reprint) 1985).

Bhuyan, S.K., *Anglo-Assamese relations, 1771–1826: A History of the Relations of Assam with the East India Company from 1771 to 1826* (Guwahati: Lawyer's Book Stall, 1974).

Bhuyan, S.K., *History of Assam from 1681–1826 A.D* (translated) (Guwahati: Depart of Historical and Antiquarian studies, 1990).

Devi, Laxmi, *Ahom Tribal Relations: A Political Study* (Gauhati: Lawyers Book Stall, 1968).

Downs, Frederick, 'Identity: The Integrative Principle', *Essays of Christianity in North East India*, (eds), M. Sangam and D.R. Syiemlieh (Delhi: Indus Publishers, 1994).

Dubey, S.M., 'Inter-Ethnic Alliance, Tribal Movements and Integration in North-East India', *Tribal Movements in India*, (ed.), K.S. Singh (New Delhi: Manohar, 1982).

Gait, E.A., *A History of Assam* (Guwahati: Spectrum Publications, Delhi, (Reprint), 2011).

Grierson, G.A., *Linguistic Survey of India*, Vol. 1 (Delhi: Low Price Publication, 2005).

Morgan, Lewis Henry, *Ancient Society* (New York: Henry Holt and Company, 1877).

Shakespear, L.W., *History of Upper Assam, Upper Burmah and North-Eastern Frontier* (London: 1914).

Part III

Gender

9

Masculine Gender Identity and Man's Modern Right among the Meiteis of Manipur

Thiyam Rabikanta Singh

In every society, the difference between males and females is the most fundamental of all distinctions between peoples; however, the male–female dichotomy is not clear-cut (Hicks and Gwynne, 1996: 181). The 'maleness' and 'femaleness', as well as the learned behaviours that are supposedly male or female, are qualities and expectations in sexual roles and sexual orientations. Here, sex is usually referred to the biological category into which a person is born as determined by chromosomal and anatomical characteristics. The term *gender* refers basically to culturally determined behaviours.

Gender identity is the individual's self-identification as male or female. It is the part of an individual's personality and a central component of (his or her) self-concept being tallied with the masculinity or femininity given in the concerned society. How an individual feels inside; like feeling of masculinity and femininity is the gender identity (Chin, 2004). Tiwari and Ghadially (2009) describe three psychological theories for acquiring gender identity. The first, biological determinism argues that femininity and masculinity follow inevitably from our physical differences as males and females. The second, social learning theory claims that the gender skills are acquired by imitation, and the third, cognitive development theory maintains that masculinity and femininity develop through a process of interaction between our experience of the world and our emerging but prestructured capacity for conceptual thinking. In identification theory based on biological determinism, boys learn 'I am what mother is not' rather than 'I am what father is', whereas girls learn 'I am what mother is'. Thus, a boy's sense of masculinity starts out with a sense of antifeminism. Social learning theory suggests that the notion of reinforcement in which reward following behaviour and punishment following behaviour directs the children to repeat or abandon certain behaviours. Children learn by imitating and modelling those around them, so children will most likely imitate those who positively reinforce (reward) their behaviour to develop to the gendered persons. Cognitive development theory holds that children learn gender through their mental efforts to organize the social world. They are active in structuring their understanding of gender roles. They approach through a stage of wanting to conform to stereotypical expectations of what females and males are like despite the question of advices from their parents or teachers. Once they become aware of their sex or gender they actively seek out opportunities to behave in ways, which they see as being 'girl-like' or 'boy-like'. Performing what they are expected to do is what being a boy or being a girl actually means. For instance, among the Meiteis of Manipur, the boys or girls are expected as 'You are a girl because you wear *phanek*. You are a boy because you wear trouser or *khudei*'. Again, as they develop and mature mentally, they rationalize that masculinity and femininity are not absolute concepts, but relative concepts.

Masculinity must be discussed with its place in the gender constructions in specific cultures because how we behave as women and men will always depend upon the existing social relations of gender. Gender role, which refers to the rights, attitudes, behaviours and relationships of men and women, includes the rule of masculinity and masculine ideology that may be expressed as masculine stereotypes. Stereotypical 'real men' masculine identity can be described as having certain traits prescribed by the society and as prohibiting certain behaviours proscribed by the same society. Masculinity scholars attempt to broaden the discourse of gender through 'men's studies'. It studies men's gendered experiences, but it tries to understand that gender does not mean female, the same way race does not mean black. Thus, such studies include men's rights movement. Men also claim for rights against sufferings of being gendered men. In short, men's studies often called 'men and masculinities' are about men, masculinity, gender and politics. The concept of plural masculinities was proposed by R.W. Connell in her influential book *Masculinities* (1995), and in the academic field today it is known as *men and masculinities*.

The present study focuses on the changing masculine gender identity and men's studies. So, an attempt is made to know the traditional masculinity and the modern men's right in moulding changing traits of redefinable males in the dynamic cultural scenario of the Meiteis in Manipur, India. The people understudy settle mainly in India, Myanmar and Bangladesh. In India, they settle mainly in the states such as Manipur, Assam and Tripura. However, they are described as autochthons of Manipur valley. The other settlement regions were established as consequences of different historical episodes. They live in agrarian societies having patrilineal clans and virilocal residence.

Methodology

The present qualitative study among the Meiteis tries to discourse the development, shift of masculine ego ideal as well as man's rights of the concerned people. Data collection was done using standard techniques such as case studies, observation and focussed interviews among different age groups – adolescents of 10–18 years and educated males ranging from 40 to 62 years of age.

Masculine Gender Identity

Masculine gender identity is fully acquired when a man exhibits gender stereotypes such as personality traits, household behaviours, occupation and physical appearance. Regarding personality traits, men acquire traits such as aggressiveness, higher-stakes risk-taking and assertiveness more commonly, while traits such as sociability, harm-avoidance and emotionality are less common. Toughness, self-reliance, and rationality are men's strength; selflessness is men's honour and risk-taking tasks and competitiveness are men's favourite actions. In domestic behaviours, men do best in household repairs while women are best in child caring. Among the Meiteis, occupations such as hunting are masculine while occupations such as weaving and pottery making are feminine. Regarding physical appearance, men are expected to be tall and broad-shouldered while women are expected to be soft and graceful. In Meitei expression, *nupathokpa* denotes maleness. Hypomasculinity means weakness, timidity, dependence and irrationality, apathy, irresponsible, submissiveness and lethargy. Hypermasculinity means fearlessness (*akiba khangdaba*), less selfish (*oijaba thidaba*), hyper-aggressive and life endangering risks. In addition, 'universal masculine' gender roles such as (1) provider: secure and provide resources and (2) protector: defend others and territory just as mentioned by Gregor (1985) are also fitted for Meitei males.

Men in Traditional Feminine Role

In the patrilineal and patriarchal Meitei society, though the tradition recognizes stereotypic male roles, there is a group of men called *nupa maibi* who are the priestesses. *Maibi* generally means a priestess wearing white blouse, white *phanek* (skirt) and a waist wrapper having a traditional extra weft design known as *sarong*. She is addressed as *ima* meaning 'mother' by people irrespective of ages. The male *maibi* is also addressed by the same pseudo-kin term. Gajrani (2004: 151–152) writes about the vital role played by the *maibi* while performing rituals in temple and in the society. She lives with certain restrictions in social life. For instance, they cannot take food which is not socially clean or prepared in the house where child birth has taken place or a food prepared by a woman in her menstruation period as such places and conditions are considered defile by the society. The *maibi* is above the common people as she or he is a person of *Lai* (god). It is believed that a *Lai* possesses the *maibi*. A man or woman becoming a *maibi* is believed to be a choice made by the *Lai*. He or she suffers psychiatric problem which is taken as a symptom of being selected by god to be a *maibi*. During *Lai haraoba* (merry-making festival of *Lai*), when he or she is selected by Lai, he or she would become hysterical while dancing, becomes frenzy and gets into a state of trance during which she utters words which sound alien. The female can be possessed by the *Lai* directly. In that case the female at the initial stage will show an abnormal behaviour by singing songs, pulling her hairs, shouting, trembling and speaking in an unusual tongue. A girl or a woman (married or unmarried) of any age is liable to be chosen by the Lai to become a *maibi*. The girl at the tender age of seven may become a *maibi* and a woman of 40 or 50 years also can be chosen as *maibi* by the *Lai*. It is believed that a *maibi* since the tender age becomes a successful *maibi* in the long run. A married *maibi* usually sleeps on the left side of the bed with her husband. The visits of *Lai* are during the nights on some fixed dates of the month. On these particular days, she sleeps alone. On these nights, the *Lai* may appear in the form of a human being and the *maibi* feels the sensation of copulation. It is said that it is more satisfying when the *Lai* appears in the human form. The *Lai* also visits the *maibi* during her menstruation but no intercourse sensation is felt by the *maibi* during this period. The husband senses the presence of the *Lai* with his wife and therefore, he leaves her alone to be comfortable with the *Lai*. The *Lai* is never happy if she bears a child as she will never be able to develop natural affection for the child and may maltreat or ignore the child. One important role of the *maibi* is to predict through divination holding a metal bell, which is believed to be the genital part of the *Lai*. She also interprets the predictions by using oracles made of metal coins.

The roles played by the *maibi* signify a feministic character. The male *maibis* also wear the same uniform of the female *maibis*. So it is a transsexual role sanctioned to males. But, an organization known as *Umanglai kanba lup* has banned the males from becoming a *maibi*. In defence, the male *maibis* claim that the first *maibi* who predicted through divination was Lord Sanamahi who later assigned this task to Goddess Leimarembi. Above all, it is not the man who chooses the profession of *maibi* but the divine beings select a person to become a *maibi*. A male *maibi* abandons female dress once he stops performing as a maibi. This is an indicative of a traditional feminine role, which is extended to the male sex through transition. But, the legendary villain called Nongban who interpreted the divine message as a *maibi* was never a feminine character. Further, researchers find many male *maibis* performing masculine roles too.

Socialization to a Male Gender

From infancy to early childhood and beyond, children learn the gender expectations. Parents at family level, is the first to enculture their children for the development of gender stereotypes. What has recently been termed *femiphobia* – an unconscious hatred and dread of the part of the self that is experienced as feminine – often ensues (Ducat, 2004). In the Meitei society, such idea of contrast identification in its initial stage is reportedly started during the second and third years of the children. Through the boy's relationship with his father who he admires, interacts with and mentors him in caring way, he is able to internalize a parental imago in which the active and penetrating aspects and the receptive and caretaking qualities of the father's parenting become a foundation for healthy and fluid masculinity gender identity. Nonetheless, the boy's relationship with his mother is also significant. Her recognition and affirmation of her son's maleness helps him to progressively differentiate from her rather than establish his sense of masculinity in opposition to her femaleness. His relationship with her is not identification but the formation of 'disidentification'.

Some of the socialized qualities and behaviours for the dichotomy of gender relation among the studied people are given below.

Age	*Male*	*Female*
3–10 years of age	Prefers toys such as gun, sling shot.	Prefers toys as doll.
	Prefers pictures and movies such as Ben 10.	One of the favourite characters is Barbie.
	Prefers blue, not pink colour.	Prefers pink coloured items.
	Enjoys in assisting father.	Playfully assist mother in cleaning, washing dishes, sweeping, etc.
	Prefers outdoor games, avoid girlish play.	Prefers indoor games and play-acting games, sometimes mimicking lady teachers, cooking or ita lakpi (friend's visit) using toy mobile phones.
	Avoids crying when hurt accidentally – nupanabu kap para (do men cry).	Avoids craziness, toughness – nupa saranu (do not imitate boys).
10–18 years of age	Pursues to use man's dress, in dull colour.	Bright and colourful woman's dresses are favourites.
	Crazy about motorbikes.	Avoids use of motorbikes
	Assigned hard work in agriculture	Assigned less hard work in agriculture
	Aggressive tendency	Tender and defensive
	Teased when they beautify their face – Nupana kerisibu homogi maóngda (comparing boys who want to beautify as transgender)	Beautification allowed
	Aphaba nupa pamdra – joke by boys asking whether the girls want good breadwinner	Thakpinaba pharaga loire – joke of girls to boy expressing their dependence to men

Men's Rights Movement

The men's modern rights movement (MRM) emerged from the men's liberation movement in the early 1970s. It is made up of a variety of groups and individuals who are commonly concerned about issues of male disadvantage, discrimination and oppression (Boyd et. al., 1996). Its activists see men as an oppressed group and believe that society and state have been 'feminized' by the women's movement. Sarah

Maddison (1999), an Australian author, argues that for most man, power is an illusion and that women are the true power holders in society through their roles as the primary careers and nurturers of children. Because of exhibiting misogynistic tendencies, this antifeminist men's rights movement have been critiqued. But the pro-feminist men's movement – which was influenced by second-wave feminism, the Black Power and student activism movement, the Anti-war movement, and LGBTQ (Lesbian, gay, bisexual, transgender, queer) social movements – generally embraces the egalitarian goals of feminism (Kimmel, 2004; Messner, 1998). They argue that socio-cultural expectations and traditional norms have forced men into rigid gender roles, limited men's ability to express themselves and restricted their choices of behaviours to be fitted for men. Among the Meiteis in Manipur, there is still no loud voice of MRM. However, interviewees of the focused interviews in the present study expressed the disadvantages and discriminating issues of men by citing good numbers of example. Some of the issues that have spawned their own group's mind are produced here.

In the patrilineal society of the Meiteis, the domestic violence by women is ignored and under-reported in part because men are reluctant to describe themselves as victims. Women are as aggressive as or more aggressive than men in relationships and that domestic violence is sex symmetrical. There are many reports of battered men in family conflicts, though the matter is not disclosed due to the fear-factor of male dignity. In one of the reported cases, a man had committed suicide in order to avoid being labelled as *nupina ngamba nupa* or *adha mora*, that is, the man under the supremacy of his wife or influenced extrovertly by his wife termed as 'half-death'. In addition, man does not speak much, whereas female shrews much taking this advantage. But the matter is not disclosed to the public. Moreover, he is insulted in the public for not able to tackle and manage family issues. Even though man is gendered to be tough and has the right to compel his wife for running the family, in its practical organization, woman continues to nag and drive her husband into total confusion.

Men's rights wishers are concerned with false accusation of rape and sexual assault and desire to protect men from the negative consequences of false accusations. Paul Elam, a psychologist and men's rights activist from Texas in the United States, founded two important websites for the MRM, 'Register her' and 'A Voice for Men' to rally against false rape accusations and divorce courts that favour mothers (http://rationalwiki.org/wiki/Paul_Elam, 6 February 2015). Women's claims are often heard and actions are taken up by mass to mob-punish the man involved. One such victim who participated in the study reported that he was charged of rape without concrete proof. He somehow managed to escape from the scene. Before truth came to light and he was found not guilty, his house was already burnt down and his family became homeless.

Among the Meiteis, there is no serious dowry-related problem, and so the voice of men's rights organization such as Save Indian Family Foundation (SIFF) against dowry harassment when women misuse legislation meant to protect them from dowry death and bride burning is not heard in Manipur. However, in situations such as *Nupi haidokpa,* which literally means relaying the news of elopement by the boy's father to the girl's family, even though the elopement is the consequence of mutual love, the boy suffers from guilt for putting his father in helpless condition for failure to meet the monetary demand made by the girl's family for 'stealing' her. He is left with no option to escape from the condition but to comply with every huge demand that is imposed to pay on the same day and afterwards.

Another view of men's right is the health issues faced by men and their shorter lifespans as compared to women as evidence of social discrimination and oppression. David Benatar (2012) suggests more money for the health research on males to reduce the disparity between men's and women's life expectancy. Higher suicide rate in man than women (Menzies, 2007), the funding of men's health issues as compared to women's including prostate cancer research receiving less funding than breast cancer research (Haywood and Ghaill, 2003; Zernike, 1998) and other instances are discriminating health problems of men. Farrel (1993) writes that women are actually perceived as the valuable gender (specially in evolutionary terms) who need to be protected and preserved at all cost, while men (a dime a dozen in evolutionary terms) are thought of as essentially disposable. Among the Meiteis, the rural men belonging to poor families usually die earlier than women, which demands research to find the cause.

Men's and father's right groups have stated that there are high levels of misattributed paternity or paternity fraud when men are parenting and supporting who are not biologically their own. Wives should not force husbands to support children fathered by another man. It does not mean remarriage or pater (social father). Among the Meiteis, if not deceived by the live partners, the tradition recognizes pater and there are four major agnatic pools known as *sairuk tinnaba* reckoning the descent line that may reflect exogamous marriage rules.

It means different descent lines of biological father and pater of a woman and the descendants of these progenitors are tabooed to intermarry, thereby reflecting as the ramification of incest relation. There are also six exogamous uterine kin pools known as *leinung pen tinnaba* under six ancestresses, even though there prevails patrilineal system of the Meiteis under seven patrilineal clans known as *yek*. But paternity fraud is a disgrace to male, and it is men's right to whine against this psychological injury.

Another interesting voice is that Christian men eventually blame the church for not being masculine enough. It means that church is geared to the needs of women. There is too much sharing of emotions, too much hugging and too much love songs to Jesus, with too many effeminate leaders giving ladies what they want; church is without testosterone and does not meet masculine needs of men. Masculine Christianity fights to champion the right and defeat the evil. It means revival: prophetic, expansionist and uncompromising. It is an interesting view of certain pro-masculine men, yet such a concept is not sprouted among the Meiteis.

Cross Occupations: A New Right against Prolonged Suppression

Traditionally there is a distinct sexual division of labour. Stern works are meant for masculine, whereas petty works are assigned to feminine and it can be expressed as *panjaona nupagi, akup atana nupigi.* For running a family, the husband is described as *hei hekpa,* who plucks fruits from big plants, whereas the wife is *hei khunbi,* who gathers the fruits dropped by her husband. So, he is the breadwinner, the income earner and she is the caregiver mother or wife. When men's roles are linked to earning potential, any threat to earning potential becomes a threat to gender identity. Male identity may intersect with ethnic identity, and so, it restricts men's occupational options. The Meitei men do not weave cloth, make pottery (specially at Andro village) and sell as vegetable/ornaments/cloths vendor.

In rural areas, simple life is restricted within the bound of masculine occupations. In urban areas when jobs are difficult to come by, men experience 'social impotence', due to the inability to fulfil socially important roles as breadwinners for the family. The stressful sense of responsibility towards their children and their psychological adaptability has taken on greater burdens. Self-worth and earning capacity even lead to late marriage of many men. In the focussed interview of educated males ranging from 40 to 62 years of age, the main cause of late marriage is found to be lack of good earning to maintain their family of procreation. A participant who is still unmarried said, *Nupi thakpa ngamkhiroida* meaning that 'I am not in a position to earn for the wife'. The traditional expectation that men will provide for the family and yet not depend on feminine work to earn money even when options are limited becomes a burden. Some individuals have adopted coping strategies despite rigid prescriptions of appropriate gender roles. Two case studies of such men are given here.

Priyo, an educated 56 years old man from Mongsangei village in Imphal West district, is a vegetable vendor at Pishumthong market. His family members include his wife, one son – who is working in a hotel – and three daughters. When he first started as a vegetable vendor among the female street sellers, there was strong objection from his family, especially his children. But he did not let them stop him as financial pressure was increasing, and his body was not fit for manual labour. He had tried running a grocery at Khwairamband market but the shop was evicted following a government policy. So, he started selling shoes at the Pishumthong market, which is located at about 3 kilometres from the former market but the business was not as successful as he anticipated. Finally, he became a green grocer at the same market where entry of male vendor is not prohibited as done at *ima keithel* (Khwairamband market). In this way, he struggled for 10 years to provide for his family. His wife who is primarily a housewife also does petty business to supplement the family income. Needless to say, he was subjected to criticisms and gossips at his choice of business, which caused him great embarrassment. But he had decided and stood firm to fight the social stigma against male green grocers. He feels that men should not be deprived the right to choose any occupational trait.

One of the most important male stereotypic roles is to be the financial provider. He would be the breadwinner, income earner of a family. The above case study clearly shows how a man has to struggle for family maintenance and how the struggle leads him to cross the line of control between socially recognized gender-bound occupations. It leads to gender strain resulting in gender role conflict (GRC) and may even reach a stage of creating family conflict undermining the man's self-esteem. Such a situation may compel the man to depend on substances but the masculine courage in him can stop him for falling into the sea of intoxicants or creating violence in the family. A Meitei man is always marginalized and abused if he makes an attempt to join a group of women. Statements such as *Nupi marakta phouyan yal'lanu* meaning 'do not mix among women as a paddy with rice' clearly reveal the boundary between the two sexes. Women also take the liberty to scold choosy customers with *nupanabu onthokna wa petkhare, nupi hek mal'ladana/nupi marai ama heli* meaning 'why so fussy like a woman?' In this way a man faces certain amount of discrimination often overlooked by the society.

Another life history of Khangembam Thambal Singh, aged 60 years, a resident of Heinoukhongnembi Konjeng Leikai Pukhrichou Mapal, Imphal (West) district and who is living with his wife, son's wife, one grandson and one granddaughter is produced here. All his three daughters were married. He studied till IV standard. His present occupation is *potloi* (bridal costume) making, though he was a *maibi* (priestess) in his earlier livelihood. He grew up as a male in his childhood, even though he possesses a soft voice. As a boy he assisted in masculine activities in agriculture. At the age of 16 while he was helping his father in a contract work at Maram Khullen, a hilly village in Senapati district, Manipur, he suffered from severe psychic disorder for about one month. During this period, he mentioned the name of a *maibi* (priestess) (as commanded by his inert supernatural being). His parents went to this *maibi* who was a man called Rajo maibi from Thangmeiband, Imphal. He diagnosed the cause of his illness as an effect of possessed by the spirits as he was destined to become a *maibi* who would act as the middleman in between man and supernatural. It is also believed that if the spiritual influenced is suppressed to avoid becoming a *maibi*, he will be diagnosed with severe psychological abnormality. So, the only remedy known to the Meiteis is to enter into the realm of *maibi*ship. Therefore, he was treated at the house of Rajo maibi, fed and cared for till he became his normal self. Like other *maibis*, he avoided the food prepared by/with the use of plants or fruits such as *heimang* (*Rhus hookerii*), reed and certain fishes as *ngakra* (*Clarias batrachus*), otherwise he would have suffered from irritating symptoms and problems such as diarrhoea or stomach pain. After full recovery, he mastered the knowledge of sacred procedure of *Lai haraoba* (merry-making festival of gods), divination, and prediction through oracles. After one and half years, he returned home where he gave lessons to 10 disciples of both sexes but retired at the age of about 40 because of some physical problems. However, he did not stop working or earning. He went into bridal decoration and make up. Potloi (bridal attire and costume of dances such as *jagoiras*) making which is done by embellishing with appliqué works is not a masculine work. But he was interested in it and mastered the skill under the guidance of a man called Kumar from Khurai village. Today he earns about five lakhs per annum as bridal dressmaker and beautician.

He opines that the sexual division of labour is good but it is not right to restrict the skill of a person based on gender. He feels that inborn talents should not be suppressed because of gender. That is why he ignored various insults from deriders particularly when he was a *maibi* and though people still talk about his present occupation, he wishes to continue it to establish gender equality in occupation.

As evident from Thambal's case, he joined a profession which is common to both sexes, even though it is tilted towards feminine pole. During this status, he faced various social abuses. As he withstand strongly, he gained the strength of taking up a women's occupation in his later part of life. He, thus, chose an occupation crossing the traditional gender barrier and expressed the desire of overcoming occupational discrimination upon male gender.

At present, whether men are employed or unemployed or underemployed, there are many working housewives. All the married male informants in the present study are found to extend help in domestic works assigned to women. Traditionally, men do not cook food at home (though traditional chef for public feast is male), fetch water, care or nurture child, mop floor, wash cloth, wash dishes or do any household chores. But all the informants from urban and semi-urban areas, whose wives are working women, help in all of these activities. A senior man also mentions that he wakes earlier than his wife, fetches water and cooks rice in the electric cooker. He does these things and afterwards bathes. When his wife has bathed, she cooks curry and arranges the meal. Another informant occasionally helps in cleaning dishes and others also do it when his wife asks for it, though it is not a daily routine work. When she finds unclean dishes, she even taunts her husband for being inconsiderate and not understanding her workload both at home and office. She wants him to share in running the family but not at the cost of his male image. An informant remarks, 'Even though *phanek* (lower garment of women) is untouchable to men in the Meitei society, how can I remain as a silent spectator when my wife's *phanek* is wet in the rain? In my nuclear family, shall I not fetch it directly or indirectly to a dry place as she and our children are not at home?' Thus, the present study finds gradual compromise in gender-bound duties at the cost of reduced traditional masculine role among the men whose wives are white-collar workers. Both sexes look towards gender equity.

Towards an Integrative Model

Though there are various explanations such as *strength theory* (Murdock and Provost, 1973) exhibiting greater strength of males in quick burst of energy, *compatibility theory* (Brown, 1970) arguing women's tasks as more compatible with child care, *economy of effort or entailment theory* (White, et. al., 1977) explaining the advantage of one sex to perform tasks that are located near each other and *expendability theory* (Ember and Ember, 1993) suggesting men rather than women doing dangerous work in a society as they are more expendable because the loss of men is less disadvantageous reproductively than the loss of women. To find out the universal and near-universal patterns of assignments to different genders, it seems not much healthy at situations wherein cross occupations are preferred. In addition, men's studies put up masculinity problems. In the male-oriented societies, why do movements such as MRM has been started? For this, certain psychological studies on the gender issues point out positive as well as negative impacts on masculinity which have been shaped by various components. It may result to coping strategies in order to fit in the changed socio-economic environments. The Integrative Model of Masculinity (Meek, 2011) brings out such impacts.

Figure 1

The Integrative Model of Masculinity after Meek (2011).

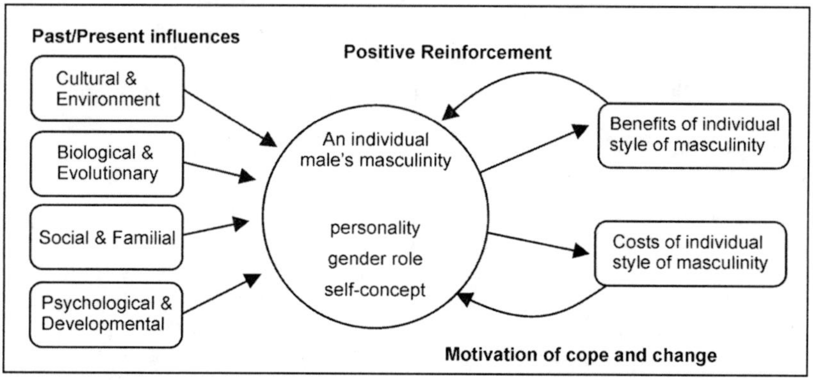

In this model, the centre is an individual man that has a certain style of masculinity composed of his personality, gender role and self-concept. On the left side are sets of influences that impact the person's masculinity. Each box (cultural and development, biological and evolutionary, social and familial, psychological and development) represents a different angle of research done on masculinity. The box on the bottom right represents the costs and negative impact of the individual's style of masculinity, which feeds back to him as motivation to cope and change. The box on the top right represents the benefits and positive impact of the individual's style of masculinity, which feeds back to him as positive reinforcement for specific behaviours or his style of masculinity.

The Integrative Model of Masculinity of Meek has the similarity of influences on the Meitei society in developing masculinity, men's modern right and certain gender anxiety towards changes in gender roles.

Conclusion

In the male-oriented society of the Meiteis, there are distinct gender identities as developed by factors such as socialization, psychological impact and social structure. For instance, among the Meiteis, social masculinity roles make no concessions for feelings and direct to distrust the inner voice. They become scared of their inner feelings and desires as these invite people's wrath or ridicule. For example, when a boy gets hurt and cry, someone may tell him that it is improper for a boy to cry. Men are not to cry loudly even over the shocking news of father's death, while women get the liberty of lamenting and weeping to her heart's content. Traditionally the male emotions were celebrated as masculine, though modern men have started to propagate male emotions as an unmanly quality just as those of computers. At a time women claimed that they are inferior sex and gender like the racism psychology of the black people. But, today men's modern rights movement finds certain discrimination and suppression on the male gender. To reduce such social inconveniences due to positive as well negative impacts of an individual as a gendered man when viewed on a comparative canvass, coping strategies towards cross occupation is a solution by redefining gender roles. But the best change preferred by both genders as revealed by the present study is tended towards gender equality just like pro-feminist rationale. Thus, both sexes will know the emotion of each other and rationalize the competent gender roles suitable in the dynamic direction of the society.

References

Benatar, David, *The Second Sexism: Discrimination Against Men and Boys* (UK: John Wiley and Sons, 2012).

Boyd, Stephen B., Longwood, Merie W. and Mark William Muesse, (eds), *Redeeming Men: Religion and Masculinities* (Louisville: Westminster John Knox Press, 1996).

Brown, Judith K., 'A Note on the Division of Labour by Sex', *American Anthropologists* Vol. 72, No. 5 (October 1970): 1073–1078.

Chin, Jean Lau, (ed.), *The Psychology of Prejudice and Discrimination: Bias based on Gender and Sexual Orientation*, Vol. 3 (Westport, CT: Praeger Publishers, 2004).

Connell, Raewyn W., *Masculinities* (Sydney: Allen & Unwin, 1995).

Ducat, Stephen J., *The Wimp Factor: Gender Gaps, Holy Wars and the Politics of Anxious Masculinity* (Boston: Beacon Press, 2004).

Ember, Carol R., and Melvin Ember, *Anthropology*, 7th ed., (New Delhi: Prentice-Hall Pvt. Ltd., 1993).

Farrel, Warren, *The Myth of Male Power* (New York: Simon & Schuster, 1993).

Gajrani, Shiv, *History, Religion and Culture of India*, Vol. 6 (Delhi: Isha Books, 2004).

Gregor, Thomas, *Anxious Pleasure: The Sexual Lives of Amazonian People* (Chicago, Ill.: University of Chicago Press, 1985).

Haywood, Chris, and Mairtin Mac an Ghaill, *Men and Masculinities: Theory, Research, and Social Practice* (UK: Open University Press, 2003).

Hicks, David, and Margaret A. Gwynne, *Cultural Anthropology* (New York: Harper Collins College Publishers, 1996).

Kimmel, Michael S., 'Profeminist Men', *Men and Masculinities: A Social, Cultural, and Historical Encyclopaedia*, (eds), Michael S. Kimmel and Amy Aronson (Santa Barbara, Calif.: ABC-CLIO, 2004): 634–635.

Maddison, Sara, 'Private Men, Public Anger: The Men's Rights Movement in Australia.' *Journal of Interdisciplinary Gender Studies*, Vol. 4, No. 2 (December 1999): 39–52.

Meek, Will, 'Integrative Model of Masculinity', 2011. http://www.psychologyofmen.org/integrative-model-of-masculinity (20 March 2015).

Menzies, Robert, 'Virtual Backlash: Representation of Men's "Rights" and Feminist "Wrongs" in Cyberspace', *Reaction and Resistance: Feminism, Law, and Social Change*, (ed.), Susan B. Boyd (Vancouver: University of British Columbia Press, 2007): 65–97.

Messner, Michael A., 'The Limits of the "Male Sex Role": An Analysis of the Men's Liberation and Men's Rights Movement's Discourse', *Gender & Society* Vol. 12, No. 3 (June 1998): 255–276.

Murdock, George P., and Caterina Provost, 'Factors in the Division of Labour by Sex: A Cross-Cultural Analysis', *Ethnology* Vol. 12, No. 2 (April 1973): 203–225.

Tiwari, Neha, and Rehana Ghadially, 'Changing Gender Identity of Emerging Adults', *Journal of Indian Academy of Applied Psychology* Vol. 35, No. 2 (July 2009): 313–321.

White, Douglas R., Michael L. Burton, and Lilyan A. Brudner, 'Entailment Theory and Method: A Cross-Cultural Analysis of the Sexual Division of Labour', *Behavior Science Research* Vol. 12, No. 1 (1977): 1–24.

Zernike, Kate, 'Feminism Has Created Progress, But Man, Oh, Man, Look What Else,' *Chicago Tribune,* 21 June 1998. http://www.articles.chicagotribune.com/keyword/mclean-hospital http://articles.chicago tribune.com/1998_06_21/features/9806210 422_1_men-and-... (27 February 2015).

10

Situating Women in Muslim Society

Study from Personal Experiences

Tahir Hussain Ansari

The study of women and Islam has attracted a lot of interest in academics. Concerns such as how one understands the situation of women in a more patriarchal religion like Islam have taken centre stage in many debates. But sadly the condition of Muslim women is more serious than women of other religions. Generally gender and community overdetermines the Muslim women's question. Whatever work is done on Muslim women, religion is seen as dominating every aspect. While studying Muslim women, undue emphasis is given to Muslim personal law. It also complicates the study of Muslim women as we do not have community-based data. The need to talk about Muslim women when one talks of marginalized communities rises from the fact that Muslim woman is a doubly marginalized community – being women and being Muslims.

Muslims in India have been generally alienated from the mainstream. The Sachar Committee Report brought the pathetic and meagre conditions of Muslims in India. The report says that Muslims are doing worse than SCs and STs. And the absence of any affirmative action to redress this issue has worsened the scenario. The survey mentioned above efforts to take a complete scenario of various aspects of a Muslim woman's life. Muslims are conspicuously absent from formal jobs. Muslim women are unlikely to finish minimum eight years of schooling. It seems financial constraint of Muslims works mainly against education of girls than boys. The case of early marriages of Muslim girls also leads to higher dropouts. But it is very sad to say that even after the committee report, the central government and the state governments in the respective states in India have failed to follow an effective measure to uplift the socio-economic condition of the Muslim community.

The socio-economic status of a family is closely linked with the level of education. Although gender disprivilege is practiced in the family even when there is a level of socio-economic upliftment, in case of economic constraint it is always the women who bear the brunt. Muslims, who also insist on maintaining some kind of segregation among the sexes, take out their girl child out of school in case of unavailability of sex segregated schools. While Muslims are working more in informal sector, Muslim women opt for home-based jobs, which will let them do housekeeping as well. Demands of the private domain restrict their mobility. Marriage, motherhood and housework are perceived as women's primary occupation pointing to the entrenched presence of a sexual division of labour.

In this chapter, I tried to discuss some social problems and issues related to the Muslim women in Northern India, which proved to be a great hurdle for their emancipation and empowerment. Some of the prominent issues are dowry (*Jahez*), girls' education, child marriage, violence against women, polygamy, *pardah* system and so on.

To understand the situation of Muslim women, we have to take into consideration the intersection of gender, class and community. The Muslim women are disempowered due to poverty, communal politics, patriarchy and personal law. There is also a tendency to find out a direct co-relation between Islam and Muslim women.

Here it is important to remind you that the condition of Muslim women varied according to their social, economic and cultural background. Generally caste system is denied in the Muslim society; but it is there, not in rigid form. Except marriages between the higher-class and lower-class Muslims, the other kinds of interaction between these two classes are normal but not very cordial. That is why here I am using class rather than caste. The conditions of higher-class Muslim women, that is, *Syeds, Sheikhs, Khans* and so on, are far better than the OBC Muslims. Majority of the Muslims belong to lower class or OBC, and their condition is the worst. Women in the higher-class societies are educationally empowered, and they are not facing most of the problems like the majority Muslim women except few social norms, that is, *pardah* system or some other dictation of the society. But the conditions of the lower-class Muslim women are very serious.

I was born in a middle-class Muslim family, and I am going to share some of the experiences, observations and the memories (which I got through different newspapers, i.e. *The Times of India*, *The Hindu*, *The Indian Express*, *Amar Ujala*, *Nai Duniya*, some books and other references for the last 20 to 25 years about the norms and traditions that are prescribed for women in Muslim society). Following are some of the remarks given by our elders about the Muslim women in the Muslim society:

> Women are all causes of *fitna/fasad* or disorder. If there is conflict or disorder in the society then it is due to woman or wealth or land property. Women are out of control if you educate them. One should not get marry to a short and fat woman or a tall thin one. You should never marry an older woman; she will bear a worse son. One should never marry to woman with hairy legs, black spot on her body, or her tongue should not have black mark. A woman should be soft spoken. She should not complain, not go out without permission, and not eat before her husband. Shc should not participate in any kind of public functions. *Burqa* or veil is compulsory for her. She has to confine herself within the household.

These are few norms of the society that I remember but still there are many such kinds of norms within the household that are followed in the Muslim society. For example, norms or traditions related to festivals or marriages are followed blindly by the people who do not have any relevance for the society and are pushing the women backward. The women who are illiterate do not support for their children's education. It becomes difficult to convince them or let them understand how education is very important for the progress and development of their children. If the parents agree for their children's education, they do not support for their daughter's education. This is still one of the major challenges for the Muslim society. I do not know how the Muslim society fails to understand the importance of education. Even Prophet Mohammad once said that for acquiring knowledge and education, one should travel to China, which was a very tough task during the sixth and seventh century. It is also said that if you educate a girl child in your family, it means you are educating the whole family.

Women from the well to do family get good education, and they get a chance to join college for higher education but learning English language is discouraged for them. It is considered that if she learns English she would be more open, which is immoral for the Muslim society.

I am not going to fall into any kind of controversies related to the rights of women in contest of Islam, but simply have discussed some of the important social issues that had been suppressing the women's rights in the Muslim society. Education is one of the important medium through which women can be empowered. But from the childhood, girl is not welcomed in our society. They are not considered equal to boys. They are discriminated in every aspect of their lives whether it is regarding their brought up or their choice of a dress or food – girls are never given freedom. Girls are not served food items such as egg, meat and dry fruits. It is assumed that if girls are given nutritious food, they would become sexually more active, which is bad for the society. If the girl is bold and behaves like a boy and mixes up with boys and falls in love, she is given a bad name and she becomes a role model for degrading moral prestige of the society while for boys it is vice versa.

When it is a matter of sending girls to the school, again there is a hue and cry in the society that whether it would be healthy for society or not, ultimately the decision are taken against the girls. As soon as she reaches the age of puberty, she is given in marriage without her consent because it is the responsibility of her parents, and they become very happy after sending their daughter to bridegroom's house. That house becomes her last resort till her death. During childhood, she is controlled by parents and after marriage by her husband and during her old age, she remains on the mercy of her children.

Here I would like to draw your attention that the condition of Muslim women is more pathetic than women of other religious communities. We cannot blame the government only, Muslim society is also responsible for not understanding the challenges of the twenty-first century, and they are not ready to cope up with the situation. They are very happy to confine in their own hole and happy with this. There are various other reasons for backwardness of Muslims, and specially Muslim women. Muslim society is still not open to accept the modern education, which is the demand of the time. We still find that the people are happy to send their children to the *Madrasas* for Arabic and Islamic study only. Muslim people are poor, and they cannot afford to send their children to English medium schools. Now our nation is providing free education for everyone. But Muslims cannot think about imparting education to their children as they expect their male children will support the family for their survival and livelihood. So in this situation, the children are compelled to leave the primary schools and join their parents to run the families. Due to poverty and gender bias, the poor parents cannot send their daughters to school. *Madrasas* are mostly imparting traditional education of Arabic, Persian, Urdu, *Quran* and Hadish. Therefore, the poor children who are getting education at *Madrasas* could not study Science, English and Mathematics, which are necessary to get a good job and secure their lives. We also find that these illiterate Muslim parents have more children. According to them, their children would run the family when they grow up. So they believe in quantity and not in quality. Hence, the number of Muslim children is more than the children in other communities in India. This may be true and I am not denying the facts. Generally, the poor and illiterate people from all communities have more children than literate and well to do families. Some orthodox Muslims may think that if they increase their population, then they would rule over India some day. But this kind of argument cannot be generalized, and this kind of notion is related to illiterate or fanatic people. We can take up the example of Sikh community in India who are hardly 2 per cent of the population of India but hold approximately 35 per cent of government jobs and mostly Class 1 jobs. The same is true for Jew community all over the world. Their population is less than Christians, Muslims, Buddhist, Zoroastrians and other religions but they are dominating over the world in the field of education, economy, science and technology. Israel as a small country in the world is dominating over the Middle East countries. Muslims as the second largest population of the world are doing worst in the world. Here I want to say that increasing population is not going to help any community for its progress and development. Quality matters and not quantity.

Islam gives equal rights to both men and women but in practice women are made to be subservient to men. It is also the interpretation of *Quran* which matters as we should limit the conservative interpretation of it. Controversial matter such as four marriages in Islam is pointed out as *sunnat-i-rasool*, which is justified by the Muslim patriarchal society. But they failed to point out the circumstances and the conditions in which Prophet Mohammad entered into four marriages. Even Islam favoured and preferred monogamy. Polygamy was permitted after the battle of *Uhud* to safeguard widows and orphans who were left alone because of the battle and to look after their property. Polygamy is not a problem if a man after marrying four women can live a happy life. But here it is also important to see that we have to control population of the nation. Islam says not to kill those children who have been already conceived. This does not include children who have not been even conceived. The most important part is to give a just and fair life to children by giving them proper education. Today it is a very costly affair to give a just and fair life to a single child, hence the reason to discourage having more than one child. Of course keeping in mind the overpopulation or population explosion in India and over the world, we should not increase the population. Overpopulation is a problem for family, society, state, nation and the world. We are having and generating very limited resources that are not going to cope with the overpopulation of the world. Therefore, we should check our population to solve the various problems of our society.

Muslims in their respective countries are following Islam but regional traditions and norms are mixed up with actual Islamic teachings and it becomes very difficult to discard it from the society. In India, some regional tradition has also entered the Muslim society. For example, in western UP among the higher-class Muslim societies the family of the boy approaches the family of the girl for marriage proposal, which is the Islamic practice. It means these kinds of marriage arrangements give more respect to the family of the girl. But in eastern UP and Bihar, it is vice versa.

Therefore in many ways, some of the evil traditions that have entered the Muslim societies have hardly any connection with Islam but they are creating hurdles for the progress of Muslim societies as a whole and women's progress in particular. It is wrongly perceived that all the bad things which are practiced by Muslims are the products of Islam. But it is not true. As once George Bernard Shaw told that Islam is the best religion but its followers are the worst. It is true that almost all religions of the world are the best but we the followers of the religions are either misusing it or not following it in proper way. Religion is used as tool in negative sense.

All the religion of the world teaches us the truth and enlightens us to differentiate between the right and wrong. But human beings have manipulated or misinterpreted it for their petty or narrow gain, for example, political, economic, social and religious gains. They forget to understand that these small materialistic gains or interests are spoiling the real ethic and moral value of the society, which is very precious for us and our society for broader vision. According to Late Dr A.P.J. Abdul Kalam, the 'Missile Man of India' and the former President of India, 'if there is peace in family, peace would be in society and if there is peace in society there would be peace in the state and if it is in the state then there would be peace in the country and if there is peace in the country there would be peace in the world'. We also have to understand that all the religions of the world were founded to establish the order and peace in the society and not to create hate and differences among the human beings.

Another social issue is *hijab* (veil) which means to maintain privacy. It was used by women to not to showcase their expensive clothes and jewellery in public. It was mainly worn to stop rich and neo-rich from showing their embellishments in a disparity-ridden society. *Hijab* or veil is used in *Quran* for Prophet's wives and not for all women. Now it is perceive that *burqa* or *hijab* is used to control women. The veil which being a part of attire has more to do with culture than religion. *Hijab* is an issue that is going out of contest. It hardly matters whether the women are putting veil or not but it is the mindset of the people that should be changed. Women should be given freedom of education. I am taking the example of Iran among the Muslim nations where we find that the women are more empowered in spite of practicing hijab or veil or other Islamic traditions. *Hijab* is seen as the marker of Islam and hence denigrated in many places. *Hijab* was seen as completely exploitative and assumed to be imposed. This led the Western countries to ban *hijab* in their respective countries. Turkey banned headscarf in school and France banning veils in public spaces are sad instances in the history of secularism. In Aligarh, I have seen Muslim women are well qualified and they are working in the offices and are practicing the so-called *hijab* or veil. *Burqa or hijab* became more controversial and understood in negative sense after Taliban's dictation and imposition of the traditional dress of *Pashtun* women on non-*Pashtuns* as well. And Americans portrayed their intervention in Afghanistan in the name of restoring democracy, which will be liberating for women. But ironically during post-Taliban regime, women did not throw off their veils. Veils for many are liberating in public spaces. *Burqa* and different forms of veil evolved over a period of time as markers of modesty and emerged not merely as an imposition. The perspective of the other also needs to be accommodated. And respecting differences does not make one a cultural relativist. Kuwaiti women elected to Parliament filed a case for their right to enter Parliament without using *hijab* and won.

To understand the condition of Muslim women, we have to see how the religion of Islam evolved. Within a larger context of patriarchy, religion is an end product of patriarchy and hence permeated by its values. The orthodox and the reactionary elements in Islam undermined the beautiful tradition of *Ijtihad* or creative interpretation in Islam. Scholars such as Asghar Ali Engineer lament the absence of interpretation of the Holy Book to fit into the present context. While core values and principles of a religion should not be changed, the laws based on these values have to undergo change over a period of time. There is a need to counter such innovations, which have been aimed to fit conveniently to a patriarchal society and instead bring forth the strong notions of equality, justice, value of education and compassion, which is the foundational values of Islam. In India, *fatwas* (the religious decrees) are issued by Deoband or other religious groups or individual *Ulemas, Qazi* or *Mufti* related to different matters for the Muslim societies time to time. These kinds of *fatwas* are setback for the Muslim women in particular and Muslim society in general. Recently (March 2015), in Malda, one *Qazi* issued the *fatwas* that the women cannot participate in any sports. Majority of the Muslims follow these religious heads very blindly because they are illiterate and they trust and believe them as the divine head or leaders of the Muslim societies. But these *fatwas* issued by narrow-minded and orthodox *Ulemas* pushing Muslims communities backward as whole and creating hurdle for their progress and development. I have come across a numbers of *fatwas* that created controversies and these are curse for Muslims. One such *fatwa* was issued by Qazi Bukhari, the Imam of Jama Masjid, New Delhi. When United States was attacking over Talibans in Afghanistan, large civilians were killed. During that period, Bukhari made the statement that the Indian Muslims should go to Afghanistan to fight (*Jihad*) against America. Shabana Azmi the film actress told Bukhari that first of all he (Bukhari) should go to Afghanistan to fight against America. Bukhari was angered and made the statement that she was a dancer/singer (*nachnewali-ganewali*), she did not know anything about Islam. (Here I am not justifying American attack over Afghanistan.) There are hundreds or thousands such kind of *fatwas* issued in India (different states) in different context at different times.

With the rise of communal politics, the Right Wing came to portray Muslim women as victims of polygamous males and extremely regressive legal code. Communal violence against Muslims during riots is not always perpetrated by men. Women have also worked alongside. Many Muslims who wanted reform in personal laws were overlooked. They were only criticized for not supporting uniform civil code. But in a situation where majority politics is in place, uniform civil code may fail to accommodate the concerns of minority communities completely. Government's non-intervention in personal law shows a lack of commitment to improve the conditions of women. The political parties in India also keep distance from the religious matter for their vote bank.

Another social evil of Muslim society in India is *Jahez* or dowry. *Quran* and *Hadish* do not mention about dowry system, which is an evil tradition that has entered the Muslim society from the Indian culture and tradition. If the bride is beautiful, then parents are lucky to give fewer dowries to the family of bridegroom. When the parents search bridegroom of high stature for their daughter, then they have to give dowry to the boy's family. If the bridegroom is an IAS officer, he demands around 40 to 50 lakh money in cash or valuable things equal to the same value. According to their respective posts and their positions in the society, the government servants demand the dowry. I have seen that even the boys who are unemployed demand not less than a bike from the family of the bride. This tradition is very much practiced in the north Indian Muslim society, especially in Bihar and eastern UP. The worst situation is that after the marriage some families of the bridegroom continue to demand dowry. It becomes more serious when in the name of *Jahez*, brides are beaten and tortured to death. Household violence is one of the factors of dowry. One of the very interesting examples that I came across was regarding a boy in my locality who decided to marry a girl without *Jahez*. The girl's family started doubting about the competency and the potentiality of the boy. There were rumours in the locality that the boy is not taking *Jahez* because he has physical defects or something is wrong with his family. The bride who brings dowry with her is welcomed in the family and is treated very cordially by the family members. There are instances where daughters of poor family could not get married, and sometimes the parents are compelled by the situations to sell off their daughters or push them to prostitution.

Marriages among cousins are prevalent among the Muslims, which check the violence against the women. When such marriages are arranged in Muslim society, the families of the boys and girls know each other and therefore the chance of violence against women is less. But if couples are well qualified, then there would be minimum violence. It is found that if the educational gap is high among the couple, then the chance of violence against women is more. In the present time, people move far away from home in search of job for better life for oneself and the family. This compelled the couple to remain in a nuclear family, and there is a chance of increases in the violence against the women in such cases.

In North India, I have noticed some of the problems and women-related issues in the lower middle class society. After reaching the age of puberty, the boys and girls are married at early ages, and boys after marriage leave their homes for livelihood. Most of them go to Gulf countries and Middle East countries where they are employed as third-grade employees. They return to their families after a gap of few years because of these few social evils have resulted. There are instances where women were found to have extramarital relations with their fathers-in-law or brothers-in-law or neighbours who are unmarried. If the only son of the family leaves for Gulf soon after his marriage, there are chances of more interaction between the father-in-law and daughter-in-law, which sometimes lead to physical intimacy and closeness. Because of the family honour, this situation remains hidden in the society even if other family members come to know. In this case also its the women who bear the brunt of the society. When, this kind of closeness and intimacy is seen by mother in law, and of course she could not bear her husband's intimacy and physical relation with her daughter-in-law. She is traumatized and she tolerates and she does not reveal it to anybody as she does not want to spoil the honour of the family which is a matter of concern for the middle class family. At the same time she is discarded by husband and daughter-in-law but she bears all the trauma and humiliation. Slowly her dignity and respect in the family is undermined and looked down upon and she could not come out of this trauma. Ultimately she loses her mental balance and is declared mad and her condition becomes more serious and pathetic. This is not a general phenomena but author has observed few cases.

Violence against women and girls is a problem of pandemic proportions. At least one out of every three women around the world has been beaten, coerced into sex or otherwise abused in her lifetime with the abuser usually someone known to her (Annan, 2006). One of the key issues addressed in the 1995 Fourth World Conference on Women in Beijing was the elimination of violence against women. Violence affects the lives of millions of women worldwide, irrespective of their socio-economic status. This has been found across all ethnic, cultural and religious barriers, impeding the rights of women to participate fully in the society.

In India the violence against Muslim women is also similar. Women are beaten and tortured in their household. There are various reasons for these kinds of violence against women, which are totally unjustified. Muslim women are victims of dowry practices, facing much harassment if not bride burning. Early marriage is also one of the important factors for unhealthy marriage and misunderstanding between couple, which led to violence, dispute and separation. The marriages in the poor and illiterate families face a lot of other problems as well. The bride who is underage could not develop understanding with the mother-in-law or father-in–law, and the arguments among the family members become a daily routine. The illiterate couple have more children, And if the father is unemployed, this further creates the problems for the family for their survival.

Muslim Women in Assam

Muslims comprise around 30 per cent population in Assam. But their overall condition is pitiable. Therefore, Muslim women in Assam are also lagging behind. In case of Assam, the victimization is at multiple levels. The hinterlands of Assam are mostly inhabited by Muslims. Muslims are left out from the mainstream; it is the Muslim women who bear the brunt. The absence of schools and poor communication takes a toll on the education of these women. Apart from this, identity-related conflicts leading to displacement also jeopardize the lives of Muslim women and children. The absence of Muslim women from the socio-political scenario of the state has been noticeable.

Although fundamentalist elements in Assam are dominating over the Muslim society and have imposed *fatwas* such as declaring women's income from government jobs as *haram* and demanding extreme seclusion of women. There is a ray of hope because day-by-day Muslims are challenging such regressive religious decrees (*fatwas*). It is a great challenge for the Muslim society to create an egalitarian society, and it cannot be fulfilled without empowering the women. Hence a struggle for an egalitarian society must be launched at two levels: within the boundary of religion and in the society outside where minorities have been at the receiving end of various injustices.

Conclusion

Muslim women have to struggle on two fronts: one against the state and another within the Muslim society against the orthodox elements to secure their emancipation and empowerment. Generally it is perceived that all social and religious evils that are prevailing in the Muslim society are the hurdles for the progress of the Muslim women and these are derived from *Quran* and *Hadish*. But some of the evils that are practiced in the Muslim society are wrongly interpreted or misunderstood. There are two kinds of interpretation, that is, conservative and liberal interpretation of *Quran* and *Hadish*. Conservative interpretation is dominating over the Muslim society over the world.

This is one of the major hurdles for the progress of the Muslim society as whole and Muslim women in particular.

Apart from the orthodoxy, many traditions and customs that have entered the Muslim society are not the products of Islam at all, but it is generally perceived and considered as Islamic orthodoxy. Education, according to *Hadish*, is obligatory for men and women, and there is clear indication that we have to acquire all kinds of knowledge about this universe and the creations of the God but education according to the demand of time is not taken seriously by the Muslim communities. This is generally believed by the Muslims that this world is illusion and the real world comes after the death, which is based on heaven and hell. So they have to focus only on real world to achieve it. If the illiterate Muslims are poor in this world, at least they are satisfied that they would secure heaven after death. It is also believed that wealth is all cause of evils and sin in the Muslim society. These are some of the challenges for the Muslim intellectuals and thinkers to change the medieval mindset of the Muslim community as a whole and to direct them on the path of progress and development. Although the pace of development and progress of the Muslim society is slow, but now they have understood the demand of the time.

References

Engineer, Asghar Ali, *Islam: Restructuring Theology* (New Delhi: Vitasta Publishing, 2012).

Engineer, Asghar Ali, 'Status of Muslim Women', *Economic and Political Weekly* Vol. 29, No. 6 (1994).

Forbes, Geraldine, *The New Cambridge History of India, Women in Modern India* (Cambridge: Cambridge University Press, 2007).

Hasan, Zoya and Ritu Menon, *Unequal Citizens: A Study of Muslim Women in India* (New Delhi: Oxford University Press, 2004).

Kofi Annan's Speech (*The Secretary General Report*) (New York: United Nations, 2006), 38.

Metcalf, Barbara D., *Islamic Contestations, Essays on Muslims in India and Pakistan* (New Delhi: Oxford University Press, 2004).

11

Does Sexuality Define Identity?

An Expository Study on Bar Dancers, Prostitutes and Eunuchs in the Works of Literature

Tripti Soni

Everybody talks about identity, our national identities, cultural identities, political identities, marginalized identities, gender identities and so on, but what makes our personal identity? Our self or may be our rejected or cancelled self, that in another term is called the Other. The identity of self is not independent. It is made by those social-cultural-political contexts in which we belong. We attribute certain traits, ideas, perceptions and the most important virtue morality to our self that are gained willingly or unwillingly from these contexts. Hence the image of self is deliberately created at conscious level in our mind. There are some more traits: that are silent, unspeakable or may be without language and stay in our unconscious mind. Those are in fact the part of our imaginations, thoughts, repression or fear developed by the chronology of experiences rather than any contexts that make our psyche. This is called the Other, which we generally pretend not to recognize. To fight for equality, freedom and rights is something acceptable in society (because it is concerned with the breakdown of the repression) and presumably related to our identity. But how does the struggle in deep psyche initiate a fight? And most importantly with whom? Isn't it a fight for seeking personal identity by knowing the notion of self and the Other? But why Other is so repressive? And if sexuality becomes a part of repression, then why it is 'a sin' to protest against sexual repression?

For instance, prostitution is treated as an illegal practice or profession in every country because of its explosive nature of sexuality in exchange of payment. Who creates prostitutes? Or whosoever has dreamt to become a prostitute? Of course not the sexuality of women and men, it is basically their poverty or marginalized identities. Some of them accidently fall into it, and some deliberately embrace it because they lack social power. Their personal identity becomes oppressive because of the people in power whose true nature is as Foucault says, 'General in nature and silent in expression, its true nature as an oppressive force is hidden'. For prostitutes their sexuality becomes their ultimate identity, but this is an unacceptable identity. This we can understand with an example, what happens to Maya? A character in the movie *Kama Sutra*, who is a maid. She was brilliant in her childhood, very quick to learn than her friend Tara who is a princess. Throughout her childhood she seeks freedom and her identity. She wears Tara's old clothes, which she doesn't like. She would like to wear new clothes (which she can't afford). She is embittered and humiliated by Tara many times but when Tara insults her on the day of her engagement with King Raj Singh, Maya sleeps with King Raj on their wedding night. This happens because Maya is always repressed. She has knowledge (of *Kama sutras*), she is full of sexuality (looks more attractive than Tara) but she lacks power. Foucault says that 'theory of desire' is always present in every relation, whether it is a sexual desire or a desire to gain power. The sublimation of her repression eventually forces her to sleep with the king, and later on she becomes his concubine (attains power). On another side, Tara is raped by her husband on their wedding night, doesn't attain sexual identity and frustrated for not developing any love and physical relationship with her own husband. Now Tara lacks power and ultimately her personal identity. Another example in relation with sexuality and power lies in the lives of bar dancers. Suketu Mehta's *Maximum City* is an enormous account of the lives of people in the slums, crime, politics and prostitution in Bombay. He raises a question when he finds people of every class in bars to shower money on bar dancers.

> Why are they doing this? What do these men get in return?
>
> And his friend Mustafa replies,

Five minutes attention. Even a garage mechanic can come here and get attention from these girls. This is one place where the classes meet, where the only thing important is the colour of your money. Because it's not just the mechanics and the taporis, it's also the rich traders and merchants of south Bombay, who are surrounded by men during the day and by their fat wives in the evening. This might be the only place in their lives where they can look directly at beautiful young girls, young enough to be their daughters. The moment the customer walks in, he's the star in his own custom-made Hindi movie song. No matter how old or ugly or fat he is, for the two hours he's in the bar, he's a movie star, he's Shah Rukh Khan. (p. 292)

Do we really think that the cost of five minutes attention is worthy of thousands of rupees? Those who have power can shower money, but due to the repression of their sexual desire the sublimation takes place by going to bars or prostitutes. What they need and they do only is to gain their sexual identity, which they consider above money. The people who lack money and subsequently power go there because they are treated equally to rich, an illusionary frame to feel power. But these people can have prostitutes not bar dancers because bar dancers are far richer than prostitutes.

Mehta's description of girls at bar and especially life of two bar dancers Monalisa and Honey is very thought-provoking. When he and famous film director Vidhu Vinod Chopra go to Sapphire, the famous Bar at Bombay, to get resources for their research on the life at bars they are astonished to see the beauty of Monalisa, who is only 20 years old. Vidhu says,

> If she were from Malabar Hill she'd be at the top of the film world. (p. 296)

Such is the role of money and power; they change us, affect our life and define our fortune and identity. Monalisa gives a very traumatic and tragic description of life in the bar to Mehta. She says,

> Most of the bar lines girls come from the villages; there are very few native Bombayites. They are brought into the bar line when they're thirteen or fourteen by their parents, an older sister, or an agent; by the time they're in their mid-twenties, they're too old for it ... three or four girls might share a room, an air-conditioned one. They all have mobile phones and some of them drive their own cars. Most of them are saving money to send to their parents in the village, to buy a house with their earnings. Behind every earner there are fifty eaters. (p. 297)

Monalisa was also brought in this profession at the age of 17 by her mother. Her mother was a waitress in a beer bar. She had an extra-marital affair, her husband left her, married again and then left her second wife too. He started to live with her again, when Monalisa started to earn and her mother didn't mind it.

Throughout her childhood she is raised in such an atmosphere where unacceptable sexuality is acceptable. She doesn't like her mother because she puts her in this profession. She even doesn't call her mother. She lives alone at her flat. Now she rarely visits her family, which lives in slums. Monalisa, like everybody, yearns for power and freedom, which money gives her. She also values for personal identity. She says,

> I am standing on my own feet; I am not leaving off anyone else. ... I earn enough. I earn with izzat. All the men give me izzat. Izzat is the most important concept in the bar line, more desirable than sex, more durable than love. (p. 300)

It seems odd that a girl whom most people would consider a prostitute says that she is earning with honour, but it doesn't. Because she feels that she earns with integrity, she never pretends to be in love with her customers if she doesn't love them, and most important she doesn't sleep with anyone with whom she is not in love. If any person falls in love with her and she doesn't, she never accepts money from him. She is true to her profession and that's why she earns with izzat. She is much better and honest than those who are in power, indulge in multiple sexual relationships, pretend that they are true to their spouse, hide their real identity which they believe is unacceptable in society and will ruin their social status and power. It is really odd to believe that we all live with 'theory of desire' and different sexual identity, those who do not accept publically call it 'a sin' or 'an illegal act' (whether they are involved or not, they denied its existence in their life.) and those who accept it, call it identity: a deep rooted identity. There is an understanding that a bachelor goes to bar dancers or prostitutes because he wants love and knowledge of sex and middle-aged man, to get attention or to gain lost excitement. Prostitutes become their girlfriends or treat them as their husbands. All of us find a way to sublimate our desires. Sigmund Freud also says that repression of sexual desire finds its sublimation into something grander or noble way. Sometimes sexual urges are promoted into religious or spiritual longings and sometimes into illegal acts (including prostitutions, extramarital affairs, crimes and drugs). Why does a prostitute do this? Because they know they can't marry or can't lead socially acceptable life. Their repressions also take place and sometimes they fall in love with their customers and provide them comfort, mentally as well as physically. Rich bar dancers even help their customers or lover with money. It gives them the feel of being in power and the sense of having personal identity.

In Foucault's term, the existence of unacceptable sexuality can't be denied by society. He rejects the legal code of power in which sexual desires and sexuality is judged by the 'law of transgression and punishment'. He rejects the legality of 'Negative relations', 'Cycle of prohibition' and 'logic of censorship' in which unacceptable sex in not permitted, its expression is prevented and its existence is denied.

The famous Northeast author Temsula Ao's short story collection *Laburnum for My Head* echoes the sense of identity in a very stirring manner. In one of her story 'Three Women', she talks about sexual identity. The three women are Lipoktula, her unmarried daughter Medemla and Medemla's adopted daughter Martha. She reveals a great secret about different sexual identity in the life of these three women. Medemla is in love with a man but they can't marry, and she decided never to get married. She is a nurse and found Martha at the hospital where her parents left her. She decides to rear her. Medemla is not only unmarried but also has never entertained any other man's overtures. She represses her sexual urges, and these repressed urges are transmitted into noble work, that is, serving the poor patients. Martha, who is originally an Ao-Naga, has a dark complexion and has always been victim of humiliation in her school and her friends tease her as she is not the real child of her mother. This knowledge hurts her identity; she feels that she belongs to no one and till now she has been living in an illusion of having an identity. Her mother and grandmother make her believe that the depth of their relations is beyond the boundaries of blood relations. She falls in love with a young boy who always likes her despite the truth of her real identity. She becomes pregnant before their marriage. The lost of her personal identity eventually leads her and forces her to discover her sexual identity. She feels that she belongs to that boy, they have been good classmates, she can trust him, he cares for her and he never cares about her origin. Some hidden forces drove them together into sexual acts. When Martha tells this to her mother, she is shocked and informed her mother Lipoktula:

> *I keep asking myself:* what is it that pulls a man and woman together and makes them so irresistible to one another? Why did I never feel that way with Imsu? And when I think back to the time after Imsutemjen's rejection of me, I realize that whatever sense of dejection and abandonment I had felt at that time, it was somehow not personal or intimate; but more like the disruption of an order of things that ought to happen in a woman's life. And after this debacle, I decided that I would

> have nothing to do with any man, ever. This has often led me to ask myself: am I abnormal or just a different kind of woman? (p. 77)

Temsula presents the deep psyche of her characters. She exposes the notion of Other, that is, unacceptable sexuality is acceptable by our psyche. While Medemla is deprived of such intense sexual urges, her daughter and even her mother have felt it intensely. Her daughter says,

> I looked at her pained expression and wondered: how could one describe the responses of a woman's body to the touch of a man she loved to such a person as my mother, who had never felt the demanding power of such love? And harder still, convince her that once you've tasted love like that, there was no stopping. (p. 77)

This cycle of prohibition and logic of censorship, though restrictive in nature yet, always drive us to do those actions that are negative and unacceptable. Opposite always attracts and curiosity never dies. Even when we rebuke a child for not doing certain things, immediately he is determined to do it with full eagerness.

Lipoktula's revelation of sexual identity remains a secret to both Martha and Medemla. Lipoktula and her husband used to work in the field. One day when her husband was not there, a man named Merensashi got an injury in the ankle in the adjoining field. She went there with hot water to give him hot fomentation for his injured foot. She noticed that he was sexually interested in her. He pulled her to the ground. Though she warned him off 'but he was like an enraged bull and his passion was brutal'. When he was done and she began to collect her clothes, something stirred him and again he took her second time. This incident had imprinted in her mind till old age. She remembers how it happens:

> Though I started to blame the man, there was a recurrent question in my mind: why had I not resisted more vigorously, screamed or even scratched his face when he was groping for my sex? I could not explain my own conduct. (p. 75)

Lipoktula can understand the inevitable force that draws a man and a woman towards one another. She never feels guilty for herself and with Martha because she knows how impulses become outrageous when a woman feels orgasm. Even being a married woman, she discovers her sexual identity with the man who according to legal code of power attempted rape on her – twice. We have seen this happening with D.H. Lawrence's *Lady Chatterley's Lover* who rejects her showy social identity and left her husband after discovering her sexual identity with another man. The law of nature supersedes the law of censorship. Lipoktula asks herself,

> Why I had not run out the moment? I understood what these intentions were that day. But each time, I only recall how contagious the crazed passion of the man was and how an inexplicable reaction to my body turned my feeble resistance to participatory submission. (p. 78)

Medemla is the child of Lipoktula and Merensashi. And Medemla's boyfriend Imsutemjen is the son of Merensashi with his wife. It is Lipoktula who stops an incestuous marriage. When she reveals the secret of her pregnancy to her mother she says,

> You know, it is always wise for a woman to keep a part of the self all to herself and sometimes she has to choose between telling the truth which destroys, and living with a lie which may remain a secret forever. (p. 75)

Lipoktula decides to keep this secret and her identity of self and shifts to Other (the rejected self). As in Freud's term projection and repression cannot be avoided, they come and display in our screen memory. The famous twentieth-century Australian feminist, theorist and journalist Germaine Greer also talks about sexual identity and sexual liberation. She believes that sexual liberation is the key to women's liberation. She tells this to *New York Times*,

> Women have somehow been separated from their libido, from there faculty of desire, from their sexuality. They have become suspicious about it. Like, beasts for example, who are castrated in farming in order to serve their master's ulterior motives – to be fattened or made docile – women have been cut off from their capacity for action. It's a process that sacrifices vigor for delicacy and succulence, and one that's got to be changed.

In her book *Sex and Destiny: The Politics of Human Fertility*, she talks about powerlessness of women. Since their childhood they are taught to be feminine and expected to behave in a particular way. In early time as well as in twentieth century, most of them are deprived from proper education so they lack knowledge. This results in powerlessness, isolation, a diminished sexuality and a lack of joy. She says,

> The ignorance and isolation of most women mean that they are incapable of making conversation: most of their communication with their spouses is a continuation of the power struggle. The result is that when wives come along to dinner parties they pervert civilized conversation about real issues into personal quarrels. The number of hostesses who wish they did not have to invite wives in legion.

Greer criticizes the Western attitude towards sexuality, fertility and family. She condemns upbringing of girls in nuclear family for the way parents feminized them since childhood. She protests against government intervention (like Foucault's legal code) in sexual behaviour and commercialization of sexuality and women's bodies. She even argues that the Western promotion of birth control in the Third World was in large part driven not by the concern for human welfare but by the traditional fear and envy of rich person (power) towards the fertility of poor. See, how power oppresses the repressed humanity (which as mentioned in the beginning 'general in nature and silent in expression'). There is a need to bring frankness and liberty in the way in which a woman sees her sexuality. Society teaches a woman to have shame on her normal conduct as well as on sexual conduct. It teaches woman to serve herself to her husband as his mother during day and please him as a prostitute at night. So the identity and power of woman lies in being a good prostitute for her husband? Why doesn't the husband play this role? Should a woman really need to have inspirations from prostitutes? Or should we need to reconsider our upbringing and family values so that difference between legal/illegal, power/knowledge and repression/liberation will be cleared to humanity. Sexual passivity comes in women because they are repressed to play a role of being good daughters, good wives and good mothers. Don't we take women's freedom for granted and of course their sexuality? Greer says in her most critically acclaimed book, *The Female Eunuch,*

> Loneliness is never more cruel than when it is felt in close propinquity with someone who has ceased to communicate. Many a housewife staring at the back of her husband's newspaper, or listening to his breathing in bed is lonelier than any spinster in a rented room. (p. 318)

Woman's secondary place in society and at home makes her feel lonely, repressed and powerless. Greer says further,

> Marriage cannot be a job as it has become. Status ought not to be measured for women in terms of attracting and snaring a man. The woman who realizes that she is bound by a million Lilliputian threads in an attitude of impotence and hatred masquerading as tranquility and love has no option but to run away, if she is not to be corrupted and extinguished utterly. Liberty is terrifying but it is also exhilarating. (p. 23)

Like Greer, famous Chinese-American author Anchee Min talks about loneliness, isolation, sexuality and sexual psychology. In her recent visit in India at 'Jaipur Literature Festival' (2015), she unravels secret of her life which she describes in her two memoirs, *Red Azalea* and *The Cooked Seed*. Anchee Min says,

> I was nine when Cultural Revolution began; I believed so wholeheartedly in Mao's communism that I happily denounced my own parents. I was brainwashed by their ideology. As a member of the Little Red Guards, I was asked to betray my favourite teacher (an anti-Maoist), an act that earned me reward. But I lived in guilt. Soon I became aware of horrified outcome of Mao's communism. All children of schools did labour work in the field as that was the system of giving education for the growth in production for the nation. At the age of seventeen I worked eighteen hours a day. Living in hunger and deprivation from any human communication or contact I became close to my commander Yan, and one day she kissed me. And the sensation was something which still thrilled me.

Anchee says that, although she has loved Yan, but their lesbian relationship only comes about because she craves for human contact. In the midst of that chaos, she had once seen her friend Little Green and her boyfriend in sexual act, and this erotic excitement had stayed in her mind. She became homosexual not because of her sexual orientation just because she has been lacking human contact, human affection, human touch and ultimately her identity. Her repressed sexual behaviour leads her into a relationship that has happened only in that particular horrified time in china. She says, 'We pretended to be each other's boyfriend to satisfy our craving for a boy'.

Her book *The Cooked Seed* describes vicissitudes of her life after moving to America at the age of 27. She learns English within three months because she has to take admission in School of the Art Institute of Chicago. There she faces insulted remarks and humiliation for being Chinese. She says,

> Americans asked me, 'Are u Chinese'? I said happily, 'yes, I m Chinese'. They said, 'Fuck you then'. Nobody talked to me. I wanted to dissect myself, do an autopsy on my flaws and my greed and my loneliness. I used to watch sex tape that I relied on my personal comfort. That was only human contact for me. I had to sleep at the rough part of the town with a Chinese immigrant who raped me.

The story of violent trauma of her life is heart-rending. Her memoirs are the real example of oppression of the people by the people in power and how the sense of loneliness and separateness dehumanize them, crushed their identity and the universe of self and 'Consciousness'. We are also aware from the fact that at the time of First and Second World Wars, soldiers were deprived of sexual pleasure, so they became bisexual and homosexual. Their sexual needs were deformed as they created different ways to satisfy their sexual needs. Greer in *The Female Eunuch* also depicts the sexual psychology of human being. She says,

> We still make love to organs and not people; that so far from realizing that people are never more idiosyncratic, never more totally there when they make love, we're never more in incommunicative, never more alone. (p. 55)

However, the structure of sexual behaviour and its deformation varies among people living in metropolis from the people who live in village. On some cases realistic analysis fails to find connection and biology finds its methods. The men in village maintain animal contact and girls had sex with eggplants and have relation with trees. Monalisa tells Mehta that girls in village are not innocent, though they can't afford education to make themselves learned; they discover sexual pleasure with trees. She says about herself,

> But I would watch music videos on TV, and they would affect my dreams. My feeling would be completed in sleep. I sleep with a pillow between my thighs; even if it touches me lightly, I'll discharge. (p. 323)

On other side men and women who are living in metros lead unhappy and less exciting life because of their mechanical routine. They wake early, have to reach office early, and come back home late, women chop vegetables for night meal in Metro train. Their children now have become out of course for them. And in the night they fall on the bed soundly, ultimately giving no chance for pleasurable little noise. They forget even the feel of tender touch from their spouse and that's why they started having extramarital affairs because they need and find the way to get intimacy with their colleagues, which later become sexual. Monalisa has a deep understanding of sexual unhappiness in the city (Bombay). She says,

> If all the areas of a person's life – work, family – are circumscribed, if the pattern has been established before they have been born, then when it comes to sex it will be similarly conditioned, its positions and its techniques preordained or hastily improvised in the darkness. A man or woman with a deadened brain could not possibly realize the peaks of pleasure of sexual life. (p. 323)

She says, even in the profession of prostitution, earlier men used to share their feelings, sometimes fell in love with prostitutes and then have sexual intimacy with feelings, now they come hastily just to satisfy their bodily needs. Monalisa is thinking to get out of this profession. She has saved enough money to open a boutique or parlour. According to her, the problem with this profession is that,

> It is all going western. It is becoming just like the discos, just like the colleges. Soon, the bar lines girls won't be wearing these full saris and dresses; it will be short-short. The customer knows what they want. In the early days, they used to come to the bar for fifteen days before asking for a girl's name; now they ask point-blank: 'Are u coming or not'? (p. 372)

Like Monalisa many women think that sex is an expression of feeling of love or intimacy with someone, and it is indeed. And the ultimate satisfaction is essential to discover sexual as well as personal identity. She wants to leave because she doesn't want to be treated like an animal, she doesn't want to bring frustration in her conduct and any deformation in her sexual behaviour. She wants love. She wants to get married if someone accepts her. Mehta says,

> Monalisa is caught between two worlds, the one she aspires to but can never be accepted in and the other, which she wishes to leave but which keeps pulling her back. She is in transit between these worlds, and it is a damned lonely journey. (p. 369)

But does this sense of love-sex-identity is same for everyone? Or the complete idea to attain sexual identity is untenable? Another bar dancer with Monalisa is Honey who feels love is the blade that cuts down the ladder towards your goal in life. Honey was featured in *Savvy Magazine* as well as in *Priya Tendulkar Show* as a highly paid bar dancer. But her secret is safe. And her secret is that she is actually he. At the age of thirteen he was brought in this profession by his neighbour. At the age of sixteen, he was the youngest of the dancers and earned 40,000 rupees per day. He also does it for living. Her mother was once caught for smuggling. She lost everything and was left with 50,000 rupees in debts. Initially his father doesn't like his son earning money by dancing in the bar wearing woman's clothes but when Honey brought home his first earning, he accepted gifts from him and shared a glass of Fanta saying, 'If my son earns, I have to drink with her'. (p. 348)

Honey is not overly feminine, but she lives two lives. She says, 'by day a man, by night a woman'. Her real name is Manoj. While speaking to her customers, she never, accidently, refers to herself in the masculine manner. How these two identities are kept apart? He tells Mehta,

> Because I've never fallen in love. Neither with a woman nor with a man. If love or even the hint of it had entered in my life, my whole life would have changed. I would have slipped into a man's tone ... I am not falling in love ... in this line we have lost our identity. (p. 360)

Honey lives with a double identity, which is fluid. She can't afford a love relationship. Initially she earned a lot by her dancing; she has bought flats for her family and a phone shop for her brother. She is in demand and everybody wants to possess her. So, for the sake to full her stomach, she has to give some liberty to her customers. She allows kissing and smooching. She can't, or won't, have sex with the customers because she cannot be identified, and this has started to affect her earning. Every time she has to say, 'today I am not in the mood' or 'I m feeling sick'. If any customer falls in love with her and calls her, she picks the phone, pretends to be Honey's sister and says, 'Honey can't come to the phone right now. She's gone to the shit house'. This image destroys a certain delicacy essential for romance, and the customer hangs up the phone.

Like her gender, Honey's sexual life is bifurcated. Manoj wants to impregnate his wife during day, while at night she has to let her customers smooch her. Honey wants breasts, smooth skin and an admirable ass. Manoj wants to grow biceps, a beard and a gut. This shifting sexual identity creates chaos in his psyche and makes him feel lonely and disillusioned. Among the customers who are aware that Honey is not a woman, some think she is a eunuch, while some others think she is a gay. But she is neither of these. Not a transvestite, or a homosexual, or a eunuch, or a cross dresser, but a man who dresses as a woman out of economic necessity. Manoj/Honey has to bear a double identity, which makes him feel tremendously lonely. Jeet Thayil's character Dimple in *Narcopolis* also suffers from the notion of fluid sexual identity. Dimple, as the name suggest, was not a girl at the time of birth. She was he. Due to economic necessity, her mother takes him to Hijra's brothel and the owner of the brothel a famous *daima*, Shantabai, castrates him at the age of nine and he becomes she. Dimple plight of her grief has been depicted in the following text,

> The daima told me to chant the goddess's name and she gave me a red sari. She made me drink whiskey. I hated the taste but I drank it. They gave me opium. The four of them held me down. They used a piece of split bamboo on my penis and testicles and held me down. The bamboo was so tight I felt nothing until afterwards, when they poured hot oil on my wound. That was when I felt the pain, and more, something strange, I was sure the pain would set me free. (p. 85)

What could be the peak of sexual repression, if somebody by birth is male, his sexual orientation will have led him towards woman but due to poverty and hunger he has to be shed? Here Dimple is far away from the notion to realize sexual identity because he is neither he nor she, he has become a eunuch. His self is not only repressed but also killed miserably. She becomes opium addict, a eunuch prostitute and an opium server at Rashid's khana. Dimple is close to being a woman because she (he) is never attracted by a woman. Due to hormonal changes she develops breasts and her arms become longer. When she consults the doctor for her longer arms,

> He didn't touch her at all, not even to shake hands, as if he knew her, knew where she lived and what she did for a living and exact amount of opium she took on a daily basis, and even if he made no normal judgment about her life, he had made a medical or personal judgment, which he had every right to. He didn't touch her but he washed his hands with soap at a sink near his desk ... he gave her a note and asked her to take it to the front desk. She paid more for fifteen minutes of the man's time than she earned in an entire night. She thought: All he did was look in a book. I wonder how much he would charge to touch me. (p. 82)

She breathes in the intoxication of opium and lives in the state of oblivion where she dreams. In her dreams she yearns for her identity, sometimes she dreams about what will be her future if she (he) has not been castrated and sometimes she dreams about her sexual identity. In dreams, she always sees a male whose organ is visible, having sex with a woman. And that dreams frighten her, and she becomes more and more addicted towards drugs. Her sexual repressions are transferred into drug addiction and her libido forces her to experience sexual act (though she also does it for living). She admits that she likes to have anal sex with men but has never felt orgasm. Dimple likes reading books to avoid her loneliness. She is self-educated. She knows about religion and has a deep understanding of sexual relationship. When Dom Ullis, a character and narrator of the novel, asks her whether it is better to be a man or a woman. She says,

> For conversation, better to be a woman, for everything else, for sex, better to be a man. Woman and man are words other people use, not me. I'm not sure what I am. Some days I'm neither, or I'm nothing. On other days I feel I'm both. (p. 18)

For sexual psychology she says,

> Women are more evolved biologically and emotionally, that's well known and it's obvious. But they confuse sex and the spirit; they don't

> separate. Men, as you know, always separate: they separate their human and dog natures. (p. 19)
>
> Men aren't interested in tenderness as much as orgasm. Isn't it true that the main goal of the sexual act, for a man, is the discharging of semen into a respectable, or even an unsuitable one if nothing is available? I don't mean to be cynical, but the truth is that the gap between men and women is unbridgeable and it extends to everything, from the taking of pleasure to the meaning of marriage. (p. 26)

The truth is shocking because it is uttered and experienced by a eunuch who has felt both sexual experiences. In the day she lives in intoxication and feels as if she is a saint who cuts himself off from the world and feels no sexual urges, and in the night being a female she tries to feel the tenderness of female orgasm which she can't afford to get. But in dreams, she gets everything, her lost male organ and the ultimate goal of performing sex from male perspective. She takes drugs so that she can sleep in the night and ultimately can experience her sexual identity because as soon as she wakes she will be nothing. Eunuchs are not supposed to involve in sexual practice, but they have sexual orientation, they yearn, they crave for sexual pleasure and activity as a physically disabled crave for taking movement from the defected part of the body. Even now science has proved it that the third gender, *hijra* (who are born without sexual organs) and eunuchs (who have been castrated) are asexual (who do not have sexual urges), moderately sexual (who are involved in sexual act but do not feel orgasm) and highly sexual (they are involved and get orgasm), though all these depend on their biological and hormonal changes inside the body. Vatsyayana, the proponent of *Kama Sutra*, the authoritative science of love making has described the sexual practices in eunuchs in details. If sexuality of two genders, male and female, is acceptable in the society and by the culture then why is the sexuality of third gender unacceptable? Their sexuality is as old as the sexuality of man and women. Earlier sexual relationship is meant to perform for reproduction but now it is for pleasure. Then, why today it seems is considered as a sin to know about sexuality of eunuchs. They are also human being like us. It is still considered that eunuchs' blessings directly reach the God and we ask them to take blessings for us. Since saints' blessings also reach the God, then eunuchs should be treated equal to saints. Can we do this? Why don't we treat them as physically disabled by showing our carefulness and providing separate reservation in education and jobs? If they are given opportunity for jobs then they won't behave indecently in public. They will know that it is shame as educated people have. They become outrageous not only because they can't feel sexual pleasure or can't get sexual identity but also because we have suppressed their personal identity. We never give them opportunity to develop the notion of self. They are Other for others and have remained Other for themselves. These deep-rooted cultural myths of right and wrong need to be changed. Even eunuchs of all over the world suffer the same existential crises.

Jia Yinghua, a Chinese historian and the author of *The Last Eunuch of China: The Life of Sun Yaoting*, speaks about the sex secrets in the court of the last emperor's Pu Yi's Forbidden City. China's last eunuch Sun Yaoting had witnessed the extravagant lifestyle of emperor Pu Yi. Sun was castrated in his youth by his father so that he could get access to the royal court of emperor. His family threw away his preserved genitals because at the time of Cultural Revolution (1966–1976) having anything from the old society could put life at risk. He died in 1996 and told his secrets to Jia, whom he trusted the most. Jia says,

> He only cried about two things; when telling me about the castration and about the loss of his 'treasure' (Chinese slang word for genitals). He never became rich, never became powerful, but he became rich in experience and secrets.

Sun Yaoting lived a very tragic life. In China, for centuries, eunuchs were the only person who had access to emperor other than family member. They were highly trusted person for emperor. If anybody wanted access to emperor, he had to talk firstly to eunuchs then to the king, and some eunuchs charged for this work and became rich. Men deliberately swapped their genitals to get the favour of the emperor but when Sun was castrated by his father, the emperor lost his kingdom and Japanese had started intervention in China. Eventually the last emperor was allowed to stay in the palace. All the eunuchs had fled with palace treasure but Sun's dream was to serve the emperor. He saw the torture and turbulent life in the reign of the last emperor, who killed all the traditional values of the kingdom. His wife was pregnant by other man and emperor himself was interested more in having sex with the eunuchs than his wife. He witnessed how emperor brutally killed the century-old tradition by involving eunuchs into sexual practices rather than to honour them for their service to their emperor. Sun Yaoting's story unveils the relation between power and powerlessness and the loss of sexual identity. Jason Godwin in *The Janissary Tree* also talks about the life of a eunuch Yashim, who was a detective at the time of Ottoman Empire (1453–1923) in 1836, who resolves the mystery of continuous barbaric murders in Istanbul. The elite Janissary corps consisted of the most efficient soldiers of Ottoman Empire, and it was attributed to Sultan Orhan's first brother Alaeddin (1326–1359) so that he could conquer more and more part of the world. It was raised under the highly restricted rules of Islam. Young boys between the ages 7 and 14 were brought into this, and their rank was divided according to their physical ability. They were not allowed to involve in sexual practices as Islam has decided a set of punishment for them. They were suppressed highly but they fought to get the favour of the emperor and to attain power. Eventually they were replaced by the new reform minded Sultan Mahmut, 2nd, who put eunuchs to serve the royal court. Yashim discovered how these soldiers were hidden in the different places in the city of Istanbul to take their revenge from the emperor and eunuchs who were given power in the court. The realization of powerlessness and sexual envy (impotent attains power where sexually active soldiers remain powerless) eventually forces them to commit murders in the city.

Thus, we see that power, knowledge and sexuality play a vital role to define personal identity. Unacceptable sexuality survives in every class of society but we never accept it because of social taboos. Powerlessness gives birth to diminished and deformed sexuality and sexual envy. Those who have power can hide negative relations because money gives them freedom and they can never be looked down. But for those who lack power it becomes a sin. Sexuality should not be the only parameter to judge personal identity and social status. Sexuality should not be the part of Other. It is our self and should not be evaluated in legal terms. The knowledge of sexual identity gives strength, freedom and power that make the path to attain personal identity. Whether it is personal or sexual identity, it is not denotative rather connotative. And we need to understand its symbolic meaning, larger contexts and must take initiatives to erode any moral stand. In my point of view there is only one sexual sin, Sexual Assault.

References

Ao, Temsula, *Laburnum for My Head Stories* (Gurgaon: Penguin Books, 2009).

Barry, Peter, *Beginning Theory* (Chennai: T.R. Publication, 1995).

Dale, William, 'Foucault's Sexuality', *The Atlas Society*. www.atlassociety.org/foucaults-sexuality (5 December 2015).

Gamm Nikki, 'The Complete Janissary', *Hurriyet Daily News*. Istanbul. http://www.hurriyetdailynews.com/the-complete janissary.aspx?pageID=238&nID=35841&NewsCatID=438 (3 December 2015).

Goodwin, Jason, *The Janissary Tree: A Novel* (New York: Farrar, 2006).

Graham, Emma, 'China Last Eunuch Spills Sex Secrets'. *Reuters*. Beijing. 16 March 2009. http://www.reuters.com/article/2009/03/16/us-china-eunuch-idUSTRE52E06H20090316 (5 December 2015).

Greer, Germaine, *The Female Eunuch* (Harper Collins e-Books. 2 February 2015).

Lindenbaum, Shirley, 'Getting the World in a Family Way'. *The New York Times*. 29 April 1984. https://www.nytimes.com/books/99/05/09/specials/greer-fertility.html (2 December 2015).

Mehta, Suketu, *Maximum City: Bombay Lost and Found* (Gurgaon: Penguin Books, 2004).

Min, Anchee, Interview with Anindita Ghosh. *Red Azalea*. Jaipur Literature Festival, Jaipur (25 January 2015).

Min, Anchee, Interview with Anuradha Sengupta, *Cultural Revolutions*. Jaipur Literature Festival, Jaipur (25 January 2015).

Min, Anchee, *Red Azalea* (New York: A & C Black, 1994).

Min, Anchee, *The Cooked Seed* (New York: A & C Black, 2013).

Min, Anchee. Interview with Ramita Navai. *In Exile*. Jaipur Literature Festival, Jaipur. (25 January 2015).

Nair, Mira, dir. *Kamasutra: A Tale of Love* (1996). (*Kama Sutra* by Vatsyayana).

Rev. of 'The Janissary Tree by Jason Goodwin: A Eunuch/Unique Novel'. *Captivating Cappadocia.Com*. http://www.captivatingcappadocia.com/the-janissary-tree-jason-goodwin-book-review/(2 December 2015).

Saxena, Piyush, 'Sexual Behaviour of a Eunuch'. http://drpiyushsaxena.com/life_of_a_eunuch/38.pdf (2 December 2015).

Thayil, Jeet, *Narcopolis* (London: Faber and Faber, 2012).

Yinghua, Jia, *The Last Eunuch of China: The Life of Sun Yaoting* (Beijing: China Intercontinental Press, 2008).

12

Role of Societal Norms in the Creation of Identity of a Female

A Study of Aruni Kashyap's The House with a Thousand Stories

Rini Banerjee

The *Rigveda* says that the entire world of noble people bows to the glory of the glorious woman so that she enlightens the world with knowledge and foresight. She is the leader of the society and provides knowledge to everyone. She is the symbol of prosperity and daughter of brilliance. She must be respected so that she destroys the tendencies of evil and hatred from the society (1.48.8). When we speak about the status of woman in the society, the vital concepts that govern the idea are the roles that she plays and her position within the social circle. It is the position that she occupies in a social group in relation to other positions held by the members of the same group. The attitude of the society towards women, the socio-religious taboos associated with women, women's own attitude and awareness towards their position in the society and the duties and responsibilities allotted to them in the society and family determine her status in the society.

In India strong patriarchal domination exists because of which the concept of equal rights and opportunities granted by the constitution to both men and women has lost its significance. As such women's life is shaped by such patriarchal traditions. In many places of our country, the birth of girls is seldom a joyous occasion and throughout their lifetime they will be expected to perform certain specific roles that the patriarchal tradition has fixed for them. Women who have been culturally trained to perform those roles even forget their autonomy and consider themselves subordinate to men.

However, the situation is somewhat different in Northeast India. Though gender inequality exists but women of northeast enjoy greater mobility and visibility compared to other parts of the country. Women of this region are known for their hard work. They are expert weavers, reapers and carriers of the rich culture. They act as equal partners to their male counterparts in every matter. Women of Assam possessed greater freedom due to the prevalence of the non-Aryan culture. Due to the assimilation of different tribal cultures since ancient times the attitudes towards women was somewhat liberal in comparison to the contemporary women of other parts of India.

Women in Assam enjoyed and still enjoy more freedom than their counterparts in other places of the country. Women of Assam from earlier times are very much active and versatile in their accomplishments. There are many instances in the history of Assam when a woman recorded her name in golden letters in the glorious pages of history and created her own identity. During the Ahom period, during the reign of Suklengmung a new post of Borpatra Gohain was created by the king on the advice of the queen Chan-Ching. Gaurinath Singha consulted his mother on the affairs of the state. Phuleswari, the chief consort of the Ahom king Siva Singha (1714–1744) was the first queen of Assam to govern the kingdom directly. The king was predicted by the astrologers that he was under the evil influence of the stars (*chatra-bhanga yoga*) as a result of which, he might lose his throne. At the advice of the chief priest, the king therefore handed over the reins of the government to his queen Phuleswari. The latter on assuming the charge of the kingdom took the name Pramatheswari, and the title *Bar-Raja* or 'Great king' and minted coins in the joint name of herself and her husband. Jaymati, daughter of Laithapana Bargohain and wife of the great Ahom king Gadadhar Singha (1681–1696), was another such politically conscious women. She knew it well that her husband was the only person who could put an end to the prevailing anarchical condition and restore peace and order in the kingdom. When the reigning king in order to make the throne safe for him was killing or maiming almost all the rival claimants, Gadapani (later known as Gadadhar Singha) at the insistence of his wife Jaymati was concealing himself in the Naga hills. Jaymati who was then pregnant was brought to the court and interrogated. But on her refusal to say anything about her husband's whereabouts, she was tortured to death. This noble sacrifice of Jaymati for her husband and her countrymen is still held in great esteem by the Assamese people.

Love of independence and freedom was not confined to the male-folk alone. It was equally strong among all classes of women. In the course of the Ahom–Mughal conflict, on one occasion, Assamese women pursued after the fleeing Mughal soldiers and beat them with bamboo rods.

It was with this background that women of Assam played their remarkable roles in the national struggle for freedom. Gandhiji had high-respect for Assamese women for their proficiency in the craft of spinning and weaving and their simplicity in dress and ornaments. Assamese women won admiration from all Congress leaders by making with their own hands all the khadi cloths required for making the canopy and covering the sides of the huge pandal erected on the occasion of the 41st session of the Indian National Congress held at Pandu near Gauhati in 1926. In the 1942 movement, more than a dozen of Assamese women – Kanaklata Barua, Bhogeswari Phukanani, Khahuli Nath, Rabati Lahon, Abali Kochuni, Golapi Chutiyani, Kon Chutiyani, Thuniki Das and others, laid down their lives at the altar of their motherland. Such proud heritage would always remain a source of inspiration to women of this part of the country to play their role in administration and politics and work for a better future. Such women succeeded in creating their individual identity with their bold decisions, steps and their sacrifice. Assam like other parts of the country has a patriarchal society, and patriarchal dominations have always played a vital role in shaping the role and identity of a woman. Hence these brave women of Assam too faced such patriarchal challenges in defining their roles but they could successfully play their part well by rejecting those challenges and became immortal.

Families in medieval Assam were mostly joint and patriarchal. Though the position of women was subordinate to men, she enjoyed great freedom in the society where the tribal outlook prevailed. They played an important role in all family affairs. Besides rearing up her children and doing her household duties, she helped cultivation in every stage except ploughing because of which she had and still has a distinct place in the economy of the family. They take an active part, mostly in eastern part of Assam, in the rearing of crops. They transplant the paddy seedlings and reap the harvest when they are ripe. All women, even the queen, were proficient in spinning and weaving. Assam does not have a separate weavers' class. Here all people weave irrespective of caste, creed or social position and almost every house contains a loom. Girls of all tribal communities choose their own husbands and even in case of arranged marriages the consent of the girl is always taken. The Bihu festival offered an occasion where grown up boys and girls mixed freely, some entering intermarriage bonds. Widow remarriage was prevalent but not among the Brahmans and the Kayasthas. Such was the social condition of Assam during the medieval period. Though Brahmans and Kayasthas were an integral part of the society, the influence of tribal traditions in Assamese society could never be ignored. Owing to such influences the women could enjoy so much freedom in the society compared to the women in other parts of India. As such they found an environment suitable for the development in every sphere of life that could help them in creating a distinct identity of their own. The very life of some of the brave women of this part is a perfect example.

Women were given an important status in the society during the Ahom rule in Assam. They were far advanced in all respect. Consequently, they were capable of sharing a space almost equal to men. While a valiant woman such as Mula Gabharu could enter the battlefield and destroy the enemy soldiers, an ordinary devdasi could rise to become the *Bar-Raja* of Ahom kingdom. These two women could create their individual identity in the society by dint of their own qualities. Though women were considered subordinate to men, yet the influence of tribal traditions of matriarchy could be felt, which could inspire these women to challenge the patriarchal norms such as women should be submissive, endowed with feminine attributes and be engaged in household activities. Mula Gabharu, a simple housewife, became a valiant warrior when she lost her husband in a battle between the Ahoms and the Mughals. According to Padmanath Gohain Barua's *Asamar Buranji,* Mula Gabharu's husband, Phrasengmung was killed in the fifth Muslim invasion of 1,527. The sixth Muslim invasion took place in 1,532 and Mula Gabharu fought with Turbak, the Muslim general in this battle. It is believed that during the gap between the two invasions, she took lessons in fighting. During a war or a battle, the womenfolk became the worst victims, they are the worst sufferers but at the same time women were rarely allowed entry in a battleground following the myth of masculinity and role of protector associated with men. But it has been found that the entire Ahom army was inspired by her valour that even after her death she continued to inspire the demoralized army. She is an unforgettable source of inspiration for the entire womenfolk as she moved beyond the gendered roles traditionally enforced upon women. She moved into a territory that is associated with masculinity and succeeded into creation of an identity of her own. The Ahom army was composed of men, and Mula Gabharu entered the battlefield with five other women. As mentioned earlier her valour had inspired them and hence it became clear that the societal norms were not rigid like any other patriarchal societies in the other parts of India that could allow an ordinary housewife to acquire military skills and skills of warfare.

Bar-Raja Phuleswari was originally a dancer at a Shiva temple who was later married to Shiva Singha. She had the reigns of the Ahom kingdom in her hands. The king Shiva Singha relegated himself to the position of a chief adviser to her. The royal umbrella of Ahom emblem of sovereignty and supremacy was jointly shared and coins were minted in the name of both. The point to be considered here is that though the king was alive, it was the queen who was the real ruler. Here we can see the interchange of gendered roles where the queen was more powerful and active than the generally accepted norm.

Even decades after the deeds of such women who established their own self-identity in which society and circumstances played a crucial role in shaping that identity, the women of Assam still continue to be in a better position than those in other parts of the country. In Aruni Kashyap's *The House with a Thousand Stories* we find women from different strata of the Assamese society. These women have different roles and modes of behaviour to follow at different places according to the society of that area. In rural areas, joint families are a moral practice. The Bishoya family of Mayong with its different branches is an influential and established family in Mayong around which the entire story of the novel revolves. In this novel, Kashyap has portrayed a rural Assamese society with its norms that shapes and moulds the roles that people particularly women need to observe. Oholya is the powerful matriarch of the Bishoya household. In spite of the existing patriarchal society in rural Assam, we find a spinster – the sole decision maker of the family. She rejects the feminine attributes of being submissive, calm and docile, which society expects from a woman. But at the same time she follows certain rigid rituals and tries to impose those rituals on every female in the household as she believes that a rural society is still less corrupted by modern outlook. There arises a conflict between her rejection of societal ideas of feminine qualities and the societal norms for a woman in a rural household. Consequently, she accuses Deepali, the mother of the narrator Pablo, of being shameless as she being a person from the city and a professor of a reputed college has lost her sense of the rituals and customs that have eroded along with the times. She says,

> modern women who don't care for the veil even before elderly man. Don't you know you shouldn't enter the bedroom during the day? It doesn't look good, and you should know that you must at least bathe if you have entered the bedroom in the day. You must not follow these rules in the city, but at least maintain some decorum in the village. (*The House with a Thousand Stories*, p. 39)

At this point she makes it clear that the society of the city and the society of the village present different norms for its people. While in the city (Guwahati) she can act as she wishes, in the village she has to follow certain rituals and customs that the society has fixed for them. If she rejects or fails to follow those, she brings disgrace to the household. However, Deepali finds such customs and rituals of the village pointless as she feels them no longer relevant. In Guwahati, Deepali's identity as fixed by the society is that of a professor of a reputed college and she enjoys a status almost equal to her husband, whereas in Mayong she is the younger sister-in-law of Oholya's younger cousin Prodip. Here her position lies much below her in-laws who are much older than her. Here her identity arises from the different relations that the society has fixed for her and has come to her by her marriage to Prodip Medhi. She is the daughter-in-law and the sister-in-law. However, her identity as the mother of Pablo and the wife of Prodip Medhi remains fixed at both the stages, though her almost equal status with her husband deteriorates as we find that it is quite objectionable to call her husband with his name.

It is quite interesting to note that nobody in the house dares to challenge or say a harsh word to Oholya, though she could rebuke and be harsh to others. She has almost adopted the character of a tyrant in the house, and everyone hardly dares to offend her. Though she rejects the feminine attributes in her character that the traditional society has laid down, she accepts the societal norms for females. She represents a contradictory idea that shapes her identity. Memory plays an important role in the novel. The narrative is not a straight laced one and often the narrator falls back upon his past to relate the present and the past. In a way we can say that past and present are intertwined together, and that the present validates its existence because of the past. So does the past have its credibility because of its inadvertent link with the present. In a way, it represents the true rhythm of life. Oholya, in order to avoid the memories of the past, adopts an attitude of a strict ritualistic and a sharp tongued woman. She adopts such an attitude not merely to avoid her past but also not to let people and family discuss her past and be remorseful, thus in a way respect and obey her. Perhaps she felt that the society of Mayong would never accept a woman who had stayed several nights at the place of the person with whom she was supposed to be married.

> the villagers were furious. They said they wouldn't come for her wedding and our family would be excommunicated. Everyone talked about it. In the early seventies things were different. The Panchayat is strong now, but was even stronger in those days. (*The House with a Thousand Stories*, p. 162)

> 'Of course the wedding didn't take place. Otherwise, why would she be hanging around here? Why would she turn into this acerbic person?' (*The House with a Thousand Stories*, p. 162). She assumed the character of a sharp tongued woman and followed strict rituals and customs and created an identity so that nobody dared to question her about the transgression of the societal norms. The conflict within herself of being a failure in love and at the same time the ominous result of transgression that she and her family faced created a fragile woman. But to assert her existence within the family, she successfully created an identity that is dominating and strict in nature. In a way, she followed some of the women of Assam as mentioned above who have their own individual identity, and Oholya too has that ability to control the entire household in a patriarchal society.

References

Barua, Hem, *The Red River and the Blue Hill* (Guwahati: LBS Publication, 1984).

Barua, S.L, *A Comprehensive History of Assam* (New Delhi: Munshiram Manoharlal Publishers, 1985).

Kashyap, Aruni, *The House with a Thousand Stories* (New Delhi: Penguin Books, 2013).

Pathak, Guptajit, *Assamese Women in Indian Independence Movement* (New Delhi: Mittal Publication, 2008).

Webber, Annette, *Feminist Peace and Conflict Theory*, http://www.uibk.ac.at (Accessed 12 March 2015).

Part IV

Other Marginal Identities and Politics

13

Conceptualizing Nature of Identity Movement

An Analysis of Telangana State

Bijayani Mishra

The demand for the creation of a separate state for Telangana is a struggle for over five decades, which claims to achieve a regional identity, integrity and inclusive growth. However, this should not isolate us from discussing and conceptualizing certain crucial facts that have been folded cold-bloodedly by both intellectuals and political pseudo-nationalists in the name of development and inclusion.

Andhra Pradesh: A Territorial Recognition for Linguistic Identity and Integrity

The State of Andhra which composed of ten districts of Circars and four Rayalaseema districts was divided from the Madras State in 1953 due to the strong agitation from Telugu-speaking community in erstwhile Madras State. In the due course, the demise of Potti Sriramulu who had sacrificed his life with fasting unto death for the creation of Telugu State, followed by unrest resulted have helped to pressurize the government to create a separate state for Telugu-speaking people. Further by 1956 the State of Andhra Pradesh (*Vishalandra*) was created by merging the State of Andhra and Hyderabad. The State Reorganization Commission which had studied the existing conditions in both the states opinionated that 'The creation of *Vishalandra* is an ideal to which numerous individuals, and public bodies, both in Andhra and Telangana, have been passionately attached over a long period of time, and unless there are strong reasons to the contrary, this sentiment is entitled to consideration'. As a matter of concern, the committee further stated that the merger would facilitate river water for the entire new state, the deficit in food supply in Telangana could be benefited from Andhra, which has surplus food grains, and Andhra gets benefit from the Singareni coal and so on. In addition, Telangana will also be able to save a great deal of expenditure on general administration, in case it is not established as a separate unit. So, the unification was projected as a win-win situation.

However, certain sections in Telangana apprehended for unification due to three main reasons: (a) unification may cause them to lose monopoly over water resources, (b) financially Hyderabad State was strong with a 5 crore annual revenue whereas the State of Andhra was having financial problems and (c) the most importantly, educational backwardness of Telangana region may result in monopoly of Andhra region in employment, which is educationally forward (Sri Krishna Committee Report, 2010: 105).

Notwithstanding with any arguments proclaimed, the committee was not supportive of immediate merger as it assumed that the Andhra State had been in existence for less than three years. So due to the immature administrative experience, the unification may lead to administrative failure. In order to avoid such trauma, the committee had recommended creating two separate states with a provision for unification after the general elections likely to be held in 1961, provided that the two-thirds of the legislatures in Hyderabad Assembly express their will for such unification. The intermediate period may 'incidentally provide an opportunity for allaying appreciations and achieving the consensus of opinion necessary for a real union between two States' (Sri Krishna Committee Report: 107).

Nehru on the other hand, believed that there would not be any difference between immediate merger or merger after the general election of 1956. In addition, the Gentlemen Agreement between political elite of both the regions had convinced the Delhi veterans to support the merger. The Gentlemen Agreement assured the creation of conducive environment for the development of Telangana region. Accordingly, the State of Andhra Pradesh was created in 1956, as the first state to be formed under linguistic identity. This move had not satisfied those dissatisfied over the educational backwardness issue. Today, the unified state for about 57 years could achieve a lot of development and global recognition for the state, but unfortunately it has also resulted in enormous unrest in the entire state due to regional imbalances.

The State of Development in Andhra Pradesh

All the three regions of Andhra Pradesh (Coastal Andhra, Rayalaseema and Telangana) have a lot of differences in its cultures, finances and social identity. However, the notion of linguistic identity keeps them together. While the Coastal Andhra due to the advanced agriculture and industries based on coast takes the lead in terms of financial development, Telangana with its intermediate advantage in both agriculture and industry stand next in the development, whereas the Rayalaseema stands at the end. Neither agriculture nor industry is prevalent in the Rayalaseema region, leaving most of the excluded to migrate in search of livelihoods. Historically, Telangana witnessed feudal oppression for a large part of time; as a result wealth is concentrated. In addition, the Nizam rulers of the Hyderabad State extorted agriculture surplus from marginal and small farming class. Landlords who were authorized to extort the surplus had employed cruel means. Such oppression and soreness had later resulted in class struggle, which had emerged in the form of armed struggle and recent struggle for Telangana identity (Haragopal, 2010). On the other hand, Andhra region under direct ruling of British has had access to modern education and Western culture, which offered a lot of space for learning and reflection.

Having understood the backwardness of Telangana region, as prescribed in Gentlemen Agreement, the Telangana Regional Council was established for planning related to socio-economic and cultural development of the region. However, the council had lost its visibility and by 1983 it was disbanded. In fact, the council lost its significance within a decade of its creation. The failure of the council was attributed to the lack of commitment from politicians to realize justified needs. This has led to the first major blow in the unification of the state in 1969 – Telangana movement (Srinivasulu, et al., 2011).

Green Revolution from the beginning of 1970s had largely helped the coastal landlords to get enormous surplus. This surplus was used for two reasons by these landlord communities including (a) to send their children to Western countries for higher studies. Upon completion of their higher studies, most of them have stayed back for jobs and started sending their earnings back to their parents and (b) the remaining surplus from agriculture was reinvested in real estate in the state capital city – Hyderabad. This had resulted in many Telanganaites, especially in the geographical purview of Greater Hyderabad, selling their lands to the coastal elite. On the other hand, due to the deprived agrarian growth among small and marginal farmers, technology usage during the Green Revolution, which resulted in decreased labour intensity, lack of proper educational attainment has resulted in increased migration of people from Andhra and Rayalaseema to Hyderabad. This has piped up reasons for Telanganaites to smell exploitation of their own resources.

Migration of different section of people to Telangana has resulted in more competition for jobs. However, industrial growth in Hyderabad could not adopt all those who are in need of employment. So, the whole spectrum of activities had resulted in creating tension among Telangana business and working class. The entire process had been articulated by the intellectuals from Telangana and students as exploitation of their resources by Andhraits. Further, the political class of Telangana had also come up with similar complains about Andhra politicians whom they had accused of not letting the Telangana region to get necessary resources for development. This political and intellectual duo had narrated that Telangana had not only being exploited financially but also politically. Their voices are unheard and the entire region had been bypassed from the development that is witnessed in the other regions. As claimed by the duo, the Telangana is the most backward region in the state and not only political tycoons from Andhra region but also each and every individual coming from non-Telangana background tagged as exploiters.

However, let us see the developmental trends in the state. Due to the abundant water supply from Krishna and Godavari rivers and thanks to Green Revolution, four districts in Andhra – Guntur, Krishna, East Godavari and West Godavari – are agriculturally well developed. In addition, the region has second largest coastline (972 kilometres) in India, which attracts a lot of sea-based industries. The fishing industry is also quite handy in the region. Out of the remaining five districts in Coastal Andhra, both Visakhapatnam and Nellore are semi-developed, whereas three districts – Srikakulam, Vizianagaram and Prakasam – are underdeveloped. The region quite frequently gets affected by floods and cyclones. The region has attracted three gigantic cyclones in 2013 alone. The Rayalaseema region which composed of four districts is the most underdeveloped in the entire state. Kurnool, one of the biggest cities in the region, was the capital for Andhra State from 1953–1956. However, the creation of Andhra Pradesh had moved the capital from Rayalaseema to Telangana. The region is neither agriculturally developed nor its industry. Though there is no external exploitation, the region is virtually more underdeveloped than the Telangana region. Except four districts in Coastal Andhra region, the remaining parts of the state are by and large equal when it comes to the question of underdevelopment and, hence, need special attention.

Intellectual Ignorance

Historically, the role of intellectuals in building and acknowledging societies is quite evident. Unfortunately, in propagation of false assumptions and failure of projecting a right way out from current crisis, the Telangana intellectuals have taken the lead. Telangana is blessed with intellectuals who have demonstrated and stood strong for the advocacy and strengthening the movement through false allegation and manipulation of truth. Taking the movement to a new horizon, these intellectuals have organized in the name of forums such as Telangana Intellectual Forum, Telangana Intellectual Joint Action Committee (JAC) and Telangana Human Rights Forum. Not only they have organized into the forms, they have also provoked other sections by their writings and speeches starting from colleges and universities to big mass stages. In addition, the occasional *dhoom dham* by various cultural teams and activists have also added up the spice. The political parties, especially Telangana Rashtra Samithi (TRS), have contributed their share since its inception and in the recent past quite heavily. All of them put together made sure to form JACs at different levels by different section of people such as the JACs of students at different university levels; JAC of Osmania University; Kakatiya University being the most strong; JACs of various journalist organizations; JACs at village level, mandal level and district level; JACs of various organizations including employees, writers, doctors, engineers, lawyers and other professional. What differs from the early stage of demand for statehood and that of the present is the increased participation of intellectuals who had pulled other sections into the gambling on a massive scale. 'Clearly, years of cultural and ideological work done by the Telangana Intellectual Forum has paid off in making Telangana a highly emotive issue' (Maringanti, 2010). Kodanda Ram, a professor of Political Science at Osmania University and the chairman of JAC at state level, and Prof. Jayasankar, who is named as an ideologue behind the movement, have played a crucial role in building the momentum. Other intellectuals such as Jadav, Haragopal, Srinivasulu and others have offered their part in building this false regionalism.

Scholars claim that the maturity in articulation of the problems is what differs now from the earlier stages of the movement (Kannabiran, et al., 2010). With the participation of intellectuals and politicians, they have taken a new horizon and new ways of agitation. Since beginning in

1950s, separatists never fought for development. They have acted within the boundary of achieving separate Telangana and moved all their arguments and took advantage from the circumstances within the boundary they drew. They never had any idea that development is something that is worth achieving with cooperation and united effects. Their argument or articulation never talks about alternative ways of development. Rather to put it this way, the struggle never aimed at development – it is always for the creation of separate state. Telanganaites were unhappy in 1950s when the two parts were merged, and they were unhappy in 1960s, 1970s, 1990s and in new millennium as well. The only solution that they keep on articulating is the demand for separate Telangana for any problem existing in the region.

It is also claimed by the intellectuals that rulers from Andhra have destroyed Telangana by exploiting local cultures and natural resources with their hegemony in the State Assembly (Kodandaram, 2007). However any rational explanation for such allegation remains unexplained except showing the current stage of development in Andhra region. The claims that their politicians have put forward need a clear logical expiation which by and large gets manifested by their political aspirations. Both Telangana and Andhra almost have equal share of political representatives in the State Assembly (119 and 123 respectively) and accordingly equal share in the Lok Sabha with 17 and 16 members respectively. However, the Telangana politicians and intellectuals blame leaders from Andhra for manipulating the state policies that were finally aimed at benefiting the coastal region and exploiting the Telangana. In addition, Chief Ministers from Andhra have ruled the state for a period of more than 16 years, whereas it is 12 years and 27 years from Telangana and Rayalaseema respectively. For most of the time, it has been leaders from Rayalaseema who ruled the state. The 16 years of rule of Andhra includes most charismatic Chief Minister of AP: N.T. Rama Rao (NTR) who had introduced a plenty of welfare schemes including a kilo rice for ₹ 2, ban on liquor and others. In fact NTR enjoyed full support from all Telangana districts.

Unfortunately, notable scholars such as Kodandaram, Haragopal and Jadhav (2010) have always narrated about Telangana debate from their emotions and sentiments as they come from the same territory. Neutrality is being missed in the entire scholarship. They have altogether failed to see the destruction that is being caused is set from the class forces. Class forces do not see any other means unless they achieve what they are aiming for. In the process, it doesn't matter whether the exploited is from Coastal Andhra or Telangana. There are plenty of incidents where the political, business and bureaucratic elites exploited the resources and deprived Coastal Andhra, and the same can be found in Telangana by the elites coming from Telangana regions. The intellectuals have clearly shown their hypocrisy by failing to understand or articulate in reality what they teach in classes. Most of the intellectuals in this occasion teach Marxism and claim to follow Marxist philosophy that strongly backup the class struggle phenomenon, however, they all see current trend being the result of cultural hegemony not of class. Accordingly, they have failed to see the atrocities or the class exploitation led by their own men.

Andhra region lacks intellectual community, who are reputed at national level. The grim resources available in the local universities have failed to produce intellectuals, whereas Hyderabad, on the other hand, being the capital city is flowed with various centrally funded universities and research institutions, which have produced enormous intellectuals. Though various intellectuals from Andhra who stay in Hyderabad acquire such intellectualism, most of them fear to express their wishes due to the hooliganism that often appear as a threat from the fellow Telanganaites. The *Samakhandhra* rallies and *maha sabha's* organized in Hyderabad by supporters of unified Andhra Pradesh frequently receive threats or mob attacks. The advocates of Telangana have projected Telangana as panacea to all the problems the region face. Accordingly, name any problem – employment, education, poverty, underdevelopment and ignorance – people from Andhra region have been named as culprits. However, when research by third party such as Sri Krishna Committee (2010) has never projected that the 'hegemony' among different regions has caused damage as proclaimed by the so-called intellectuals from Telangana region. Sri Krishna Committee also proclaimed that many districts in Telangana are comparatively more developed and better irrigated than those in Rayalaseema and the north of Coastal Andhra.

The ideologues and politicians on the one hand projected false reflections of current trends, and on the other hand they have also offered false promises to project bright future for the newly established state in order to motivate more people to join the movement for a separate state – a dalit or someone from lower caste to become the head of the government and to deepen ties between political leaders and common man leading to more transparency and accountable democratic government. Due to the rapid industrilization there was assumption that people from all the sections would get equal share. This would further create more employment opportunities for youths who have already failed in open competitive market. However, TRS which sets to seal most of the seats in the region or Congress which may ultimately get benefit has no intention to realize the promises manifested above. Many dalit bahujans in the state believe that TRS is a party of Velamas, a predominant caste in Telangana after Reddy and Kammas (Lorraine, 2013). It is believed that this caste will replace the domination of Kamma in newly formed Telangana State. So, domination of certain advanced sections is inevitable. Where domination prevails inclusion doesn't become a reality. In addition TRS is well known for its nepotism where his family alone bags three MLAs.

Politics of Telangana

So far the political leaders who acted for the creation of Telangana movement seem to patronize their political interests. For example, in the general election of 1971, Chenna Reddy won a majority of seats in Telangana with a slogan for separate Telangana under Telangana Prajan Samiti (TPS) party. However, after his election victory, he merged his party with Congress, which helped him to build his political career. As a result, later he got a chance to become Chief Minister twice and Governor of Utter Pradesh, Punjab, Rajasthan and Tamil Nadu. This entire episode postponed the Telangana agitation for 30 years to rise again later in 2001 after the formation of Telangana Rashtra Samithi (TRS) by K. Chandrasekhar Rao (KCR). As everyone in the state is well aware, the party was formed over issues related to ministerial portfolios in the then existing TDP government. KCR, a veteran politician with four time winning history from Siddipet assembly constituency in Mahabubnagar district, had worked with Telugu Desam Party (TDP) for about 18 years. He was part of TDP government during the entire period when the resources in Telangana had claimed to be exploited. Rao had earlier enjoyed a cabinet and Deputy Speaker positions in the TDP government. However, after failing to get a desired cabinet berth - Ministry for Labour - during the last TDP government, Rao had come out of the party and formed TRS with a clear aim of achieving separate Telangana. Surprisingly, Rao who had initially failed to fight against such exploitation that the Telangana region witnessed took advantage of the movement, when he was not offered a cabinet berth as he expected. Such fact however is always kept in dark by Telangana intellectuals who argue that 'The Telangana Rashtra Samithi (TRS) party emergence from (this) deep-rooted discontentment and deprivation' (Haragopal, 2010: 57). And many in Andhra region credit this development for the failure of Naidu who had not accomplished the demand of Rao for an impressive cabinet berth.

TRS as a political party was somehow effective in the initial days of its inception. Such effectiveness was being caused by (i) KCR's anger over the then existing TDP government, which denied him a ministry position of his choice and (ii) rebirth of the movement in which many activists and intellectuals were eager to take part. After Naxal attack on the Chief Minister Naidu, he had proposed a prematured poll in order to grab the sympathy vote, which had resulted in a drastic fall out for Babu. During the election of 2004, TRS has had an alliance with Congress Party, and both of them agreed to get benefit from each other where Congress gets benefit using the Telangana label and TRS gets benefit from the larger political identify and support from a larger political party, which can by and large offer a separate Telangana state. Y.S. Rajasekhara Reddy (YSR) up on whom the Congress Party had relied in the state had stood out and took the party to a thumping victory in the election. Benefiting from such alliance, TRS had supported the UPA government at the centre and Y.S. Rajasekhara Reddy government at state.

With a clear majority in the State Assembly, the YSR-led Congress reintroduced a series of welfare schemes that have benefited a large section of masses. Meanwhile, KCR and his other party leader Narendra got cabinet positions at the centre for their loyalty towards Congress. In addition to the welfare schemes at the centre, state government had introduced a number of welfare schemes aiming at poor and agrarian masses such as Rajiv Aarogya Shree, Fees Reimburse Scheme, free electricity for farmers, a kilo rice for two rupees and other schemes. These schemes could crack the notion of underdevelopment by benefiting masses and other excluded groups in the state including in Telangana. With the mileage from welfare schemes, YSR is considered as one of the best ruler ever in the state who could break the dilemma between underdevelopment and hegemony. In addition, being a dominant ruler from Rayalaseema faction background, YSR could keep all sections happy across the state. Due to his charisma and dominance, region has never become an issue of discussion during his rule. His priorities have sidelined the need for separate Telangana in order to attain inclusion of various deprived sections. In addition, the centre which had promised Telangana has largely maintained silence. In spite of TRS's participation in the government, no major affords were initiated by the government towards the formation of separate Telangana. Critics including the intellectuals, activists and loyalists have built pressure on TRS to withdraw from Congress as a matter of repression. Accordingly, TRS withdrew from both the state and central government and stood nowhere in the political territory. The welfare schemes have been undoing the proclaimed Telangana sentiment. YSR being the strong symbol of Congress in the state has gone in the general election in 2009 with a single point formula of welfare and development. This time Congress had contested alone without any alliance. On the other hand, TRS had patterned with TDP and the communist parties to form *Mahakutami.* However, the election mandate was so clear that the Congress led by YSR had succeeded as single largest party with a clear majority in the State Assembly, and the State of Andhra Pradesh stood as a single largest state to send a maximum number of MPs from a state to form Congress-led UPA government II at the centre. In the State Assembly, TRS was restricted to less than 20 seats. TDP emerged as opposition party. This electoral consensus demonstrate how people across the regions including Telangana view and support the development and welfare against regionalism. With the same spirit, YSR expected to carry forward the same momentum with more welfare schemes. However, his sudden demise in 2009 led to the current crisis. The opportunistic KCR, who until then maintained silence, restarted the movement for separate statehood, which induces a few days of fasting that resulted in the decision of Congress High Command to initiate the process for the creation of Telangana State on 9 December.

Though the centre's move was not an expected output for the bifurcation, the game resulted in agitation in other parts of the state in Rayalaseema and Andhra regions. In addition, political leaders from both the regions including several central ministers have shown their opposition for bifurcation. With such sudden outrage from public and the party men from the state, Congress at centre had to rethink about its decision and accordingly stepped back. However, YSR Congress Party led by Y.S. Jaganmohan Reddy was rising in the state especially in Rayalaseema and Andhra regions, and election surveys predicted Jaganmohan Reddy to win a large proportion of seats both in the state and at the centre in the next election. TRS will bag majority of seats in Telangana literally leaving Congress on crossroads in the state. There is no way that Congress is going to fetch seats in Seemandhra. However, with the Telangana card, Congress can win a significant portion of seats in the region. Accordingly, in order to manage next election and get a proportion of seats from the Telangana region, Congress again brought back the game plan of Telangana with a strategy. This strategy includes merger of TRS with Congress after the creation of Telangana State or TRS offering unconditional support to

UPA III government, which will be headed by Rahul Gandhi. Based on the agreement, the Congress Working Committee (CWC) has cleared the Telangana bill on 31 July 2013.

The 30 July clearance of Telangana Bill by CWC has enormously resulted in a strong *Samikhandhra* movement, which resulted in literally halting of both the regions – Andhra and Rayalaseema. Everyday hundreds of thousands of people have participated in the agitation on a voluntary basis from each district. Various forms of agitation were led by different sections of population in headquarter of each district, in addition to the village-level and mandal-level agitations. It was found that the popular media or intellectuals have obscured the agitations carried out in Andhra and Rayalaseema regions. The agitations carried out in Hyderabad as part of the Telangana movement were aggressively covered by media due to the sensitivity in the capital city, whereas the agitations part of the *Samikhandhra* movement have not been adequately covered in national media as the movement largely worked in the peripheral areas other than the state capital where the presence of national media doesn't exist.

As part of Telangana movement, the protests were financed by both politicians and traders for their political and economic gains respectively in order to paralyse monopoly on the resources (Maringanti, 2010). Whereas the movement carried out by *Samikhandhra* loyalists for about 60 days was more a democratic movement where employees from both public and private boycotted their offices and stayed on roads. A new edition of agitation has started when the movement was inculcated in various universities in these two regions including Andhra University, Visakhapatnam' Nagarjuna University, Guntur, Sri Venkateswara University, Tirupathi; and Sri Krishnadevaraya University, Anantapur. Properties of the political leaders who won from Andhra and support Telangana State have been attacked. Accusing the Pradesh Congress Committee Chief Botsa Satyanarayana Rao who represents Vizianagaram district, one of the backward districts of Coastal Andhra, as the main culprit who believed to have assured Congress High Command for supporting the creation of separate Telangana State. A severe attack was executed on his property, which resulted in the imposition of curfew in the area. The entire movement against the proposal for the creation of a separate state could produce vibrations within the state political mechanisms; however, the central government which contemplates its political mileage superior to the majority wish has ignored the movement.

It is fair to calculate that the lives of these people are at stake. There is no doubt about that. But who should be blamed for this depravedness is a larger question that needs answer. Should we blame a well set four districts in Coastal Andhra that have had a clear planning and natural resources including the canal water that they have received from the government policies or should we blame the leaders and other pressure groups from the Andhra for making all possible resources available for their prosperity or should we blame the other side for lacking such pressure groups to manage the resources. Ironically, their pressure groups only aimed at separate state not for development while together. Whoever is culprit of this tragedy, it is the common man at stake.

Way Forward

There is a demand for the creation of a separate Hyderabad State as Muslim population in the city feared the growing popularity of BJP in Telangana and the advantages that the party may get from the bifurcation. There is no end for such demands. Soon we will see separate Rayalaseema movement getting strengthened with a notion that people from Coastal Andhra may betray the interests of Rayalaseema region. Congress or BJP will have its quick calculations for mileage and move a bill in the Parliament for supporting such movement as well.

For its political mileage on one hand, the government at the centre is moving actively to pass the bill in the Parliament, whereas demands such as creation of a separate state for Vidharba, which was unanimously approved by Maharashtra State Assembly and First SRC, or many such demands are not considered. As per the conservative estimation, there are a total of twenty demands for the creation of new states. Though the creation of a separate state of Telangana may fulfil the desires of political leaders, but on a larger outlook the question of exploitation remains unanswered. When the systems adopt oppression as a game in which no exceptions exist, the creation of Telangana with such game plan is a mere moving away, not eliminating the game of oppression, as the internal hierarchies any system processes would never allow any inclusion of those claims to be excluded or exploited.

The long projected hegemony by intellectuals and political duo and struggle to end that leaves several unanswered questions, whereas central governments election *hungama* to create Telangana should be wisely questioned by all politicians and citizens. Congress Party in 1950s with a socialistic vision seems to uphold the spirit of democracy.

The merger of the two regions was under complete scrutiny of Telangana Assembly, and as the majority opinionated the State of Andhra Pradesh was created (Srikanth, 2013). But the then adamant Congress-led UPA Government at the centre was interested to entertain neither the democratic interests from the State Assembly nor popular majority from the affected people. The final decision to bifurcate the state is more the result of a cold political calculation that led the party to choose the best alternative in terms of votes (Lorraine, 2013).

On the other hand, the expert committee formed on this matter headed by Justice S.N. Sri Krishna has opinionated that 'Consultation on the Situation in Andhra Pradesh' has resulted in diverse views from different sections and regions. After thorough discussion and deliberation with various stakeholders, the committee has expressed that there are six way to get out of the present crisis. However, out of the six the committee has viewed that keeping 'the State united by simultaneously providing certain definite constitutional/statutory measures for socio-economic development and political empowerment of the Telangana region – creation of a statutorily empowered Telangana Regional Council' was worth consideration (Sri Krishna Committee Report, 2010: 454). Political parties such as the CPI (M) have consistently rejected the formation of a new state, arguing that the neglect of the region can be rectified by focusing on prioritized development of the backward areas in Andhra Pradesh, whereas YSR Congress Party headed by Jaganmohan Reddy argues that the present state of proposed division is embedded in political interest. As a result, growth in both regions will be descended.

It is a clear vindication by the Congress government for the creation of separate state after its compromising political deal with KCR who had agreed to merge his TRS party with Congress before the next election, immediately after passing the bill in the Parliament. This merger would bring light for the Rahul-led Congress with a few seats from Telangana region in the next election. The noble intention of Constitution of India and Article 3 that supports changes of boundaries and the creation of a new state is once again misused for personal and political mileage.

As it stands today, the Andhra Pradesh is the only state that is divided based for the political mileage. Every political party has its own aspiration through the separation or safeguard the status-quo. The struggle once started as a peasant and mass movement is now transformed as a political or rather a gamble to attain larger figures in the ensuing general elections.

References

Haragopal, G., 'The Telangana People's Movement: The Unfolding Political Culture', *Economic and Political Weekly* Vol. XLV, No. 42 (2010): 51–60.

Jadhav, Keshav Rao, ''Backwardization of Telangana', *Economic and Political Weekly* Vol. XLV, No. 13 (2010): 15–20.

Kodandaram, M., 'Movement for Telangana State: A Struggle for Autonomy', *Economic and Political Weekly*, Vol. XLII, No. 2 (2007): 90–94.

Kannabiran, Kalpana, Ramdas, Sagari R., Madhusudhan, N., Aashalatha, S., and Kumar Pavan M., 'On the Telangana Trail', *Economic and Political Weekly* Vol. XLV, No. 13 (2010): 69–82.

Lorraine, Hohler, 'A Telangana State? An Illustrative Analysis of the Stakes in Modifying Internal Borders', *Economic and Political Weekly* Vol. XLVIII, No. 34 (2013): 31–35.

Maringanti, Anant, 'Telangana: Righting Historical Wrongs or Getting the Future Right?', *Economic and Political Weekly* Vol. XLVI, No. 4 (2010): 33–38.

Srikanth, H., 'Construction and Consolidation of the Telangana Identity', *Economic and Political Weekly* Vol. XLVIII, Nos. 45/46 (2013): 39–45.

Sri Krishna Committee Report, 'Committee for Consultations on the Situation in Andhra Pradesh'. http://pib.nic.in/archieve/others/2011/jan/d2011010502.pdf (30 December 2010).

Srinivasulu, K., Basavaiah, M. Channa, and Ravinder, D., 'Sri Krishna Committee: Thorough But Unviable', *Economic and Political Weekly* Vol. XLVI, No. 10 (2011): 16–18.

14

Occupation of the Marginalized

A Study of Urban Informal Sector in Tezpur Town of Assam

Biman Kumar Nath

Indian states and major cities have witnessed rapid urbanization without any proportionate improvement in urban infrastructure. The urbanization which is taking place is not solely the result of industrialization. It can be attributed to urban bias in the investment of capital, finance and allocation of productive resources. The level of urbanization has increased from 27.8 per cent in 2001 to 31.15 per cent in 2011. The same trend of the country is also visible in the states. For example, the growth of urbanization in Assam is increasing from 12.9 per cent to 14.8 per cent over the same period. However, the growth of decadal urban and rural population is 27.61 per cent and 15.31 per cent respectively (Census, 2011). Consequently, the various demographic features of the urbanization process have resulted in a substantial increase in urban labour force. Thus, the growing labour force remains unemployed and underemployed, which finally settles in the urban informal sector (UIS) in variety of activities. The empirical scenario of urban labour market in Assam reflects coexistence of a small, well-organized formal sector with a large informal sector. The formal sector is characterized by relatively high earnings and attractive employment condition, while the informal sector is characterized by low and volatile earnings. Research efforts in urban employment as well as labour market in the past have most often focused on the organized sector.

Concept and Approaches

It emerges as an extensively researched topic prior to 1970s when it became a stylized fact that the informal or broadly unorganized sector is often the most important employment opportunity in developing nations. The models of sectoral dualism put forth by Lewis (1954) and Fei and Ranis (1961, 1964) proved to be ineffective since the 1970s when broad-based employment generation is concerned. Those classical theories assumed that informal sector would gradually disappear with the process of economic development. However, the contemporary evidence negates this truth, and informal sector now acts as a potential candidate capable of creating widespread income and employment. The developing countries face the problems of poverty and employment creation coupled with malnutrition, hunger, inequalities and so on. By this time, there is limited scope for generating adequate formal sector employment. It is resulting in failure to keep pace with continuously rising unemployment in the last few decades. The process of informalization is a transitory phenomenon, which is expanded and diversified to many economic activities as the development process is taking momentum. The jobless growth introduced by Structural Adjustment Programme (SAP) sincerely compelled the private sectors to squeeze their employability to maintain competitiveness and cost-efficiency. This trend is observed in developing nations where informal sector sits in a permanent chair and employability is a debatable issue. However, the nature of informality does not coincide between developing and developed nations. In developing countries, it can be considered as a survival instrument or 'employer of last resort' for the poor people where no alternative avenues are available for them. On the other hand, the enterprises in informal sector of developed countries provide more autonomy, flexibility and freedom as compared to formal sector. The International labour Organization (ILO) started the first employment mission in Kenya in 1972 and found that the traditional sector of Kenya included some profitable enterprises and marginal activities, which they referred to as 'informal sector'. But the term *informal sector* is first coined by a social anthropologist Keith Hart (1973). While doing a research on labour market of Accra, Ghana, he found that there were sections of labour force that did not fit into the conventional category of the working class that is formal sector. Those were local day labourers who offered their services at certain places in the city. And Hart labelled them as 'informal sector' workers in contrast to the formal sector comprising regular wage-earning workers. Recognizing informal sector as a relative term, Bose (1978) examines that informal sector is exploited by formal sector, and backwardness of informal sector is responsible for the stagnancy of formal sector. The informal sector is exploited by formal sector through marketing system by purchasing goods from informal sector at negligible prices and makes huge profit by selling at higher prices. Moreover, the informal sector is also at disadvantageous position in purchasing inputs at sky-high price from the black market. On the other hand, formal sector can get their inputs at controlled and subsidized price. This view is also supported by few scholars (Harriss, 1982; Romatet, 1983) by stating that subcontracting system is a medium of exploitation that usually prevails in the informal sector. But for the dynamic growth of both the sectors, there is a requirement of simultaneous development (ILO, 1972; Papola, 1981).

About the Study Area and Methodology

Tezpur, which is known for its mythological stories and cultural peculiarities, is situated in the middle Assam where both the people from Upper and Lower Assam do reside since time immemorial. Many studies are undertaken in Guwahati by scholars who are mostly confined to particular segment of informal workers such as construction workers or milk producers (Saikia, 2009). The district is surrounded by Lakhimpur in the east, Darrang in the west, Bhutan and Arunachal Pradesh in the north and Brahmaputra in the south. The entire district is divided into three subdivisions, namely Tezpur, Biswanath Chariali and Gohpur with seven revenue circles and fourteen development blocks.

The study is mainly empirical in nature. It is primarily based on the analysis of primary data with pretested questionnaires canvassed among 246 informal sector workers in Tezpur town of Assam. Workers are selected from each of the following activities: (i) Construction, (ii) Rickshaw pulling, (iii) Auto-repair and transport, (iv) Hotel and restaurant, (v) Petty trading and (vi) Domestic services and other informal sector activities. The sample is carefully chosen so as to give adequate representation to both male and female workers, as well as indigenous/local and migrant workers. The collected data are recorded in a statistical package, and accordingly tabulations are made to analyse for desired objectives.

The Sample Informal Sector Workers in Tezpur Town: A Brief Socio-economic Profile

The sample workers are surveyed in 25 different sublocations of the town. Diverse communities having different castes reside in the town. However, field survey is made on those particular places where municipalities do exist to go through the definition of UIS. Among the 246 informal sector workers including self-employed and working in other enterprises, highest participation is found with OBC followed by General and SC communities. Most of the migrants and natives of informal sector workers do stay in the sublocations, which is evident in Table 1. As a growing city with rapid urbanization, many economic activities are accelerated in Tezpur town including construction, trading, hotels, financial intermediation and others. A comparatively less amount of house rent pulls the workers to stay in those rent houses, which are distant from the main town.

Table 1

Caste-wise Distribution of Sample Informal Sector Worker

Sublocation	*Caste*				*Total*
	General	*OBC*	*SC*	*ST*	
Murhateteli	0	8	2	1	11
Kamarchuburi	6	3	25	1	35
Mazgaon	5	2	12	6	25
Bamunchuburi	12	14	11	0	39
Saikia Chuburi	20	17	1	0	38
Basantipur	20	1	3	0	24
Darjipatti	0	10	0	0	10
Ganeshmil Chariali	0	7	0	0	7
Pahumara Chuburi	1	0	0	0	1
Police reserve	0	1	0	0	1
Polo field	0	1	0	0	1
Joymati Pathar	5	5	1	0	11
Nepali Patty	0	2	0	0	2
Kachari Gaon	2	1	3	0	6
Haidur patty	0	7	4	0	11
Tribeni	0	2	1	2	5
Gharpara Chuburi	4	0	0	0	4
Usha Nagar	1	2	0	0	3
Ratnapur	0	1	0	0	1

Cont'd...

...Cont'd

Parbatia	1	2	0	0	3
Rupom	1	0	0	0	1
Basantipur	0	1	0	0	1
Mission Chariali	3	2	0	1	6
Vartak	1	0	0	0	1
L.B. Road	1	0	0	0	1
Total	83	89	63	11	248

Source: Field Survey.

Immigration in Assam is evident in many writings. It can be traced back to the opening of capitalist economy in the post Ahom rule period when immigrants from many places of Mainland India and also from East Pakistan settled their lives in every nook and corner of the state. Declining land/man ratio and poverty in the rural areas are two basic push factors of migration within the state and participation in UIS. Of the total workers, nearly 89 per cent reported that they are native and most of them are native to the state (Table 2). However, in the lower circuit of UIS such as barbers and shoe makers, the predominance of migrant is found (nearly 11%) to be more than that of other occupations.

Table 2

Cross-tabulation of Migration and Sex of the Respondent

Sex	*Are You a Migrant to This place*		*Total*
	Yes	*No*	
Male	26 (12%)	176 (88%)	202
Female	1 (2%)	43 (98%)	44
Total	27 (11%)	219 (89%)	246

Source: Field Survey.

Vulnerability and Security

A significant share of the informal sector workers are deprived of benefits or security, similar is the case of those who are engaged in informal employment in the formal sector. But employment analysts argue that degree of vulnerability is higher in case of informal employment in the informal sector than that of informal employment in the formal sector. Many workers are sometimes physically abused either at the workplace or outside the workplace.

Table 3

Physical Abuse at the Workplace of Sample Workers

Religion	*Have You Ever Been Abused Physically at Your Workplace*		*Total*
	Yes	*No*	
Hindu	48 (25%)	143 (74%)	191
Muslim	25 (55%)	20 (44%)	45
Others	5 (50%)	5 (50%)	10
Total	78 (31%)	168 (69%)	246

Source: Field Survey.

Table 3 shows that 31 per cent of the workers are physically abused at their workplace either by the employers or by the customers. Cross-religion figures indicate that 55 per cent of the Muslim workers are abused physically which is the highest followed by Hindu and other religions. But the workers who used to work under an individual or in some household are found to be less abused than that of self-employed (Table 4). It can be simply perceived that people work under an individual or in a household do have some informal agreement for which both the parties benefited. On the other hand, self-employed people do not have such kind and any unknown may physically abuse them.

Table 4

Physical Abuse of Cross-employer Employees in Informal Sector

Nature of Employer	*Have You Ever Been Abused Physically at Your Workplace*		
	Yes	*No*	*Total*
In a household	8	13	21
By an individual	0	14	14
Self-employed	58	153	211
Total	66	180	246

Source: Field Survey.

A large number of studies suggest variations in earnings of entrepreneurs across different activities in unorganized sector (Samal, 1989; Upadhyay, 2007). The earnings of the respondents are collected and recorded in SPSS by classifying three categories of income. The result shows that wide variation do exist within the respondent's income. Of the total, 16 per cent and 56 per cent of the workers get income within ₹ 1,000 to ₹ 2,000 and ₹ 2,000 to ₹ 5,000. A meagre 27 per cent reported that they earn more than ₹ 5,000 per month from their source of livelihood (Table 5). Moreover, earning discrimination of the employees as well as workers is remarkable. It is quite surprising that there are no female workers who earn income more than ₹ 5,000.

Table 5

Earnings of Sample Respondents in Three Income Slabs

	Earning Slab Per Month			*Total*
	1,000–2,000	*2,000–5,000*	*5,000–10,000*	
Male	4 (1.98%)	130 (64.35%)	68 (33.67%)	202
Female	36 (81.18%)	8 (18.18%)	NA	44
Total	40 (16.26%)	138 (56.09%)	68 (27.64%)	246

Source: Field Survey (Figures in the bracket indicates row percentage).

The public distribution system is having positive impact in rural India, which is evident from 66th round of NSS data.

Table 6

Public Distribution System of the UIS Workers in Sample Area

	Have You Purchased Any Item from the PDS in the Last 30 Days		*Total*
	Yes	*No*	
Male	64 (31.84%)	137 (68.15%)	201
Female	5 (11.11%)	40 (88.89%)	45
Total	69 (28.04%)	177 (71.96%)	246

Source: Field Survey (Figures in the bracket indicates row percentage).

But due to the problem of identification of UIS workers, it is not been able to accelerate the pace of development. Most of the surveyed workers belong to distant places which can otherwise be stated as migrant within the state. It is sometimes difficult for them to get any below poverty line (BPL) or APL card to entertain the benefits of PDS since most of the workers do have their own home in different districts of the state. The male workers of the survey show that 68 per cent of them do not entertain PDS either for being a migrant or not interested in the low quality items. Of the total female workers, only 11 per cent entertain the benefits. In a nutshell, PDS system in the study area is not able to achieve any success results towards the betterment of UIS workers.

Concluding Remarks

The informal sector as a whole suffers from a number of structural deficiencies. Since it is occupying a bulk of workforce, it is needs to be systematically protected, which require utmost attention from the government. Of course, there are numerous common problems and characteristics between formal and informal sector. But, it is seen in many subnational-level studies that heterogeneity in informal sector does exist even within a state. Therefore, uniform policy prescription cannot be suggested. Development in all dimensions in Tezpur, being a growing major town of Assam, is required. Higher labour market flexibility, higher employment generation with low capital and use of family labour like factors show its superiority over formal counterpart. Thus, the development of livelihood conditions of the workers in terms of many securities is the need of the hour. Identification of unorganized sector workers instead of BPL population should be given prominence by the national statistics. In that situation, it may be possible to trickle down the policies exclusively to the actual beneficiaries.

References

Bose, A.N., 'Informal Sector: Problems and Prospects', *Nagarlok*, Vol. 12, No. 2 (1980): 24–25.

Fei, John C.H. and Gustav Ranis, *Development of the Labour Surplus Economy: Theory and Policy* (New York: R.D. Irwin, 1964).

Government of India, *Primary Census Abstract* (New Delhi: Office of the Registrar General and Census Commissioner, 2011).

Harriss, John, 'Character of an Urban Economy: Small Scale Production and Labour Markets in Coimbatore', *Economic and Political Weekly*, Vol. XVII, Nos. 23/24, (2004): 945–1002.

Hart, K., 'Informal Income Opportunities and Urban Employment in Ghana', *Journal of Modern African Studies* Vol. 11 (March 1973): 68.

International Labour Office, Employment, Incomes and Inequality : A Strategy for Incveasing productive Employment in Kenya (Geneva: ILO. 1972)

Lewis, W.A., 'Economic Development with Unlimited Supplies of Labour', *Manchester School of Economic and Social Studies*, Vol. 23, No. 2 (June 1954).

Papola T.S., *Urban Informal Sector in a Developing Economy* (New Delhi: Vikas Publishing, 1981).

Papola T.S., and Sahu Partha Pratim, 'Growth and Structure of Employment in India Long-Term And Post-Reform Performance and the Emerging Challenge' (New Delhi: ISID 2012).

Ranis, Gustav and Fei, John C.H., *'A Theory of Economic Development'*, The American Review, Vol. 1 (September 1961) 533–564.

Romatet, Emmanuel, 'Calcutta's Informal Sector: Theory and Reality', *Economic and Political Weekly*, Vol. XVIII, No. 20 (December 1983): 2115–2128.

Saikia, J., 'Economics of Informal Milk Producing Units in Guwahati City' (Unpublished PhD Thesis, NEHU, 2009): 35–57.

Samal, K.C., *Urban Informal Sector: An Exploration of the Informal Sector in a Small City of Orissa* (Delhi: Manak Publications Pvt. Ltd., 1990).

Todaro, M.P., 'A Model of Labour Migration and Urban Unemployment in Less Developed Countries', *American Economic Review*, Vol. 59 (March 1969).

Upadhyay, Vandana, 'Employment and Earnings in Urban Informal Sector: A Study on Arunachal Pradesh', *VVGNLI Research Studies* (2007).

15

Social Networking Sites

A Boon or Curse for Society

Jhumpa Dey and Sekhar Kanti Sarkar

Social networking site (SNS) is a valuable tool, which has become widely popular in today's society. These are virtual communities where users can create individual public profiles, interact with real-life friends and meet other people based on shared interests. They are seen as a 'global consumer phenomenon' with an exponential rise in usage within the last few years. People today can't imagine living without social networking. It has become a daily routine no matter where you are. Also, it is interesting to know how mobile phones are shaping the use of social networks today. Those who do not get enough time to access their desktops often use a mobile device to stay connected with their friends. What's even more interesting is that adults are using social networks more than the younger demographic today, something which has never happened before the last year or so.

The mass appeal of social networks on the Internet could potentially be a cause for concern, particularly when attending to the gradually increasing amount of time people spend online. SNSs are 'web-based services that allow individuals to construct a public or semi-public profile within a bounded system, articulate a list of other users with whom they share a connection, and view and traverse their list of connections and those made by others within the system'.

In terms of SNS history, the first social networking site (*Six Degrees*) was launched in 1997, based on the idea that everybody is linked with everybody else via six degrees of separation, and initially referred to as the 'small world problem'. In 2004, the most successful current SNS, *Facebook*, was established as a closed virtual community for Harvard students. The site expanded very quickly and *Facebook* currently has more than 500 million users, of whom 50 per cent log on to it every day. Furthermore, the overall time spent on *Facebook* increased by 56 per cent from 2007 to 2008.

Definition of SNSs

A social networking website is an online platform that allows users to create a public profile and interact with other users on the website. Social networking websites usually have a new user input a list of people with whom they share a connection and then allow the people on the list to confirm or deny the connection. After connections are established, the new user can search the networks of his connections to make more connections. A social networking site may also be known as a social website or a social networking website.

Review of Literature

As the social media and the related activities are rapidly developing, the numbers of involved women users are more than the number of men now. Due to this fact, there are many possible changes that could be experienced within the future media. Due to the increasing trend of social media usage by women, social media such as newspapers, movies, magazines and social networking sites would have a huge impact on the shaping of social patterns (Thompson, 2011). It is necessary to analyse some of the quotes that are related to the social media and the aspect of gender when viewing the issue of social media and how the gender influences media. It is also necessary to analyse the aspect of women taking charge of the media, the increasing popularity of social media, and the relationship between age, gender and the social media (Thompson, 2011). In order to complete analysing the influences between social media activities and the aspect of gender, it is helpful not only to consider the number of the social media users and the length of the time they spent on social media but also to compare the modern social media with the previous media. As mentioned earlier, social media communication patterns have been shaping the ideology of audiences and also been shaped by the gender of users. Many media communication methods have a very deep connection to the aspect of gender in different cultures (Donald A. MacKenzie, 1985). There is another study done by the *TIME* group that evaluates the factors behind the fact that women belongs to *Pinterest* and *Google* belongs to men. This study indicates that around 83 per cent of the users of *Pinterest* were actually women, and approximate two-thirds of *Google+* users are men. (Wagstaff, 2012). This study however raises a question on whether this fact means the female users dominated the social media and male users have less impact on the media (Dines, 2002). According to the results of this study, the reason behind this surprising fact is that *Google+* has less female friendly form of content than *Pinterest*, and its functions are more focused on academic contents instead of social networking. Many of research studies have indicated that a specific gender group tends to use the social networks more than others with different purpose. According to the article *The Social Media Gender Gap*, female users usually make more purchasing decisions and spend longer time on the online shopping than male users (Hoffman, 2008). Due to this fact, the female users are the major group where the advertisers could get more benefits from. A majority of these researchers still indicate that although both user groups of gender use social media frequently, women are still 'the ones that hold down the fort' (Hoffman, 2008). Chakraborty (2012) in her paper entitled 'Activities and Reasons for Using Social Networking Sites by the Research Scholars in NEHU: A Study on *Facebook* and Research Gate' reveals that most of the respondents from social science background used SNSs for education and research point of view and scholars from pure science think that SNS has no role on research and education. Mahajan (2009) in her article entitled 'Use of Social Networking in a Linguistically and Culturally Rich India' explored the usage, impact and problems related to social networking sites on the social and cultural values in India where she described the top most social networking websites of India along with their bad and good factors.

Methodology

Empirical data were collected through the survey method of the primary data for which a questionnaire was developed using both open- and close-ended questions based on the objectives of the proposed study and distributed randomly among the target group of the population. For secondary data, available resources were discussed and analysed for collection of data. Again the dearth of available resources shows light on this fact that a very few studies have been done on the subject and thus scope remains open for further studies. This study will also involve observations – both direct and participation method where direct observation will be made with the youth group. An extensive literature search was conducted using the academic database *Web of Knowledge* as well as *Google Scholar*. The following search terms as well as their derivatives were entered: social network, online network, addiction, compulsive, excessive, use, abuse, motivation and personality. Studies were included if they: (i) included empirical data, (ii) made reference to usage patterns, (iii) motivations or usage, (iv) personality traits of users, (v) negative consequences of use and (vi) impacts.

Data Analysis

The data analysis was done on the following parameters:

- Gender wise
- Age wise
- Period or duration of using SNSs
- Purpose of membership in SNSs

Findings

1. The outcomes of this study were that majority of the users use SNSs for personal uses as messaging, chatting, media sharing, browsing friends, pages and sharing files, pages, blogs, and so on. *Facebook* and *WhatsApp* are the most popular one and majority will be using SNSs through mobiles. Its use is time consuming.
2. The main reasons for this usage were staying in touch with friends and using them to make new friends. This was more common among boys than girls. Girls preferred to use these sites in order to maintain contacts with actual friends rather than making new ones. Furthermore, half of the teenagers in this sample visited their SNS at least once a day which is indicative of the fact that in order to keep an attractive profile, frequent visits are necessary and this is a factor that facilitates potential excessive use. The findings indicated that majority of males and females had SNS profiles from which more than half of them used SNSs on a daily basis. Mostly the respondents were engaged in reading/responding to comments on their SNS page and/or posts to one's wall, sending/responding to messages/invites and browsing friends' profiles/walls/pages. Usage of SNSs has also been found to differ with regard to age group. The study revealed that teenagers' friends' networks were larger and that their friends were more similar to themselves with regard to age. Furthermore, older users' networks were smaller and more

dispersed age-wise. In reviewing SNS usage patterns, it indicates that overall, regular SNS use has increased substantially over the last few years.

3. In addition to this, the findings of the presented studies indicate that compared to the general population, teenagers and students make most use of SNSs by utilizing the inherent Web 2.0 features.
4. SNSs tend to be used mostly for social purposes of which extracting further information from friends' pages appears particularly pleasurable. A large number of users used SNSs for the maintenance of offline relationships. Females used SNSs for communication with peer group members, entertainment and passing time, whereas men used it in an instrumental way for social compensation, learning and social identity gratifications. Seeking friends, social support, information and entertainment were found to be the most significant motivations for SNS usage.
5. In terms of socio-demographics, the studies presented indicate that overall SNS usage patterns differ. Furthermore, men tend to disclose more personal information on SNS sites relative to women. Also, more women were found to use *MySpace* and *WhatsApp* specifically relative to men. Moreover, usage patterns were found to differ between genders as a function of personality. In addition to this, it was found that males were more likely to be addicted to SNS games specifically relative to females.
6. In general, research suggests that SNSs are used for social purposes. Overall, the maintenance of connections to offline network members was emphasized rather than the establishment of new ties. With regard to this, SNS users nourish bridging social resources through a variety of heterogeneous connections to other SNS users. This appeared to be beneficial for them with regard to sharing knowledge and prospective future possibilities related to employment and related areas.
7. In this regard, the pursuit of weak ties on SNSs is of great benefit and thus coincides with the satisfaction of the members' needs. At the same time, it is experienced as gratifying. Therefore, rather than seeking emotional support, individuals make use of SNSs in order to communicate and stay in touch not only with family and friends, but also with more distant acquaintances, therefore sustaining weak ties with potentially advantageous environments. The benefits of large online social networks may potentially lead people to excessively engage in using them, which, in turn, may purport addictive behaviours too.

In addition to this, motivations for usage as well as a wider variety of negative correlates related to excessive SNS use need to be addressed.

Boon or Curse for the Society

Whether social networking sites (SNSs) are a boon or curse for the society depend on the users as how they utilize the services of SNSs. Let us see some of the positive traits of the social networking sites:

1. Students can produce and retain information, as social networking sites offer lots of opportunities for learning and interaction. Students are exploring and experiencing the world not only by books and assignments but also by adapting social media. In today's world, contacts, networks and communications are also very important. Students are making a network with professionals for job opportunities and internships.
2. SNSs are a comfortable way of communication for shy teens. This can boost their self-esteem and confidence. SNSs provide teens with unusual interest and hobbies, are a place to share information and enthusiasm and help them to enrich and manage their social lives. Teens who are differently abled and have other challenges can communicate with other teens with similar problems.
3. SNSs are an excellent tool for business exposure to the public at a much lower cost than any traditional marketing. In India nowadays there are numbers of social networking sites that deals on marketing such as *Amazon, Snapdeal, HomeShop, Olx.in, Craftsvilla* and other sites. These sites have each and every category starting from clothing to grocery, real estate and so on that help targeting new customers and make brand more popular, which has turned to be a threat for the retail outlets in the market. Social media can improve customer services and enable business to gain new information about their customers. Many companies are developing interactive communities that connect individuals to share business needs and experiences.
4. Valuable aid for solving crime: Police are beginning to investigate gang-related crimes on social media networks. It is a form of political influence as it is a true voice of people. Being a powerful force for change, it has a potential to influence the outcomes of political decisions.
5. SNSs have the power to wipe out the distances. We can reconnect with our kith and kin internationally without spending money on ISD calls by using e-mails and *Skype*. As Internet provides many

free online services, we can connect to our dear ones at all times. Internet social networking even helps people get married. There are no boundaries or borders for a person to connect with other people living even in other continent.

6. Social media has transformed the market. Brands have the ability to engage the customers with products, and social media helps to make good brand image. Social networking sites are a powerful tool of communication. Social networking keeps us to know the latest events happening around the world. Many top most companies directly approach candidates through social networking sites and offer jobs. We can able to interact with people of authority who might help us in our careers. And also it helps us to enhance our communication skills. It gives us a platform to share our views, opinions and thoughts. It does keep a person updated about the latest happenings in the world. Surely it is a boon for society, if used judiciously.
7. Teachers and professors are making groups to extend classroom discussion to posting assignments, tests and quizzes, to assisting with homework outside of the classroom setting.

Negative traits of the social networking sites are as follows:

The study also highlights a number of potential negative correlates.

1. People who extensively use SNS, that is, people who spent more time on SNSs are less involved with their real-life communities. According to the study assessing the relationships between *SNSs* usage and academic performance, SNSs users had lower grade point averages and spent less time in studying than students who did not use this SNS. It had a negative impact, namely procrastination, distraction and poor time management. SNS usage can lead to a variety of negative consequences that imply a potential decrease in the involvement in real-life communities and worse academic performance, as well as relationship problems.
2. Social media can be very distracting and harmful for students. Students share personal information, comment on someone's post, which may be harmful for them, always glued with their mobiles, tablets and computer, which is a wastage of time and may spoil their performance.
3. Online bullying and harassment, also known as cyber bullying, may be the biggest danger for teens. There are cases of falling as a prey for online predators, an online sex crime against minors. Also there is a decrease in interaction between friends and family.

4. Consumers can post negative comments on social media sites, which may damage your prospects with new clients. Threat of hackers is a terrible issue on SNSs. Choosing among different social media sites might be a tough task for business owner because selecting the wrong one may affect the success of the business.
5. Personal information is not secured in some social websites. Due to the vast improvement in social networking, the numbers of users have increased, so this is directly proportional to the number of websites. In the same way, some fake websites are being created to harm people, not only fake sites but even the trusted sites are hacked easily nowadays due to loopholes. Due to this the data are leaked, which contains passwords of banks and conversations.
6. Whatever shown on SNSs are considered to be true, which are not always, whether it is photo of an animal or nature or people. Sometimes people are not able to decide whether the information or photos available are fake or real, for example, there are various job-related portals that are fake. This can hamper the decision-making capacity of the job seekers.
7. SNSs sometimes lead to misconception. People post often scathing opinions that are based on misconception or false facts and they are not bothered to check, thus influencing others in a similar matter.
8. The security issues – physical as well as those related to computers – are increasing as the teenagers do not understand the effective usage of social networking. Personal lives are getting affected as they have started sharing their personal things on these sites.

On these sites people make friends and spend long hours chatting with them whom they have never seen or met. Young generations are becoming more and more addicted to these sites. Somewhere the real social life is getting affected very badly as they find it more comfortable to chat online with a stranger than finding time to meet friends or relatives. Recently there was a case where a girl attempted suicide after reading a message from her boyfriend. Such incidents are increasing day by day.

In addition to the above-mentioned implications and suggestions for further study, specific attention needs to be paid while selecting larger samples that are representative of a broader population so as to increase the external validity of the study.

Rights of Women

Women are entitled to equal enjoyment and protection of all human rights and fundamental freedoms that include among others: The right to life, right to equality, right to liberty and security of person, right to equal protection under the law, right to be free from all forms of discrimination, right to the highest attainable standard of physical and mental health, right to just and favourable conditions of work, right not to be subjected to torture, or other cruel, inhuman or degrading treatment or punishment.

To highlight and to have a greater insight as how social networking sites is contributing in highlighting the issues as well as protecting the rights of the marginalized gender, that is, women section of the society. For the said purpose, following two of the case studies were undertaken.

Case Study

A girl from Guwahati was molested by a group of men when she came out of a bar on busy G.S. Road in Guwahati, Assam, on 9 July 2012 at around 9 pm–10 pm. The incident was captured on camera by a journalist of a Guwahati-based local news channel. The video went viral on SNSs, and there was a nationwide outrage. The editor-in-chief of the local news channel uploaded the video and faced wide criticism for uploading it in *YouTube*. He was also criticized because the reporter of the channel continued shooting the video instead of helping the girl. There was a series of protest on 14 and 15 July 2012 in which many NGOs and civil society groups participated. Meanwhile youth from Assam were also campaigning on the *Facebook* against the incident, and such online communities organized themselves in the SNS and mobilized themselves to demonstrate protest on the streets on 15 July 2012. The youth under the aegis of *Music and Peace* organization and *Facebook community* gathered at the incident site on G.S. Road and took out a rally. They shouted slogans of *Soch Badlo Kapde nahi* and *Respect Woman.* Their rally started from that exact place where the incident took place. This incident can be perhaps regarded as the beginning of cyber activism in Assam. The protest demonstrations on the streets got a huge offline response as well, while the online youth groups stepped out of the cyber world to physically participate in the same. The news was covered by the national media and renowned journalists and personalities from India and abroad commented in social media on the issue. The Chief Minister of Assam, Tarun Gogoi, ordered probe and arrest of the culprits. The editor-in-chief resigned on 17 July 2012. The reporter of the news channel who was alleged of instigating the crime was also taken under police custody for further investigation.

Thus from the above case study and its observations, it can be traced that SNSs have immense power to influence the masses and communication, and IT revolution has further increased its importance. The violation of rights of the victim, that is, of the girl was hugely showcased and highlighted at the same time by the media and SNSs that drew huge attention of the nation. This ultimately led to the protest and rallies by the people, women organizations, NGOs and so on, which finally led the authority to take severe action against the culprits. Such is the power of this so-called high tech instrument – social networking sites. Due to the active involvement of SNSs, within a day the incident catered to the eyes and interest of the people through which justice was given to the victim's rights and self-esteem. At present, the state of art of Information and Communication Technology has enabled a transformation in the approach of activists and activisms. Research is beginning to explore how activist groups across the world are using social media to facilitate public engagement and collective action. Internet has the potential to increase the speed, reach and effectiveness of activist-related communication as well as mobilization efforts, and as a result it has a positive impact on activism in general. In these protests, the social media tools provided a common platform for the people of Assam to raise concerns about issues relating to their interest in the cyber world and perhaps as a result protest demonstrations and huge rallies were also carried out in the physical world. In the series of these protests, the participation of the people was particularly influenced by the SNSs, which was used to publicize, organize and create awareness among the people, particularly among the people of Assam. It is also seen that the users tend to publicize and organize events online and offline through the medium, which indeed have revolutionized the modus operandi of collective activities by increasing the effectiveness and speed of the intended communication.

Nowadays people rely on SNSs to know about the happenings in the society. Media are able to reach to common people, and undoubtedly media has attained the role of a very powerful organ virtually in all spheres of life. SNSs have a myriad of different goals, which range from entertainment to information, marketing, education and so on. The result is that news is available in various interesting colour. For instance, the *NIRBHAYA* case documentary that has been made, based on the interview of the convicted, has created a storm across the country and abroad. Though for various reasons, the telecast of the film has been stopped but the public poll through the SNSs says some different story and speaks that the same documentary has been shown in some foreign nations. Everyday latest updates on this particular story are available through SNSs. These instances throw a light on the fact that if the users wish to bring about a constructive change in the society, they can certainly execute that through the positive use of the SNSs.

Violence against women in any form is a global pandemic, and the instances of deprivation of this marginalized gender of their rights are horrific. Though the scenario is changing day by day and nowadays the social networking sites are highlighting the issues worldwide instantly but yet the cognitive procedures of the society at large have to be changed, which will take a very long time to process. In India SNSs need to be sensitized to gender issues where it should play a proactive role in inculcating gender sensitivity in the country and must ensure that women are not depicted in poor light and in creating public awareness on the rights and privileges of women as well. Constitutional and legal rights should also be advertised and discussed regularly. As their role should be to expose and generate awareness against society's ills and evils, therefore their role should be still more effective.

Conclusion

In conclusion, social networks on the Internet are iridescent Web 2.0 phenomena that offer the potential to become part of, and make use of, collective intelligence. The findings indicate that SNSs are predominantly used for social purposes, mostly related to the maintenance of established offline networks. Moreover, extraverts appear to use social networking sites for social enhancement, whereas introverts use it for social compensation, each of which appears to be related to greater usage, as does low conscientiousness and high narcissism. Negative correlates of SNS usage include the decrease in real-life social community participation and academic achievement, as well as relationship problems, each of which may be indicative of potential addiction.

The immediacy of social media and its potential to make information viral with a time period was unimaginable, and now it has thrown up unique opportunities and challenges. The dynamics will keep changing as more users from the rural and semi-urban populace adopt this influential domain of information exchange. Whether SNSs are a boon or curse for present era depend completely on the users as how they use them. But children and teenagers must be guided by their guardians and well wishers as they rarely know the difference between the good and bad. Whereas those who are using SNS must take extra precaution while uploading their personal information. The issue here is not to demean social networking but the way of handling it relies in our hands. Whether SNS should operate our lives or vice versa. Conversing with people personally over phone, getting engaged in face-to-face communication and using social networking judiciously will obviously lead to balance one's life. Social networks are definitely a boon to the society, but too much exposure to it can affect the social progress. While efforts are on to collate data on the proliferation of use of the social media in the county. It is also imperative for all stakeholders to collectively work towards ensuring maintenance of law and order and protection of individuals and companies from the anti-social impacts of social media.

References

Andreas M. Kaplan and Michael Haenlein, 'Users of the World, Unite! The Challenges and Opportunities of Social Media,' *Business Horizons* Vol. 53, No. 1 (2010): 60–61. http://dx.doi.org/10.1016/j.bushor.

Braiser, R., 'The Social Networking Paradigm Shift and Internet Fraud'. http://thetargetgroup.wordpress.com/.../the – social networking-paradigm-shift-and-internet-fraud (20101.). Chakraborty, Nirmali, 'Activities and Reasons for Using Social Networking Sites by Research Scholars in NEHU: A Study on Facebook' (Paper presented at 8th Convention Planner, Sikkim University, Gangtok, 1–3 March 2012).

Dines, Gail, *Gender, Race and Class in Media: A Text-Reader*, Vol. I (New Delhi: Sage, 2002).

Edwards, Waelde, (ed.), 3rd, *Law and the Internet* (Oxford: Hart Publishing Ltd, 2009).

'Hate Speech on the Internet', http://www.osce.org/publications/rfm/2004/12/12239_94_en.pdf

Hoffman, A., Men are from Video Games, Women are from Social Networks (Available at : http://blog.summation.net/2008/03/men-are-from_vi.html.

http://www.emaxhealth.com/1275/can-social-networking-sites-facebook-cause-stress

http://www.indiasocial.in/mobile-social-networking-in-india/

http://www.telegraph.co.uk

J. Bullas, '5 ways to integrate social media into your company's DNA,' <http://www.jeffbullas.com/2010/12/23/5-ways-to-integrate-social-media-into-your-companys-dna/>

'Legal Issues Raised in Social Networking Sites', http://articles.technology.findlaw.com/2007/Sep/18/10966.html (15 December 2010).

Mackenzie, Donald A. and Wajcman, Judy, *The Social Shaping of Technology: How the Refrigerator got its Hum* (UK: Open University Press, 1985).

Mahajan, Preeti, 'Use of Social Networking Sites in a Linguistically and Culturally Rich India', *The International Information & library Review* Vol. 41 (2009): 129–136.

'Right to Privacy and Media Law', http://webcache.googleusercontent.com/search?q=cache:KPPnmU86VMJ:www.indialawjournal.com/volume2/issue_1/article_by_Rituj_and_Suchi.html+right+to+privacy+and+media+law+in+india&cd=6&hl=en&ct=clnk&gl=in

SAS, 'Social Media Metrics: Listening, Understanding and Predicting the Impacts of Social Media on Your Business,' *eMetrics* (San Jose, CA: SAS Social Media Analytics, 2010).

Singh, K.P., and Gill, Malkeet Singh, 'Use of Social networking Sites by the Research Scholars: A Study of Guru Nanak Dev University, Amritsar', *Library Herald* Vol. 49, No. 3 (2011): 229–241.

Thompson, Rachel, *A Walk in the Snark* (New York: Booktrope, 2015 (2011)).

'Understanding the Legal Issues in the Social Networking Sites', http://articles.technology.findlaw.com/2007/Sep/18/10966.html (4 November 2001).

Wagstaff, Keith, 'Come Here Often', *TIME*, Vol. 179, issue 12, 3.26.2012.

16

Conceptualizing 'Self' as a Social Product

An Analysis among the Migrant Labourers in Kerala

Prasad R.

Migration is an enduring theme of human history. The movement of people for food, shelter, better living and for other reasons had started from the prehistoric period. The process of migration is continuing along with those factors that are promoting human movement. As Lee (1966) puts forward, this movement is basically due to the lack of economic opportunities, religious and political persecution, and environmental hazards, which push and compel people to leave their homeland in search of a livelihood. Also the people are pulled or attracted towards regions with better economic prospects, religious and political freedom, and benign environment. Thus, a wide range of factors act behind the decision to migrate. Primarily these movements were within a geographical territory or the boarders of the nation. However, sooner than later the people began to move overseas, which ultimately resulted in high rate of international migration or emigration. As estimated, throughout the world there are more than 214 million international migrants and approximately 750 million internal migrants who rely on migration as an effective and immediate strategy to reduce poverty, escape conflict and improve the prospects for their families (Sutherland, 2013). Apart from demographic aspects, remittance from migration is often seen as a scale for development. The income from migration is contributing to the economic development of the nations across the globe. The top remittance receiving countries through migration for the year 2012 are India ($70 billion), China ($66 billion), Philippines and Mexico ($24 billion), and other large recipients include Nigeria, Egypt, Pakistan, Bangladesh, Vietnam and Lebanon (World Bank, 2012).

The UNDP Human Development Report of 2005 states that apart from migration overseas, there are four times as many internal migrants in the world. The Census data of India 2001 estimates 309 million Indians are migrating internally. Deshinkar and Akter (2009) analyse that the internal migrants contribute 10 per cent to the national GDP. Apart from economic benefits and demographic changes, the internal migrants are excluded from the cultural, social and political life of society (UNESCO, 2013). Indian society is diverse from region to region. The migrants are differentiated according to gender, caste, class, ethnicity, language and religion. When a person leaves the homeland and settles or works in a different social and linguistic background, he or she becomes a minority group over there. The identity of a migrant person has changed from the place of origin to the destination region.

Methodology

This chapter is based on the analysis of both the primary and secondary data. Existing literature is analysed to understand the condition of migrant labourers in Kerala and to get a theoretical knowledge about self and 'identity'. To get a firsthand knowledge about the problem, migrant labourers and social activists who are working for the welfare of the migrant labourers were interviewed. Apart from that, Malayalam newspaper reports related to migrant labourers were critically analysed. The internal migration[1] towards Kerala comprises migrants from southern and northern parts of India. Majority of them are basically from the north and northeastern parts of India. Hence this chapter focuses on the migrant labourers from the north and northeastern parts of India.

Kerala Migration

People of Kerala began to out-migrate (migrating outside Kerala but within India) and emigrate (outside India) significantly after the independence (Zachariah and Rajan, 2012). As a result of the massive labour demand in the Middle East and Western Countries of the world, educated, skilled and unskilled people of Kerala began to emigrate. Survey records of the Centre for Development Studies, Thiruvananthapuram, estimate that in 2008 around 21.9 lakh population of Kerala are living outside India. Out of these, 88.5 per cent are working in the Gulf countries, 4.7 per cent are working in the United States, 1.8 per cent in United Kingdom and the rest were settled in different parts of the world. Apart from high emigration rates, large numbers of Kerala population are working in different states of India. Approximately 9,14,387 people of Kerala migrated to different parts of India (Zachariah and Rajan, 2012). Thus, both emigration and outmigration to other Indian states have contributed to the outflow of people from Kerala.

During the latter half of 1980s, high educational standard of Kerala had produced a large number of qualified people but the job opportunity in Kerala remained low. The migration of professionally qualified people has led to the phenomenon called 'brain drain[2]'. But the outflow of skilled and unskilled labourers had made gaps in the domestic labour market. For better economic benefits, large number of labour class people began to migrate to different places. Also the increased educational standard of Kerala had made 'white-collar[3]' job culture among the educated youth. As a result of this, the youth became reluctant to do 'blue-collar[4]' job. These new trends, which took off during 1980s, had created gaps at the lower-class structure. There occurred huge shortage of manual labour power. Due to this workers from other states began to migrate towards Kerala. Over the last three decades, large number of migrant labourers from other states began to occupy the lower-class position. Primarily people from nearby states of Tamil Nadu, Andhra Pradesh and Karnataka were employed in skilled and unskilled labour sector. But during 1990s migrants, from north and northeastern parts of India began to occupy the labour gap. This labour power is widely seen as replacing the earlier (Kumar, 2011).

Migrant Labourers and Economy

In India, the changes happened at the structural level made vast differences in wage rates. States such as Kerala, Tamil Nadu, Himachal Pradesh, Haryana and Punjab have comparatively high wage rates, both in the agriculture and non-agriculture sectors. Wage rates in Gujarat, Maharashtra and West Bengal were lower than the national average (Reddy, 2015). Thus the people from the rural villages are forced to migrate to urban centres for better wages.

> Lakshman[5], is from Assam, for the past eight years he is working under a construction contractor in Kerala. At home he does farming but it is hard to live with the income from agriculture alone. Working in construction sector over there gives around two hundred and fifty to three hundred and fifty rupees but in Kerala wages is around seven hundred to seven hundred and fifty rupees. During weekends the remittance is send to his father's account. With the remittance he bought some more land, a new bike and done some maintenance to home. Other family members are doing farming at home. (Interview Excerpt 30 March 2014)

The availability of job coupled with higher wage rates attracts the unskilled and semi-skilled labourers to find fortune in a new place. Kerala has now become a dream land for many labourers. The Labour Department of Kerala Government[6] estimates more than 25 lakh Domestic Migrant Labourers (DML)[7] in Kerala (Narayana and Venkiteswaran, 2013). But debates over this estimation argue that there are more than 50 lakh migrant workers. They are now seen in every nook and corner of Kerala. They are employed in construction sector, factories, hotels, farming, domestic works and others. They become an unavoidable part in the labour market of Kerala. The migrant labourer in Kerala does not constitute a homogenous category, they are diverse. This heterogeneous category comprises wide range of people predominantly males from different parts of India. While the numbers are few from Punjab, Haryana, Gujarat, Maharashtra and so on, the largest proportion hail from West Bengal (20%), Bihar (18.10%), Assam (17.28%), and Uttar Pradesh (14.83%) (Narayana and Venkiteswaran, 2013).

Table 1

Region and Age wise Distribution of Domestic Migrant Labourers in Kerala

State	*Age Group Distribution*						*Percentage Share*
	Below 18	*18–23*	*24–29*	*30–35*	*36 and above*	*Not reported*	
Uttar Pradesh	00	38.53	38.53	15.60	7.34	0	14.83
Assam	1.57	50.39	34.65	10.24	2.36	0.79	17.28
West Bengal	1.36	46.26	29.25	14.97	7.48	0.68	20.00
Bihar	0.75	34.59	33.08	21.05	9.03	1.50	18.10
Orissa	2.04	34.69	30.61	20.41	10.20	2.04	6.67
Others	1.18	37.65	37.65	14.71	8.82	0	23.13
Total	1.09	40.95	34.29	15.65	7.35	0.68	100

Source: Narayana and Venkiteswaran (2013).

The flow of migrant labourers to Kerala is increasing day by day. The majority of the migrants are youth who are selling their labour power for higher wages. Their presence has boosted the industrial and construction sector of Kerala.

> Before the arrival of labourers from Assam, West Bengal and Odisha there were 200 sawmills in Perumbavoor of Ernakulum district. But after 2002 around 800 new industrial units emerged with the availability of labour force in this region. (Mathrubhumi 16 July)

On an average annually these people are sending home remittance of around ₹ 70,000 (Narayana and Venkiteswaran, 2013). The migrants are earning a better living than what they used to in their homeland. Economically migration is helping the workers to have higher earnings. At the same time, the Kerala society is economically developing and enhancing its urbanization process by making use of the manpower of the migrants. The testimony of a construction contractor clearly shows the impact migration had made in the labour market of Kerala.

> Now ten 'hindi people' are working under me. They are sheltered in a room leased by me. Whenever I need labourers they are ready to do work. So, now there is no need to search for labourers. (Interview Excerpt 9 May 2014).

Thus migration is a reliable means for both the homeland and host land.[8] The former is being satisfied with remittance and the later enhancing its urbanization process. It is true that migration is contributing to the economic development of both the homeland and the host land. But the migrants are away from their family and working in a new society which is socially, culturally and linguistically different. More than economic achievement, it is highly relevant to analyse the social impact made by migration.

Self and Identity

Discussions on self and identity became popular during the twentieth century. Debates on both take two major forms: psychodynamic and sociological. The 'Psychodynamic' tradition emerges with Freud's theory of identification through which the child comes to assimilate external persons or objects, usually the superego of the parent. Psychodynamic theory stresses the inner core of a psychic structure as having a continuous identity (Scott and Marshall, 2009). The sociological tradition of identity theory is linked to symbolic interactionism and emerges from the pragmatic theory of the self discussed by

William James and George Herbert Mead. The self is a distinctively human capacity, which enables people to reflect on their nature and the social world through communication and language. Self is often seen as a process with two phases: the 'I', which is inner, knower, subjective, creative, determining and unknowable; and the 'Me', which is the more known, outer, determined and social phase. Identification, here, is a process of naming, of placing ourselves in socially constructed categories, with language holding a central position in this process. For Goffman and Peter Berger, identity is stated clearly to be 'socially bestowed, socially sustained and socially transformed' (Richard Jerkins, 1996).

According to Richard Jenkins (1996), identity is an integral part of social life. He states that social identity is 'our understanding of who we are and of who other people are, and, reciprocally, other people's understanding of themselves and of others'. Identities are concerned not just with our own impressions of ourselves but also with our impression of others, and others' impression about us. Identity is both internal and external. The former is what we think we are and the later is what others think we are. Identities are formed and stabilized in a dialectical relationship between these internal and external factors.

Migrant Labourers and Social Interaction

Migration is often celebrated as a means of economic development. Because it improves the economic condition of the homeland through remittance and increases the urbanization process of the host land. But through migration, the migrants become a part of a new social and cultural setting. The social background of northern parts of India is entirely different from south. They are diverse at the social, cultural and linguistic level.

The migrant labourers are often linguistically categorized as *Hindi people*. But among them there are people who speak Assamese, Bangla, Oriya, Gujarati and several other tribal languages. Also there are people who don't know Hindi language. Normally migrants use their local language to have conversations among themselves. Since Hindi is not known to all natives, it is often seen difficult to have interactions between the migrants and natives. Only those migrants who get chance to mingle with the native people learns the local language Malayalam. This is totally different from their language.

> Gopal is a middle aged man from Odisha. He is on his way back to home to take part in election. He has been working in Kerala for the past eleven years. But he hasn't learned Malayalam because he is dealing with

> migrant labourers who speak Hindi. Only one mason is a Malayali[9] and all others are Hindi speaking including one Tamil mason helper. (Interview Excerpt 30 March 2014)

The linguistic difference controls the interaction of the migrants with the natives. Only those who are getting a chance to mingle with the local people are learning the Malayalam language. But parallel to this the native society is also making changes in its nature of social formation and practices. In certain parts of Kerala especially in Perumbavoor[10] region of Ernakulam district, the name boards and service boards of shops and transport buses are printed in Hindi, Oriya, Bangla and Assamese languages. This ultimately attracts the migrants towards the right choices. Though the language barrier constrains their social interactions, over the past two decades these migrants are playing a major role in the social and economic structure of Kerala. Living in a new social context with different social, cultural and linguistic background has transformed them into an 'ethnic category'. Based on this evolved categorization, it is significant to analyse how the migrants see themselves and how the native people see them in a new social setting.

Outlook towards Migrant Labourers

> Anil is a plumbing contractor of Kerala. Three migrant workers from Northern parts of India are working under him. He is very happy about them because they are dedicated in their work than the local workers. But he says that, he never employ these 'hindi people' in houses which are already occupied instead to newly building houses. He is concerned about the risk of crime and robbery. (Interview Excerpt 6 April 2014)

The contractor is highly satisfied about the work done by the migrant labourers but he is highly concerned about their character. Even though these people are working for him, their identity is being questioned. He is bothered about the risks of robbery and crime involved in dealing with the migrants. The migrants are often subjected to under suspicion. The manpower of the migrant labourers is used but their self is questioned.

> Bhaskar is a local politician of Kerala who is working for the welfare of the unskilled in his region. He is having a strong opinion that these migrants are thieves. They are real threat to the local society. These people have to be send back home. (Interview Excerpt 23 October 2014)

The common attitude the native people have towards the migrants is a sense of *other*. Though the migrant labourers are the citizens of India, they are seen as people from unknown land. Ultimately the identity native people has towards the migrants is mirrored in their interactions.

> Pradeep, is now 25 years old, he hails from Assam. He reached Tamil Nadu at the age of 18. He worked there under a contractor and learned the construction work. He later migrated to Kerala and began to take works of his own. His relatives and some village mates are now working under him. He feels that not all the peoples are having a negative attitude towards them but there are a few. He recollects one incident that happened at a construction site in Trivandrum district. He asked drinking water from a nearby house owner but the door close and denied water. (Interview Excerpt 27 July 2014)

The social interactions at the micro level reflect the attitude of native people towards the migrants. At the same time, the migrants get a clear picture about how the natives look upon them. A sense of self is formed among the migrants on the basis of the attitude of native people towards them. The reflection of the migrants is based on the generated understanding of the self. Through the active interactions among the native people, the understanding of the self is shared. But parallel to this self at the micro level, a social image is formulated at the macro level.

Media and Migrant Labourers

Media is the main channel that creates an outlook to any incident in the society. Like so, media plays a major role in presenting the migrants before the public. *Gang of Burglars from Bengal* is the title of a special article published on the front page of a supplementary Malayalam newspaper (*Metro Manorama Kochi*, 23 October 2012). The report covers a quarter of the front page with the pictorial representation of migrant labourers as cruel individuals. It reports that a group of thieves from Jellangi, a notorious village famous for robbery and illegal currencies in the Murshidabad district of West Bengal, had migrated to Kerala. The report is a call for the native peoples to be vigilant towards the migrant labourers. There may be truth in it but rather than making people cautious, it makes the native people suspicious towards the whole migrant labourers. There can be burglars and illegal currency carriers but that does not mean all are like. Rather than finding the culprits, all the migrants are stigmatized. Knowingly or unknowingly this alienates the migrants from the common society.

In media, Murshidabad is the focal area around which all the suspicions revolve. This place is near to Bangladesh. One can reach

Bangladesh crossing the river Jalangi flowing through Murshidabad district of West Bengal. It is the same route through which the illegal Bangladeshis are entering West Bengal and from there to Kerala. On their journey towards Bengal, agents are changing them to Indian Citizens with duplicate Indian Identity Cards (ID)[11] (*Metro Manorama Kochi*, 23 October 2012). The citizenship of the migrant labourers is questioned here. Indian Constitution through Article 19 confirms that 'All citizens shall have the right ... to move freely throughout the territory of India; to reside and settle in any part of the territory of India'. But through this kind of illegal entries, the local people become doubtful about the citizenship of the migrants. The local people are hesitant about the presence of criminals among the migrant labourers. An identity card is the only thing which validates the citizenship of a migrant but it is questioned. Even an Indian citizen with a valid ID is being approached with an aura of suspicion.

> Construction companies are interested in the Bangladeshi workers. Because they are illegal they became more flunkeys. Since it is difficult to go back, they stay here for continuous two-three years with the employer. There are intermediate agents to collect monthly earnings. (*Malayala Manorama* 29 November 2013)

This kind of favourable condition is compelling the illegal labourers from Bangladesh to find their fortune in an unknown land far away from the homeland. Adding to this, there are incidents where several Bangladeshi labourers were arrested and deported. Rather than implementing effective measures, the media knowingly or unknowingly burdens the migrant labourers by presenting them as illegal.

The newspaper report titled *Spreading of Dangerous Epidemics by the Bhai* (*Metro Manorama Kochi* 18 May 2012) highlights the idea that the migrant labourers are the major source in spreading dangerous epidemics such as malaria, dengue fever, chicken guinea, typhoid, cholera and leprosy. They are represented as the carriers of dangerous diseases, which were once eradicated from Kerala. This report is only one among several similar newspaper reports that presents migrants as unhygienic and carriers of diseases. But these reports intentionally or unintentionally sideline the fate of the migrant labourers who were forced to live in substandard living conditions. The migrant labourers are vulnerable in all dimensions (Kumar, 2011). They are vulnerable not only in their settlements but also at their worksites. Lack of safety measures at worksites and ineffective welfare measures makes their condition worse. But media is often blind towards these aspects.

> Fr. Jacob is a Christian priest who is working among the migrant labourers in Kerala. He feels that the migrant labourer's major focus is to earn as much as they can. So they are ready to negotiate with the living conditions. This opportunity is made use of by the contractors and house owners who provide substandard living conditions. Now there are several makeshift shelters in Ernakulam district specially meant for the migrants. (Interview Excerpt 17 May 2014)

As a result of low-quality living conditions, they are often being exposed to dangerous diseases. This jeopardizes the life of migrant labourers.

> Twenty minutes into the raid, a doctor arrived on the site and two tanker lorries of water were brought to clean the toilets, from which emanated a pungent smell. The unhygienic conditions of migrant worker's camp at a construction site in Kakkanad of Ernakulam district led to the closure of one such camp that housed 150 people in a room. All of them cooked, ate and slept in the same space that could be called a small hall. A single bathroom and toilet facility was present for use by all of them ... the toilets were unhygienic with no proper drainage. Open septic tank pits merged with a make-shift drain outside that stagnated, giving the whole area a stench. (*Hindu*, 12 June 2012)

These conditions expose migrant labourers to a state of risk. Primarily it is a risk to their lives. Also it indirectly affects the society in which they are living. Media is often reluctant to report the problems faced by the migrant labourers. Ultimately all these aspects create a negative impression about the migrants among the native people.

Ethnic Identity Formation

People from diverse geographical, linguistic and social background are working in Kerala. The social status (caste and religion) they enjoy at their homeland is unequal; the language used in social interactions at homeland is different. But through migration all are brought under the umbrella word *bhai*. For the local people, all the migrants from north and northeastern parts of India are *bhai*.

> Krishna is from Assam and he is working in Kerala for the past ten years. He keeps a good relationship with the local people. He says that, '... I am bhai to all. It does not matter whether I am younger or older than them'. (Interview Excerpt 10 December 2014)

A single word has transformed into a symbol to give a common identity to all with common characteristics. Migrant labourers who are heterogeneous socially, culturally and linguistically became a homogenous category under the word *bhai*. Thus within their heterogeneity, they becomes an ethnic category. Also if anything done wrong by a single person will become a burden to all. The literal meaning of the Hindi word *bhai* is brother. Since the migrant labourers are from the same country it is true that a brotherhood relationship exists between migrants and the local people. But when the relationship becomes practical, the word gets different meaning. *Bhai* in the new context becomes a symbol of ethnic identity to a group of people who are doing all the manual labour. Thus, a common identity is tagged to the migrants from north and northeastern parts of India. A term which is representative of brotherhood at one place becomes a symbol for manual workforce identity at another place. The word *bhai* gives an ethnic identity to the whole labourers. This new identity stigmatizes them as people who are unhygienic, illegal and criminals.

The migrants are regionally and linguistically different. There are persons who speak Bangla, Gujarati and tribal regional languages but through migration the native people brand them as *bhai* with Hindi language as the means for communication. As a result, this *bhai* is sometimes called as *Hindi people*. A person who doesn't know Hindi language is treated the same way. Thus along with the common identity of *bhai,* a common linguistic characteristic is attributed. With this new ethnic identity coupled with linguistic categorization, *bhai* are treated as uncivilized persons without any health and hygienic consciousness. This makes an impression that the *bhai* are the carriers of dangerous epidemics. The *bhai* were often evaluated as criminals who are having hidden intentions. The media reports most of the time convey a negative identity to the migrant labourers.

This ultimately gives an ethnic identity to the migrant labourers. Ethnicity refers to the way in which social and cultural differences, language and ancestry combine as a dimension of social action and social organization and form a socially reproduced system of classification. The centre of gravity of 'ethnic' is ancestry, culture and language (Fenton, 1999). The social identity that the native people have towards the migrant labourers is a group of people, commonly termed as *bhai,* with same cultural background, having common regional origin of North India and with a common linguistic background of Hindi. This ethnic group of people is stratified into the lower-class position of the society. They become the manual labour force of Kerala. The natives have prejudices about the intentions of these labourers. They are often treated as offenders. The *bhai* is portrayed as real threat and responsible for all the problems in the native society. The identity of the *bhai* is often stigmatized. They are labelled as uncultured and uncivilized people.

The conflict between internal and external identity makes the ethnic group stigmatized. Erving Goffman was interested in the gap between what a person ought to be and what a person actually is. Anyone who has a gap between these two identities is stigmatized (Ritzer, 1988). The internal identity a migrant labourer keeps is different from the external identity which is understood by the outside world. Thus, the migrant labourers are stigmatized as uncivilized people and uncultured people with the intention of committing crime.

Discussion

The migration of the skilled and unskilled labourers from north and northeastern parts of India is giving a new identity to them. The interaction with the local people at the destination area formulates a new self identity to the migrants. Even though there is only minimum level of interaction between the migrant labourers and native people, due to linguistic and social differences, a kind of social identity is constituted. The identity the native people have about the migrants is based on the understanding that they have through personal experiences, shared knowledge and media reports. This identity ultimately results in the formation of an ethnic categorization of the migrant labourers. The identity, the people of Kerala attribute towards the migrants, is primarily sceptic and stigmatized. The labourers through the process of migration become a part of a completely different social and linguistic atmosphere. The native people categorize them under a common identity called *bhai*. The term *bhai* become a symbol of unification where socially and linguistically heterogeneous group is unified into a single group with attributed characteristics. But this social attitude of native people towards the migrants gets reflected in the social interactions, and it affects the self of the migrant labourers.

> Rafeek is a school student from Jharkand and he is now in Kerala spending his vacation time with his brother. Rafeek often helps his brother, who is a street vendor in Kerala. He is disturbed about the attitude of Kerala people towards the migrant as 'hindi people' though the people of Kerala are themselves migrants. He says that the people from Jharkand and Bihar work together, play together and live together but they don't have any problem. The problem is with Malayalis who look them as outsiders. (Interview Excerpt 4 May 2014)

Rafeek likes Kerala as a safe place to live with nice climate but the self he holds through the interaction with the native people makes him feel alienated. A self of otherness is experienced by him within his country. He knows that the people see him as a person from an alien land.

> Krishna is having a good relation with the local people around him. But he does not go to Thiruvananthapuram city centre during weekends to spend leisure time. He knows that there are so many risks involved in it. He doesn't want to get into trouble. He feels that something wrong done by a single person will affect all. (Interview Excerpt 10 December 2014)

A sense of identity and self is continuously created and recreated through the interaction between the migrants and native people. Even a person who has good relation with the native people is disturbed about the risky situations that will affect his safe zone. He does not want to go out and get into trouble. This social self makes them avoid the situations which are not safe. A sense of social self is actively created and shared through the personal interactions with the native people and interactions that the migrants keep among them.

Conclusion

The migrant labourers from different parts of India are coming to Kerala for a better living. The internal migrants are willing to do any job and often employed in all kinds of manual jobs. The migration process gives people a new social life, which is socially, linguistically and economically diverse. Even though the migrants work, earn and live along with the native people, they fail to create a true self of them and the native people fail to make a true understanding about the migrants. Although the migrant labourers are from different parts of India, they are socially, culturally, regionally and linguistically diverse, still these labourers are categorized as *bhai* in local terms throughout Kerala. Thus, migration gives a homogenous identity to a group which is heterogeneous. Through migration a new ethnic identity is attributed to the labourers. The social identity towards the *bhai* is sceptic and stigmatized. But this new ethnic categorization results in a sense of *otherness* to migrants. At one side, the migrant's labour power is used but on the other hand they are treated as *other*. The formation of *other* occurs both at the micro and macro level. At the macro level, media is playing a major role in the creating an outlook about migrants in the public sphere, and this identity is alienating. At the micro level, the interpersonal relations become a reflection of the categorization and stigmatization. Eventually their citizenship gets questioned. Through the process of migration, a citizen within his country is forced to live as a second-class citizen.[12]

Acknowledgement

I am sincerely grateful to Dr Saji P. Jacob, Loyola College of Social Sciences, Thiruvananthapuram, for his guidance and assistance in my ventures. Also I am extremely thankful to the Jesuit migrant welfare organization Jeevika of Kalady, Ernakulam district, for their support and providing me articles from their archive.

Notes

1. Internal migration is of two types: inter-state migration and intra-state migration. Even though people of Kerala are moving to other states, here internal migration is used to represent the migration of people from other states to Kerala.
2. It is the process of the emigration of highly trained or qualified people from a particular country.
3. The work done in an office or administrative setting with less physical labour.
4. The type of work which involves manual labour.
5. The names used in all the interview extracts are pseudo names.
6. Kerala Labour Department has the official data about migrant labourers based on the study done by Gulati Institute of Finance and Taxation (GIFT). For more details refer Narayan D and C.S. Venkiteswaran.
7. It is the term used by Narayan D. and C.S. Venkiteswaran to represent all migrant labourers in their study for the Labour Ministry of Kerala.
8. The migrant receiving place is termed as host land and the place from where the migrants come is called as homeland.
9. *Malayali* is a term used to denote the people of Kerala. It means that one who speaks the Malayalam language.
10. Large number of migrants is living around this place. The plywood industries, rice mills and other factories working near to this area give better employment opportunities for the migrants.
11. The documents commonly used by the migrant labourers to prove their citizenship are Voter Identity card, Aadhaar Card, Pan Card, Bank Passbook and other such documents.
12. It is a person who is systematically discriminated within a state or other political jurisdiction, despite their nominal status as a citizen or legal resident there.

References

Appelrouth, Scott, and Laura Desfor Edles, *Sociological Theory in the Contemporary Era: Text and Readings* (USA: Sage, 2011).

Deshinkar, P., and Shaheen Akter, 'Migration and Human Development in India'. HRDP 2009/13. 2009. http://purochioe.rrojasdatabank.info/HDRP_2009_13.pdf (14 February 2015).

Fenton, Steve, *Ethnicity: Racism, Class and Culture* (Hong Kong: Macmillan, 1999).

Haralambos and Holborn, *Sociology Themes and Perspectives*, 5th edition (London: Collins, 2000).

Jenkins, Richard, *Social Identity* (London: Routledge, 1996).

Kumar, N. Ajith, *Vulnerability of the Migrants and Responsiveness of the State: The Case of Unskilled Migrant Laborers in Kerala, India*. Working Paper No. 26 (Centre for Socio Economic and Environmental Studies, 2011).

Lee, E.S., 'A Theory of Migration', Demography 3(1) (1966), 47–57.

Malayala Manorama (29 November 2013).

Mathrubhumi (16 July 2013).

Metro Manorama Kochi (18 May 2012).

Metro Manorama Kochi (23 October 2012).

Narayan, D., and C.S. Venkiteswaran, *Domestic Migrant Labour in Kerala* (GIFT: Government of Kerala, 2013).

R., Smith Eliot, and Diane M. Mackie, *Social Psychology*, 3rd edition (Hove: Psychology Press, 2007).

Rajan, S. Irudaya, and Marie Percot, (eds), *Dynamics of Indian Migration: Historical and Current Perspectives* (New Delhi: Routledge, 2011).

Reddy, A. Amarender, 'Growth, Structural Change and Wage Rates in Rural India', *Economic and Political Weekly* Vol. 50, No.2 (2015): 56–65.

Ritzer, George, *Sociological Theory*, 2nd edition (Singapore: McGraw, 1988).

Ritzer, George, and Barry Smart, (eds), *Handbook of Social Theory* (London: Sage, 2001).

Scott, John, and Gordon Marshall. *A Dictionary of Sociology* (New York: Oxford Press, 2009).

Sutherland, Peter, D., 'Migration is Development: How Migration Matters to the Post-2015 Debate.' *Migration and Development*, Vol. 2, No. 2 (2013): 151–156.

The Hindu (12 June 2012).

UNESCO, *Social Inclusion of Internal Migrants in India* (New Delhi: UNESCO, 2013).

World Bank, 'Press Release'. 2012. http://www.worldbank.org/en/news/press-release/2012/11/20/developing-countries-to-receive-over–400-billion-remittances–2012-world-bank-report (14 February 2015).

Zachariah, K.C., and S. Irudaya Rajan, *Kerala's Gulf Connection: 1998–2011* (New Delhi: Orient Blackswan, 2012).

Index